THE MIGHTY W

Howard Jacobson was born in 1942 and educated at Cambridge University. He has worked as a lecturer in England and Australia and now works full-time as a novelist and critic. He is the author of *Coming From Behind* (1983), *Peeping Tom* (1984), *Redback* (1986), *The Very Model of a Man* (1992), *No More Mister Nice Guy* (1998) and four works of non-fiction.

Howard Jacobson

THE MIGHTY WALZER

A Novel

BLOOMSBURY
NEW YORK · BERLIN · LONDON · SYDNEY

The extract from "Ping-Pong in New York" © Jerome Charyn
(published in *Antaeus*, Special Essay Issue, No. 21/22) is reproduced by
kind permission of Jerome Charyn and The Ecco Press.

Published by Bloomsbury USA, New York

All papers used by Bloomsbury USA are natural, recyclable products made
from wood grown in well-managed forests. The manufacturing processes
conform to the environmental regulations of the country of origin.

LIBRARY OF CONGRESS CATALOGING-IN-PUBLICATION DATA HAS BEEN APPLIED FOR.

ISBN: 978-1-60819-685-2

First published in the United Kingdom in 1999 by Jonathan Cape Ltd.
Paperback edition published in the United Kingdom in 2000 by Vintage

First U.S. Edition 2011

1 3 5 7 9 10 8 6 4 2

Printed in the U.S.A. by Quad/Graphics, Fairfield, Pennsylvania

For the boys of the J. L. B.
and G. O. S. J. ping-pong teams,
remembering the glory days.

where dreams and retail collide

Nike ad

BOOK I

ONE

The racket may be of any size, shape or weight.

4.1 *The Rules*

SMALL BEGINNINGS. The principle of the oak tree, and the secret of the successful artist, politician, sportsman. Nice and easy does it. A box of Woolworths watercolours for your birthday, a volume of Churchill's speeches, a cricket bat or a pair of boxing gloves in your Christmas stocking. And then the slow awakening of genius.

Softly, softly, catchee monkey.

No small beginnings or slow awakenings for me, though. My sporting life was shot through with grandiosity from day one.

Grandiosity was in the family. On my father's side. Normally, when I speak of 'the family' I seem to mean my father's side. Make what you like of that. My mother's side went in for reserve. And that too was something my sporting life was shot through with from day one. Can you be simultaneously grandiose and reserved? Not without great cost to yourself, you can't. But let's stick to my father's side to begin with, if only because my mother's side wouldn't want to be intruding itself on anyone's notice so early in the piece.

3

And let's pin it to a date. August 5, 1933. Dates are important in sport. They remind us that achievement is relative. One day someone will run a mile in zero time; thanks to improved diet and training methods they will cross the tape before they've left the blocks. But back in the fifties four minutes looked pretty fast. On August 5, 1933, the first ever World Yo-Yo Championships were held in the Higher Broughton Assembly Rooms, not far from where the River Irwell loops the loop at Kersal Dale, on the Manchester/Salford borders. From my grandparents' chicken-coop house in Hightown my father could walk to the Higher Broughton Assembly Rooms in twenty minutes. That was on an ordinary day. On August 5, 1933, he walked it in zero time. Excitement. He was twelve years old. And carrying his Yo-Yo in a brown Rexine travelling-bag.

The Yo-Yo craze had swept the country the year before. Cometh the hour, cometh the toy. A Yo-Yo was the perfect Depression analgesic. Every unemployed person could afford to own one. It passed the time while you were hanging around on corners or standing in a bread queue. And it conveyed a powerful subliminal message – nothing stays down for ever. It's even possible that in some sort of way Yo-Yos were seen as an antidote to Fascism. Not just because of the multiplicity of bright colours they came in but because they bred individualism, introversion even. A kid playing with his Yo-Yo was a kid not marching behind Oswald Mosley. This may have been one of the reasons the Yo-Yo craze lasted so much longer in Manchester, which was a Black Shirt stronghold, than anywhere else. Though for the most likely explanation of Manchester's irresistible rise to Yo-Yo capital of the world you need look no further than the weaver's shuttle. They'd been spinning cotton here for two hundred and fifty years; they'd been weavers of wool, slubbers of silk, distaffers of haberdashery, ribboners and elasticators, for centuries prior to that. Wristiness was in their blood the way grandiosity was in mine. Playing with a

Yo-Yo was no more than they'd been trained to do since the Middle Ages.

In the face of an adeptness as ancient and inwrought as that, it was fantastical of my poor father to suppose he had a hope of impressing at the World Championships, let alone of lifting the title itself, on which he'd set his heart. He may have been Mancunian in the sense that he'd begun his life in a Manchester hospital bed – 'It's a lad!' were the very first words he heard, 'and a biggun' too' – but there had been no other Mancunian of any size in our family before him, and you can't expect to barge into an alien culture and lift all it knows of touch and artistry in a single generation. Bug country, that was where we came from, the fields and marshes of the rock-choked River Bug, Letichev, Vinnitsa, Kamenets Podolski – around there. And all we'd been doing since the Middle Ages was growing beetroot and running away from Cossacks.

He couldn't count on much support at the Assembly Rooms either. The only person he'd told that he was competing was his father. And he only told him on the morning of the competition.

I imagine my grandfather sitting in his rocking-chair, looking into space, listening to the ticking of a clock. Grandfather clock, you see. That's how we make our associations. Though in fact he wasn't anybody's grandfather then. The rocking-chair won't be accurate either – that too belongs to a later time. But I'd be right about him looking into space. The one thing he wouldn't have been doing was reading. There were no books and no newspapers on my father's side. I don't mean few, I mean none. Although he owned reading-glasses towards the end of his life, and liked opening and closing them, I never once saw my father reading anything except the instructions that came with whatever new shmondrie he was playing with and the notes my mother wrote (in capital letters and on lined paper) to help him with his patter when he was standing on the back of his lorry pitching out chalk ornaments on Oswestry market. He was so unfamiliar with books that when I presented him with mine (mine, ha! – some book, forty pages of black and white diagrams and dotted lines, illustrating the hows of the high-toss service and the topspin lob), he marvelled that I'd gone to the expense of having a special copy printed with the dedication for my father, Joel Walzer, who taught me to aim high. 'Dad, it's not a special copy,' I had to explain to him, 'they're all dedicated to you. It's called a print run.'

'All of them? Sheesh! That's very nice of you, Oliver.'

After that he took it everywhere with him – he would have taken the whole print run everywhere with him had it been practical – even to bed, my mother told me, where he'd sit up and stare at it for hours on end. 'I think I'm beginning to get the hang of this,' he told her one night. I asked her if she knew how far he'd got. Yes, she did as a matter of fact. He'd got to the bottom of the page opposite the dedication to him, where it says 'This book is copyright. Apart from any fair dealing for the purposes of private study, research, criticism, or review, no part may be reproduced . . . without the prior permission of the publisher.'

But then who has time for books when they've a living to earn? And when their head's full of big plans.

And big disappointments.

What my grandfather actually said on the morning I imagine him looking bookless into space I know from my father. He said, 'Keep your voice down.'

'It's all right, she's upstairs.'

'And stairs don't have ears? Use your loaf. Do you want to kill her?'

He did quite want to kill her, yes. They both did. But the real issue was did he want her to kill him. 'No,' he said.

'Then hob saichel! Keep your voice down. What time are you on?'

My father wasn't sure what time he was on. Only that he was contestant No. 180.

'My advice to you,' my grandfather whispered to him, looking anxiously at the ceiling, above which prowled the snorting beast, my grandmother, 'is not to watch the previous one hundred and seventy-nine. Go somewhere quiet. See if you can find a dark place to sit, or better still lie down. And don't show your face till they call your number. Now geh gesunterhait. If I can get away to come and watch you, I will. But if I can't, have mazel.'

He knew about nerves, my grandfather. Not as much as my mother's side knew about nerves, but he knew specifically about stage nerves, which they didn't. He had once auditioned to be a Midget Minstrel for the Children's Black and White Christy Minstrel Troupe. It's been said of all the men in my family – father's side, father's side – that we are built like brick shithouses. The shit part I take to be gratuitous; the house, however, gets something about our rectilineal outline. Even as a boy my grandfather was well on the way to being that hugely comical hexahedral shape, like a walking sugar cube (except, of course, that as a Christy Minstrel he was expected to be black), which he subsequently bequeathed to my father and indeed to me. That was what failed him his audition. You can't be a Midget Minstrel at five feet nine and three-quarter inches in all directions. He could have made it as a lyric tenor maybe, but for my grandfather these were the Jolson not the Caruso years. What he wanted was to jerk around, to be loose-limbed, not to stand like a shlump in a monkey-suit and hit high notes. He liked blacking-up, rolling his eyes, playing the banjo, telling Mr Interlocutor jokes and tap-dancing. Photographs still in my possession suggest that his glove work must have been excellent and that he could have out-horripilated anyone in the business. No small mastery of Western ways for someone who had been carried all the way from Zvenigorodka tied in a shawl like a leaking picnic lunch only a dozen years before.

No doubt, as he put his arms around my father and wished him mazel, he was remembering the day mazel had deserted him. 'You're too big, son,' they'd told him. 'You've got a kid's voice in a man's body. Come back and try the seniors when you've got a voice that goes with your build.' But who could afford to hang around in those days? Many years later, when it no longer mattered, he was able to make light of it. 'You don't understand, Charlie. I coulda had class. I coulda been a shvartzer.' But in 1933 he was less philosophical. In 1933 he was a machinist with a bad back and olive hollows round his eyes, grafting in a poorly lit raincoat factory in Strangeways, next door to the prison. ('Me and God together – He works in strange ways, and so do I.') His head wasn't filled with darky melodies any more, only the sound of sirens. Sometimes he would switch off his machine, thinking that the siren he heard was signalling knocking-off time, whereas it was still only four o'clock – pitch-black outside but still only four o'clock – and the siren was coming from the prison, warning of a break-out.

He womanized. What was he supposed to do, sweating in the shadow of a phallic prison six days a week? He was built like a prison himself – a brick shithouse – entertained grandiose illusions, wore a wicked Rupert of Hentzau moustache, was full of juice and jokes, and loved to look down and see appreciation swimming in the eyes of another man's unclothed wife – what else was he ever going to do with his life except womanize it away?

And since he womanized, my grandmother tyrannized. Isn't that how it goes?

He chases skirt, so she gives what for.

Her giving what for embraced her children as well as her husband. Whether it extended to her grandchildren too I can't remember. I was scared of her, I know that. But that was mainly because she was swarthy and reminded me of a gypsy. Of all of us she was the only one who looked as though she still had mud from the Bug and the Dniester on her. And some of the old religion mixed in with it. Every Passover and Yom Kippur, according to my father, she'd box the family's ears. Every Succoth and Shevuoth the same. Every Chanukkah and Purim. Good yomtov, klop! 'But at least that way,' he said, 'we got to know the festivals.'

This was why there was so much whispering afoot on the morning my father confided to his father his intention of competing in the World Yo-Yo Championships – August 5, 1933, was a Saturday, and Saturday, by my grandmother's reckoning, was meant to be a day of rest from everything except her.

It's my understanding of the thirties that when it came to observance we Walzers were essentially no different from most other families who'd made it over from some sucking bog outside Proskurov the generation before. We'd done it, that's where we stood on the question. We'd done observant, now we were ready to do forgetful. If a Cohen wanted to change his name to Cornwallis, that was his affair. It was no mystery to any of us how come Hyman Kravtchik could go to bed one night as himself and the next morning wake as Henry Kay De Ville Chadwick. Enough with the ringlets and the fringes. Enough with the medieval magic. But we still bris'd and barmitzvah'd – klop! – and the seventh day was still the seventh day. Nothing fanatical; no sitting nodding in the dark or denying yourself hot food; no imaginary pieces of string beyond which you didn't dare push the pram; and if you had to travel to see someone sick, you travelled – *and* you bought them fruit. All else being equal, though – which was where my grandmother put her foot down and k'vitshed and klogged and cried veh iz mir! and tore her hair and clutched her heart and tore everyone else's hair – you rested. And even my father could see that competing in the World Yo-Yo Championships on a Shabbes wasn't resting.

But that was not the reason, not the primary reason he slipped out of the house with his Yo-Yo concealed inside a holdall. Naturally, unless he meant for his mother to burst a couple of blood vessels – his, not hers – he wouldn't have wanted her to see what he was carrying. But he didn't want *anyone* to see what he was carrying. His Yo-Yo was a secret weapon which no one at all knew about and which he would unveil for the first time only at the World Championships themselves. It might cross your mind, in that case, to wonder whether his trouser pocket wouldn't have served just as well as a hiding place, better even in that it wouldn't have attracted anything like so much notice. Have I not said that my father was grandiose? The truth is, the Yo-Yo with which he was planning to storm the World Championships, the Yo-Yo he had not simply gone out and bought from a toy shop like every other competitor but had spent weeks constructing, taking sheets of plywood and a fretsaw and a pot of glue to bed with him, working at night under his blankets so that not even his brothers should know what he was about, was on a scale utterly disproportionate to anything we normally associate with the contents of a boy's trouser pocket.

This was why he was so confident. He had read and re-read the rules of the competition. (The last big piece of reading he ever did.) Nowhere did it say that a Yo-Yo had to approximate to the size of a cricket ball. Nowhere did it say that you couldn't walk the dog with a Yo-Yo as big as a bicycle wheel.

When my father died, almost sixty years to the day after he'd competed in the first ever World Yo-Yo Championships, and in a house still not much more than a twenty-minute walk from where the River Irwell tries to hang itself on Kersal Dale – people I didn't recognize stopped me in the street to tell me how much they'd loved him. 'He had a big heart, your father,' they all wanted me to know. They looked at me in a peculiar and personal way when they said this, as though his big-heartedness might have been lost on me, not a virtue I valued, or as though it was the one thing I hadn't inherited from him. Grandiosity yes, big-heartedness no.

One of his old friends, Merton Bobker, to whom my father had

lent money before Merton won the pools and was in a position to
pay the loan back (which he didn't do), actually held me by the
sleeve and wouldn't release me until I gave him tangible proof I'd
grasped the difference. 'There are plenty of big dealers around,' he
said. He was dripping at the eyes and mouth, like an abandoned
labrador. 'You understand? In this town big dealers come cheap.
But your father was a big *man*. Get me?'

He was a big boy, too, in the get me sense. Everybody who
witnessed the shlemozzle he caused at the World Championships
reckoned he came out of it with great credit. Even his father, who
managed to make it to the Assembly Rooms after all, Shabbes or
no Shabbes, did what fathers don't always do and hugged him
afterwards, telling him that by the only standards that counted
he was the real winner.

What had happened was this:

He had taken my grandfather's advice and not watched the one
hundred and seventy-nine contestants prior to him. He had even
found a dark room in the bowels of the Assembly Rooms, where
he'd gone into a mild trance of premonitory euphoria, imagining
what it would be like when he was the World Champion. As a
consequence he missed his number when it was called and had
to publicly plead with the competition referee to be allowed to
perform out of sequence. So by the time he finally made it on
to the stage, carrying his brown Rexine travelling-bag, he was
already a character.

Don't forget that in stature he was the same comical assemblage
of sturdy right angles as my grandfather. In his square hand-me-
down jacket and with his tie knotted clumsily at his throat he
would have looked more like a parcel than a boy.

As for the spectators, remember that they had been there most
of the day, sitting on uncomfortable seats, suffering the August
humidity, and frankly beginning to lose any capacity to tell one
loop the loop from another. What were they ever going to do,
from the moment my father gave them his big smile and hauled

his chariot-wheel of a Yo-Yo out of his bag, but stomp their feet and cheer?

After that, as the *Manchester Evening News* reported it, 'the competition descended into such mayhem that the city will be fortunate if it is ever given a comparable event to stage again.'

Allow for the hyperbole of the press. My father may have been the reason Manchester has never been given the Olympic Games, but even so allow for the hyperbole of the press. In fact, nothing occurred that was any more than boisterous. They'd taken to him, that was all. They thought he was plucky, and maybe a bit simple. But worth egging on, either way. From my father's point of view all the hullabaloo was no more than he'd been expecting. He tried to loosen his tie but couldn't budge the knot. He tried to roll up his sleeve to his elbow but couldn't get it past his forearm. Perspiring heavily now – something else we do grandly in our family – he tested the tension of the string, clawed his fingers around the Yo-Yo, turned over his wrist and let it go. His stance was the conventional one, much like an ocean angler casting a line, legs slightly apart, the Yo-Yo propelled backhand from a height more or less level with his temple. He waited, knees sprung, shoulders braced, for the Yo-Yo to return fizzing in to his hand. How long did he wait? How long did it seem he waited? 'Alles shvartz yoren!' All the black years. An eternity.

I have often wondered if he exaggerated, to make it a grander débâcle than it actually was. Surely it came back up a little bit? But no. He always insisted there was no movement whatsoever, nothing, not so much as a quiver along the line. It just lay there at his feet, twenty inches in diameter, five or six pounds in weight, as inert as a dead fish, except that a dead fish had once known life.

He re-wound and tried again.

Same thing?

'A worse thing.' This time it didn't even fizz down the string. It just dropped like a stone.

Thirty, forty, fifty years on, he could tell you where he'd gone wrong. He hadn't allowed for the atmospheric conditions. It was a muggy Manchester day, the hammocks of cloud, bagging with the weight of warm Pennine rain, so low you could touch them. The string had sweated, become wet, and by the late afternoon lost its tensility. Something any experienced cotton worker would have thought of. But there you are – Rome wasn't built in a day.

On the other hand, he was giving pleasure, wasn't he? Listen to the crowd! And at the last it's all about giving pleasure, isn't it?

How hooked we've been been on the pleasure principle in our family! Pleasure, pleasure. But never for ourselves. The pleasure principle we've been hooked on, we Walzer men – even my grandfather looking down at the gratitude swimming in the eyes of another man's wife – is the principle of giving it. As long as people say thank-you and remember us – that's all we have ever asked.

The more the crowd whistled the more my father grinned. He stared accusingly at his stricken Yo-Yo, shrugged his square shoulders, and pointed an imaginary pistol at his brain. He seemed to be as amused as they were. To them it looked as if he had done exactly what he had meant to do. It was as if, although that wasn't how anyone in Broughton Park spoke in those days, he had deliberately set out to deconstruct the Yo-Yo.

'Third and final attempt,' the tournament referee warned him.

I see the tournament referee, although my father never once described him to me. Round shouldered and blubbery, prematurely bald, with sad sea-lion moustaches and a broken-hearted demeanour. They upset easily in Manchester. It might be a climatic thing. Or a class thing. They nurse a deep hurt. And those who make it their business to adjudicate, to let a little equity into the universal unfairness of life, nurse a deeper hurt than most. I hear his defeated vowels, his cadences of hopelessness – 'Third and final attempt' – meaning try if you must, but you're a dead man.

A dead boy the size of a dead man.

When all's said and done, there are only two ways of getting a Yo-Yo into play – vertical or horizontal; you throw it down or you throw it out. Having failed with the vertical pass, my father concluded his programme with the horizontal . . .

Most of the spectators had the foresight to cover their faces or duck the moment my father let go. Despite its great size, therefore, his Yo-Yo did no one any damage as it at last spun the way a Yo-Yo should, whirring out into the hall with a sound like the beating of a pheasant's wings, a meteor loosed from its orbit, cooling the air it travelled through, until it broke from its umbilical cord with a snap like a knuckle cracking, and flew free.

As luck would have it, it was his own father who stuck out a hand and caught it. Luck? Perhaps not. Who else in the hall had a hand big enough to pull off the catch?

He was carrying it under his arm when he met up with my father after the event. 'Here,' he said. 'Take your tsatske.'

That was once my favourite word. Tsatske. When I was very small anybody could make me laugh just by saying it. It was like being tickled. Tsatske. Tsatske.

A tsatske is a toy or plaything, a shmondrie, a bauble, a whifflery, a nothing. It can also mean a nebbish, a nobody, and by extension, a tart. Not a serious tart, not the sort of high-class call-girl you'd think of ruining your reputation as a carefree shtupper and family man for, more of a dizzy broad, a toy or a plaything, a shmontse to help you through the tedium of a wet Manchester afternoon.

But no definition is able to render the charge of fatuousness and triviality which I always heard in the word. A person who owned a tsatske was forever, it seemed to me, lost to seriousness and dignity. The way you were when you were being tickled.

Maybe I knew I was going to be forever lost to seriousness and dignity myself.

TWO

•

Before using a racket for the first time in a match a player shall, if so requested, show both sides of the blade to his opponent.

4.8 *The Rules*

I WAS A natural. Ping-pong just came to me.

One day, when I was eleven, I brought home a little white celluloid ping-pong ball I'd found bobbing on the boating lake in Heaton Park and began hitting it against the living-room wall with a book. I still remember the make of the ball. It was a Halex ★★★. A competition ball. Don't ask me what a competition ball was doing in a lake in Heaton Park. Perhaps God had put it there. For what it's worth I can still remember the title of the book as well – *Dr Jekyll and Mr Hyde* by Robert Louis Stevenson, in the soft green pitted-leatherette Collins Classics series which my mother's side was helping me collect. I already had about thirty of them lined up alphabetically according to author on a shelf over my bed – Austens, Jane; Brontës, Anne; Brontës, Charlotte; Brontës, Emily; Burneys, Fanny; Eliots, George; Gaskells, Mrs; Mitfords, Miss. You don't need a degree in English Literature to work out that I must have chosen to hit the ball with Stevenson, Robert Louis, not because he came last in the line but because he was the only man I had.

What with the flexi-dimpling on the book and the glossy whorls of plaster on the living-room wall there was no knowing what even a Halex ★★★ was going to do. Hit the eye of the same whorl as many times as you like, the ball will not come back to you at the same speed or with the same spin twice. I don't care how good your opponent is, he won't surprise you the way a plaster whorl will. In my own manual to ping-pong – long out of date now, and long out of print – I recommend a Collins Classic and an Artexed wall as the ideal surfaces for familiarizing a young player with the caprices of the game. As for the table you push up against the wall – there again, the more grooves and scratches in it the better.

Where my feel for the game came from, how I knew from my very first hit how to angle the book, how to chop, how to flick, how to half-volley, how to move – because yes, I had suddenly become a mover too – was a mystery to me. I'd never been a ball-player. I dropped catches. I mis-kicked. I allowed balls to be dribbled through my legs. Like an old man snoozing by an open fire, I dreamed in front of a gaping goal. Like a young girl counting the hairs on her first love's chest, I lay on my back making daisy-chains on the long-leg boundary. You know the story – if you're a reader you *are* the story: when the teams came to be picked I was the booby prize, the one you had to have because there was no one left. Sometimes I wasn't picked at all; simply ignored, turned tail on, left smarting in the mud while the chosen ones ran off riotously to play. Hurtful, but at least safe. If the truth is told, I was frightened of balls and philosophically dismayed by them. Sphericality – was that it? Not knowing where a ball ended and where it began, not being able to tell the front from the back? I'm not looking for fancy excuses; it's possible that my fear of balls proceeded from nothing more complex than the good relations other boys enjoyed with them. I don't know where I was at the time or why I hadn't been invited, but somewhere along the line, some time between my seventh and eighth birthdays, boys and balls had met at a party, hit it off, and been going steady ever since, leaving me to stay home on my own or play gooseberry. Ping-pong didn't change that. Not all at once, anyway. But it met me half-way. It made concessions to my solitary nature. Ping-pong is airless and cramped and repetitive and self-absorbed, and so was I.

But we sniffed greatness in each other.

I'd always been short of people to play with. I had two sisters, both older than me. My father had been away in the army when I was born and now worked long hours. My mother and her sisters and their mother were my company but they were sedentary and introspective and no less frightened of balls than I was. We listened to the *Morning Story* and later in the day to *Woman's Hour* on the radio together, did crosswords and jigsaws together, pored over old family photographs together, played hangman and snap! and noughts and crosses together, and on special occasions snakes and ladders or hoop-la on a board nailed to my bedroom door. I also seem to recall that they bathed me a lot. Otherwise, when it came to the rough-and-tumble necessary to summon up the blood and stiffen the spirit of a growing boy, they weren't much use. We had moved from Cheetham Hill to Heaton Park a couple of years before, far enough to lose contact with my old friends, and I was slow at making new ones. The other catch with our new address was that there were prefabs in the park just opposite us – built by German prisoners of war – and every time I went out a gang of prefab boys threw stones at me. For the time being, until I was able to enjoy the protection of a gang of my own, or until the prefabs were pulled down, my mother much preferred it that when I wasn't at school I stayed in the house.

The only person not happy with this arrangement, apart from the prefab boys, was my father. 'A stone's going to kill him?'

In protection of my skin, my mother was as fierce as a tigress. 'Does it have to kill him? Isn't it enough he loses an eye?'

'They're little kids. They can't throw that hard.'

'Joel, these are not Yiddisher boys. When did you hear of a shaygets who couldn't throw hard?'

'So let him learn to throw hard back. I'll take him out in the park and teach him.'

'You'll find time to take him out in the park? And you'll be here to put his eye back?'

Most arguments came quickly to an end the moment my mother postulated my father finding time or being in.

They were still young – my mother was still glamorous in that slightly orientalized, simultaneously petite and fleshy Polish style (with little round white fish-ball cheeks) that drove Russian men wild – and I'd like to think they were still in love, but without doubt my father suffered from what his side – dodging all questions of morality – called ants in his pants. He was driving a coach at the time, working for a firm that hired out buses to schools for field trips, and to social clubs for boozy nights out. So he necessarily went to far-flung destinations and worked long hours. Even allowing for that, though, his bus was frequently seen in some odd places at some odd times.

The markets came later, following calls my mother made to the bus company. But it wasn't long before his market lorry was seen in some odd places too.

That men were by nature grandiose and unreliable, that they had ants in their pants, that they made you promises which they immediately broke, that they forgot you and half the time forgot their own children, was an assumption that no woman on my mother's side so much as thought about questioning. That was just the way of it. It barely merited remark. And yet both my sisters were religiously educated to believe that no greater good awaited them than a man. Figure that out. And while you're at it, figure out how come not a woman on my mother's side – not my highly strung mother herself, not my palpitating aunties, not my small-boned fatalistic Polish grandmother – ever taught me to think of their sex with anything but suspicion. They chased me down the snakes and up the ladders, they floated me in my little bath, and they whispered to me of all the Jezebels who were already out there, growing their nails, waiting for the hour when I would offer them my heart and they would pluck it out.

All in all, given the threat from the prefab boys and the cruel intentions of women, ping-pong for one was my safest option by a mile. The noise drove my sisters crazy, but my mother shushed them into leaving me alone. As long as I was hitting a ball against a wall I was out of their hair, wasn't I?

Plock, plock. Kerplock, plock, if you want to be onomato-poeically pedantic about it, these being the days before sponge or sandwich. It began early. I had just started grammar school, a forty-minute walk and train ride away, so if I was going to get my regular hour's practice in I had to begin at seven at least. And then, as soon as I was back from school, plock, plock, plock. Another hour on the balls of my feet. I loved it. The sound, the self-absorption, the growing mastery. And the nursing of a secret dream – to be impregnable, plock, to be the greatest, plock, and to win, thereby, plock, plock, the respect of men and the love of beautiful women with little white fish-ball cheeks.

So they hadn't succeeded in frightening me off women, my mother's side? Of course they hadn't. You can't float a boy in a bath and tell him about Jezebels with purple nails and then expect him not to want one.

Plock, plock. How they would roar when I snatched one title after another off Ogimura and brought the trophies back to the mantelpieces of Europe! 21–0, 21–0, 21–1 – a flawless perfor-mance but for Ogimura's fluked net return on the last-but-one point of the final game, when a moment of rash but under-standable complacency caused me to take my eye off the ball and survey the ecstatic, entirely female crowd. How they would cluster around my dressing room, waiting for me to come out to sign autographs, pressing their soft, perfectly spherical breasts into my stone chest, retracting their bloody claws . . .

By the time such folderols as bats and nets came into the house I was already an accomplished player with every stroke in the game. And I still wouldn't play with anything except my *Dr Jekyll and Mr Hyde*. My mother's side, of course, presented no sort of test. I could have hit them off the dining table with a bookmark, never mind a book. My father's side put up a stiffer resistance, but they too had no answer in the end to the amount of backspin I could impart with the leatherette, let alone to the speed and accuracy of my attacking shots. Neighbours were brought in to marvel at what I could do and to try their hand against me. I fancy that my father was even secretly putting money on me. 'A tusheroon says the kid'll pulverize you. And he won't even be using a bat!'

If I'm right about that then he must have cleaned up nicely in the early days. Nobody who hadn't seen me play could have been anything but certain of beating me, so little did I look like a person who knew how to win, so completely, on the surface at least, was I the child of my mother. Even at the table I was diffident and apologetic, blushing if I happened to lose a point, and blushing even more when I took it.

I blushed with such violence in these years that I must have been in danger of combusting. Heat, that's what I remember most about being a boy – how like it was to being the kettle that spluttered and steamed all day on my grandmother's fire. So long as I was only practising on my own against the wall I was able to exercise a measure of control over my temperature – about eighty degrees Fahrenheit in the immediate vicinity of the ball, never more than that. But as soon as I played against another person the ovens came on. It wasn't fear of losing – I knew I couldn't lose. It was the exposure. Call it compound contradictory existential bashfulness. 1) – I was ashamed of existing, and 2) – I was ashamed of existing so successfully. Five, six unbeatable backhands on the run and my hand would be on fire with consciousness of its temerity; a couple more and there'd be smoke pouring out of *Dr Jekyll and Mr Hyde*. At the end of a pasting I'd handed out to Lol Kersh, an older kid with a purple birthmark and a stamp collection from across the street, his father, who had come to watch, demanded a closer look at my unconventional bat. He'd smelt the fumes. 'I've rumbled you, you little mamzer,' he said. 'You've baked that book like a conker. Show me, show me. I bet it's as hard as a brick.' But when he inspected it he found that it was soft – very hot and very wet, but soft. As, in the face of his false accusation, was I.

Shy – even the word is shaming. And I was beginning to shame everyone around me.

One night I overheard my uncle Motty ask my father – it's still not easy for me to reproduce his words, however long ago he spoke them – 'When's that genius kid of yours going to come out of his shell?'

What was I in his eyes – a snail, a tortoise, a whelk?

We were at a wedding. Not a real fresh virginal wedding, but a silver or a ruby wedding. I can't remember whose. I probably never knew. I kept my head down at family get-togethers. Especially if it was my father's side that was getting together. I wasn't equipped to handle their ramping verve.

'Well halloa dair, Amos,' was how my grandfather greeted me.

I was never certain that he knew who I was. That's the terrible contradiction at the heart of shyness. You think everybody's looking and you fear no one is.

'My name's Oliver,' I said.

He rolled his eyes, retracting the pupils and showing me the whites. Then he pinched my cheek. 'Oliver,' he said – as though coining a diminutive, as though my actual name for outside of the family, gentile use was Olive – 'Oliver, help your Zadie to that chair.'

We were still on the street outside the Higher Broughton Assembly Rooms, waiting to clap in the happy couple. So a chair . . . ?

'What chair, Grandpa?'

He had me again. 'Wotcher, Olive*ler*!' And he was off, looking for more descendants to torment.

And then there was the dancing . . .

Considering the shape we were – for the Walzer women, too, were built like brick shithouses – you'd have thought we might have passed on dancing, left it to the Yakipaks who lived in the south of the city, the svelte Sephardim with their slithery Spanish and Portuguese hips. Fat chance. A band played us into the hall and no sooner was the soup served than my uncles were out of their seats, buttoning up their dinner jackets, as though that would somehow make them lighter, steering my aunties around the dance floor the way my father drove his bus, fast on the bends and heavy on the clutch. Thereafter it needed no more than a thimbleful of sweet red wine for us to be back at the convergence of the Bug and the Dniester, throwing glasses over our shoulders and leaping on to tables to dance the kasatske. Make no mistake, a kasatske may sound like a tsatske from Kazalinsk, but there was nothing footling or fatuous about the way we did it, down on the heels of our dancing pumps, our arms folded, our jackets tight across our backs, our short stout Kamenets Podolski shanks going like pistons.

When I say *our* . . .

In fact it was what we'd assimilated in Higher Broughton that I dreaded more than what we'd brought from Podolia. The polka and the mazurka had a certain sad elegance of yesteryear about them; the sight of a forebear slapping his thighs and shouting 'Hoy!' stirred ancient fertility associations – in these I could almost forget myself. But the hokey-cokey, and worse still, the conga – what were such trashy plebeian tortures invented for but my humiliation? Come on, Oliveler, join the line, join the line!

Join a line, me? Be *seen* in a line, me?

And who did I think was looking? Irrational, I acknowledge it. Why would anyone have been looking specifically at me? And who was there to look anyway, given that everyone was *in* the line? But what's reason got to do with anything.

On the night in question I was standing in a corner at the back of the hall practising ping-pong shots with an imaginary ball and trying to be invisible when the conga suddenly snaked my way, a deadly centipede of Walzers shrieking 'Ayayayay, conga!' and kicking its legs out. I turned the colour of Kamenets beetroot and ran for it. At one exit my grandfather was saying 'Well halloa dair, Amos,' to a small bewildered square-shouldered brick shithouse of a girl in a frilly pink dress. Close by the other my father was down on one knee, impressing a cluster of cousins by lifting chairs one-handed. The combination of himself in a tight dinner suit and a crowd to watch him was always fatal for my father. Down he'd go and up would come the chair. Nothing remarkable about that? I haven't finished. Once he'd limbered up lifting empty chairs, he'd start on chairs that had my aunties in them. Not the introspective weightless aunties on my mother's side, either, but rollicking Walzer aunties with round knees and deep chests. Three inches . . . six inches . . . a foot off the floor! *One-handed*! Oy a broch, Joel, you'll rupture yourself! 'Do you want me to tell you something, Oliver? – Solomon didn't have the kaych your father has.' I knew who they meant. They meant that Samson didn't have my father's kaych. And I also knew what my father did for an encore. A chair with an aunty sitting on it, plus me sitting on the aunty.

I took the only path that was clear, to the men's room, where I came upon my uncle Motty standing at a urinal, shaking his penis to get the last drop out of it, actually banging it the way you bang a near-empty ketchup bottle. My uncle Motty was the next Walzer brother down from my father. He was more placid than the others. A sofa to put his feet up on, a few quid in his pocket, the odd shtup – nothing serious, as long as it was with someone not his wife – and he was happy. When you looked at Motty's big blond face you couldn't understand why anyone found life difficult. Which made it difficult for me to look at him. He winked at me. 'Jew in a restaurant,' he said without preamble. 'Says to waiter – "Hey, you got matzo balls?" Waiter says, "No, I always walk like this."' He waited for me to laugh. I couldn't do it. I wanted to but I couldn't find the mechanism. Not for a smile either. Where to look, that was the problem. If I looked away it would be rude. If I looked at him I'd be looking at his penis – also big and blond, and still refusing to yield up its last reserves, no matter how hard my uncle Motty shook it. I turned an even deeper red and ran for it again.

It was shortly after this encounter that I overheard him wondering how much longer I was going to cower in my shell. Unfortunately for me, the phrase struck a chord with my father. 'Hello – are you in there?' he'd ask, rapping me on the head as he passed me on the stairs – hardly a tactic to get a whelk or a tortoise to show its face, let alone to tickle out a shrinking invert like me. But my father wasn't a man for gentle coaxing. Having a son in a shell seemed to infuriate him to such a degree that I knew it wouldn't be long before he resorted to trying to beat me out of it. He was a beater, my father? Let's just say he had been klopped by his own mother and that these were, as a matter of course, klopping times. In the nineteen-forties and fifties we were all klopped. And are now the better for it? What do you think?

In the meantime, my sisters too wanted to get in on the act. I'd crawl out of bed in the morning and find a plate of lettuce outside my bedroom door. I'd put my foot in a shoe and find it full of broken eggshells. One morning I woke to the sight of a terrapin making eyes at me on my pillow. A gift tag was tied to one of its forelegs. 'Hi, I'm Tilly,' it read. 'Can I be your girlfriend?'

I was twelve now, and spending an increasing amount of time on my own. When I wasn't knocking a ball against a wall with a book I was running to the toilet where I'd lock myself away for hours on end, also with a book.

'How long's he been in there this time?' – my father, back from work, not even bothering to enquire where I was. He *knew* where I was.

'Days!' – my sisters, wanting to stir it.

'What's he doing in there?'

'Reading' – my mother, wanting to calm it.

'Reading? Reading what?'

'A book, Joel, what do you think?'

'The time he spends in there he could have written a book.'

'The time you spend away you could have written twenty books.'

'It isn't normal. You can't tell me it's good for you, sitting on top of your own chazzerei for that long.'

'Normal? Let's not talk about normal. Eat your tea.'

My mother understood the needs of a retiring nature. The way my father's side could move their bowels and be back out in the world again in sixty seconds flat had always disgusted her. To her way of thinking there should at least have been a cooling-off period, a fifteen-or twenty-minute interregnum between a motion and the resumption of normal activities, much as the laws of sexual hygiene insisted on an interval of pollution separating menstruation and intercourse. The three hours I was taking may have been excessive, she allowed, but then I was a boy and boys had other matters to attend to in a toilet. No names, no details. I'd be over it soon. In the meantime, loz aleyn, leave the boy alone.

Easier said than done. I was in a shell and I was in the toilet. 'He's always hiding,' my father said. 'He's always *in* something. The only time I see him is when he's giving a ping-pong ball a zetz, and then he's in a trance.'

Didn't he like me playing ping-pong? Hadn't I won money for him? Yes. But he wanted me out in the world more. Why wasn't I playing in a club? Why wasn't I playing for a team? Why didn't I play with a bat now, like a normal kid? Why didn't I have a girlfriend? Why was I sitting for hours over my own chazzerei? Why was I blushing all the time? Why did I show him up in front of his brothers? Why was I such a kuni-lemele?

Kuni-lemele. If tsatske was my most favourite word as a child, kuni-lemele was my least. In itself it didn't denote anything much more offensive than oafishness. A kuni-lemele is a rustic simpleton. Not quite the village idiot, more the shtetl shlemiel. There can even be a bit of affection in the word. Not on my father's lips, though. When my father called me a kuni-lemele he filled his mouth with a quivering kuni-lemele milksop substance, a curdled yellow jelly that shrank from the touch and trailed slime, like the underbelly of a slug.

That was what I heard, anyway.

It was in order to de-kuni-lemelize me, to get me out in the world, whether I shrank from it or not, that my father borrowed the coach one weekend for a family outing to Blackpool, where a boys' weekly comic just happened to be sponsoring a giant nationwide ping-pong gala. My sisters were jumping up and down on the back seat of the bus, blowing kisses at male motorists on our tail. My mother was sitting with her mother in the seat behind my father, och un veh-ing together, and I was up beside him so that I could smell the diesel and see how the gears and the pedals worked and thereby get a taste for manly things. Mistake. Putting me up there just meant that when we pulled into a petrol station I was in harm's way. In those days petrol stations weren't self-service. Nor were those who filled you up merely anonymous pump attendants. Running a garage was a profession then; drive in for a couple of gallons and you were negotiating with men of substance – a retired naval officer who loved cars, a barrister lending a relative a helping hand over the long weekend. It was my misfortune to run into a wing commander. 'Cheer up,' he called to me, after switching off the pump and exchanging pleasantries with my father. 'Cheer up – it may never happen.'

'It already has,' I said.

He had a red, raging, humourless face, the way they always do, the homicidal depressives who tell you to cheer up.

He looked bemused. 'What has?'

This was a longer conversation than I had the courage for. But I was in now. 'The thing you said may never happen . . .'

I waited for him to catch up. It's possible I allowed my contempt for his slowness to show, even through my own intense embarrassment.

'. . . it already has.'

'Has what?'

'Happened.'

That's all I said. Happened. Not happened, you shmuck. Not happened, you fucking psychopath. Just *it already has*, and then *happened*.

I watched his mouth vanish. So far he had been addressing me from the driver's side, now he came around the bus and climbed up on to the running-board. My window was open and his face was so close to mine I could count the hairs on his facetious aviator's tash.

'See this garage?' he said. 'See that workshop? See those fields behind it? See those fences? See those trees? See that grass? See those houses at the end of that lane? All mine. Every stick and stone. Every brick. Mine. I own the lot. All of it. So don't you think you can be smart with me, son.'

Where is that mysterious far-away realm to which the diffident fly to find courage? Our secret; even from ourselves. 'What about the birds?' I was aghast at hearing myself saying. 'Are they yours, too?'

That did it. All at once I was in a universe of total silence, not broken even by the tweeting of my impertinent birds. A raging silence vibrating fearfully to the throbbing of our hearts. All our hearts – mine, his, my father's, my sisters', my mother's, my grandmother's. Maybe one of us was going to have a heart

27

attack. Maybe we all were. Then I realized there was a finger in my face. Actually *in* my face. And that it had a voice.

'You little snot-nose,' it said. 'I could buy and sell you a hundred times over. You wouldn't make a dent in my bank balance. I spend more on manure in a day than it'd cost me to buy you . . .'

Then, abruptly, silence again. The finger was gone and my adversary with it. Gone without another word to any of us. Disappeared inside their workshop the pair of them, no doubt, to calculate their value in spanners and jacks.

Now here's a question: Why, if this incident so incensed my father – and take my word for it, it did, it did – why didn't he land one on the wing commander who was responsible for it, instead of on me who wasn't?

It wasn't a punch. I'm not saying my father laid me out. But no sooner had he returned to the driver's seat than he let fly with a backhand Ogimura would have been proud of, a humdinging swipe that caught me on the mouth, bringing tears to my eyes and silencing my sisters, who were just getting ready to start spluttering with laughter again. From my mother and her mother it drew a conjoined gasp. 'Oh, Joel!' my mother said.

He revved the bus out of the garage forecourt – 'Oh, Joel,' he jeered – and swung out on to the Blackpool road, careless of the traffic. We were at that stage of the journey where a penny was usually offered to the first person who saw the Tower, but there was no family fun of that sort today. I sat with my head down, determined not to cry, but promising myself that one day I would put a knife in my father's heart, supposing I could ever find it. He looked stonily ahead, no doubt promising himself some similar reward in relation to me. When he finally spoke it was to justify what he'd done. 'You and your long farkrimt face,' he said. 'I'm sick of you showing me up. You'll treat people with respect when you're out with me, you stuck-up little . . .' But he didn't finish. He wasn't a swearer.

Looking back, I think I did the right thing not asking how I could be simultaneously diffident and arrogant, stuck in and stuck up. It could only have led to another klop. And who knows, to the bus spinning out of control and the whole family being wiped out.

So we drove the rest of the way in silence until we arrived at the Tower.

For northerners in search of their first good time in the ten or fifteen years after the War, Blackpool was where you always went looking, and the Tower Ballroom was where you invariably found it. In the Tower Ballroom you smooched your first smooch, kissed your first kiss, missed your first last bus home. For me the Tower Ballroom was where I first saw a row of twenty ping-pong tables, every one of them in use. It's a sight, I have to say, going on recent experience, that still has the power to move me. People who love the spectacle of football speak of that heart-stopping moment when you come up out of the darkness of the stands and suddenly find yourself looking down upon the luminous verdure of the turf. Cricket, baseball, rugby, bowls – the same. In the end it's the arena we come for, the landscape. And the landscape of sport is always green. Always and forever green. The colour of the Elysian Fields. Our only glimpse of Paradise. Which was what I saw when I walked into the Tower Ballroom. The Holy City. Avalon. The olive garden of the Hesperides and twenty separate ping-pong balls going plock. The music of the spheres.

It wasn't a tournament. You just went over to a table and took your turn. Winners stayed on for a maximum of three games, losers went to the back of the queue and waited for another crack. But it wasn't about winning and losing. It was about being spotted for potential. A dozen senior players and coaches wandered between the tables looking for kids who had what it took. Or to whom they believed they could teach what it took. This was big-break time. If you were to have any chance of snatching the title from Ogimura or some other inscrutable pen-hander in the future, this is where it would have to begin.

And here was me with *Dr Jekyll and Mr Hyde* already smoking in my hand and a cut mouth to remind me that less than an hour before I'd been publicly humiliated by a man I was no longer prepared to regard as my father. Some preparation for my big break that was.

He – *he* – had dropped us off at the Tower and then gone to have some repairs done to the bus. Tactful of him. My sisters were out on the Golden Mile, rolling pennies and looking for men. Tactful of them, too. As usual, the ones who felt most keenly for one's suffering were the only ones who didn't have the nous to get out of the way. So I was stuck, on my first ever ping-pong outing, with a mother and a granny.

'They look nice boys on that table,' my mother said. 'Why don't you join them?'

In my heart I knew I was not going to join anyone. I wasn't a joiner. It wasn't going to happen like that for me. It would all unfold in some other way. It would be the same with the Jezebels. I would not meet them at a dance. I would meet them some other way. And what was it I wanted, then, from ping-pong and from Jezebels, that was not what others wanted, that could not be initiated or satisfied in the ordinary way? Nothing. That is what has been so disappointing about my life – at the last, after all the blushing and the shrinking, all the exceptional hesitancy and reluctance, there is nothing I have ever wanted other than to lift the cup and fuck the girl.

It's possible, then, that the man who was no longer my father was within his rights to nail me for a stuck-up prick and zetz me as hard as he did?

Anything's possible.

What I also knew in my heart, now I was here, was that I wouldn't have the courage to bat with a book. I looked around

30

at the other kids. Several of them wore tracksuits. Some seemed to have their parents with them (though not their grannies), acting as trainers, muttering to them between points – 'Concentrate, concentrate! Keep it simple!' – dumb-showing strokes from the sidelines. And all of them, of course, used bats. But did I see anyone I couldn't have licked? A few who might have pushed me hard, maybe. A tall kid with an over-pronounced follow-through, who hit the ball with plenty of topspin, but all you'd have to do with him was counter-hit from close to the table and you'd have the ball past him while he was still putting the final flourish to his previous stroke. A heavy chopper who was winning applause from bystanders for his showy retrieving, but where would he be when I got the ball to stop dead at the net? And perhaps the toughest of them, if only because he was the most determined, a round-faced boy in shorts who bounced around the table a lot, doing breathing exercises, refusing to accept that a ball was ever out of his reach. He'd take the longest to beat, because of the pleasure there would be in wearing him out. Death by push shot. *Dr Jekyll and Mr Hyde* itched in my palm. So no, I didn't see anyone I couldn't have licked. But I still didn't have the nerve to line up with my book.

It doesn't make much sense, does it? First they'd have laughed, then I'd have wiped the laughter off their faces. Game, set and match to me, with the moral victory thrown in. My trouble was that I couldn't think long term – all I could hear was the snorting of that initial mockery, instead of the soft purrings of my own satisfaction in the end.

That's the difference between a winner and a loser.

'So how did it go?' the man who was still not my father asked on the way back.

Behind me, the bus had fallen very quiet again.

'I didn't play,' I said.

'You didn't play! We went all the way to Blackpool and you didn't play!'

'He was upset,' my grandmother put in.

'I wasn't upset. I just didn't want to play.'

'Didn't want to play, or couldn't play? Didn't want to play, or wouldn't come out of your shell?'

(Something else my sisters had been doing while they were on the loose in Blackpool – collecting shells from the beach to slip into my pocket when we were back on the bus.)

'I don't think they'd have let me play with my book.'

'Did you ask?'

'No.'

'No. 'Course not. Why ask? Too much of a kuni-lemele to ask. Better to hide in a corner and go red. Or maybe you were sitting on the Benghazi smelling your own chazzerei the whole time you were there.'

'Joel!' my mother said.

'I don't know,' I said, 'if I want to play with a book any more.'

'Fine. So get a bat.'

'I don't know if I'll be any good with a bat.'

'Right!' he said. That was the end of it. Right meant discussion over. In arguments with my mother, right meant that the bus would be parked in some very odd places that night. In arguments with me, right usually meant no more than that he'd lost interest.

But a couple of days later I came home from school to find the bus outside the house and my father sitting on the garden wall waiting for me. Never in my life had I seen my father sitting on this, or any other, garden wall. 'Right!' he said. 'We're going out.'

He had a queer elsewhere expression on his face. As though he had decided that I no longer existed and was going to address all future comments to a ghost boy standing behind me.

'Where are we going?'

'You'll see when we get there.'

32

I should have noticed that he was carrying a brown holdall but I was too anxious about what was happening to notice anything. My father was never home at this time of the day. He never sat on walls. He never took me anywhere. And he never talked to ghosts.

'Is Ma all right?' I asked.

'Everybody's all right. Hop in.'

Everybody was all right but my father was taking me somewhere. Was he taking me to be adopted?

He drove without speaking, but calmly. Up Blackley New Road, past the reservoirs where other boys' fathers took them fishing, around the biscuit factory which always smelt of malted milk and which I therefore thought a woman's breasts would smell like once I next got to suckle some, and then slowly by the gates of Crumpsall Hospital.

A hospital – was that it? Electric-shock treatment to get me out of the toilet? A lobotomy?

But we didn't stop at the hospital. Nor at the Jews' Cemetery which abutted it. So it was life we were chasing, was it? More frightening still.

After about fifteen minutes he slowed down alongside some playing fields, peered out of my window, then drove another fifty yards before pulling in by a building that resembled a cricket pavilion.

'Out,' he said.

'What are we doing?' I asked.

'*We're* not doing anything. *You're* joining the Akiva.'

I'd heard of the Akiva. The Akiva Social Club. Hadn't one of my aunties on my father's side once been treasurer, prior to rumours that she'd been caught shmuckling subscriptions? All hushed up. Hadn't another of the Walzer women found a husband there – someone else's husband – at a Chanukkah dance? Also hushed up. How could *I* join the Akiva? The Akiva was for grown-up sophisticates and socialites. I was twelve. You don't need a shmuckling treasurer for a club that has twelve-year-olds as members. Nor an adulterous dance floor . . .

Aha – a dance floor! So that was it. A dance floor. Forget the lobotomy; the man I could no longer call a man let alone a father had dragged me from my home and was now going to deposit me into the middle of a hokey-cokey – in my school blazer! Come on, Oliveler, join the line, join the line.

'No,' I said. It was a small protest but at least I made it. 'No.'

He took me by the arm. 'Don't make this difficult for yourself,' he warned me.

What happened next seemed to happen very quickly. One minute we were signing forms; then I was shaking the hand of someone preternaturally affable, in a painfully obvious wig, and with a still more painfully obvious hearing-aid; then I was walking down a long passage with my father; then he was turning the handle of a door.

The door opened on to a ping-pong room. There were about half a dozen people in there, two playing, the rest sitting around. They were all older than me, I saw that at once. What I also saw was that they were not sophisticates or socialites. No one had told me that in any club the table tennis room is always where the nebbishes and nishtikeits hang out, but I was able to make an immediate assessment along those lines unaided, for all that I was a running river of no-hoper embarrassment myself.

For their part, they greeted my arrival as though a bad smell had entered the room. I know now it wasn't personal. Over the years I have seen that look a thousand times. Just when you think you've got the table to yourselves for the evening, mapped out a competition and started to relax into a little light male conversation – chipping, moodying, fannying – in walks a kuni-lemele with his dad.

But I knew from the pressure on my shoulders that there was no point in hanging back.

'Play,' my father said. 'I'll be in the bus waiting for you. I'll wait as long as it takes. But don't come back out in under two hours.'

'I'm not prepared,' I said. 'I haven't brought my book.'

Only then did I notice that he was carrying a holdall. 'You said you didn't want to play with a book any more,' he said. 'So here.' He unzipped the bag and brought out a bat. The biggest bat I had ever seen in my life. A good eighteen inches in diameter, as heavy as a hockey stick, its surface coated with coarse sandpaper, so that what? – so that I should make the sparks fly?

'Nah. Geh gesunterhait. Win.'

And he shoved me into the room.

Some time later I learnt that my father had made the bat with parts from his precious Yo-Yo which he'd been hoarding for over twenty years.

So he loved me after all.

THREE

The 'free hand' is the hand not carrying the racket.

5.5 *The Rules*

W E NOW ENTER an embarrassing phase even by the standards of this history of embarrassments. I can at least promise brevity.

My father was right to want to prise me out. Out of my shell and out of the lavatory. But I was further in than he knew.

Sometimes I wondered whether I was further in than any boy had ever been. Somebody had to be the World Shell-Skulking Champion, somebody had to hold the record for time sitting steaming on top of his own chazzerei – why shouldn't it have been me?

Somebody had to have had the most disgusting imagination in history, as well, and the scummiest ever habits to go with it; and there I yielded to no one, man or boy. I had some way to go yet before I became the ping-pong player I had it in me to be; but I was already the Ogimura of filth.

The hand that built the Yo-Yo built the bat, but the hand that rocked the cradle moved the hand that wasn't carrying a bat. You understand me?

Take time.

So far I've shovelled whatever blame I can on to my father's side. Now it's my mother's side's turn. In an important sense, it wasn't me who was bolting the lavatory door and making love to myself for sessions which I considered brutally foreshortened if they failed to exceed three hours. It was them.

I choose my words carefully. *Love*.

I was a pupil at a boys-only grammar school with vague Church of England associations and a motto taken from Seneca – POTENTISSIMUS EST, QUI SE HABET IN POTESTATE – which translated roughly into HE IS MOST POWERFUL WHO TAKES HIMSELF IN HAND. Which was what we did. We took ourselves in hand from nine in the morning until four in the afternoon, with no more than thirty minutes off for lunch. Prayers at assembly, 'Gaudeamus Igitur', 'Let Us Now Praise Famous Men', and then six and a half hours of self-love, singly, together, in teams competitively, in teams callisthenically, in the playground, in the showers, in the library, in the gym, under the coconut mat, up the wallbars, over the vaulting-horse, behind the cricket nets, behind the blackboard, under the desks, in the inkwells beneath the very noses of our teachers. St Onan's Church of England Grammar School for Boy Perverts, Radcliffe.

Jerking or jacking off, was what the other boys called it. Their prerogative. They were less nice in their vocabulary than I was; they came from less particular homes; and they treated themselves with less respect. It's not for me to judge. I can only state that there was nothing jacky or jerky in what I was doing. And nothing to justify the idea of off, either. I stayed on. May God be my witness, I stayed on.

Alone. The other thing some of the less nice boys did was to disobey the school motto and take hold of someone else. I never went along with that. Such a practice was against the Kamenets

Podolski faith which still pulsed faintly in my blood. Besides, I had no taste for it. I didn't like what Church of England boys looked like. I preferred me.

Love – I don't know what else to call it. I fell for myself. I swore eternal fidelity to myself, made myself promises I would never be able to keep. Jerk? No flesh has ever been shown steadier or more silky consideration than I showed to mine. Except that it wasn't really me who was showing it. It was *them*. My mother's side. They were the ones making promises they would never be able to keep.

Was I engaged, then, in multiple incest? Most definitely yes, if showing silky consideration to yourself while viewing photographs of your mother's side, alive and dead, is incest. But incest isn't the half of it. Oh, no. Incest isn't the quarter of it. Not even when it's multiple and mortuary incest. And if I am to accept my responsibility for the damnable things that were thought inside that shell and done behind that door, they must accept theirs.

I've promised brevity so I won't waste time on all the usual psycho family biog stuff – the circumcision carried out by an aspen-leaf Mohel with delirium tremens and dirt beneath his fingernails; the bloody bandages; the mother's guilt drying up the mother's milk; the furious denunciation of God and His ways; the bet-hedging remorse, expressed in renewed prayers and promises; the pledge to make it up to the boy and his putz, to be over-and-above solicitous to the boy, and over-and-above over-and-above solicitous to his putz, for ever and ever Amen. Yes, I was fussed over. Yes, I was lovingly washed and exquisitely talcum'd and meticulously dried, as though the wound had never healed and never would heal. And yes, yes I was – to employ the humiliating idiom of my mother's side – held out over the lavatory come pee-pee time, confidentially squeezed and shaken and squeezed again like a hose-pipe during a hose-pipe ban. But that's normal. What was exceptional was the number of women doing it.

My father was serving in the army when I was born. Driving a truck and re-styling his officers' trousers. ('You look like a tailor, Walzer,' they'd observed, 'take these in.' And he did.) It was news of me that got him out of going overseas where the fighting was. And by the time he'd completed his compassionate leave there was no fighting left. But there is driving and tailoring to be done even in peacetime, so he wasn't demobbed immediately. Which meant that the world I was just starting to see the right way up was exclusively populated by females. I had two sisters. My mother had three sisters, one of whom, Fay, lived with us in the absence of my father, while the other two limited their visits to a dozen times a day, more often than not in the company of their mother. So how many women is that?

There was a grandfather on my mother's side, but he was one of the reasons all the women came to us. He drank. Isaac Saffron, shicker to us, piss-pot to you. I'm still keeping it brief. He drank, actually pulled pints in the manner of a shaygets behind a bar in Collyhurst so he could be close to the supply, bet on the dogs, treated my grandmother like a domestic, klopped my aunties, and on one famous occasion – the straw that broke the camel's back – drove out a party of my mother's friends who had been sitting around in paper hats celebrating her eighteenth birthday. 'There'll be no bloody atheists in this house,' he shouted, stumbling into the furniture and threatening to burn the place down. I have several photographs of my grandfather. He is handsome in the early ones, a little Polski princeling with sleepy eyes, a voluptuous mouth and dainty hands and feet. By the time there are photographs that have me in them as well he has lost his looks to alcohol. But in one regard nothing changes – in all of them he has his fists clenched.

The atheism charge was a reference to the free-thinking company my mother kept and provides a clue, over and above her delicate yet fleshy oval beauty, to why my father was so keen to marry her. She knew communists, she dated doctors, she hummed Tchaikovsky, she corresponded with men who were fighting with the International Brigade in Spain, and she read books. It wasn't that she opened the door to the mind for my father; it was that she kept it closed. If he married her he'd be able to go on never reading a book himself. *She* could look after all that.

It was the best sort of match: they loved each other for what they didn't have in common. For her part, she loved him because he brought the lightness of inconsequentiality into her life, entertained her with tsatskes, and wasn't frightened of anything.

She was still only eighteen when they married, and he was hardly much older than that himself. Immediately after the wedding he drove her away in a big chocolate and cream shooting-brake which he'd coach-built for her with his own hands, along the lines of the mobster getaway saloons he'd seen in George Raft movies. My grandmother was unable to join the crowd of well-wishers waving them off. She stood with her back to the street, her face buried in her hands, praying aloud that they should be delivered from the evil eye – 'Kayn aynhoreh zol nit zayn!' My aunties, too, trembled for their sister. A husband, laughter, a big car – how much further could she push her luck?

The Shrinking Violets was the name my father gave his sisters-in-law. He always alluded to them collectively – 'What, no Shrinking Violets for tea tonight?' or 'I hope we can at least go to that together, just the two of us, without the Shrinking Violets in tow' – as though they were an established showbiz group like the Andrews Sisters. Inevitably you pictured them on stage with a big band singing 'Bei Mir Bist Du Shain', which was ludicrous since it was actually impossible to picture them on stage doing anything.

They were frightened of everything, my mother's side. A stroll in the park, the tweet of a bird, the approach of a stranger. Let a moth come in through an open window on a summer's night and beat its wings in a lampshade, and their lives hung in doubt before them. A thread finer than cobweb attached them to life, finer than gossamer.

(And here's something interesting – in its earliest days that was what ping-pong was called: Gossima.)

After my grandmother died, a whole wardrobe of unworn garments was discovered, some of it dating back to when she was a bride herself. Dozens of 'best' dresses on their original hangers, drawers of long skirts and high-buttoned blouses still folded as the shop-girls had folded them fifty years before, shoes in their boxes, silk stockings, items of underwear that had never been taken out of their wrappings. Gifts, most of them. Gifts she was unable to accept in her heart. She wasn't worthy. Gifts were for other people. And 'best' was always for some future time which, like the Messiah, was never meant to come. Be seen by the Almighty risking the presumption of a 'best' frock, and the heavens would come down on you.

She was good company for a small boy. She turned Cheetham Hill into a Polish shtetl for me. The street signs said Waterloo Road, Elizabeth Street, St James's Road, but we were in Sowalki. She wore furry boots in all weathers, and a scarf tied around her head against the wind howling across the steppes from Siberia. We crossed the roads slowly, watching where we put our feet, as though we were traversing muddy fields, our eyes peeled for the wolves waiting to pounce on us from the forest that was Mandley Park. She taught me to krich – to hobble along like a little old peasant with a back bent from years of carrying sacks of matzo meal. We kriched along together. Where she took me, no one spoke English. Or minded when she poked at their merchandise, showing me how you recognized bad fruit, how you opened up a hen's legs and stuck your nose into its rectum to be certain it was fresh. She held my hand tightly, protected me from all dangers, and filled my head full of alarms. She wasn't much taller than me either. When she patted me or kissed me I could look straight into her inconsolable blue eyes. It was like having a little girlfriend, ten times my age. And foreign to boot. I adored her.

I adored them all. Not my sisters. No one adores his sisters. But that still left me with five – a mother, a granny, and three aunties (the Shrinking Violets) – all fine-boned and fluttering. My seraglio.

One by one, and to everybody's astonishment, the Shrinking Violets found men who wanted to marry them. But that was much later. When I was growing up they each had the letter S for spinster emblazoned on their chests. I'm not being critical of the single state. They could have worn their S with pride. Instead of being mortified when a baby goo-gooed at them on a bus, they could have taken it in their arms and kissed it. 'Not for me, though I'm sure you're nice for someone else,' they could have told it. Instead of turning crimson when a shop-girl offered to assist them they could have said, 'No thank you, I will do as I mean to go on doing, and assist myself.' What, after all, did they fear that babies and shop-girls had over them? Knowledge of the mystic meaning of the letter S, that's what.

Babies and shop assistants behaved irrationally, made sudden movements towards you, like spiders, and a sudden movement is to an S for spinster what a cross rubbed with garlic is to a vampire.

On Saturdays they used to take me to town, sometimes to buy me a jigsaw, new rubber rings for the hoop-la board, a whole book of crosswords, a new Collins Classic to add to my collection, but in the main to replenish their supplies of S brand haberdashery – yards of spiritless elastic and broken-hearted lace, spinster zips, spinster fasteners, spinster hooks and eyes, all the cheerless wherewithal to repair their lumpy brassieres and granny stockings and God knows what else. That was the fun part. It was the bus journey there and back I dreaded. Did we ever, my three S-emblazoned aunties and I, enjoy a single carefree bus ride? Not that I recall. If there wasn't a goo-gooing baby to embarrass and frighten us there was a drunk, or a madman, or an invalid we didn't know how to help, or a jeering gang of prefab boys. Irrational movers, all of them. From whom we had no choice but to leap. As a consequence, we drew notice to ourselves the way black holes suck in the stray matter of the universe. Notice and misadventure. We'd upset the conductor, we'd drop money, we'd lose our tickets, we'd stand on people's feet, we'd fall into the invalid and spill him off the bus. And the blushing of one of us would set off the blushing of the others. Off we'd go – red, red, red, red – like traffic lights that are running against you. There is no hiding place on a bus. You either jump off or you suffer the exposure. And we were of no assistance to one another. The shy are tyrants. They are consumed by their own appetite for suffering. Nothing else matters. No one else exists. We lowered our eyes and individually burned, leaving the others to die in their own flames.

Back in my parents' or my grandparents' house, where nobody was looking, the ordinary affections could be resumed. I could dote on my aunties and, more to the point, they could dote on me.

Did they 'hold me out'? I must be scrupulous here; I owe that to the love we bore one another. I don't know whether they held me out. I can't remember and I am not prepared to say I have suppressed the memory. (Why would I want to add the burden of suppression to everything I already do remember?) But that I was capable of being held out they were, if you can understand me, more conscious than I believe they ought to have been. It's a matter of degrees of awareness. There was another odious euphemism to which I was subjected as a little boy. *In-between.* Shaming but true – the thing I had that made me not my sisters, the thing the shaking Mohel had taken a dirty-fingered moon-shaped slice out of and which thereafter and for evermore needed scrupulous bathing and talcuming, the thing I was held out by, did not, in our house, go by any of the usual anatomical or nursery-rhyme names – a penis or the intromittent organ, say; a winkle or John Thomas – no, what I had was an *in-between*. And everybody knew it.

In the end, the point is not whether my seraglio of women should or should not have enjoyed familiarity with my in-between, understood what it was and where it was – in the end the only point that matters is that with my father away and my grandfather permanently drunk and the Violets shrinking from every approach, mine was the only in-between between them.

Enough said. Whatever harm I did them, the measure of the harm they had done me was the box of family photographs I was now smuggling into the lavatory as many times a day as I could get away with. And if you think a box of family photographs simply means a box of family photographs, you've got another think coming.

The box itself nags at my conscience like an undiscovered weapon used to commit an unconfessed crime. Is it still where I left it? Will it ever be found? After all this time, *should* it ever be found?

It was a chocolate box originally, a de luxe beau monde two-storey coffret, padded, scented, covered in pink velvet and lined with crimson silk. It had once cradled two pounds of the best quality Austro-Hungarian marzipan. An aged and toothless admirer, a fourth or fifth cousin on the non-Walzer side, had embarrassed Fay with it, and she had disembarrassed herself of it on to me. The lid showed a scene from one of Mozart's operas. I doubt if it was *Il Seraglio*. Pink ribbons were sewn into the velvet, and with these you secured the lid or released it. When I'd finished what I was doing I'd tie a bow with the pink ribbons, listen to be sure the coast was clear, make a dash across the landing from the lavatory to my bedroom, and stuff the box in a suitcase under my bed.

Now for the contents. I have said that these were family

photographs. Naturally I mean that they were photographs of my mother's side of the family – photographs of my mother herself, my grandmother, and the Shrinking Violets; some of them studio studies, but, in the main, snaps I had taken with my little box camera during one of our peregrinations around Sowalki, or on a blushing trip to Lewis's at the top of Market Street. Photographs that had men in them were of course no use to me. Nor were group photographs of any sort. One woman at a time was how I liked it. And not necessarily alive. I had a good one of my grandmother's mother Cheena, for example, looking pensive in a feathered hat. And another of my great-great-aunt Sophia, come to Bialystok in her rustling finery to pose against a painted forest and gain immortality in the putrefying imagination of a twelve-year-old boy still half a century away from being born.

Is it such a sin, jacking off, as the Church of England boys put it, over loved ones? In its own clumsy way, doesn't beating one's meat over the female branches of the family tree show a certain groping genealogical respect? If you're gonna spill, spill over your own.

That would have been my defence, had the marzipan box gone on containing only what I have so far described. But I have, and had, no defence. No defence, no excuse, no rationale, no sanity.

Soon, satiated with the aplasticity of the photographs themselves, I added to my scented coffret of concupiscence the following: a magnifying glass, a pair of kitchen scissors, a tube of glue, and pages of particular appeal torn from *Span*, a pin-up magazine I had fallen into the habit of buying, the minute I was able to lose the hand of a Violet, from a soft-porno shop on Deansgate, immediately opposite Manchester Cathedral. All porno was soft then. Girls hitching up their skirts, showing a suspender, looking down at their own disarrangement in astonishment, unable to account for how a breast with an unaroused nipple, or a star where the nipple should have been, had slipped its moorings. No split beavers in those days. No beaver of any sort unless you went for *Health and Efficiency* and then you had to put up with the volleyball and the rest of the family. Otherwise not a hint of a hair, let alone a labium. That was what the magnifying glass was for. To see if I could detect where a hair had once been. And the scissors . . . and the glue . . . ?

Ah, the scissors and the glue . . .

On its own, *Span* was nothing, a half-hearted iniquity no matter how filthy the ever-irked, all-judging proprietor of the soft-porno shop tried to make me feel, refusing me a brown paper bag, daring me to check my change, not taking his eyes off me as I stuffed the magazine into my shirt. What were they to me, these hard-faced yekeltehs with dead eyes and thin lips who resembled no one so much as the mothers of the prefab boys who threw stones at me when I left the house? What they did with their bodies on the other hand, their lewd gestures, the shamelessness with which they bent over or found pretexts for letting you see up their skirts or down their blouses . . . that was something else. Be strictly logical about it and you'd have to say that their bodily contortions perfectly matched their facial expressions; that only women who looked as though they lived in prefabs and brought their kids up to throw stones could have cared so little for the aesthetics of the human form. But since when did lewdness ever have anything to do with a perfect match? Disparity – that, surely, is where lewdness has always found its home. An elegant woman in an inelegant pose, a demure face on an obscenely splayed body. Where's the shock of seeing reserve thrown to the winds, if there was never any reserve there in the first place? Well, I was the one to ask. I had lived for twelve years in a reservation of reserve. There were things I understood. As, for example, that there would have been no erotic pay-off whatsoever in cutting out the faces of the women on my father's side and attaching them to the bodies of the toerags who flashed the lot for *Span*. This is not to say that they were in any way toeraggy themselves, only that they were already uninhibited rompers. For this to work, it had to be the refined, sensitive oval faces of my mother's side – faces utterly dear to me – that I desecrated.

Yes, I am saying what it looks as though I'm saying. Much like a sweet little girl playing with her cut-out dolls – except that a sweet little girl will mix and match on the dining-room table or on a sunlit lawn in the company of other ambrosial chits her own age, whereas I was stewing it alone and malodorous in the lavatory – I changed the outfits worn by the women I revered, got them to open their legs and show me the tops of their stockings, the lace on their pants, turned them round and bent them over, enticed them into peignoirs and babydoll pyjamas, cut them into French maids, naughty nurses, leggy belles from St Trinian's, cowgirls who couldn't stay on a horse or keep their tushes in their chaparejos.

And I did this even to my little Polish grandmother?

Especially to my little Polish grandmother.

Scissoring with the utmost care, I cut around the contours of her face, freeing her from the gross contingencies of Piccadilly or Cheetham Hill, then slowly, lovingly, I separated her head from her body. Now she was mine to love as only I knew how to love her. Up on to six-inch high heels I hoiked her, fishnetted, frilly-knickered, fingering a cane; out of an upper-storey window I leaned her, a wanton housewife in a scant pinny, shaking out a feather duster and jiggling her introverted-nippled breasts; down on a scarlet bed I laid her, wearing her peasant scarf as always, God-fearing, inconsolably blue-eyed, sixty-five years of age, but in her 'best' at last – a gossamer négligé of ankle length, through which, with the help of my magnifying glass, I could just make out where the snatch should have been.

Trying to find some saving grace in all this, I can only thank the Almighty in whom my grandmother placed her trust that split-beaver shots were not around when I was twelve.

I repeat, too, that I never co-opted a single page of *Health and Efficiency* to my cause. I come from a culture which attaches a near religious significance to the family and sanctifies the old: I wasn't going to have a grandmother of mine kriching after a volleyball on some beach in Scandinavia.

FOUR

Exceptionally, strict observance of the prescribed method
of service may be waived where the umpire is notified,
before play begins, that compliance is prevented by physical disability.

7.7 *The Rules*

IN FAIRNESS TO them, the Akiva ping-pong players, on whose
mercies my father had thrown me, could have given me a
much harder time of it than they did.

They could have left me standing there for the whole evening,
for example, the way I was left standing on the touchline at
St Onan's, instead of just for the first hour. I wouldn't have
complained. I wasn't in any position to complain. What rights
did I have? It was their table. They were grown men, some of
them, sort of. And I was wearing a school blazer enjoining me
to take a firm hold of myself, a comic strip bat in my hand.

As it turned out, it was the bat that broke the ice.

When I say they were grown men, some of them, sort of, I
mean to render not so much the uncertainties of an unusually
apprehensive twelve-year-old, as the approximateness of the
company itself. If I were to encounter them again as they were
then, myself as I am now, I think I would still be struck by how
sort of they were. And it was the most sort of of them all – a

tall, baby-bald man in his forties, I reckoned, who neither played nor sat down, but circumnavigated the room the whole time in a buttoned-up blue raincoat and heavy shoes, talking and laughing to himself – who finally addressed me. He'd climbed up on to the little stage, presumably to win attention for his cleverness (there is always a little stage in the room where people play table tennis, just as there is always a scullery where the janitor keeps the mops), and was standing where the comedian would have stood. 'Someone's gotta tell you, so I will – you're in the wrong club, son.' He had a queer quick stuttering delivery, like an automatic weapon that cut out after every other round. 'We don't play lacrosse here. Why don't you get your old man to take you to the YMCA?'

It pleases me to recall that no one was amused. 'Nisht, Gershom, nisht,' I heard one of them say. Leaving me to roast was one thing, being outright rude to me was another.

'Come and have a hit,' the 'nisht, Gershom, nisht' person invited me, after Gershom had shrugged his shoulders and gone on another self-communing ramble round the room. 'But not with that bat. You'll shneid the ball.'

He handed me his bat. A Victor Barna: nipple-brown rubber pimples, medium fast, smooth stubby wooden handle with no tape or strapping around it. It slid into my grip like the hand of an old friend. In an earlier life I must have played with a Victor Barna. Owner of the best backhand there has ever been, and winner of more world championship titles than any other player before or since, Victor Barna first took the men's singles in 1929–30, lost it the following year to Miklos Szabados, then recaptured and held on to it for four years running, defeating Szabados (in the finals, twice), Kolar and Bellak. Players, from the sound of it, from roughly the same neck of the woods as my father's side; the Bug, the Dniester, the Danube – Slavs and Magyars whichever way you cut us. In an earlier life could I have been Victor Barna?

I took off my jacket and stood at the table, not daring to pop my head out of my burning shell and look around me, scalded, abashed, suffocating, certain that no one would give me a game. And certainly no one wanted to. The likeliest was the owner of the Barna bat, but then how could he play me if I had his bat? Twink, I'd heard the others call him, when he'd done something worthy of remark, or suffered a reverse, on the table. 'Shot, Twink.' 'Unlucky, Twink.' Otherwise, Theo. 'You going to Laps' later, Theo?' So he had two names: a social name and a ping-pong name. He was lanky, very thin, sixteen or seventeen years old, with an asthmatic cough, a little face that was all but shut out by a cascade of Tony Curtis quiffs, and good looping attacking shots. Whenever he over-hit or netted, he coughed up something phlegmy from his lungs and banged his bat against his leg. I was impressed by his ability to use the width of the table and find the edges. Not overawed, just impressed.

It was Theo . . . no, Twink . . . no, Theo, for this was a social act . . . yes, but ping-pong related – it was Twink who, having lent me his bat, got me a game. 'Go on, Aishky, give the teapot lid a knock. What'll it cost you?'

Aishky looked like Esau – strong armed, superfluously freckled, an angry mob of red hair overrunning his shirt and fanning out around his neck and shoulders. But it was Esau's father Isaac who was the short-sighted one as I recall, so in that regard Aishky was more like him. He wore inch-thick bulletproof lenses in his glasses, which he had to wipe between points.

We fell immediately into a lengthy version of the knock-up, forehand drive against forehand drive, backhand against backhand, no scoring, no one trying to win a point, simply keeping the ball in play. How did I understand this convention, how did I know, without ever having been taught any of the interpersonal skills of ping-pong, not to try to pass or thwart Aishky, not to try to out-fox or out-chop him, but just to keep it going, plock, plock; plock, plock; plock, plock; plock, plock? Reincarnation.

In an earlier life I *had* been Victor Barna. Even if Victor Barna himself was not dead yet.

Since I did understand the convention, though, it was wrong of me to break it. But what could I do? We'd been knocking up for ten minutes and he hadn't yet acknowledged I existed. He was hitting the ball automatically, with half his eye on it – and half an eye for Aishky was a quarter of an eye for anybody else – continuing his conversation with Twink/Theo and the rest of them about some bird with big bristles he'd been seen dancing with in the Azlap on Oxford Road on Saturday night. (Bristles, notice, not bristols. In fifties Manchester we thought of women as bristling with breast.) 'What was she like?' he wanted to know. 'I had my bins off, I couldn't see her. Was she fair?' Plock.

'Meers,' the others teased him. 'A dog. But if you were happy . . .'

'Who says I was happy?' Plock.

'You had your eyes closed.'

'I was asleep.' Plock.

'Nebach. You missed seeing the bristles to end all bristles.'

'What do you mean I missed seeing them?' Plock.

'She had them out.'

'On the dance floor?' Plock.

'Sure.'

'Out of her bra?' Plock.

'Completely.'

'You're moodying me.' Plock.

'I'm not.'

'Moody-merchant!' Plock.

'She had them *completely out of her bra*, Aishky. How many more times?'

'Both of them?' Plock.

'What's with the both? You think there were only two?'

'My mazel! I'd been trying to get those bristles out all night. That's why I was so tired. Now you're telling me I slept through them.' Plock. Plock.

Tcheppehing, we called this in those days. Anglicized to chipping. Verbal lumberjacking. I loved it. How much longer before I would be allowed to join in? Be one of the boys at last? 'What the eye doesn't see, the heart doesn't grieve over,' I thought of contributing. But I didn't have the balls.

In the meantime my opponent was still taking no more notice of me than if I'd been the plaster whorl I practised against at home; less, because you had to watch a whorl. So when a ball finally did sit up for hitting I hit it, not diagonally in the direction it had come from, making it easy for him to return by reflex, without looking and while still tcheppehing his chinas, and not with a nice high friendly topspin bounce either, but straight down the line and flat – a shot that is all feint and deviance – and faster than the speed of light.

Years later, even after he had lost two fingers from his right hand in an accident in a phone box and had taught himself to play again with his left, right up until the time he lost a further two fingers, this time from his left hand, in an explosion at a retail bedding warehouse, Aishky Mistofsky was still recounting the story of how we'd met. 'To tell you the emmes, that night I'd gone along to the club for a quiet game of kalooki. I didn't feel like running around. My nerves were giving me trouble. And I'd just come out of a bath. Yes, I had my bat with me, but that didn't mean anything. Anyone who knows me will tell you I don't go anywhere without my bat. Anyway, I get to the card room and no one's turned up yet, so I think I may as well take a kuk at the table tennis room. How far is it to walk? The usual gang's there – Sheeny Waxman, Twink Starr, Louis Marks, Gershom Finkel, all nice people. And we're sitting around, having a knock and a nobbel, when suddenly – and you'll split your sides at this – in walks this kid carrying a bat as big as the Empire State Building, challenges me to a game and starts shmeissing the ball past me. I'm telling you I've never seen a ball hit faster. And this is just the knock-up! I think OK, Chaim Yankel, say your prayers, and

I start zetzing the ball myself. Makes no difference. I hit it hard, he hits it back twice as hard. Then he puts a chop on it. Oy! – I see it spinning backwards in the air. And fizzing. Like Superman's chopped it. That's it. I put my bat down, look across at Twink Starr, whose mouth has fallen half-way off his face, and I say, "OK, maestro, so you give the teapot lid a knock. What'll it cost you?" But we both knew a legend had been born.'

Sweet of him. Doubly sweet of him, considering the tragedy of his own career. But the reality was more mundane. They woke up to the fact that I could play a bit, that was all that happened. They took an interest in me. All of them except Gershom Finkel who said, 'He's got brawn but no timing. He's a shtarker, nothing else.'

'Do me a favour, Gershom,' Aishky said to him. 'You know as well as I do that you can't hit a ball that hard unless you know how to time it.'

'Depends how it comes to you. You were feeding his strengths. You never played him short.'

'Easier said than done.'

'I don't say what I can't do. I could clean the kid up with my wrong hand.'

(Where am I while all this is going on? I'm standing there like a kuni-lemele, counting the pimples on Twink's bat, shell-locked, listening to the patter of my perspiration on the club floor.)

'So do it,' Aishky dared him. 'I'd like to see you.'

'I'm in my coat,' Gershom said. 'I'm not taking my coat off.'

'Keep it on. If you can clean him up with your wrong hand, you can clean him up in your coat.'

'I don't have anything to prove,' Gershom said. 'And I don't give free lessons.' Whereupon he went walkabout again.

'Ignore him,' Aishky advised me. 'He used to be a great player. Now he's just a mamzer.'

'What do you mean a *great* player?' Twink put in. 'One of the *greatest*. The guy was mustard. He played for England twice.

54

And made it to the quarter-finals in Baden the year Bergmann won. It may even have been Bergmann who beat him. That's how good he was. Louis'll know. Louis, who beat Gershom in Baden in '39?'

I hadn't taken much notice of Louis. He hadn't played, that was why. I hadn't seen what he was made of. He'd scored a few games and laughed hysterically at the bristle jokes, groaning with pain because he'd hurt his ribs and pulled muscles in his back and chest and laughing made them worse; but I hadn't otherwise been aware of him. It was hard to tell how old he was. He lifted weights – which was how he had come to have damaged most of the muscles in his body – and this gave him the torso of a man in his twenties. But in the face he was a fifteen-year-old boy, a grinner, almost as shy as I was, with a mass of black hair that had never been combed and that muddy Dniester complexion that put me off my grandmother on my father's side. Test him with a name or a date, though, and his skin shone like a Yakipak's.

'Baden was '37 not '39!' he retorted. Why retort? He had only been asked a question. But I had noticed that no one spoke in a normal voice here. There was no discourse. Everyone shouted. Not in anger, but in a sort of perpetual sorrow that everyone else should be so wrong about everything for so much of the time.

'Does it matter when it was? I'm asking you who beat him.'

'I'm telling you – Sol Schiff, the finger-spinner. 26–24 in the third.'

'So who beat Schiff?'

'Who do you think! Bergmann. But not easily. No one beat Schiff easily. No one could handle his finger-spin service.'

'I thought they'd banned Sol Schiff's service,' Aishky said.

'Later – that was later. You're thinking of the Americans.'

'Why would I be thinking of the Americans?'

'Because they banned it.'

'Louis, do me a favour – was it banned or wasn't it?'

'It was banned in America, I've told you, but not in Baden. It took the International Federation another few years to wake up.'

'That means that if the World Championships had been held in America –'

Twink saw where Aishky was heading. '– And Gershom had been drawn against Schiff there –'

Louis laughed wildly. It was almost a sob. '– He'd have been given a walk-over, yeah. And maybe gone on to take the title. But what's the point of talking? He didn't.'

We exchanged crestfallen expressions, then turned our eyes as one man on the strange loping buttoned-up figure of Gershom Finkel, wispily bald in that manner that suggests the hairs are yet to come rather than that they've been and gone, still circumnavigating the room and still muttering and laughing sarcastically to himself. We were all thinking the same thing. Was this any way for a great ping-pong player to have ended up?

My father was waiting for me as he'd promised, asleep on the wheel of his bus. I'd been in the club four hours. I was surprised I recognized him.

'So how was it?' he wanted to know.

'They've all got something wrong with them,' I said.

He let go of the wheel and banged the side of his head with the heel of his hand. An upward brushing movement, as though he wanted to clear unwelcome matter from his brain. *They've all got something wrong with them.* He hated that sort of talk. Judgements, judgements. The stuff I'd picked up from my mother and the Violets. We couldn't say boo to a goose, any of us, but we knew what we thought of the goose, oh yes.

'I didn't ask what they were like,' he said. 'I asked how it went.'

'It went well,' I said. 'They've asked me to play for the team.'

'Ah!' Now he was pleased with me. 'Thank you.' He drove on in silence for a few minutes, looking at me out of the corner of his eye. Pride? Did I see pride? Then he asked, 'And how was the bat?'

You can't hurt your own father on the one occasion he's pleased with you. 'It was good,' I said. 'Better than the book.'

'Ah! Thank you.' More silence, and then, 'You had a good night, then?'

'Yeah.'

'Thank you.'

Why did he keep on thanking me? I can only suppose it was because I'd put him in the right, at last. Proved that I was his true son and heir. Proved that he knew how to do the best for me. There was so much unaccustomed harmony between us, at any rate, that instead of turning left at Middleton Road he turned right, kept on going past the park and the mills and pulled up in front of a detached white-washed cottage by the rubberworks in Rhodes. 'Home, James,' he said.

I had to explain to him that this wasn't where we lived.

He took a moment or two to get his bearings, then he said, 'You're right. Thank you. Thank you.'

'So how was it?' my mother wanted to know. My aunties, too, who had stayed around at our place later than usual, waiting for me to come home. Waiting to kvell.

'They've all got something wrong with them,' I said.

'Such as what?' Tell us, tell us.

'Bits missing.'

'We don't believe you.' Love and laughter, for the bright boy. We don't believe you, but tell us, tell us anyway.

'They have. They've all got bits missing. Broken ribs. Tuberculosis.'

'Tuberculosis?'

This was a tactical error on my part. My mother was all for

me playing ping-pong because she believed it was safe. No one got hurt playing ping-pong. Now I was telling her the game was riddled with infectious diseases.

'Well, not tuberculosis exactly,' I corrected myself. 'More like asthma.'

'If they've got asthma they shouldn't be playing.'

'Ma, none of them should be playing. One of them's about a hundred and won't take his coat off. Another's blind.'

'Blind?'

'He was the one I beat.'

How they laughed. They loved it when I was wicked, my mother's side. It empowered them. We'd get into a huddle and we'd call the goose for all sorts.

But that always encouraged me to go too far. 'The other one I beat,' I went on, 'was dead.'

'Zei gezunt,' my mother said. 'You're overexcited. Go to bed.'

By morning the atmosphere had changed. My mother had worked out that playing for a team entailed travelling. 'I'm not sure I like the idea of you charging off God knows where at your age,' she said, over cheese on toast. That was breakfast. The entire time I lived in my mother's and father's house I ate only cheese on toast for breakfast. We had a corona of melted cheese around our hearts, each of us. My father died of melted cheese in every artery. Yet my mother was worried that I'd come to harm playing ping-pong for the Akiva Social Club.

'I think we travel as a team,' I told her.

'Travel as a team how? In an aeroplane?'

'Ma, this is the Manchester and District Table Tennis League, Third Division. The furthest we go is Stockport.' I didn't know this for a fact. I was guessing.

'Stockport! And how are you supposed to get back from Stockport?'

'In a car, I imagine. One of the team drives us, Ma.'

'Which one of the team? The blind one?'

Funny she should have guessed that.

Pending certification by the League Secretary – and it took about ten days for my registration form to be received and scrutinized, my three-shilling postal order to be cashed, and for Aishky Mistofsky, who was Club Secretary, to be given the all-clear – I could practise with the team but not play for it.

In those days, when ping-pong players grew on trees, before – but let's not start the Jeremiah stuff; we all know that Greater Manchester is no longer Eden – a team numbered five, with five more clamouring to get a game. Prior to me, the Akiva Social Club – positioned neither at the very top nor at the very bottom of the Third Division North, but enjoying the middle of her favours – consisted of Aishky Mistofsky, Theo/Twink Starr, the Marks brothers – Louis and Selwyn – and Sheeny Waxman. Selwyn, the younger of the Markses, and the nearest to me in age of the whole bunch, I'd met briefly on my first night in the club without realizing he was Louis's brother. The word met might be stretching things a bit. He'd spoken to no one the whole time, not even Louis, so engrossed was he in rehearsing his shots. He played along in dumb show with whoever was on the table, hitting the ball exactly as they did and punishing himself when they missed. Although in rehearsal his repertory of strokes was prodigious, the moment it came to actual play he lost the nerve to try any of them, and was reduced to the safest of all safe shots, the backhand almost-horizontal shove, which he executed with the greatest deliberation from every corner of the table, never taking his eye off the ball, but to an accompaniment of all manner of insults against himself, as though his own timidity was a lasting shame to him. In appearance he was slight and undernourished; and apart from a premature moustache which grew with cruel disregard for shape or uniformity – a couple of dozen individual spikes of various lengths and colours – he was as white all over as a box of new balls, like a person who had never been seen by the sun.

Sheeny Waxman, notwithstanding Aishky Mistofsky's *post hoc* recollection that he'd been of our company on the night my talent was divulged, was an unknown quantity to me. He was very short, with a pronounced tic, and enjoyed a reputation as a head jockey – that was all I knew about him. A very short twitching head jockey with a terrific forehand. When I asked what a head jockey was they all laughed at me. 'Something like a linguist,' Theo confided, whereupon they all laughed again. As for Sheeny Waxman's forehand, only Louis Marks, on our team, had a forehand that could equal it. And Louis Marks was injured. Hence me.

I was going round to the Akiva almost every night now. If my father was home he would drive me. Otherwise I caught a local train from Bowker Vale to Woodlands Road, one or other of my aunties accompanying me to the station, just in case the prefab boys thought of launching an assault.

How anyone could have supposed that the prefab boys would have been deterred by a Shrinking Violet I can't imagine, but the ploy worked. The one time I was stoned was the one time I'd persuaded my mother I was now big enough to walk to the station on my own.

Usually Aishky Mistofsky drove me back. I'd promised my mother that if I didn't have a lift I would ring home and wait for someone to collect me. The trains stopped early and she didn't want me wandering in the dead of night. Not through that part of Manchester with all its shaygets perils. I didn't of course tell her that Aishky Mistofsky was indeed the blind one and that I was never in more danger than when he drove me home.

I had quickly grown fond of Aishky, in the gooey way a little kid grows fond of a big kid. I liked his gingery beaky face, which he brought very close to mine on account of his short-sightedness, and which he pressed right up against the windscreen of his Austin A40, for the same reason. I liked the way he laughed, throwing his head back and showing the red hairs at his throat – an action that didn't so much register the funniness or smartness of something someone had said, as the uncomplicated pleasure he took in someone being there to say something to him at all. And I liked the way he played ping-pong, earnestly, with a resolute arm, as though he owed something to the ball. He never defended, not even when that was the one sure way of beating his opponent. He liked to hit, rhythmically, conventionally, the bat starting low down, arcing predictably, and finishing high up, and if that didn't happen to be what it took to win that night, so he lost.

In this he was the very opposite of his best friend, Twink Starr, whose great strength was his ability to find the edge of the table, but who would grit his teeth, chew his tongue, alter the whole nature of his game – pushing, chopping, half-volleying, sweating buckets, coughing up phlegm – if that was the only way to win the match. But I'm running ahead of myself. Before there were any matches – at least as far as I was concerned – I had to be kitted out. 'For starters,' Twink reminded me, 'you can't go on borrowing my bat – you'll need your own.'

'What do you mean for starters?' Aishky queried. 'What else does he need?'

This was the other big difference between them. Aishky Mistofsky played in the clothes he came home from work in. He took off his jacket, rolled up his sleeves and changed his shoes, that was all. He didn't even loosen his tie. Whereas Twink Starr turned up already panting and dancing, like a prize fighter, in a hooded tracksuit, with a towel round his neck. Under the tracksuit, which he peeled off in stages, he wore a crested Fred Perry shirt, pleated shorts and long white socks with a blue stripe in them. In his bag he carried an asthma spray, two sets of sweatbands, a change of shirt and a small lawn-cotton hand towel with his own monograph sewn into it – *TS*. When the going got tough he would tuck this into his shorts like a waiter's tea cloth, so that he could dry the handle of his bat between points. Years later, professional tennis players competing for more prize money in a single fortnight than Twink Starr and Aishky Mistofsky could hope to earn between them in a lifetime would, as a matter of course, tuck lawn-cotton hand towels into their shorts. But before Twink Starr no racket-player had ever thought of doing such a thing.

'You want him to play in long hasen, like you?'

'What's wrong with long hasen?'

'You don't win in them, Aishky, that's what's wrong with them. And you have to keep them up with braces.'

'Barna won in long hasen.'

'That was the past, Aishky. Don't talk to me about the past. This kid's got a future – he has to have shorts.'

'The next thing you'll be saying, he has to have a Fred Perry shirt.'

'Well he can't play in his school blazer, can he, you potz.'

They took me to Alec Watson and Mitchell's in Market Street and continued to fight out their differences in front of the asssistants. 'Here,' Aishky called from the cricket counter, 'what about a jockstrap and a box to go in it?' And then from the football counter, 'And maybe some shin pads . . .'

'You're a meshuggener,' Twink shouted back across the shop. He was helping me choose a cover for my bat. Zip or stud, that was the issue. 'Do you hear what I'm saying? You're a meshuggener. You haven't won a match in a month. But you know what to wear, suddenly. You don't even look after your bat properly. You carry it around in a plastic bag with your sandwiches. I'm the one who has to pick the crumbs out of your pimples for you. You don't even know they're there. You don't even notice them. But you're an example to the kid!'

Aishky was in his element, shouting and being shouted at in a public place. His beaky face shone with bashfulness and audacity mixed. 'What about these?' he called out. He was now in the boxing section. 'You wouldn't want him to spiel without these, would you?' He was holding up a box of gum-shields.

'Do me a favour,' Twink said. It wasn't a retort. More a philosophical expostulation, to no one in particular.

I too was in my element. It was flattering to be argued over like this by two grown men, sort of. And I loved being in their element. It made me feel I was coming to the end of being a kid. A whole new world was opening to me, one in which *you* embarrassed the shop assistants. It beat having aunties all ends up.

Which reminded me: I was only a short walk across Corporation Street from the soft-porno shop opposite the Cathedral; if there was some way I could give Aishky and Twink the slip for ten minutes, leave them to argue over my ping-pong wardrobe without me, I could be back before the contemptuous behind-the-counter judge, stammering out a request for the latest *Span*.

I hadn't finished with all that, now that I was coming to the end of being a kid and had a team to play for?

Do me a favour.

FIVE

All matches shall start not later than 7.30 p.m.; the penalty for late starts shall be 2/6 for every fifteen minutes or part thereof.

> 29(a) *Match Procedure*, The Manchester and District
> Table Tennis League

The sets of any player not present by 9.00 p.m. shall go by default to the opposing team, and the defaulting team be fined 1/- per player then absent.

> 29(d) *Match Procedure*, The Manchester and District
> Table Tennis League

M Y FIRST LEAGUE match was against the Allied Jam and Marmalade Sports and Social Club (the A. J. M.), just this side of Dukinfield. It was November. The blue-black month, smoky with fireworks and fog. To give ourselves plenty of time to get there, Aishky Mistofsky had suggested that he pick me up from home at six o'clock. I was worried about this arrangement. I knew that my mother and my aunties would come to the window to wave me off and I didn't want them to see Aishky with his blind face pressed to the windscreen. Not knowing how to raise this with him directly, I'd mentioned it to Twink who came up with the idea that he'd change seats with Aishky as soon as they arrived at our place, drive around the corner himself (which he reckoned he could just about manage, although he hadn't learnt to drive yet), and then change back again once we were out of view. The explanation he'd give Aishky was that he was soft on my aunty Fay, whom he'd seen shopping with me in Lewis's, and wanted to impress her with the sight of him sitting up like a mensch in his own Austin A40. Aishky would not be able to refuse him this. Impressing a woman with the aim of getting her to show you her bristles – even when the bristles in question happened to belong to someone you knew's aunty – was a sacred undertaking: if you called yourself a friend you ministered to it. Besides, a bristle out for one was a bristle out for all. In a verbal culture, what goes around comes around. If you don't cop the feel yourself, you at least get to hear about it.

The subterfuge part worked fine. I bounded down the path in my new baggy burgundy tracksuit, a wildly rhetorical $\mathcal{A}$ for Akiva (embroidered for me by Fay) dilating over my pumping heart; my mother, my grandmother and my aunties waved from the lounge window; and Twink, sitting at the wheel of Aishky's Austin, leaned across and opened the passenger door for me. One more wave and we were off – Dukinfield here we come. Looking back, I suppose it's just possible that Twink really had seen and fallen for my aunty Fay and wanted to impress her, because he revved the Austin hard, reversed thirty yards down the street, and slammed into a lamppost.

We were lucky. In the fog and with fireworks going off, no one in my house heard the bang. And we hadn't done serious damage to the Austin. A smashed offside rear light, that was all. And a small dent in the bumper. The damage to our nerves, though, would take much longer to assess. 'This is something I don't need,' Aishky said, after he'd walked round the car a couple of dozen times, looking for scratches.

Although he was the younger of the two, Twink Starr was

generally considerate of Aishky's nervous system. When he saw Aishky getting overexcited he would go out of his way to settle him down, sending out calming signals to the rest of us with his hands and taking Aishky aside and reasoning with him in a loud and extravagant manner, like an uncle. Tonight, though, following his counter-attacker's instincts, he went immediately into aggressive mode. 'Aishk, what are you inspecting the bonnet for? Don't give yourself the platz. How could I have damaged the bonnet?'

'Suddenly you know about cars? You don't know forward gear from reverse gear but you're Stirling Moss all of a sudden.'

'You don't have to be Stirling Moss, Aishk, to know you're not supposed to park in reverse. Doesn't your jam jar have neutral?'

'I don't need this,' Aishky repeated, getting back behind the wheel.

'I'll pay,' Twink told him. 'Do me a favour – don't make a gantse megilleh out of it. Whatever it costs, I'll pay.'

'What'll you pay with? Buttons?'

This was an allusion to Twink's profession. He worked a button machine in a shirt factory in Derby Street, just behind the ice-rink. In the sense that our generation was meant to have put working at a machine behind us, the allusion was cruel. You're a nebbish – that was what Aishky was implying. Which was rich, coming from him, a cutter in a holdall factory. I took it as a proof of the esteem in which Twink held Aishky that he didn't play the nebbish card back, but simply fell silent, looking down and shaking his head.

'Anyway, it's not the money,' Aishky relented, 'it's the aggravation.'

He was right: it was the aggravation we didn't need. Not on match night. My first ever match at that. Needless to say, I felt it was all my fault. If I'd had the courage to face down my family on the question of being driven to Dukinfield by a blind man, none of this would have happened.

The aggravation was getting to Selwyn Marks, too, whose morale was already shot on account of his not having won a match for six weeks. He sat bunched up in the back seat, shivering and yammering something about bad omens.

'Selwyn, do me a favour – shtum up!' Twink told him. 'We don't need any meshuggener omens to explain why you're going to lose tonight. Push, push, push. Listen to me – if you want to win a game of table tennis before you die, try playing some shots.'

'I'm not having this,' Aishky said. We were on Deansgate, making slow progress in the fog. He braked suddenly, without giving any signals. Behind us cars honked and swerved. 'Leave the kid, alone,' he said, 'or we won't be playing anywhere.'

Fortuitously, he'd pulled up dead outside my soft-porno shop. Through the fog I could see that the latest *Span* was in the window. A golfing issue. The cover showed the mother of a prefab boy teeing off and thereby uncovering a suspender. Playing golf in stockings – why was that so . . . whatever it was? A great yearning for the warmth and comforts of home overcame me. What was I doing out in the fog with these tsedraiters when I could have been back in the bosom of my family, sitting in the toilet with my scented chocolate box, religiously gluing aunty Fay's serious spinsterly face to the body of a woman who I bet couldn't sink a six-inch putt without showing the tops of her stockings?

'Push, push, push,' Twink repeated.

'Genug is genug,' Aishky said. 'Loz the kid alone.'

I wasn't sure, but I thought it was just possible that Selwyn had started to blubber.

The aggravation was getting to us all right. The only member of our team who might have been assumed to be in good shape was Sheeny Waxman who was making his own way to Dukinfield.

He couldn't have been faring any worse than us, that was for sure. We lost our way in Gorton and then again in Audenshaw.

The fog thickened. Bangers kept going off, rattling Aishky's nerves. A half-spent Roman candle landed on the bonnet of the car, singeing the wiper blades. Once we nearly went into the canal at Guide Bridge, and shortly afterwards, taking what he thought was a turning on to Dukinfield Park Road, Aishky drove into someone's private drive and would have gone into the garage had another car not been parked there already.

'It's just a question, Aishky,' Twink said, 'but what kind of a meshuggas is this? Is this meant to be a short cut or something?'

Aishky had had it. He jumped out of the car. 'You do better.'

Twink started to climb across.

'No you don't,' Aishky said, jumping back in. 'We're not going all the way to fucking Dukinfield in reverse.'

It was the first and only time I ever heard him swear. Culturally, we weren't swearers. Not my father, not my aunties who called my putz an in-between, not Aishky, and not, as a general rule, Twink either. So it shows how fraught we were getting. 'What do you mean all the way to fucking Dukinfield? I thought we were *in* fucking Dukinfield!'

'Let me out,' Selwyn said. 'The fog's making me feel sick.'

'The fog's making *you* feel sick? Who's the asthmatic here? Push, push, push . . .'

At this point the owner of the house came out to see why there were four meshuggeners, two of them in tracksuits, screaming obscenities at one another in his drive.

By the time we found the Jam and Marmalade factory it was 8.45, which meant that the opposition was within fifteen minutes of being able to claim our eight games by default. Sheeny Waxman was waiting for us in the car park. He was sitting in the back seat of his car with his arm around a young woman. I hadn't met him before but the atmosphere wasn't conducive to formal introductions. He didn't bother to get out of the car. 'Noo?' he said, winding down his window and looking at his watch. 'Did you have a barmitzvah to go to first?'

I've often wondered if he meant mine. I was to see a lot of Sheeny Waxman over the next few years – he worked for my father for a while – but I never learnt to be comfortable with him. He always made me feel underage. There was some certainty about him that I was never able to gain upon. Maybe it had to do with the amount of time he'd been something like a linguist – a head jockey. He'd had a head start.

I couldn't cope with his tic. How had he managed to turn this disability into an advantage? Normally when a person twitches badly he's the one who's embarrassed. But when Sheeny's face went into spasm it was as though it was you who was being obliterated. The right eye closed, the head jerked backwards, the muscles in the neck tightened, and you felt it was your fault for not being able to hold his attention.

The prematurely gravelly voice threw me too. The only person I knew who had a voice as hoarse and phlegmy as Sheeny Waxman's was my grandfather on my mother's side, but nobody thought he was putting it on to arouse women. Why it should have worked for Sheeny Waxman I never understood. Unless it was fear. When Sheeny Waxman flashed his cuff-links, went into spasm, and growled from his seat at the Kardomah, ''Ello doll, new to town are you?' a woman must have thought the Head of the Five Families was making a move on her.

He'd been here, at Allied Jam and Marmalade, since 7.30, played his two matches, won them both, and had spent the last twenty minutes in the car park looking out for us.

Aishky was angry with him. It wasn't good manners to turn up for an away match and then walk out on your hosts. What were they doing now, the home team, twiddling their thumbs?

'What they're doing now, Aishky, is polishing off the cakes you couldn't get here in time to eat and counting off the minutes before they can claim the match. You want to get in there and get your jacket off instead of giving me a rollocking. Eh, Cynthia?'

'Is that his girlfriend?' I asked, rather inconsequentially, as we hurried towards the clubhouse.

'Never seen her before,' Aishky said.

I didn't say that I thought I had. That I thought I'd seen her on the cover of *Span*, swinging a golf club.

'Sheeny Waxman doesn't have girlfriends,' Twink added. 'He has opportunities.'

'Which he takes,' Aishky concluded. With some bitterness, I thought. 'Now can we think about table tennis?'

It was a sticky situation. Our opponents had given us up and were on the point of writing *walk-over* on the official scoresheet. Legally, we could claim our last man had arrived with five minutes to spare, but no one knew where we stood, morally, in the matter of our last man being in fact our four last men. What saved us – not that it made any difference to the outcome – was the universal ping-pong player's appetite for competition. The jam and marmalade makers wanted a game. They wanted to win. And given the fog-wash that was on us after two and three-quarter hours on the road, they couldn't see anything to stop them.

The room was icy. There were radiators on every wall, great glossy cream cobra coils of burbling iron, much like the ones we jacked off behind at school, but the room stayed cold. The radiators were there for us to lose the ball behind, not to provide warmth. This was my first lesson in the ergonomics of ping-pong: every feature and dimension of the playing area must contribute to your discomfort; every item of fixed or moveable furniture is where it is for no other purpose than that you should lose your ball behind it.

Never mind Gossima – Tribulation, that should have been ping-pong's *nom de jeu*. No wonder the game came naturally to sun-starved Slavs and Magyars. Tribulation was also the name of their native countries. And no wonder the game came naturally to me, cramped in my clammy shell.

Another law bearing on the playing environment of the game called Tribulation states that there must always be steps within two yards of the table or two bounces of the ball, whichever makes for greater inconvenience. Steps going up or steps going down. The Allied Jam and Marmalade ping-pong team played in a room that had steps going down *and* steps going up. The steps down, which no one had yet contrived a system for even partially blocking off during play, led to a small scullery-cum-kitchen, where there were buckets and beer crates and old stoves and gas pipes and cans of paint and boxes of tiles and stacked wooden benches with cross-supports ideal not only for losing your ball behind but for injuring yourself while you were searching for it. The steps up led of course to the stage, which sloped away in a manner that must have made it vexatious for the chorus of the Jam and Marmalade annual panto, but more importantly ensured that a ping-pong ball once up there would never come rolling down again. Since the ball ended up on the stage as often as it ended up on the table, why was no one posted there to retrieve it? And why was no one stationed at the bottom of the scullery steps with his hands cupped? These are questions only a person who has never played ping-pong competitively, or never lived within a thousand disheartening miles of the choking River Bug, would ever dream of asking.

I spent what was left of the evening on my knees, getting my own ball back and, because I was the youngest, getting everyone else's back to boot. I had grazed elbows. I had cobwebs in my hair. I had fog in my lungs. And I was cold. Sweltering in my shell, freezing out of it. Should it be any surprise I didn't win?

I'm not making excuses for myself. I was beaten fairly and squarely. Squarely, anyway. Twice. The first defeats I had ever suffered since I'd found the little white ball bobbing on the lake in Heaton Park. Were they good players, then, the two who did me? No. They were not good players. Neither of them was a good player. What they were was canny. They'd seen action. One of them must have been an employee of the jam factory since it was built in 1891. He made less of a concession to athleticism than Aishky did. Aishky at least wore plimsolls. Aishky at least took off his jacket. Jack Cartwright played in a cardigan with leather buttons and never moved his feet. He held his bat pen-hand, like Ogimura, but he didn't have Ogimura's flashing shots. Strictly speaking he didn't have any shots, not even a backhand push like Selwyn Marks's. He simply blocked the ball. Stabbed at it. Poked it dead. Whatever I put on the ball was what came back. If I hit it hard and flat, hard and flat was what I had to deal with. If I chopped the ball in half, half was all I saw of it. It wasn't Jack Cartwright who beat me, it was me who beat me. But that didn't stop me feeling a prize fool, dancing around in my brand new shorts and Fred Perry shirt, breathing hard and sweating profusely, unable to get a ball past a narcissistic old cacker who chewed at his false teeth throughout the match, who wore bracelets for arthritis on each wrist, who resembled J. B. Priestley for portliness and consciousness of sagacity, and who in truth might as well have been J. B. Priestley's cadaver for all the vital principle he demonstrated in body.

An anachronism – J. B. Priestley would still have been alive on the night Cartwright cleaned me up. But you know that dead-fart Yorkshire torpor I'm talking about.

Bob Battrick, my second victor, at least shuffled around the table. But he too did me for savvy. Placing – that was his genius. He knew how to wear me out and cramp me up, pushing me out wide then bringing me in to the net, then pushing me out wide again, then tempting me back in to the net only to fire an awkwardly rearing ball into my stomach. All this with an octagonal cork bat and a square stance and a half-volley. Each time he caught me out he'd give a little skip and hold up his hand as though to apologize for his craftiness.

If losing to Battrick was still more humiliating than losing to Cartwright – and I don't intend to relay the score in either instance (look it up in the archives if you have a taste for statistics) – it was because of the expression of pity that never left his face the whole time I was playing him. 'Better luck next time, me duck,' he said as we shook hands, by which I took him to mean that he'd been doing his utmost to give me every point but that I'd lacked the nous to take a single one of them.

Back in Aishky's Austin a hangdog silence reigned. We'd all lost.

'No post mortems, thank you very much,' Aishky had said as we'd trooped back out into the fog. 'I don't want post mortems.'

'I bet you don't,' Twink replied.

'What does that mean?'

'What do you think it means?'

'If I'd played the way you played tonight I'd keep it shut. What was it again – 21–6, 21–19, after you'd been 19–11 up on your own service? But you had to win with a smash, didn't you!'

'I thought no post mortems,' Twink said.

None of us had any reason to be proud. Aishky, too, had thrown away apparently unassailable leads, wanting to win with a smash. And Selwyn had barely got a ball over the net. But then if Twink hadn't crashed the car . . .

The first person to break the silence on the drive back was Selwyn. 'Anti-Semites,' he said.

Aishky went for the brakes. 'Where?'

'Back there.'

'Back where?'

'Where we've just been. Anti-Semites.'

'Are you telling me that's why you lost now,' Twink said, 'because they were anti-Semites? I suppose the net was anti-Semitic.'

'I'm not saying it's why I lost. I'm just saying it's what they are.'

'You're meshugge,' Aishky said. 'They were nice people.'

'Then why did they call Oliver Mordechai?'

'Mordechai! Who called him Mordechai?'

'The one with the shmatte bat.'

Aishky and Twink wanted to hear it from the horse's mouth. 'Oliver, did he call you Mordechai?'

'Not that I remember. Why would he have called me Mordechai, anyway?'

'Because he's an anti-Semite. Mordechai the Jew.'

'I never even spoke to him,' I said. 'Except after the game.'

'And what did you say to him then?'

'I dunno. "Well played," I suppose.'

'And what did he say to you?'

'I suppose the same.'

'No he didn't. I heard him. He said, "Better luck next time, Mordechai."'

'No,' I said. 'He said, "Better luck next time, me duck." Me duck, not Mordechai.'

But there was no budging Selwyn Marks. 'Anti-Semites,' he muttered to himself for the rest of the journey home. The last of the night's fireworks fried and spluttered in the fog. 'Yiddenfeits,' he said.

So how did I react to this first setback to my sporting ambitions? Let's leave me out of it for the moment. Others suffered that night.

A couple of weeks later, which was about the normal time it took for poor people's mail to be delivered in those days, Aishky Mistofsky, in his role as club secretary, received a notification from the Manchester and District Table Tennis League informing him that the League was in receipt of a solicitor's letter on behalf of Miss Cynthia Cartwright, an employee at the Allied Jam and Marmalade works canteen. On the night of the alleged offence Miss Cartwright had been serving tea and cakes, as she regularly did at home matches, to a visiting team from the Akiva Social Club in Crumpsall. In the course of the evening, and while waiting for the majority of the visiting team to arrive, she had struck up an acquaintance with a Mr Sheeny Waxman who offered to drive her home. Miss Cartwright freely admitted that in return for the lift she was prepared to let Mr Waxman kiss her in the back seat of his motor car. But she wanted it to go no further than that, especially on a first date. Angry with her refusals, Mr Waxman drove her to Miles Platting, a considerable distance from her home, requested that she allow him to perform an indecent act upon her, and when she again refused he unceremoniously ordered her to get out of his car. Given the lateness of the hour and the inclemency of the weather, Miss Cartwright viewed this as a grave discourtesy on Mr Waxman's part, and sought his suspension from the League, a written apology, and the cost of her taxi fare back to Dukinfield.

Since there were no witnesses and it came down to one person's word against another's, the League could do no more than refer the matter to the Akiva Social Club and leave it to take whatever steps it thought necessary. I happened to be at the club, practising, when these steps were taken.

'Anti–Semites!' Twink said.

'Yiddenfeits!' Aishky said.

Then we went on playing.

And that was that?

Not quite.

In private Aishky led Sheeny Waxman aside and warned him against taking liberties.

Sheeny listened unperturbed. He couldn't see what the fuss was about. Why hadn't the slag just let him eat her in Miles Platting and saved herself the trouble?

SIX

For more serious offences, such as swearing or throwing a
racket, it may be appropriate to warn the player formally
that any repetition will incur a penalty, interrupting play
if necessary, and showing that he has done so by holding
up a yellow card so that it is clearly visible to the player
and to spectators.

18.1.7 *The International Table Tennis Federation Handbook
for Match Officials, 1993*

... Spectators? what spectators?

But I am allowing my disappointments to run ahead of me
again. That nobody was there to behold and marvel – no roaring
Jezebels with retractable claws and fluttering pink autograph
albums – should count as a consolation, a godsend, when all
there was to behold and marvel at was me being trounced. They
wouldn't be there later, though, when trouncing was in my gift
and no god would have dared say boo to me – there lay the pity
of it. I fulfilled my destiny, I did everything my genes told me to
do, I became king of the tsatskes, but a king without a kingdom,
a king with no subjects.

Back, back ... One disillusionment at a time. So how did I
react to the Allied Jam and Marmalade catastrophe, the hitherto
unknown ignominy of having someone at the opposite end of

the table get to twenty-one before I did?

Badly.

Badly while it was happening – though I hope I was able to conceal it, hope that no one saw I was playing through tears, blinded. But far worse afterwards.

My mother was waiting up for me. She had already rung every hospital in Manchester twice. 'Look at the time,' she cried. 'We've been worried sick. We've been at our wits' end.'

We nothing. My father was snoring on the couch, sleeping the innocent self-absorbed sleep of the grandiose. A smile twitched his mouth open. Where he was, thousands were cheering him.

I didn't answer my mother. Make her pay. That's what mothers are for.

'We thought you'd crashed.'

'I did crash,' I said. Then I went upstairs to bed, refusing cocoa, and thought about putting an end to myself with my pillow.

It's no fun, losing. Not until you've done a fair bit of winning, it's not. Then of course it can be the most terrific fun in the whole wide world. Pain fun. But the perversion of embracing loss was beyond me at this stage. I was a deviant boy, but as yet not that deviant. You have to own something before you can start finessing around the business of throwing it away.

And this night I believed I owned nothing. I was worthless. And conscious of more shame – I, already the very mollusc of mortification – than I had ever experienced before. I lay in my bed and relived every point I'd lost. A mortal fear gripped me: I would bear these losses like scars for the rest of my life; I would know no relief from them; I would go on playing and re-playing them for ever.

When I closed my eyes I fell through space, down, down into a sucking colourless cone of infinitely narrowing circles; no fires in this hell, only repetition and reduction. Ring upon ring of it, round and round, lower and lower. When I forced my eyes open – for it was a temptation, that spiral, a ride to remember – the darkness pulsed above me, shifting shapes, emptiness opening and closing its gumless mouth as in a fever, now weightless as death, now heavy as disgrace.

When it falls, grandiosity, it falls big.

I tried desperately to free my mind from its own devils, to think about something other than itself, someone other than itself. But what and who else was there to think about? Girls? – none. Friends? – my only friends were ping-pong players now. School? – poof, school! Holidays? – none till next summer. I hadn't anything to look forward to. That was the most devastating effect of my double defeat – it robbed me of a future, left me without a single cheerful event to anticipate. Hence the thought of self-suffocation with my pillow. There was nothing left to live for.

That I began to spend even longer periods in the toilet with my glue and scissors will come as no surprise to those who remember what it is to be a boy who has been beaten. I compounded shame with shame, heat with heat. I see now that I was attempting to transfer my humiliation, collage it on to someone else. Had I been able to get my hands on a photograph of Bob Battrick I would have cut up my aunty Fay and laid her across his knee with her *Span*-poached pants down. 'Fancy a paddling, me duck?'

And people say that sport is a healthy activity for the young.

I didn't suffocate myself. Though it might have been better for the short-term future of my parents' marriage if I had. They were arguing over me again. What was the point of his coming home early, my father wanted to know, if he couldn't get into his own toilet?

Then he didn't get back until four in the morning. My mother was waiting up for him, just as she'd waited up for me. Only for him she hadn't rung every hospital in Manchester. We were all awake. We could feel the floorboards vibrating to her pacing.

'And where have *you* been?'

'Me?'

'No – Yashki Diddle. Where have you been?'

'Out.'

'Out doing what, Joel?'

'Out looking for somewhere to have a Jimmy Riddle.'

'That's it! You've taken your last ride, Joel.'

We heard no more that night, not a squeak from either of them, but the following morning, finding me already locked in the toilet, he began breaking the door down with his bare hands. 'You've got ten seconds to get out of there. Ten . . . nine . . .'

Ten seconds? How was I going to put all the photographs away, screw up the gluepot, close the scissors, tie a bow in the ribbon, do up my pants, hide the box, in ten seconds? It was impossible. I was done for.

'. . . eight . . . seven . . .'

What saved me was the sound of my mother on the blower to the bus company. There was a terrible calm in her voice, like the quiet that must have fallen over the Steppes the night before The Hun rode in. She was explaining that the stress of the job had turned her husband into an alcoholic, that he was arriving home rolling drunk at all hours of the night, that he was leaving the bus parked in the middle of the road – not just *in* it but *across* it – that the neighbours were up in arms and were threatening violence against him, against his family and, more to the point – let's get practical now – against the bus; hence she felt it was her responsibility, though she was a loyal and loving wife – no, *because* she was a loyal and loving wife – to bring matters to a head before someone, not least a coachload of innocent passengers, got killed.

Not everything she asserted was untrue. The bus wasn't popular with the neighbours. Every three or four months a new petition would be posted through our letter-box, signed by everyone in the avenue, including babies, demanding that my father consider other people's right to light and quiet and park his monstrosity somewhere else. In the lake in Heaton Park, preferably. My father was always more upset by these expressions of public dissatisfaction than the rest of us were. He was the one who wanted only to give pleasure. He discussed the possibility of widening our path and getting rid of the garden shed. Getting rid of the garden even. 'So that'll be our view, will it,' my mother had said, 'your bus!'

Without any real expectation of swaying her, he had offered to have it spray-painted green.

But the alcoholism charge was pure invention. My father only ever drank at Walzer weddings, sweet red wine, a fairy thimbleful, and then most of that got spilled over his sisters during the kasatske. Not that truth was the issue here. My father belonged to a generation of men who did not expect their wives to ring up their places of employ. He'd reached 'four' when he heard what she was doing. By what should have been 'three' he was downstairs ripping the phone off the wall and hurling it across the room.

But the moral damage had already been done. He was out of a job.

'Don't you ever again dare . . .' I heard him threaten.

'And don't *you* ever again dare . . .' I heard her threaten back.

'Don't you ever don't-you-ever me . . .'

'And don't *you* ever don't-you-ever don't-you-ever me . . .'

To my knowledge it was the most serious fight they'd had. The nearest they'd come to raising their hands to each other. The telephone with its amputated wires lay smashed and hapless on the floor, like a corpse spilling its intestines. My father left the house and wasn't seen or heard from for two days. When he returned he was staggering. 'I'll show you drunk,' he jeered, flicking out a tongue I'd never seen before. He didn't look like anyone I knew.

'Come one step nearer and I'll call the police,' my mother warned him.

'What with? You haven't got a phone any more, remember. Ha! Ha!'

'I've got a voice, Joel.'

'So you have. And I've heard you use it, too. Very effective. Very refined. All those words. Such words you have, you and your kuni-lemele sisters and the Kazi Kid. And where would he happen to be at the moment? Don't tell me. On the kazi.'

'I'm not,' I protested. 'I'm here.'

'Go to your room,' my mother said.

'That's right, do what your mother tells you. Go to the kazi. In fact I'll take you there . . .'

'Get back, Joel.'

'Or you'll do what, Sadie?'

Or she'd do what she did – which was run out into the street, screaming, 'Police! Police!'

All this because I'd lost at ping-pong.

The best market within range of Manchester in those days – and I'm talking takings now, not local colour – was Stockport. If your family somehow got its hands on a stall at Stockport you knew your future was secured. You could start thinking about taking elocution lessons and moving to Wilmslow. Men slept in their vans overnight to secure a pitch on Stockport market, and then drew knives on one another if there wasn't enough space to go round. According to market mythology, the Toby Mush who went from stall to stall in policeman's boots, with a clinking leather rent-collector's bag on his shoulder, deciding who got to stand where at Stockport, was afflicted with a blind eye and a bent right arm, so many backhanders did he take possession of on market days. But every market was reputed to be run the same way. The Toby was the godfather. 'First rule of the gaffs,' my father advised me in later years, when he was regularly hauling me off against my will to markets all over the country, 'always shmeer the

Toby. If you don't look after the Toby, the Toby won't look after you.'

Just how well he looked after the Toby on his first attempt at getting on to Stockport market I have no idea, but it must have been well enough because by nine o'clock he was set up with a trestle table, four iron bars and a length of tarpaulin on a square yard of favoured cobblestone close to the public facilities. It helped that he was built like a brick shithouse himself. A slighter man might have found a breadknife protruding from his shoulder-blades, as a polite warning against trying for this pitch again. But you couldn't have got a breadknife into my father's back. That was why my mother had had to resort to the telephone.

They were on speaking terms again. Monosyllabic, but at least speaking. She had given him an old faded pink and yellow candlewick bedcover to spread out on the stall. Even before he'd drawing-pinned it on to the trestle table there were women fighting for it. That was how good a gaff Stockport was.

And he sold it? Of course he sold it. 'I'd have sold my own gatkes,' he said, 'if anyone had asked for them.'

A salesman suddenly.

His other advice to me in later years was, 'Always make a nice flash.' He made a nice flash, a lovely flash, that morning. The proof of which was that by midday it was all gone.

A tycoon suddenly.

True, he didn't have, as he put it Mancunianly himself, 'a very lot' to get rid of. All the soft toys he could squeeze into a couple of cardboard boxes that weren't too bulky to carry on a bus. Not his bus. He no longer had a bus. On a red, double-decker public bus. Which he had to wait for in the cold at five in the morning. On two red, double-decker buses, because the first one only took him to Cannon Street, from where he had to shlepp his boxes up Market Street to Piccadilly and wait, still in the freezing cold, for the second one to take him to Stockport. No picnic. No picnic, having a wife who loses you your job. And a son who's never out of the Benghazi.

He'd bought the toys from a warehouse near to where my grandfather used to labour in the shadow of Strangeways, imagining he could hear the sirens signalling knocking-off time. In those days all the warehouses were owned by fellow refugees from the Podolski Plateau. Asians *qua* Asians hadn't even started on the markets yet. One muffled-up Indian selling nylons on a scrap of waste ground behind Victoria Station, that was the extent of their penetration. Otherwise all unserer – one-time beetroot farmers rising from the Podolian swamps. Peddling, markets, wholesaling, importing, next generation in the professions – that was the way of it. The old merry-go-round. That it was a cycle not a progression, that mud-nostalgia would once again exert its shtetl pull, none of us could ever have imagined. We were on the move then, upwards and onwards, conscious of not a single impediment. If anything, we Walzers were slower than many. My father started markets when other Yiddeles his age were opening cash and carries, and I was playing ping-pong when others my size were preparing themselves for the law. But then *we* had big hearts, we Walzer men.

And big ideas.

If soft toys weren't quite a big idea they were certainly a bright one. Christmas was coming, the season of soft toys. And my father was good with toys. He understood them. Could relate to them. Tsatskes, remember. Had things panned out differently he might have made it as one of the world's great puppeteers. Or ventriloquists. At Stockport he sat a stuffed parrot on his shoulder, called out 'Aha, Jim lad!', and engaged in proxy conversation with mothers trundling their trolleyloads of snot-strewn progeny. Why northern gentile children were always snotty in those days I don't know. It might have been a parenting fad. But the sight of them never put my father off. He was a humanitarian. Few other Bug and Dniester marketmen had such a natural way with the big-spending northern proletarian poor. 'I say! I say, Mrs Woman!' he'd get the parrot to squawk. 'Take me home with you and I'll keep you warm at night. I'm very cheap, you know. How cheap? Cheep-cheep. Love you.'

And Mrs Woman would glow with the compliment, tell the proxy parrot he was cheeky and open her purse.

'The one thing you never do even when you're selling toys,' my father used to tell me, 'is appeal directly to the godforbids themselves. I don't approve of that.'

By the time the Christmas tree had gone from the market square and the little lights no longer twinkled under the tarpaulins he'd earned enough to put a deposit on a small van. Had found a second market in Garston at the Speke end of Liverpool. And had hit upon another bright idea. What were these soft toys anyway? Half a yard of furry Draylon, a fistful of flock filling, a couple of buttons for the eyeballs and a triangle of scarlet felt for the tongue. Machining was in the family. Why give the money to a wholesaler when he could knock up the gear himself? By he he meant we.

At first the cutting-out was done by my grandfather on my father's side. He was retired now and sitting staring into space. Now he really did have a grandfather chair. But he hadn't lost any of the old mind-numbing skills. He'd cut out and partially machine; then the toys would come to us to be stuffed and to have their features sewn on by hand; then they'd go back to my grandfather to have their remaining seams stitched up and, where necessary, their looks improved; then they'd come back to us for bagging. That was my job: blowing open the polythene bag, popping in a yellow Gestetner'd WARNING slip giving notice, as was required by law, that the toy was not fire-proof, that the dye was not suck-proof, that the eyes were a danger to children under twelve, that the bag itself presented a threat to the life of anyone idle enough to think of putting it over his head, and then sealing it with a sufficient number of staples to rip open the hand of any ordinarily inadvertent adult.

Clearly we couldn't go on like this. The toys were flying there and back so often they were virtually second-hand by the time I came to bag them. But it wasn't only the wastefulness of our system of manufacture that finally decided my father against going on employing my grandfather. Not aesthetics exactly, but something like aesthetics also had a bit to do with it. No matter what animal he was meant to be machining, my grandfather couldn't stop himself turning it into a version of a golliwog. Not just the monkeys, but the pandas and the kittens and the polar bears too, the whole bestiary, came back with fuzzy hair and rolling eyes and white Mr Interlocutor gloves on their paws.

The times were less nice then. Amos and Andy were on television once a week. A Black and White Minstrel show still turned up regularly at the Ardwick Hippodrome and drew large audiences of utterly well-meaning Stephen Foster fans. My father could have specialized in golliwogs and got away with it in Stockport. But somehow or other one of my grandfather's creations landed on the desk of Robertson's Jams and Marmalades who came carrying briefcases to see my father on his market stall and threatened him with a lawsuit for breach of copyright. And you know by now how little my father liked upsetting people.

Queer, the trouble we always seemed to be having around jam and marmalade. And we didn't even touch the stuff. Cheese — that was what we put on our toast. Melted killer cheese.

Without my grandfather we were stymied as far as soft toy production went. My father had tailoring skills himself, but he couldn't be expected to make the stock *and* sell it. And the few he did try his hand at all came out hunch-backed. Buy me and I'll keep you warm at night, cheep-cheep, I love you, was all very well, but not if the bunny-wunny with a pink ribbon round its neck looked like Quasimodo. He ran my mother up a pair of curtains for their bedroom with what was left of the spotted furry

Draylon and that was it with the cuddly stuff. Soft toys don't sell that well after Christmas anyway. Besides, my father had already come up with another bright idea. Coffee tables. He'd seen them in the warehouses, he'd seen other grafters pitching them out on Garston, and he couldn't see why he couldn't make them himself. What was a coffee table when all was said and done? An oval of chipboard, four screw-on angled spindle legs, a sheet of glass and a strip of plastic beading. He could do it easy. By he he meant we.

And by we he meant me. Him and me. All very well getting the girls and the infirm to help with the teddies, appropriate even, given how infirm and girlish teddies themselves were. But there was nothing fluffy about a coffee table – coffee tables were carpentry, and carpentry was what men did. Measuring, sawing, screwing, gluing. (How much did he know about me and glue?)

There was a further aspect of coffee tabling he needed me for. Artwork. I was the grammar school boy. I knew something about pictures, didn't I? Paintings. All that malarkey. The coffee tables my father had watched the pitchers clearing out on Garston market – 'Not five pounds, not four pounds, not even three pounds, here, look, I'll tell you what I'll do . . .' – were illustrated, showing scenes from *Swan Lake* and *The Nutcracker* under their glass tops. My father didn't know what the ballets were called, or even that they were ballets. They were pictures, that was all, and someone had to choose them. Me. The one with all the green books.

Leaving aside the crazed salacious collages I made in the privacy of the lavatory, what did I know about art? Well, I knew that my grandmother's reverend head on a naughty schoolgirl's torso wouldn't be a seller in Catholic Liverpool. I knew that there were no famous paintings of ping-pong players in action. And I knew I could do better than *Swan Lake*. I had the regulation art tastes of a shell-shrinker my age. I revered a couple of Rembrandt self-portraits, as well as *The Nightwatch* and the person in the gold helmet; I owned a jigsaw puzzle of Brueghel's *Tower of Babel*; and I was stirred at some deep and upsetting level by Bosch's nightmare demons with flowers in their bums. Enough there to be going along with, wouldn't you have said, for a coffee table company limited in its production capacity by the space available after supper on the living-room floor.

We soon got to the bottom of the omnipresence of *The Nutcracker* and *Swan Lake*. They were the only prints of a suitable size you could pick up. No printer cheap enough to keep our tables competitive had Brueghel's *Tower of Babel* in stock. Nor *The Nightwatch*. We enjoyed some good fortune with the Bosch, though. One small firm in Eccles was so taken with the flowers in the bum they were prepared to have one of their artists copy it. But we had to order five hundred. 'Done,' my father said. We still have them. Somewhere under the stairs of my mother's house is a soggy cobwebbed oblong carton containing four hundred and ninety-nine barely-look-alike Bosch posters printed in the primary colours. We never sold a single one. The public knows what it likes and it knew it didn't like a coffee table showing Bosch's *Garden of Earthly Delights*, chiefly anal, under glass. What it liked was *Swan Lake*. Also anal, but melodic. The only Bosch table in existence is owned by me. 'Keep that one for yourself,' my father said ironically as we dismantled the three dozen we had made, substituting the art people wanted for the art they didn't. 'Consider it an early wedding present.'

A better early wedding present would have been to leave me alone.

To get on with what?

To get on with ping-pong for a start.

I'd been wrong to think there was nothing left to live for after losing in the fog in Dukinfield. There was getting even left to live for. There was passing on the pain and beating someone else left to live for. In short, there was next week.

Thus the beauty of playing in a league was quickly made manifest to me. In a league there is never a last chance. Never a final, once and for all deciding match. Play in a league and you do not have to come face to face with your maker. Next week you might thrash your maker.

The week after Dukinfield was a home match. Against the Post Office. I was told we played better at home. I could have figured that out for myself. We would have played better on an ice floe in the Arctic Circle so long as we hadn't had to spend an hour in Aishky's Austin beforehand.

As though it took a special interest in our progress and had committed our fixture list to memory, the fog which had lifted immediately after Dukinfield began to fall again. 'You're not going out in that on your own,' my mother said. 'Your father will drive you.'

'What in?' my father asked.

Losing a bus is like losing a limb: it takes a while to remember you no longer have it. More than once I'd seen my father pat his face clean, throw on a tie and go whistling out of the house only to return disconsolately half a minute later.

'Then your sisters will take you.'

'No!' I said.

'Ah, Ma, no!' they said together.

They no more wanted to be seen with me in my tracksuit than I wanted to be seen with them in their ballooning net petticoats and ankle socks and Olive Oyle high heels.

So there was nothing else for it. My mother and the Violets accompanied me on the train from Bowker Vale and waited for me in the card room at the Akiva. It's an ill wind. There was a dance on in the card room that night and it was here that my aunty Dolly, the oldest of the Violets – though she had come out in nothing more alluring under her maroon overcoat than

89

a yellow cardigan with a button missing, and the S for Spinster throbbing on her chest – met the man who would one day take her out of herself, make her heart dance, and then break it. Gershom Finkel.

I went all phlegmy seeing Twink and Aishky again. I coughed, blaming the fog, but it was puppy love that was guggling up at the back of my throat. I hadn't realized how much I'd missed them. They hadn't turned up for practice after the jam and marmalade fiasco. Aishky had had to lie down all week, and Twink had blown his life savings on a trip to London to hear Giuseppe di Stefano sing Rudolfo at Covent Garden. Di Stefano was his favourite living lyric tenor. Aishky thought Mario Lanza but Twink laughed in his face. That shreier! Not counting those who had long jossed it like Caruso, and those who had recently jossed it like Gigli (though he'd always been too much of a crooner for Twink's taste), it went di Stefano one, Björling two, Ferruccio Tagliavini three . . .

Over Del Monaco?

. . . Tagliavini three, Mario Del Monaco four, Richard Tucker five . . .

And then Mario Lanza?

Twink snorted. Mario Lanza, Aishk, didn't make it into the top twenty.

Sheeny Waxman wanted to put in a vote for Bill Haley.

'Do me a favour,' Twink said.

I tried a joke myself. 'Where would you rate Victor Barna?'

Twink looked nonplussed. 'As a table tennis player . . . ? You're moodying me.' Then he got it. 'Dependable, but not up there with the very best of them. He can be a bit flat for me. But definitely above Lanza.'

He was in high spirits, limber, laundered, up there with the best of them himself, ready to take on anybody. Opera lifted him, warmed him through, cleared his asthma, put arias in his hair. He'd unearthed some rare and precious 78s of John McCormack while he was in the Smoke, including Act I of Boito's *Mefistofele* and the exquisite and almost impossible to find 'Pur Dicesti' by Antonio Lotti, both in mint condition. It was Twink's ambition to own the biggest collection of recordings of lyric tenors in the country. Already it was second to none in Prestwich. 'I've got stuff even the BBC don't know where to lay their hands on,' he told me. 'They ring *me*. How do you like that?' So he was well on his way.

I noticed that his bat looked as laundered as he did. The pimples sat up unusually flexuous and nipply. 'Have you shampooed your bat?' I asked.

'Listen to the kid! Have I shampooed my bat? Shmerel! I bought new rubbers from Lillywhites. Fatter pimples. I decided to change my game while I was away.'

He was magnificent that night. Going on a hunch, Aishky put him in at number one, which was strictly Sheeny's spot according to recent form, to say nothing of its being what Aishky had promised me when he'd signed me up. But Twink didn't let him down. He hit like di Stefano. Full of chest, but sweet. No screamers, just winner after winner stroked sweetly off a thrumming blade, lovely smooth high bouncing legatos, picked up early and pitched perfectly on the line.

His form affected the rest of us. Aishky found the rhythm that had deserted him the week before. He could do no wrong. Even when he was manoeuvred out of position and was forced to try his infamous behind-the-back retrieval – a shot Twink was forever begging him to forgo, because it looked smart-arsed and would upset the goyim – he pulled off an unbelievably acute angled return that left his opponent open-mouthed, with his hands on his hips. 'The ball's stuck to my bat,' he whispered to me, beaming, as he changed ends. 'It's on elastic.'

Selwyn Marks won handsomely, by his standards, as well. Striking his thigh and sometimes even his head with his bat, and berating himself as always – 'Make your mind up, play the shot you mean to play, what's the point of starting to hit if you don't hit, come on, watch the ball, come ON, COME ON!' – but actually playing shots tonight, actually trying to get the ball past his opponent instead of just keeping it in play and hoping.

'Geh, Selwyn!' Sheeny Waxman called out after a couple of exaggeratedly effective forehand smashes, whereupon a circle of pink appeared in each of Selwyn's cheeks and he smashed the next five forehands into the net.

'No,' he yelled to himself. 'NO!' And netted two more.

'Steady, Selwyn,' Sheeny called. 'Take it a point at a time.' And the crisis was over. Having thrown away a 19–12 lead to end up on 19 all he reverted to what he did best and pushed his way to a 21–19 win. 'Better,' he said to himself even as he was shaking hands. 'BETTER!'

Sheeny, ticking and flicking, won easily. That goes without saying. He should have been playing in a higher division. But that would have meant practising a couple of nights a week, keeping himself in shape. And Sheeny was otherwise engaged. He had an air of wasted brilliance about him. Could do better, they'd written on his school reports. Does himself no justice. Performs below his potential. He carried that one around in his wallet and showed it to the girls he chatted up in the Kardomah. 'I wouldn't mind performing below your potential, darling.' Be careful not to underestimate me – that was the challenge he threw out. I'm not the low-life you take me to be. Not *only* the low-life you take me to be. I have a say in the matter.

And I? How was I on my first ever home appearance?

I beggared belief. Need I say more? I made a pauper of credulity.

Whatever embellishments Aishky went on adding to the famous story of how I'd turned up at the Akiva carrying a bat as big as the Empire State Building and zetzed my way into club legend, I was never an out-and-out come-what-may hitter. My game was built around control and demoralization. I loved

92

ping-pong most when I felt the fight go out of my opponent. You can hear it sometimes. Hear their self-belief crack, hear their heart break. Like a twig snapping in a moon-frozen forest. The fight goes out of players differently. Some give up in a fit of irritation as soon as you've bamboozled them with a couple of spin serves. Others decide you hit too fiercely for them and settle for admiring what you can do. 'Shot, son. Too good.' Or they sense the night's luck is running your way and can't be bothered to resist it. But nothing hollows out a player more than when you soak up everything he's got. Think Ali on the ropes against George Foreman. You stand back and let them do their worst, take the lot – go on, hit harder, harder, go on, is that it, is that all you've got? – and then kapow! All very well releasing my backhand and thinking I was Victor Barna. I did that only once the ball sat up, begging for it to be over, a superiority I'd achieved at a distance of ten or twenty feet from the table, chopping deep and low in the manner of Richard Bergmann, the little Austrian defender who stood so far back he was almost in the next room, and who had become World Champion at the age of seventeen.

Had he been a bit taller, and looked a little bit less like some of my cousins on my mother's side, Bergmann would have been my hero. As it was, I'd gone to the trouble of learning many of his reflections on ping-pong off by heart. Such as, 'You should at all times be able to vary your style of play and go back to defending of your OWN ACCORD.' In other words, defence wasn't a recourse, forced on you by the will of your opponent. It was your choice (like Sheeny's to become a low-life), made in your own time and in reference to no one but yourself. Was that true of Ali, holding on and covering up for so long in that Zaire night? Maybe not. Maybe he defended of Foreman's accord. In which case little Richard's will was more fearsome than big Ali's.

Something else Bergmann said which I'd committed to memory: 'Practise until you have a feeling of absolute safety, that certain "I can't miss" feeling.' He was talking about the backhand defensive chop. Of all table tennis strokes, this is the one it's easiest to have that 'I can't miss feeling' about. If you don't have an absolutely safe backhand chop you might as well forget ping-pong as a career. That was true of the game as it was played in my time, anyway. Now – but in every way now's different.

Precisely because it does (or should) come naturally, precisely because it's an intimate, easily camouflaged stroke played without discernible risk close to your body, you can't demoralize an opponent with a backhand chop alone. To break a spirit comprehensively you need to be able to chop with your forehand. Of all table tennis strokes the forehand chop is the loveliest – speaking classically now, speaking of grace and elegance, speaking of music and poetry – and the most deadly. To execute a forehand chop you must leave the sanctuary of your body, go out on a limb, risk your reach and your balance, expose yourself. Get a forehand chop wrong and everyone can see it. Ditto get a forehand chop right. Not just see it either; execute the forehand chop to perfection, take the ball into custody on your forehand, cradle it, coddle it, suspend its trajectory for a millionth of a second, caress it, make it yours, put your name on it, and your opponent will shudder like a patient on an anaesthetist's table, feeling fingers pulling at his heart. You shudder yourself at that moment of suspension and possession, as though futurity, with its adoring millions, has paused to lay flowers on your grave. Yes, it is the loveliest and the most arrogant of all ping-pong strokes because it infinitesimally arrests the game and controverts its logic. In this way it is crucially different from a counter-hit, however unexpected, for a counter-hit merely answers like with like, whereas the forehand chop refuses your opponent's entire vocabulary. It is insouciant. Egotistical. Imperious. Soul destroying.

And I played it as though I'd invented it. 'You must be able to execute this stroke in your sleep, on the roof of a burning house, in a blizzard and on the high seas with a north-west gale blowing,' Bergmann said. I went one better: I executed it in the face of Gershom Finkel's sneering.

He missed the first game of my first match. I count that as significant. It meant that I was able to get my chop going, free of the evil influence of his detraction. He wandered round the club on match nights, unable to watch, unable not to watch, unable to stay in the room, unable to leave it, as though an invisible devil with a pitchfork were goading him from one hellish circle to the next. Who knows, had we compared sightings we might have discovered that he was in the ping-pong room at the same time he was in the billiard room, and in the billiard room at the same time he was in the card room, that even as he was sneering at me he was dancing – still in his buttoned-up navy coat, still laughing mirthlessly to himself – with my aunty Dolly.

He turned up – some bodily form of him turned up – just as I was completing victory number one. He ducked in, between points, like a bailiff, stood at the far end of the room where I couldn't fail to see him, and clapped ironically, dead knuckles on a dead palm, when the match was over. You can always tell when someone from your own side would much rather you had lost. Though it might be stretching language a bit to say that Gershom Finkel was on our side. He wandered off again for Twink's and Aishky's second matches. Went dancing, presumably. Put his dead hand between my poor aunty Dolly's quaking shoulder-blades. How did he know when to come back? Who told him that I was about to go on again?

'I'll umpire this one if you like,' he said, testing the net for height, and twanging it for tautness, before sitting down.

No one likes umpiring. No one undertakes the job willingly. Least of all, my team-mates told me later, Gershom Finkel. 'The mamzer's never umpired a game in his life,' Sheeny reckoned.

'Once,' Louis Marks corrected him. 'Three years ago, when Johnny Leach came to play an exhibition match in the club. He called him for foul-serving as well.'

As well. The phrase tells its own story. 'When you're ready, gentlemen . . . Away call. No, it's tails. Walzer to serve. Love all. Foul serve, love–one.' That was about the way it went. I exaggerate only slightly. To be fair to Gershom – though I can't think of any good reason to be fair to Gershom – he cautioned me about my serve before calling it. Cautioned me once, called me twice, and then, to rub salt in, rose from his chair, stood behind me, breathed into my neck, and showed me what I was doing wrong. My serving palm was not flat, there was the problem. 'In the delivery of the service,' the rules stated, 'the free hand of any two-handed player shall be open and flat, with the fingers straight and together, thumb free and the ball resting on the palm without being cupped or pinched in any way by the fingers.'

Make a rule and you'll always find a life-hating pedant who will interpret it ungenerously. Later emendations of the rules – having just such an umpire as Gershom Finkel in mind – removed the emphasis from 'the precise degree of flatness of the server's free hand'. What's so special about flatness, when all is said and done? Illegal spin, that was what the no cupped-palm rule existed to prevent. Sol Schiff's legacy. Diabolically concealed finger-spin. The thing that had once dashed Gershom's own hopes. But just because the four fingers of my free hand were not lying dead straight and together, like the corpses of four little Victorian pauper babies, it didn't mean I was doing a Sol Schiff.

This could have been the end of me. Mortification in front of friends; mortification in front of strangers; my confidence shot down just as it was taking flight; and a palpable ineptitude demonstrated in the area where I was most sensitive – in the matter of what I did with my free hand. I thought I would burn up. There is nowhere to hide on a ping-pong table. I have said that about a bus, but compared to a ping-pong table a bus is a haven of hideaways. I lost control of my mouth which began to skid horribly across my face. I was within a whisker of throwing my bat down, covering my shame, and running out of the Akiva for ever. So what stopped me? Not my own presence of mind, that's for sure. I was a shell-skulker, a lavatory-stewer, a secret cutter-up of aunties and grandmas – I *had* no presence of mind. What saved me was the generosity of my opponent. Dave. They were all Dave or Derek, the Post Office team. Derek Lockwood, Dave Clayton, Derek Hargreaves. This one was Dave Hancocks. I was lucky in him. He let Gershom's first decision go. Took the point. Not gladly. But took it. You don't look a gift-horse. But after the second call he deliberately hit his next return off the table and subsequently dribbled his own service into the net. Thereafter, whenever Gershom fouled me, Dave Hancocks threw away the next point.

But where did this leave me? Ought I to be deliberately netting my returns to thank him for netting his? Where did reciprocity end in a situation like this? I looked to Aishky. 'Dave Hancocks is one of ping-pong's gentlemen,' he whispered to me. 'He isn't looking for any favours. Just play your game.'

Twink too had some advice for me. 'Don't insult the guy by holding back,' he said.

Easier said than done. I was falling in love with the man. He had saved me from humiliation. He had stuck it to Gershom in the most demonstrative way possible, short of smacking him in the face. And he praised me, once I had recovered sufficiently to be able to play some shots, in a manner that sent little warm shivers – love-warm, not shame-warm – down my legs. 'Shot, kid,' he said, and I tingled. 'Unlucky,' he said, shaking his head and smiling, and I fear that I tingled even more.

There was something of the foot soldier about Dave Hancocks. Strong stocky legs, a low centre of gravity, resolution, dependability. You could imagine him walking across the Alps with Hannibal, carrying the General's sandwiches. He had a Roman profile too. And a head perhaps a little too large for his body. Anyone wanting to be picky about Dave Hancocks's appearance might have wondered whether he wasn't too much like a dwarf – not exactly a dwarf but too much like one – to be considered handsome. For my part I can only state that I have always admired the Roman-dwarf look on a man. I suppose I was responsive to the shape because it was a refined and more mobile version of my father's side. I had been brought up to believe that a big head on a square squat body was a mark of manliness.

Under other circumstances, later in my career, and without Gershom around to vex the chemistry, I would gladly have lost to Dave Hancocks. 'Unlucky,' he would have said, 'unlucky, kid,' and I would have gone soft inside his strong consolatory handshake. Of course I didn't know at the time that I wanted to yield to him. What I am describing comes to a man only after many years of reflection; and I refer to it for no other reason than that it is interesting to me to realize that the corrupt germ of voluptuous defeatism was lodged in my system so early.

As it was, I had to make do with the lesser voluptuousness of beating him. It was plenty to be going on with. 'Very well played,' he said, looking up at me, shaking my hand and bowing. He was wonderfully courteous. A postal clerk by day, a little dark top-heavy troubadour of ping-pong by night.

'Yes, very well played,' Aishky and Twink chorused.

We all knew what we knew. That I'd beaten Gershom Finkel as well as Dave Hancocks.

When he'd finished filling out the scorecard, Gershom Finkel came over to where I was sitting with my towel on my head. I felt it go dark around me. 'I don't mind spending a bit of time helping you to get that serve right,' he said.

I didn't come out of my towel. I felt very calm in there. Very calm for me. It was as if I'd been born with ringing ears and suddenly they'd stopped. I could hear the world clearly at last. I heard Aishky taking the net down. I heard Twink zipping up the legs of his tracksuit and humming 'Che gelida manina' to himself. Then, 'Fuck off, Gershom,' I heard myself say.

It's a wonderful moment in the life of a shy young person when he swears at a fully grown adult for the first time. It's like a miracle cure. It's like waking up with strong legs on your second morning in Lourdes. Speaking for myself it was as though I had all at once become a man.

So I stayed under the towel a little longer, just in case it wasn't true.

I had a lot to trawl through before I could get to sleep that night. The perfect loveliness of winning. The confirmation of that old Walzer conviction – that I was destined for great things. My storm-resistant forehand chop, which I actually replayed as I lay on my bed, chopping at shadows. The kindness of my friends. My acceptance, signalled by the consideration shown to me by the Roman dwarf, into the affections of men. But most of all I kept saying over and over again, because they were sweeter than any words I had ever previously heard myself utter, 'Fuck off, Gershom . . . Fuck off, Gershom . . . Fuck off, Gershom . . .'

SEVEN

THIRD DIVISION NORTH
LEADING INDIVIDUAL AVERAGES

	P	W	L	%
O. Walzer (Akiva Social Club)	32	30	2	94
S. Waxman (Akiva Social Club)	40	37	3	93
D. Bromley (Freeman, Hardy & Willis T. T. C.)	42	37	5	88
D. Lockwood (Prestwich Hospital)	38	33	5	86
T. Starr (Akiva Social Club)	44	37	7	84
A. Mistofsky (Akiva Social Club)	44	35	9	80
D. Flewers (Water Board)	38	29	9	76
J. Cartwright (A. J. M.)	40	30	10	75

Manchester and District Table Tennis League, Official Handbook,
Season 1956/57

T HAT WAS HOW the season went for us. Forgive the sin of pride. But percentages are percentages.

Having come of age against the Post Office I never lost another league match. What the figures don't reveal is that I was never once taken to three games either. And never once to deuce. I was unbeatable. Until I took my revenge against him at home, Jack Cartwright was sitting pretty on top of the averages. Played thirty, won thirty. All without raising a sweat. The first of those subsequent ten defeats was inflicted by me. 21–5, 21–3. Funny how some scores you always remember. He must have had trouble forgetting too; he made the averages by the skin of his clicking teeth and retired at the end of the season. Fall to your prayers, old man.

Yes, there was needle in it. Aishky had made the brave but wise decision not to play Sheeny in the return match against Allied Jam and Marmalade. The Miles Platting Affair, for which Cynthia Cartwright had received neither compensation nor apology, still rumbled on. 'When I see that little pervert Waxman again I'll break his bloody nose, rules or no rules,' Jack Cartwright was reported to have been going round saying.

This confirmed Selwyn Marks's darkest suspicions. 'There you are, didn't I tell you? Nose. "I'll break his bloody *nose*." Didn't I say they were anti-Semites?'

'Selwyn, everyone's got a nose,' Aishky said.

'Yeah, yeah. And everyone's got a chin too. But he isn't saying, "I'll break his chin," is he? He's saying nose. *Nose*.'

To be on the safe side Aishky rested Selwyn as well. We were running hot, heading the table, certain of promotion. We could afford to risk Louis and go in a man short. We'd forgotten what it was like to lose.

Even with Sheeny and Selwyn out of the way the confrontation turned ugly. Our opponents came wanting to find fault with us, and to be honest that wasn't difficult to do. For a start we were never well supplied with match balls. As Club Secretary it was up to Aishky to see to it that there was always a box of new ★★★ balls to hand on match night. Week after week we ran out, discovered that the box was empty, or that it was full of used balls and cracked balls, balls of a lower denomination, two-star, one-star, no star at all, balls with dents in them or with ill-fitting seams, balls through which you could see a pin-prick of light, balls which inexplicably rattled or sighed, balls which seemed all right, which defied the most scrupulous investigation and testing, but which plocked hollow the moment you struck them. It wasn't meanness that stopped Aishky going out and stocking up with new match balls. It was indifference. He no more understood the reason for a high quality ball than he understood why Twink needed to play in a Fred Perry shirt and short hasen. He himself could have played with a hard-boiled egg and not noticed the difference.

Two plocks into his knock-up with Twink, Jack Cartwright was asking for a new ball. Aishky emptied a long box of used and grubby pills on to the table. Jack Cartwright rolled each of them in turn with his bat, round and round as though he were trying to get an ancient stain out of the table, his ear cocked like a wise old rat's, pressing until the table threatened to give way and his pimples squeaked. A golf ball wouldn't have survived that kind of treatment. 'Nope,' he said. 'Nope . . . nope . . . nope . . . nope.'

'Those are all we've got,' Aishky laughed.

Cartwright went over to the patchwork of leather elbow protectors that was his jacket and brought out the rule book from its inside pocket. It too was well worn, like a miser's cashbook. 'Balls . . .' he said aloud, leafing through. 'Balls . . .'

It was Twink who felt the humiliation most keenly. He had been skipping around the room during Cartwright's interrogation of our stock of balls, running on the spot and practising attacking shots, anxious to keep his muscles stretched and his temperature even. Now he was furious with Aishky. 'How many times have I told you about this?' he said.

Aishky shrugged. Tomorrow he would need a long lie down, but tonight he could shrug. 'If balls are so important to you,' he said, 'why don't you carry some around yourself?'

'You know why,' Twink said.

'Yeah – because you're a nudnik. Because you like kopdreinish.'

Twink shook his head. 'Believe me, Aishky, if you think this gives me any pleasure . . .'

'If it doesn't give you any pleasure, then stop. You look after the balls. I nominate you. Theo Starr, *Ball Shamess*.'

'Aishky, please. Keep your voice down. You know why I can't carry balls in my kit.'

'Say it. I want to hear you say it.'

Twink lowered his eyes. He could be very girlish. 'The dog.'

'The dog!' Aishky looked at each of us in turn. Our friend was a madman. Did we hear? 'The dog!' Then of Twink himself he asked, 'What's the dog got to do with it?'

'You know what.'

'I want to hear you say it.'

Twink fluttered again. 'I'm frightened of the dog swallowing a ball,' he said. 'You know what happened to Jackie Strulovitch's dog.'

'Moody-merchant! That was a marble.'

'No it wasn't, Aishky. It was a table tennis ball. Jackie Strulovitch's dog choked to death on a Barna ★★★.'

'So because I don't have a dog I've got to shlepp boxes of balls around with me?'

'Aishky, you're the team captain,' Twink said. And then with slow and awful deliberateness, 'Go. And. Get. A. Box. Of. Balls.'

He had that wild Bug and Dniester us-and-them look in his eyes. When one of *us* looked like that it was in the belief that we could magic words and that none of *them* would hear what we were saying.

Aishky consulted his watch. 'It's eight o'clock at night. Where am I going to get a box of balls? The off-licence?'

'Aishk, get in your car,' Twink said. 'Drive over to the Maccabi. And beg them for a box of balls.'

Aishky threw him the keys.

'Aishky, I'm in my shorts.'

'So? Put your hasen on.'

'Aishky, I suffer from asthma. You're asking me to go out in the cold in my shorts when I'm sweating?'

'You want the balls, you go for them.'

'Aishky, you know I can't drive.'

Now Aishky stood up. 'Thank you,' he said. He reminded me of my father. 'Thank you for admitting there is something you can't do.'

And he drove to the Maccabi on Middleton Road and begged them for a box of match balls.

Then there was the problem of the slippery floor. Why the floor of a room that was used only for table tennis, storing mops, and a once-a-year Chanukkah party had to be so highly polished that even a twelve-year-old could admire his moustache in it, no responsible person at the Akiva was able to explain. They were nice old boards and the caretaker took pride in them. Ask the caretaker . . . except don't. The club had never had a caretaker who took better care. Just loz him ein. Leave him alone. Who can understand the mind of a caretaker? What he did, he did. You don't upset the shaygets.

We'd got used to the problem ourselves. We'd spit on the floor between points and rub our shoes in the puddle. For visiting teams we provided a wet cloth. Only tonight Aishky had mislaid the cloth.

'On my life, Aishky,' Twink said, the minute Aishky was back from the Maccabi, 'if you don't find that cloth I'll rip the shirt off your back.'

'Don't do that, Sonny Jim,' Jack Cartwright said. 'Just wait till one of us goes over and breaks a leg, then we can sue you for all you've got.'

It was a good job Selwyn had been told to stay at home. 'Did you hear that? *Sue* you for all you've *got!*'

And as if the balls and the floorboards weren't enough, we slipped up on refreshments as well. At the best of times hospitality wasn't our strong suit. A cup of weak tea and a sweet biscuit each was the most we were usually able to dig up. Once again the problem wasn't meanness. Aishky just wasn't a fresser. He liked a big lunch, and there was always something hot waiting for him when he got home to his mother after a match, otherwise he didn't think about food. 'You want delicatessen, you go and buy delicatessen,' he told Twink. But Twink wasn't much of a picker either.

Tonight though – and what made it worse was that the A. J. M. was famously hospitable: milky Nescafés, PG Tips, hot chocolates, Lucozades, bitter lemons, club sodas and all the jam fancies and marmalade doughnuts you could eat – tonight, though, the element in our kettle had broken and because Passover was in the wind all we had to offer in the way of solids was a box of dry matzos and a bag of kichels. In fact a kichel is a delicacy, provided you have the right expectations of what it is you are eating and are given a strong cup of tea or a glass of sweet red wine to dunk it in. But there was no tea and no wine.

'Bit hard on your teeth, these,' Jack Cartwright said, coughing one up. For a minute I thought he was going to go into his rule book again. 'Kichels . . . kichels . . .' What he actually did was ask where the bathroom was so he could wash his mouth out with water.

But by then he was a spent force. By then I'd taken him out 21–5, 21–3, to pay him back for the misery he'd caused me on Bonfire Night, and the trouble he was trying to make for Sheeny Waxman, and the fuss he'd made over the balls and the floor, and for being an anti-Semite.

The markets were going well, too. My father had given us a couple of weeks of anxiety after we'd found him collapsed one morning with his head in the fireplace. Overwork. He'd been up all night finishing an order for twenty-five coffee tables. Grandiosity again – now he was making for other marketmen! It was a lucky escape. There was a diadem of winking embers around his head when we found him, like a halo round a saint in an illuminated manuscript. And he still had tacks for the beading in his mouth. It was a miracle he hadn't burned or choked. Or burned *and* choked. But at least that had put an end to manufacturing on a large and impersonal scale. Now when we gathered round the dining-room table as a family it was to pop together plastic poppet necklaces, or to assemble travellers' refreshment packs – a sponge, a face cloth, a comb, a tube of toothpaste and a shoe brush – or to weigh out bags of chocolate truffles which my father was able to buy cheaply in bulk on account of their having changed colour. Fershimmelt was the precise term. Anything too fershimmelt we threw away. My father wasn't in the business of poisoning his punters. But between too fershimmelt and pretty appalling to look at there was some leeway. That was where I came in. I sat half-way down the production line and wiped the discolouration off the so-so truffles with one of the sponges from a traveller's refreshment pack.

I didn't have to be over-nice about it. The truffles were only plunder – one of the lines my father tossed out from the side of his lorry for pennies, sometimes even for nothing, depending on how much it took to get the crowd in the mood. Yes, there was a lorry now, and crowds. In no time at all my father had gone from being one of those shtumkopfs who stand behind their stalls with their hands in their pockets waiting for the punters to finger their tsatskes – allow me an exaggeration, I know he was never that shtum – to being a fully fledged pitcher who called the punters to him. Not a mock auctioneer or a run-out worker – he was always strictly above board: 'Who's a liar!' he would laugh whenever he promised them that this 'really was the last one' – but a showman who blew whistles and juggled plates and told jokes and confetti'd the crowd with free pens and cheap bags of chocolates ('Out they go! See if I care!'), and was variously known as Cheap Johnnie, Honest Jo and Mad Jack.

He had come to an understanding of what sort of marketman he was now, too. No more searching around for lines. He was in swag – end of story. And swag took in chalk love-in-a-cottage wall plaques and shepherd and shepherdess figurines and hot-water bottles that burst when you filled them with hot water and torches that didn't work in the dark and plastic colanders with no holes in them and hula hoops and shockproof deep-sea divers' watches and jardinières and folding chairs that could kill when they sprang shut and dolls that sometimes said 'Mama' but more often than not didn't and leatherette writing-pad compendiums and dictionaries that had no definitions in them and plastic potties to go under the bed ('That's why they're called gesunders, Mrs Woman') and pairs of peeling brass candlesticks and salt and pepper shakers in the shape of pelicans and polar bears and sheer nylon stockings for women with short Far Eastern legs (fine for the Walzer women) and three-dimensional paintings of the Last Supper and musical fish-bowls and fountains that played when the phone rang and of course Swan Lake coffee tables (made by someone else) and poppet necklaces and travellers' refreshment packs and bags of discoloured truffles, 'ramped and stamped by the British Institute of Public Health and Hygiene'.

Was there such an institution? I never found out. If there was he could only have come to hear of its existence from my mother. She coached him. He was the one with the warm shaygets-loving personality but she was the one with the words. 'Ramped and stamped,' though, was his. He must have picked it up in the army. Similarly the joke about there being nothing he wouldn't do for his wife, and there being nothing his wife wouldn't do for him, and that that was how they went through life together, doing nothing for one another. He couldn't tell that one enough. It was as though it surprised even him every time he told it, as though it revealed some paradox at the heart of language itself which he never ever saw coming. He enjoyed a perfect rapport with his punters. They never saw it coming either. They'd stand there half a day, some of them, open mouthed in the Garston or Oswestry rain, listening to the routine repeat itself like di Stefano singing 'O Soave fanciulla' on Twink's turntable, and horse-laughing, if anything the more ungovernably, the better they got to know it. 'And that's how we go through life together . . .' He'd even wait for them to peer into the jiggery-pokery of language themselves, pounce on the punch-line before it could ambush them. He'd direct them in it, sometimes, like Toscanini. 'One, two, three . . . *doing nothing for one another.*'

Otherwise everything came from my mother. She'd write out his material for him in big letters on a lined absorbent note-pad – made in Albania and selling for sixpence a dozen with a Porker Pen Set thrown in – and he'd sit and commit it to memory. 'Not two pounds, not one pound, not even ten shillings . . . Here, I'll tell you what I'll do, today and today only . . .'

'*Only,*' my mother would get him to repeat. 'Give it some emphasis. Make it sound as though it really is *only* for today.'

'Only . . . today *only.*'

It really was a marriage made in heaven.

It's a funny thing about swag – you begin by being ashamed of yourself for dealing in it, feeling pity and not a little contempt for the discernment of those who buy it, and not only buy it but actually appear to like it and want it, need it even, but in the end you too succumb to it. Swag is viral. I say is but in truth I don't know how swag is now. I live a long way from any English market. Of course the carnival masks and the plastic gondolas are no different in spirit from the swag we sold, but I have nothing to do with the swagmen in whose shops and on whose stalls you find them. In my swag days, at any rate, the stuff was virulent. If you hung around it long enough you caught it.

At first none of us believed there could be a market for the gear my father was bringing back from the warehouses. 'Look at these!' we would say, scampering around in the back of the van, ripping open boxes of ornamental Dutch pee-pee boys with Chinese faces, and flowery wall plates that said 'Too Grand Ma', and brass mirrors in the design of a ship's porthole. Who was this stuff for? In time we came to realize. It was for us.

Bit by bit my mother started to make exceptions, creeping in a line here and a line there. A musical pedal bin – we could do with that. A pouffe in the shape of a grand piano – we could definitely use that. A black resin bare-breasted mermaid, six feet high, riding a dolphin and holding up a trident the prongs of which were each wired to take a seventy-five watt bulb – 'I'm sorry but I think it's lovely.' Latherless soap with sharp edges found its way into the house, talcum powder that smelt of the urine of the Siberian tiger, paper handkerchiefs that blew apart when you sneezed in them. Before long my mother was writing on lined Albanian notepads as a matter of course, she who had once corresponded with the heroes of the Spanish Civil War on the finest scented paper.

(To this day I receive absorbent letters from her which I have to collect personally from the sorting office, no Italian postman being willing to risk splintering himself on her Romanian envelopes.)

I'm not saying we had lived according to chaste design principles in the pre-swag years. Given where we came from, how could we not have been stirred by whatever moved suddenly or shone? It wasn't so long ago that we'd have swapped an entire bank of the Dniester for a string of coloured beads. So yes, gaudy we had always been. But gaudiness can have its own cultural integrity and consistency. Now, though, under the influence of swag, we became confused.

Aesthetically confused.

Whether we also became morally confused is the big question. I believe it depressed us – I'll go that far. I believe the ugliness of the tsatskes we sold, and then surrounded ourselves with, demoralized us.

But I was the only one in our family who thought that. And some would say that I ended up the most demoralized of us all. So who am I to insist I was right?

Except that I was.

I am, of course, describing a slow process. We didn't overnight go down with swag. In the beginning, or at least once my father recovered from his headlong fall into the fireplace, we were in the pink. My mother was delighted that the bus had now gone from our lives. My sisters were pleased to earn a bit of train-to-town and cappuccino money bagging face cloths. Aunty Dolly might just have found herself a boyfriend though no one was betting on anything yet, least of all my grandmother who didn't count her chickens even after they were hatched. And I had become a famous boy ping-pong player with my picture in the *Manchester Evening News* most weeks under such headlines as, 'Winning streak goes on and on for new hope' and 'Akiva chopper tipped for bigger things'.

So I was out of my shell?

Don't rush me. I was coming out.

I had less time to be in there, that's for sure. Practice at the Akiva on Sunday mornings. Matches mid-week. Maybe more practice with the Marks brothers who had just come to live next door (right next door, amazingly) and had a table in their garden – no more than a couple of sheets of plywood balanced on dustbins, it's true, but a table none the less, and the better, as far as practice went, for being uneven in bounce and exposed to all weathers. Then there was the occasional evening comparing tenors at Twink's place. And Saturdays and school holidays doing the markets with Cheap Johnnie.

The old man didn't expect much from me at first. He was somewhat disillusioned by me, I think, after the Bosch episode. And he already had a floorman, a blond amateur wrestler called Mike Sieff, who was good at helping to get an edge, banging boxes and blowing up and bursting paper bags and pretending to be in a fight with my father over the prices he was knocking stuff down at – 'What's the matter with you? Have you gone mad, has the sun got to you?' – and otherwise clowning and tcheppehing with him in the vein of Abbott and Costello. He knew how to move the gear out as well. 'Over there and over here and over here and over there and another one over here!' he'd shout, like a man who had lost his senses himself, clapping his enormous hands together as though they were the bellows that fanned the impulse to buy.

So all I had to do, thank God, was help put the stall up around the van if it was raining and otherwise do the general dogsbodying, fetch tea and sandwiches, open cartons, run for change, buy Mike Sieff a paper for the drive home, and maybe dive into the toilets with a *Span* from the filthy magazine stall (where there was definitely no shouting 'Over here and over there!' – as quiet as the grave, the filthy magazine stall, the owner always in a raincoat, even when the sun shone, so that his punters should feel at ease); or I'd just mope about, dreaming of chopping my way into that exceptional fate that was ticking away, louder and louder now – tick, tock, plick, plock – waiting to explode under me and blow me out of the trivial common into magnificent exceptionalness, pre-eminence, immunity from all things footling.

Some journalists were saying I should be given a trial for the national junior side, never mind Lancashire. Things were moving. By now Ogimura must have been feeling my breath on his neck. I imagined him in a little paper house at the foot of a triangular mountain, troubled in the arms of his geisha, scrutinizing my photograph in the *Manchester Evening News*. The geisha too was agitated by my photograph. Her kimono fluttered, parted, showing her suspenders. The rain fell on the little blue willow-pattern bridge outside the little paper house. Plick, plock. And pattered on the glass roof of the municipal toilet. I dived out to wrestle with the tarpaulin. But not before I had heard a sword coming out of its scabbard with a scraping sound like a razor scratching at a throat, and seen a stain the colour of dark plum slowly spreading up the paper walls of the little blue house.

There were worse ways of spending a wet Saturday.

Then one Thursday night my father came home looking very white. We all wondered what the matter was. He'd been looking this colour just before he fell into the fireplace with tacks in his mouth.

'Mike Sieff,' he said. 'That's what the matter is.'

He ate his supper in silence. Cheese blintzes with cauliflower cheese. Followed by macaroni cheese. Followed by cheese and biscuits.

'I sacked him,' he said, pushing his plate away, then, changing his mind, 'Any more cheese?' he asked.

What had happened was this. He had suspected Mike Sieff of tealeafing for some time. He had no actual proof. He hadn't seen Mike Sieff take anything. 'But you know how you just feel it?' That was how he just felt it. However, you can't go up to someone and say I feel you've been tealeafing from me. And he wanted to give him the benefit of the doubt. The Sieffs were from the same bend in the Bug as the Walzers. Besides, the boy was a shtarker, with triangular shoulders and a straight golden neck like a bull's. My father was built like a brick shithouse, but even a man who was built like two brick shithouses would have thought twice about tangling with Mike Sieff. But the feeling was nagging and nagging at him. He knew Sieff was up to something. And then, late this afternoon, as they were packing up, he distinctly saw a five-pound note go from the hand of a punter into the hand of Mike Sieff and not go from there into my father's apron. That was it. No more feeling – he'd seen it.

'Mike, open your hand,' he said.

'Why?'

'Mike, just open your hand.'

Mike opened his other hand.

'Not that one, Mike.'

'What is this, Joel?'

'Mike, I saw you take a flim. Open up your hand.'

'That's a serious accusation, Joel.'

'Just open it.'

'If you're going to accuse me of something,' Mike said, 'I'd like you to accuse me in front of a witness.'

'Right!' One of my father's rights. Who would I rather have been at that moment – Mike Sieff with his deltoid shoulders, or my father set on his course? Hard to say. But it's a formidable thing to be able to say 'Right!' – and to mean it.

My mother quaked for him. My mother's side had never said 'Right!' and meant it in their lives. 'Oh, Joel,' she said. 'You didn't!'

'Didn't what?'

'You didn't accuse him in front of somebody.'

'Dead right, I did.'

'Right!' he'd said, and leapt down from his van . . .

'Oh, Joel,' my mother said. 'You didn't.'

'Didn't what?'

'Leap from the van.'

Dead right, he did. 'And I don't want you to move a muscle,' he told Mike Sieff. 'I want that hand kept where I can see it.'

Then he called out, 'Katz!'

On Thursdays Katz the Kurtain King worked the next pitch to my father's . . .

'Oh, Joel, you didn't?'

'Didn't what?'

'You didn't accuse him in front of Katz?'

'Do you think I'm mad?' Katz had the biggest mouth in Manchester. Tell Katz your troubles on a Monday and the whole town knew about them the weekend before. So avid was Katz to burble out what he knew, his words liquefied in his throat and came out as spray. That was the price you paid for listening to gossip from Katz – you risked blinding by aspersion. Accuse Mike Sieff in front of Katz? No, all my father wanted Katz to do was keep an eye on the stall while he frogmarched that snake in the grass Sieff to the Toby's office. Not that Katz hadn't earwigged plenty already.

Snakes, frogs, earwigs – when my father's righteousness was engaged, you could hear the moral undergrowth tick louder than my ambition.

I had a question this time. 'When you say you frogmarched him . . .'

Yep, he frogmarched him. Took him by his pumping arm ('Oy a broch, you should have felt that arm!') and led him past the packing-up grafters, past Linoleum Les staggering under the rolls of his floor-cloth as though he were a factory trying to make off with the chimney, past the bedding boys folding up their sheets like housemaids, past the crockery twins from Leeds – Abe and Izzy, impossible to tell apart and always the last to finish pitching because they wanted to sell out and have an empty van to bundle skirt into – past the *Span* man silent in his mac, past the fruit and veg and flowers, through the café and into the Toby's den.

'Right, now you can open that hand,' my father said.

And Mike Sieff did . . .

And . . . ?

Empty.

'Oh, Joel, it wasn't!'

It was. My father's eyes told us it was. Empty. Untenanted. Void. And not just any old void. In Manchester just as you can have a very lot you can have a very void.

So what did he do then?

'I thought I'd seen him bend down just before I collared him. So I told him to take his shoes off.'

'You didn't!'

He did.

And?

Very empty.

And then?

And then his socks.

'You didn't!'

He did. Empty ditto. Very, very empty. And then his pockets.

Empty ditto. And then his shirt. And then his vest. And then his trousers . . .

'Mr Walzer, are you sure about this?' the Toby had said. ('First rule of the gaffs, always look after the Toby.')

Sure he was sure. Now the trousers please.

We were all gathered round by now, the Shrinking Violets and my grandmother as well, all staring at Mike Sieff stripped down to his underpants, wondering where my father would have the courage to search for the missing fiver next.

He smiled strangely.

It was the Violets, this time, who said, in one voice, 'Joel, you didn't!'

My sisters had their knuckles in their mouths. I could barely breathe. My mother was on the point of fainting. We didn't know much about the law in our family, in either of our families, but we guessed that a man accused of theft and made to prove his innocence by baring everything stood to gain a very lot in any civil court. This was leaving aside any payment he might choose to exact with his bare fists.

We waited.

We were ruined, were we, was that why our provider and protector had come home whiter than a dead man? We were finished?

Well?

'Any more of that cheese?' my father asked.

'Joel, don't do this to me,' my mother said.

He nibbled on a corner of crumbling Caerphilly, taking his time. 'I think all the ladies should leave the room,' he said at last.

'Joel!'

He was only teasing. Well? Well, he'd begun to panic, he didn't mind admitting that. He was running out of options. Correction – he'd *run* out of options. But he'd seen what he'd seen, and if you can't believe the evidence of your own eyes what can you believe? The pants came off.

We averted our eyes, as much from one another as from the accused.

Funny, my sisters thought, concentrating to a degree that was unusual for them, funny that Mike Sieff should have agreed to this. He didn't have to, did he? My father couldn't make him. The Toby couldn't make him. The Toby wasn't police, when all was said and done. My father lowered his head. 'The lobbess was enjoying it,' he said. Enjoying my father's discomfiture, that is. What he didn't say, but what I know as a fellow sportsman must have been the case, was that Mike Sieff was enjoying parading his own nakedness too, rubbing my father's nose in it, so to speak. I would have done the same to Ogimura, given half the chance. Cop this, slant-eyes!

And did the five-pound note in question float down between his golden legs when the wrestler dropped his drawers? Of course it didn't.

'Satisfied, Joel?' he said. He stood, in my father's words, with everything apart. As though to say, feast your eyes all you like and then tell me: 1) where you think I'm concealing your miserable flim now and 2) what someone as magnificent as I am would want with anything of yours anyway. Which, again in my father's words, was his big mistake. Because my father did feast his eyes on him, took him in from the tops of his fingers to the tips of his toes. Well built, he'd give him that. Not handsome, his eyes were too frog-like, his head was too small for his body (like a snake's, like the snake in the grass he was) for him to be handsome, and we Walzers liked a big head. But below the neck, sure, well put together. And not the usual colour for someone whose grandparents were born on the Bug but who wasn't a shaygets. Big yellow feet. Big yellow hands. Big yellow fingers. Wrestler's fingers. Wrestler's thumbs even. One of which had been bent back in the ring – a submission hold, he'd told my father – and was protected with a thick roll of bandage. Funny that you needed a bandage on a bent thumb.

And funny how long, now he came to think of it, Mike Sieff had been wearing it. Three weeks, was it? Four weeks? Five? Relief leapt like a flame in my father's heart. He had seen what he'd seen. 'Mike,' he said, 'I'd like you to take off that bandage.'

No! We didn't dare believe that the story had a happy ending after all. No! Not the bandage!

Yes. Oh, yes, the bandage. And that, my friends, was it. Finito. From anguish to joy in a single bound. And vice versa for Mike Sieff. He started to whine. Covered himself – not such a shtarker all of a sudden! – and started to shiver. Pleaded poverty. Illness. Worry. Overwork. Absent-mindedness. Accident even – the fiver had somehow got in there of its own accord, crawled up his thumb in some way he couldn't explain. Along with the three others my father found, rolled like cigarette papers and coiled inside the bandage like sleeping adders. 'On my mother and father's life, Joel, I'd have paid you back. I intended to. Honest to God.'

'Oh, Joel, maybe he would have.' Pity time for my mother's side. After the elation, the compassion.

'*Oh, Joel!* Do you have any idea how much he must have been ganvying all these months? It's enough I didn't call the police. And then do you know what he had the chutzpah to ask me for? Holiday pay. He whines all the way back in the van, gringeing and sniffing and wiping his nose on his sleeve and saying he's sorry, and he's never done anything like this in his life before, and please will I not tell his family, and please will I not mention it to his chinas, and then he says will I drop him off at Lapidus's and can he have his holiday pay now? How do you like it! Holiday pay!'

'Did you drop him off naked at Laps',' my sisters wanted to know, 'or had you given him his trousers back by then?'

'Never mind his trousers,' I said. 'What about his bandage?'

We all wanted to get in on the act.

'I don't know what *you're* looking so pleased about,' my father

117

said to me. 'You'll have to take off school tomorrow. I haven't got a floorman.'

'Me!'

'You. You've seen what you have to do enough times. "A lady over here and a lady over there! And again! And another!" Your mother can write it out for you if you've forgotten. I'd go to bed and practise if I were you.'

'It'll be good for him,' I heard my father saying, long after I'd retired to my room. 'It'll get him out of that shell of his.'

'The boy's sensitive,' my mother said. 'He'll come out in his own good time.'

'Then it'll get him off the kazi,' was my father's final word on the matter.

It's wrong of me to load my bashfulness on to my mother's side. It's unfair to them and to me. Some of the things I was shy about I was right to be shy about. Being a child, for example. It was preposterous being a child and having thoughts. The only time being a child is any good, that's to say has anything of nature about it, is when it's mindless. Wordsworth's Idiot Boy. Once the blank misgivings start, those obstinate questionings of sense and outward things, the blushing starts as well. And for some of us the misgivings start sooner than for others. As long as I'd been a child, as I remember it, I'd been ashamed of myself. The short pants, the squeaky voice, the teaty little mouth, the rubbery little in-between, the heat, the untestedness, the all to come and nothing had.

If I could have felt it looked right, me standing there confronting the edge, clapping my hands and shouting 'And again, and another, let's be having you, ooh, Mrs Woman, please . . .' I'd have made a better stab at it. I wanted to be able to do it. It passed through my mind sometimes that I had it in me to go all the way, to progress from the floor to the side of the van, to oust my own father who didn't even write his own material and become the greatest pitcher the gaffs had ever seen, the grafter to end all grafters, a spinner of such quicksilver spiel that people would come to listen to me from all corners of the globe, not just Joe Public but fellow pros – priests, professors, healers, comedians, mountebanks, evangelists, dictators – anxious to see with their own eyes the heights to which rabble-rousing could be raised, and of course the Jezebels with their retractable blood-red nails in legions as limitless as the sea, all with their purple throats thrown back and their soft funnelled mouths open and pulsing, like a thousand baby birds clamouring to be fed.

But that was in the future, when I would be a man. As yet I wasn't even ready to start at the beginning. How could I call a grown woman 'darling' at my age? ''Ee'are darling.' Preposterous. How could I look a man old enough to be my uncle Motty in the eyes and address him as 'cock'? Yes, there were younger boys than me on the markets, working the vegetable and flower stalls usually, prefab sorts of boys, rapscallions, lads (and no one had ever thought of me as a 'lad'), from whose cherubic lips flowed a stream of loves and dears and wotchercocks and I'll tell you what I'll do guvenors – but they were the idiot boys. They suffered no disjunction. It would never have occurred to them to think there was anything amiss in swapping familiarities with grown-ups when you were possessed of no better credentials than a rubbery little in-between. So they were no example to me. They were of another species.

I tried, but it must have been a ghastly spectacle.

'What was that?' my father shouted down from his eminence, cupping his ear in a comical exaggerated fashion. He had a whistle in his mouth and wore a stupid striped Wee Willie Winkie hat with a woolly bobble on the end of it. On Fridays he was Mad Jack.

'I think there might be a lady at the back who would like one,' I repeated, in what I hoped was a slightly louder voice.

'Oh, you suspect we have a lady to the rear who would care to make a purchase? Do we have a lady aft who is considering her position? Well when you've made your mind up, Mrs Woman, perhaps you would step forward and have a word with Little Lord Fauntleroy here.'

Little Lord Fauntleroy. My own father!

I was meant to be whipping up a frenzy. The phantom lady at the back is always eager to buy what the pitcher is selling long before he's ready to sell it. Not exactly abstruse psychology. Stay, illusion! If she and the other phantoms like her are prepared to fork out seventeen-and-six for the jardinière in the form of a dying swan, imagine the mayhem – 'Look, I'll tell you what I'm going to do, I'm not just going to sell one, I'm not just going to sell two, I'm going to clear the whole jolly lot, never mind seventeen-and-six, never even mind fifteen shillings' – when the price plummets to ten bob for the pair, the pair!

Over here and over there! All hell should break loose. And did when Mike Sieff leapt up and down and clapped his hands and burst paper bags. But with Little Lord Fauntleroy agitating the edge, selling all at once became a transaction of embarrassments. I communicated my diffidence. Suddenly people were reluctant to shove their hands in the air. Normally thick-skinned punters, regulars who knew the routines and their own roles in them, began to blush when my father chipped them. It was as if the fairy of mortification had waved her wand and hey presto! – the gaff was awash with Shrinking Violets.

My father did what he could with me. Sometimes, to break the calamitous spell of bashfulness I'd cast, he'd leave me in it, leave me to carry out the nest of cardboard suitcases with the rust-loving hinges to the non-existent punter at the back – 'Sold!' – leave me to go wandering at the furthest fringes of the edge and return, if I ever found the courage to return, with the cases concealed somewhere about my person. By turning me into the joke, some of the fun of the fair might just come back. I knew what he was up to. I understood the necessity to tease me. But that didn't mean I could ever get my face right. I'd give anything, today, to be able to look my father in the eyes and say, 'Go on, go on, Cheap Johnnie, make a shlemiel of me, let me be your stooge. I can take it, I can take a joke against myself. I have to take a joke against myself, otherwise I am madder than Mad Jack myself.' But it's too late for that. And anyway, my face would let me down again.

This would never have gone on for long, even if I'd been good at it. There was no question of my being removed from school and turned into a marketman. Education was God. Education would stop us ever having to be beetroot farmers again. Or swagmen. And my father didn't want me with him all the time, anyway. I cramped his style. The van was starting to turn up at some strange places, just as the bus once had. He was on first-name terms with the women who buttered the fat wedges of toast in every transport café between Manchester and north Wales, north Wales and Worksop, and Worksop back to Manchester again via Sheffield and the Snake Pass. They knew when he was coming and prepared special treats for him, liver and onion fry-ups, cheese and ham pies with double cheese, bread and butter puddings of which they gave him extra portions wrapped in foil to take home to my mother. Ha! Sometimes he'd slip me some loose change so that I could play the pinball machines while he discussed his dietary requirements with them in the kitchens. Sometimes they'd come out from behind the stoves and counters, wipe their hands on their aprons, kiss me and tell me how lucky I was to have such a wonderful father.

Now it was his turn to look bashful.

I was in his way.

Let's be even-handed about it – we were in each other's way.

So when he came to hear that Sheeny Waxman had fallen out with Sam Sam the Bedding Man and was looking for a job he jumped at him. Sheeny was reckoned to be one of the best pitchers in the country. The sizes of the edges he pulled were legendary. London Boys were known to come up just to watch Sheeny work, and to go back whistling through their teeth. His trick was to start sedately, ringing a little dinner bell and engaging individual punters in a confusion of free gifts and part-exchanges, and then turn progressively more demented. In this his natural tics and twitches were of inestimable help to him. As was his fastidious taste in sharp suits, white shirts with detachable collars, and matching ties and handkerchiefs. Short as he was, you could see and hear him from everywhere; whatever else you were doing you dropped, wherever else you were going was suddenly of no account, such an irresistible spectacle was he, frothing and jerking in his downy mohair whistle, one parrot-eye closed, hoarse and golden like an aristocratic dwarf, a scion of some Nordic royal family, gone mad and reduced to knocking out swag on English markets because of centuries of syphilis and in-breeding.

Of course there was no point hiring someone with Sheeny Waxman's reputation to work the floor, assuming he'd ever have consented to play second fiddle to another pitcher anyway, but my father made it clear he didn't in the least mind stepping down in order, in his own words, 'to defer to a master'.

'*I'm* not ongeblozzen with pride,' he told me, pointedly. '*I* don't think I know everything. *I* don't think I'm too good for everybody. *I* don't think there's nobody I can learn from.'

EIGHT

The principle of becoming better and stronger is very simple. If you improve, you become strong. How to make improvement is very, very difficult, however.

> Zoltan Berczic (one-time national coach of the
> Hungarian Table Tennis team)

M Y FATHER'S POINTEDNESS apart, it gave me a queer satisfaction to have Sheeny Waxman working for us. It altered the relations between this and that. It put my separate worlds in harmony and in some way that I couldn't properly explain made me feel more important and grown up.

Maybe there was nothing to explain; maybe having Sheeny on the family payroll simply flattered me with the illusion that I'd bought a share in his haunts, that I'd put my name down, so to speak, for the Ritz and the Plaza and the Kardomah, especially the Kardomah where hoarse-voiced men in camel coats croaked lewd propositions to women young enough to be their granddaughters.

The Kardomah had its own unofficial prep school. Laps'. Only after you'd submitted yourself to an undefined period of continuous assessment at Laps' − social audacity alone was the criterion: volubility, brazenness, wideness as we called it − were you considered up to doing the Kardomah. And even then you may have shot your bolt too soon, in which event it was back to Laps' for another indeterminate stint. No one I knew could remember when there hadn't been a chip shop called Lapidus's on Bury Old Road. It was institutional. Tell your parents you'd been at Laps' when they caught you creeping up the stairs after midnight and all your sins were remitted. Yes, you could get yourself into deep waters at Laps', but at least you were swimming between the flags. At Laps' one of our own, one of unserer, was always there to save us.

Not infrequently, successful graduates of Laps' – Sheeny Waxman, for one – would drop in to see how we were getting on, leaving the roofs of their cars down and their engines running, acknowledging greetings from juvenile versions of themselves, dispensing advice, alluding briefly to their own apprenticeships, in the manner of great men returning to their old schools on speech days. The closer you were to graduating yourself, the more you recognized these sentimental homecomings for what they were – acts of late-night desperation, the final foray before the lights went out in Manchester and all that remained was the ignominy of an empty bed. Laps' gave you one more go, there lay the beguilement of the place even for those who thought they had put it behind them; at Laps' there was always just the possibility of cashing in on someone else's mishap, or of simply doing a deal. On Saturday nights, especially, the atmosphere of bazaar and barter on the pavement outside Laps' was so fervid that motorists strange to the area would stop to consult their maps, imagining that they'd taken a wrong turning and driven into the Lebanon. It's a measure of how miffed Sheeny must have been by Cynthia Cartwright's refusal to accommodate him on my debut night that he dumped her in the middle of Miles Platting instead of bringing her back to Bury Old Road and exchanging her for someone more amenable at Laps'. Not that there had to be a swap. Sometimes you would simply drop off a non-performer altruistically, as a kindness to a fellow head jockey. Because it was understood that women were a perverse species, who would with some and wouldn't with others.

So on top of everything else it was, Lapidus's chip shop was a hotbed of early feminism, too? You could say that. Certainly anyone listening to Selwyn Marks on the injustices suffered by Ruth Aarons would have been impressed by the humanity and understanding a boy his age was able to show towards a woman he had never met.

We were sitting in the back room of Laps', sharing a big plate of pickle meat, sweet and sour cucumbers, mustard and chips. Funnily enough, Sheeny Waxman happened to pop his head into the room as we were talking. With Sheeny you always saw his stiff snow-white cuffs, and then his gold shield links engraved with his initials, before you saw him. It was a Kardomah thing; at the Kardomah you led with your cuffs, filled your mouth with phlegm, tugged at the lapels of the coat which you wore loose and empty-sleeved around your shoulders, then made your pitch.

'So who's this Ruth Aarons?' Sheeny wanted to know.

'No one you've shtupped,' Selwyn said.

Sheeny twitched. Maybe he hadn't. He'd be surprised, but maybe he hadn't.

'Anything here?' He didn't expect an answer. What would kids like us know, anyway? After checking the room out for himself, he ratcheted his neck up out of his collar, jerked a handful of our chips into his mouth, and left.

'Big shot,' Selwyn said.

'I like him,' I said. I didn't go on to say, 'And my father slips him his pay-packet.'

So who was this Ruth Aarons?

'Who won the Women's World Table Tennis Championships in 1935/6?' Selwyn asked me.

'Ruth Aarons?' I hazarded.

'Correct. And in 1936/7?'

I hesitated. I could feel a trick question coming on. 'Not Ruth Aarons?'

'Ha!' Selwyn banged the table, causing Lotte to look up from behind the fryer. Any trouble in the back room at Laps' and Lotte had you out. Selwyn, who was already flushed with indignation on behalf of Ruth Aarons, flushed further under Lotte's stare. '*Not* Ruth Aarons is a very good answer,' he said. '*Not* Ruth Aarons. Not nobody.'

'How come?' I asked. 'Were there no women players that year?'

'If there were no women players that year, explain to me how Votrubcova was able to win the mixed doubles with Vana, and Depetrisova was able to win the women's doubles with Votrubcova.'

I couldn't.

'The best women players in the world were there. All of them. Including Ruth Aarons who'd won it the year before and was playing better than ever. But do you know what it says in the record books under Women's Singles 1936/7?'

'Not Nobody?'

'Worse. It says "Title Vacant".' He waited for the information to sink in. 'How do you like that? – TITLE VACANT!'

Was I meant to be amazed by this, or crestfallen, or outraged? I plastered mustard over a slice of pickled meat, folded it around a wedge of cucumber, and tried an expression that was a combination of all three.

'There was a final, you see,' Selwyn went on. 'Between Ruth Aarons and Trude Pritzi, but no winner.'

'They didn't finish?'

'They weren't allowed to finish. They were disqualified.'

Selwyn's eyes bulged so violently I wondered what the women could possibly have been disqualified for. Not unladylike behaviour, I hoped.

'Well,' Selwyn said, 'you're not all that wide of the mark.

Pushing. That's what they were disqualified for. Pushing. After one hour and forty-five minutes of chiselling the umpire looked at his watch, said "Jude Raus!", and called it a day.'

I was familiar with the one hour forty-five minute rule. Anybody who knew anything about ping-pong had heard of the marathon battle between Erhlich of Poland and Paneth of Romania at the Worlds in Prague in '36. For two hours and five minutes they pushed the ball back and forth before either of them won a point. Two hours and five minutes and it was 1–0. By 1–1 the crowds had all gone home. Assuming a tight finish, the possibility arose of a five-game match lasting more than a fortnight: a computation that took no account of the need to sleep. Thereafter the International Table Tennis Federation decided on limiting all matches to one hour and forty-five minutes on pain of disqualification.

So Ruth and Trude got theirs. Tough, but rules are rules. However, I had a fair idea that 'Jude Raus!' was an interpolation all of Selwyn's own.

'But if both girls were disqualified . . .'

'Ruth Aarons was the holder of the title. Until someone took it off her it was hers. And if all Pritzi was prepared to do was chisel, what was wrong with Aarons chiselling back. "You want it, Trude? Then come and take it." Tactics. Suddenly you're not allowed tactics . . . If your name happens to be Aarons.'

'Selwyn . . .'

'You know where these Championships were held?' He looked around the room as though it wasn't safe to talk about these things still, not even in Laps'. He lowered his voice. 'Baden.'

I wasn't the mine of ping-pong information the Marks brothers were but I was in possession of a few essential facts, especially when they related to my nearly-hero Richard Bergmann, as for example that Baden was where the seventeen-year-old Bergmann became World Champion for the first time. 'Bergmann, Selwyn.' I rubbed my nose. 'Bergmann!'

'Exactly. They couldn't give both titles to a Jew. Not in Baden. Not in 1937.'

I shook my head.

'She was a golden girl,' Selwyn went on. 'I see what you're thinking. A golden girl with a name like Ruth Aarons? Girls called Ruth Aarons are dark little meerskeits with a big shnozz and thick glasses. Well that's your problem. She was a golden girl with blonde ringlets, a beautiful figure and a scintillating personality. But Baden finished her. Trude Pritzi went to London the next year and won the title. Ruth Aarons never played in a World Championships again. The yiddenfeits did for her.'

There turned out to be something prophetic about this conversation. A fortnight later the yiddenfeits did for Selwyn.

Years after the one hour and forty-five minute fiasco an expedite law was devised, of such complexity that it was altogether better for one's long-term peace of mind to be disqualified and have done. How were you ever supposed to remember which was the twelfth shot on your own service and the thirteenth return of your opponent's? Now I wouldn't be surprised to hear that people play with calculators in their pockets. But at the time that Selwyn himself was disqualified from a tournament the Law of Expedition had yet to be hammered out. An umpire suddenly got twitchy and you were a goner, that was how it worked then.

He was right to feel he'd been hard done by, since if he was guilty of slow play so was his opponent. All you could say in the umpire's favour was that Selwyn's off the table tactics were slow also. 'It's my religion,' Selwyn complained afterwards. 'You know what will happen next if we aren't allowed to practise our religion while we're playing? They'll disqualify us because of our names. Starr – you're disqualified! Mistofsky – you're disqualified. Walzer – you're disqualified. The way they did with Aarons.'

But none of us could quite go along with him in the matter of his having to read a ruling from the Talmud between every point, or holding up his hand to re-arrange his fringes just as his opponent was about to serve.

Even his own brother wouldn't back him. 'You don't bother with that stuff at home,' he said. 'At home you piss in your yarmulke.'

'I've never pissed in my yarmulke.'

'And you torture the cat with your tzitzits.'

'We don't have a cat.'

'Did I say our cat? Any cat. I've seen you whipping cats with the fringes of your tzitzits. I've seen you tying their paws up.'

'I don't go near cats. I'm frightened of cats. They're treife.'

'What do you care about treife? You sneak bacon sandwiches into your bedroom in your yarmulke.'

'Is that after I've pissed in it or before?'

'What's the matter with you? What gets into you as soon as you come out of the house? What are you trying to do – start a pogrom?'

'Start one? That's good,' Selwyn said. 'Start one! Next you'll tell me that six million is an exaggeration.'

It was good for me that Selwyn was out of the tournament. We were at opposite ends of the draw. If he'd gone on making it through we'd have been looking at a showdown in the final. No problems about beating him – I'd never come close to losing to Selwyn Marks even in practice – but I didn't want to win my first title that way. If I was going to be Manchester Closed Junior Champion I wanted to take out someone who wasn't one of us in the final, someone who didn't live next door to me, someone who didn't have the murky waters of the Bug or Dniester flowing through his veins . . . what am I trying to say? – someone who was white.

Wasn't Selwyn white? Only in a manner of speaking. Selwyn was pale. White only by default. What I had in mind was white white, *foreign* white.

It shouldn't be that hard to understand. My ambition was to be crowned conclusive champion of Somewhere Else, not champion of Our Street.

This was my debut tournament. There'd been others I could have entered earlier in the season but Aishky had advised me to keep myself a secret for the big one.

I was hurt by the idea that I was still an unknown quantity. 'I'm hardly a secret, Aishk,' I said. 'I'm in the papers every week.'

'Sure, sure, but most of these kids haven't seen you with their own eyes yet. Think surprise element. It'll be like Nagasaki. Pow!'

Was Nagasaki where Ogimura lived, I wondered. The paper house breathed and shivered. The champion lay motionless on his futon, staring at the ceiling. *Swish* went the geisha's kimono. *Snap* went her suspender.

If I'd been saving myself for the big one, it follows that I'd been saving the big one for me. Turning out once a week for a league match was one thing, but a *tournament*! – everyone who was anyone in Manchester ping-pong, the League Secretary, the League Chairman, the League President, for God's sake (men who had crossed ping-pong bats embroidered on the breast pockets of their blazers), to say nothing of players from higher divisions, strokemakers and tantrum-throwers and rule-benders whose gamesmanship was the stuff of legend, veterans of the sport, scouts, coaches, international selectors, commentators, and who could guess how many members of the ping-pong watching public, all gathered in one place and at one time and with one purpose . . . To see me? Of course I did not really think that. But then again, of course I really did.

Within a week of the tournament I'd lost all capacity to sleep. I couldn't even remember how to shut my eyes. The night before, I climbed into my bed like Cinderella stepping up into her pumpkin, quaking and overdressed, already in my tracksuit in case I suddenly found the trick of sleeping again and overdid it. I needn't have worried. By six in the morning I was on Oxford Road waiting for the University to open.

I checked and re-checked my registration form. By the Sports Hall, Manchester University, it did mean *this* Manchester University . . . ? There was bound to be a Manchester in the United States of America, and another in Canada, and probably a third in Rhodesia, and they were all bound to have a university, but that wouldn't make any sense, would it, choosing one of those as the venue for *our* Manchester Closed?

Assuming it was *our* Manchester Closed.

I walked around Rusholme. Sat on a park bench. Refused one of the dawn whores – I think. Blushed in the event that I hadn't. Blushed in the event that I had. Then found somewhere to have tea and toast. By the time I made it back to the University I was no longer early. Not late, just no longer early. I registered, nodded to a few people I recognized, pushed open the swing doors of the Sports Hall and pow! like Aishky had said, and I hadn't even begun yet, pow! – all the exhilaration I'd felt when I first saw a room full of green tables in action in the Tower in Blackpool returned. Green, the green of the foothills to Heaven, wherever I looked. Eden. The Happy Valley. The Garden of the Hesperides. Hush, hear the nymphs – for they too had woken sleepless and turned up early – plock plock, plock plock, plock plock.

Shocking, how small the tables looked when there were so many of them in a single space. But wasn't that the allure of the game for those of us who loved it? The confinement. No margin for error, and all the violence of competitive sport bounded by a nutshell. No spillage – there was the fatal beauty of ping-pong. No overflow or exorbitance. So there is no point blaming the players for being repressed. The game is repressed.

Plock plock, plock plock, went the shy Hesperides, and this time the music of the westernmost meadow on earth was for me.

There was my name, my certification, on the draw, accompanied by an asterisk to denote that I was seeded. I'd never before seen a draw, or even thought that as a tangible thing, a physical chart, actual sheets of paper which you could touch and rustle, a draw existed. So that was a draw! I loved it. I was transfixed by the artwork: the grand all-embracing brackets – Me against Him, and then Him gone, dropped from the picture, and Me against Someone Else – the empty dotted lines issuing from the noses of the brackets like spikes from the snouts of marlins, decreasing, narrowing, closing like jaws on that last incontrovertible horizontal. Every time I won a round I took up a seat within sight of the board so that I could verify the written proof of my advance. The mathematics of a draw staggered me. One hundred and twenty-eight players reducible to just one after only seven rounds. In that computation I saw the future, how little it took, sum-wise, to be the last man standing.

I was intoxicated by the tumult. It made me tremble. Made my stomach lurch with apprehension. So many wills, so many separate ambitions, so many arms going, enough piston power to light up the whole of Manchester on a winter's afternoon. On the green battlefield of my soul the two sides of my family took up their positions. 'Impossible,' my mother and my aunties whispered, 'impossible to expect to prevail against so many. Just do well. Get close. Lose honourably. No shame in that. Sleep, you are going to sleep. We will count to ten and when you awake you will remember nothing, my darling, but the will to lose . . . nine . . . ten . . . lose!' But then the Walzers grabbed me for a hokey-cokey, conga'd me past the draw where my seeded name kept on greedily coming – Walzer, O*; Walzer, O*; Walzer, O* – emboldening me with the least imaginative, and to tell the truth the least flattering, of all expressions of optimism – 'Someone has to win, why shouldn't it be you?'

I won.

Someone had to.

So potent was the magic which my mother's side worked on

me – it is more captivating, when all is said and done, to be told that victory is not indiscriminate, but yours to throw away – that I can only suppose every other boy had a mother's side working against him too. The closer I got to the final the more my aunties wheedled. My ears were wet with them. Their fingers paddled in my heart. I threw away leads, I served into the net on match point to me, I missed sitters – 'That's it, like that, my darling, just like that' – but my opponents' aunties must have loved them more, because for every sitter I missed, they missed two.

For the final itself all the lesser tables were cleared away and just one master table – the best and greenest table I had ever played on (a Jacques International Match Play Executive, I think it was called) – was erected in the centre of the hall. Then two hundred and eleven chairs were arranged around it.

I can be precise about the number. I counted them.

'Do you think they've made a mistake?' I asked Aishky.

Twink and Aishky had been knocked out of the senior tournament earlier in the day – if I haven't mentioned a senior tournament that's because I had no eyes for it – but they were staying on to give me encouragement. I doubt I was adequately grateful to them at the time. It takes courage to stay on at a tournament when it has no more use for you. And there were other things they could have been doing on a Saturday night. They were better friends to me than I deserved.

'A mistake in what sense?' Aishky wondered.

In the sense that two hundred and eleven chairs were hardly sufficient to seat a thousand spectators, was what I wanted to say. But I could hear in advance how that was going to sound. A man may think in thousands but he should never speak in them. I make no apologies for the wildness of my expectations. What did I know about tournaments? Wimbledon – that was my only model. All right, the Manchester Closed was not the All England, and table tennis was not lawn tennis, but I believed I'd made allowances for the difference. I was only thinking thousands, not tens of thousands.

I let the subject drop. Aishky looked concerned for me. He had mistaken my grandiosity for finals' nerves. He nodded in the direction of my opponent, Nils Hagtvet, who was lying across three chairs (three more chairs, I noted) underneath the draw, a packet of Stuyvesant's on his belly, blowing smoke rings. 'He's more nervous than you are,' Aishky said. 'He's a ball chaser. He hasn't hit one all day. He knows what you're going to do to him.'

'Does he?'

Now I did have finals' nerves. Was I up to beating a boy who could blow smoke rings?

More than that, was I up to beating someone quite so elongated? I had wanted to meet an incontrovertibly white boy in the finals. Be sure you really want what you want before you ask for it. Nils Hagtvet was the whitest and most extruded boy I had ever seen. He could have come out of a machine for rolling vermicelli. Where he actually came from no one seemed to know, but he played in a higher division than I did, for Tootal Ties.

Twink echoed Aishky's concern. 'Do yourself a favour,' he advised me, 'take a long shower. And then see if you can find somewhere dark to lie down for half an hour. Don't think about anything.'

It was the same advice my grandfather had given my father on the morning of the World Yo-Yo Championships. Except that Aishky added, 'And don't play with your putz.'

I knew better than to play with my putz before a match.

But in the event, I did something worse.

I went looking for chairs. Not with the intention of carrying them out into the arena myself, I should make plain, but just so as I'd know where they were when the multitude turned restive.

*　　*　　*

'Well?'

My grandmother, my mother and my aunty Fay were waiting for me when I got home.

I shrugged.

'Never mind,' they said. My seraglio of despairing counsel. How prompt they were with their siren consolations.

Too prompt, on this occasion.

'I won,' I said.

'You won?'

'I won.'

'You won?'

'I won. Big deal.'

'Well it is a big deal.' Now we could reverse roles. Now they could console me for discovering that victory was a trollop. Had my father been here, instead of broken down in the forecourt of a transport café outside Welshpool, he'd have given me a backhander for winning with so little grace. You pays your money . . .

I showed them my silver cup.

'Oh, that's beautiful,' my mother said.

'Swag,' I said.

They passed it from one to the other, peering under and over their spectacles to see if there was an inscription. Not a good eye between the three of them.

'I take it in to get my name engraved next week,' I said.

They all said 'ah!' as though I'd told them something upsetting.

'So how many people did you beat?' Aunty Fay asked.

'Seven.'

My grandmother shook her head. 'Seven,' she repeated. She seemed to see a challenge to the Almighty in it. 'Seven,' she said again, meaning no good could come of so big a number.

And she was right. No good had come of it.

I hadn't won well, then? The crowds hadn't cheered me to

the rafters? The girls hadn't scratched me with their nails?

Crowds? Girls?

Why did it matter to me that of the two hundred and eleven chairs arranged around the Jacques International Match Play Executive the better part of two hundred remained unoccupied?

Because it made me feel I was in possession of a skill no one valued.

I needed the confirmation of others, then, did I? I placed no philosophical value on the ping-pongness of ping-pong for itself?

Yes and no. Perhaps what had really gone wrong was that my opponent, Nils Hagtvet, was an oaf, and that my ascendancy over him – as a player, and I like to think as a moral being – reawoke section two of my old compound contradictory existential bashfulness, that's to say my shame at existing so successfully. It was like being back on the kitchen table at home making mincemeat of one of my father's associates, while *Dr Jekyll and Mr Hyde* smoked in my hand and my cheeks burned with consciousness of my own effrontery.

Nils Hagtvet's speciality was a freeze serve. Taking up a position as far to one corner of the table as was possible without disappearing from it altogether, he would touch the playing surface with the ball, hitch up his shorts, exaggerate the flatness of his palm, freeze into a crouch, and then in a sudden spasm would toss the ball high enough for him to pass his bat under it twice before imparting what appeared to be the most terrifying spin to it on the third attempt. That he would occasionally miss the ball altogether was not surprising given the complexity of the manoeuvre. Fine, so long as the percentages favoured him. But what you would never have guessed until you faced one of Nils Hagtvet's serves was that there was no spin on it whatsoever. No spin, no speed, no angle, nothing. How long did it take for him to crouch, hitch, freeze, and spasm? Forty-five seconds?

A minute? Humiliating for him, then, when you disdainfully smashed it past him before he'd even completed his convulsive follow-through.

In the first game he never won a single point on his service. And modesty forbids me telling how many I lost on mine. I couldn't bear it. The contrast between us was too cruel. I kept reminding myself that he'd reached the final, that he'd beaten other players, that I had no reason therefore to be pitying him. But then I'd see him scampering after balls I'd hit at medium pace, falling over himself in a tangle of his own making, his arms in his way, his legs too long and queerly ineffectual in little white cotton schoolgirl's socks that barely covered his ankles and kept vanishing inside his plimsolls, from which, after calling a let, he would periodically have to retrieve them. Never mind too cruel, it was too farcical. Didn't it count against me, somehow, to be thrashing someone as inept as this? Wasn't I inevitably implicated in the farce?

As we approached the conclusion of the first game sadness took hold of him. He began to turn away from the ball as it came towards him, as though wanting to distance himself from his shots, or in the hope that help might come to him from some other quarter. We changed ends, not looking at each other. But I heard his heart beating and I could smell self-disgust on him. It dawned on me that without trying I could win the next game to love. Worse than that even: I would have to try if I was *not* to win the next game to love.

Had I been all Walzer I surely would have moved in for the kill. But I wasn't all Walzer. I was part Saffron, too. Part mollusc. Part whelk. Part milksop.

I pretended to be bamboozled suddenly by his serves, raising my hand in acknowledgement of his canny play. I faked bemusement and fatigue. I stopped hitting and began to push. If nothing else that would prolong the match. Spare us both our blushes. And give the thirteen spectators something to get excited about.

It doesn't pay to tamper with your game. Before I knew it I had pushed a dozen balls into the net (balls I hadn't meant to push into the net), Nils Hagtvet had sufficiently recovered his composure as to remember how to stay upright and to push back, the umpire was warning us for slow play, and I had lost the second game.

A shame for Selwyn Marks that he hadn't hung around after his own demise; he would have been in his element now. Told you so, told you so – 'Walzer, you're disqualified.' Same umpire, too. Though there was more even-handedness about tonight's warning. Wake up or you'll both be out. But Hagtvet might have seen his salvation in that. At least that way he wouldn't be going down in the archives as a loser. *Title Vacant* was what the records would have read, not *Winner: Oliver Walzer; Runner-up: Nils Hagtvet*.

Except that having nicked the second game, Nils Hagtvet was now dreaming of making history himself. He took up extreme positions, miles back or miles wide, glared fixedly at me, hitched his shorts, and went into freeze posture – and that not just for his service but for mine as well. Ludicrous. All I had to do was serve short or into the opposite corner and he was a goner. Shaming. But he hung on. Actually thought he was in with a chance. Threw menacing glances at me, hurled himself from one side of the table to the other, charged and leapt until I too was having to scramble for every ball. Ludicrous. Shaming. Mortifying.

He implicated me in his folly to the end. At 20–8 in my favour – so I was cruising anyway – he crashed into the table and put his knee out. When they presented me with the cup he was still lying twisted on the floor, howling.

Years later he remained unshakable in his conviction that but for that smashed knee he would have walked all over me.

I could have done without running into Gershom Finkel on my way back to the changing rooms.

It was hot in the Sports Hall but he hadn't removed his raincoat. He extended his hand. 'You nearly blew that,' he said, laughing.

'Fuck off, Gershom,' I thought. But what I said was, 'Nice of you to come.'

I hadn't noticed him in the audience. That was how deeply Nils Hagtvet had embroiled me in unseemly contest.

'We were passing,' he said.

'We?'

'Dolly and Dora. We're on the way to the Ritz, so we thought we'd pop in to see if you needed any encouragement. A good job we did.'

'Are they here?'

Was that why I'd nearly blown it, because my aunties were in the vicinity?

'They're in the car outside. They couldn't bear to watch. Why don't you come out and tell them you've won?'

He was blowing, himself. Not exactly excited – he was too laconic ever to be excited – but staccato, spluttering, like a wet firework.

'You tell them, Gershom,' I said. 'Say, "Oliver won". I have to take a shower.'

'Don't you want to show them your trophy?'

'I'll show them later,' I said.

'Can I see, then?'

I gave him my cup. He felt its weight, turned it upside down, laughed and handed it back to me.

'We're off dancing,' he said.

Only later did I realize how disturbed I'd been by the size of that 'we'.

No, no good had come of my win. It left me feeling too much like my old self. I was Champion of Manchester – never mind the Junior and never mind the Closed – but nothing had changed. I still hadn't found my way out.

It's possible I was expecting too much too soon. Bit by bit hope crept up on me again. Next time there would be crowds. Next time I would play without being ashamed because I was good, and then being ashamed because I was bad. Show me a game to love in the future and I would seize it.

My voice began to deepen, that helped. I still couldn't croak like Sheeny Waxman, but I was on the way. Attacked by a hail of missiles from the prefabs while ambling down Sheepfoot Lane in a dream of glory, I stood my ground and hurled back whatever I could find. A stone struck. The first gentile blood I'd ever drawn. Maddened by the sight of it I threw still more ferociously and struck again. Two of them – I'd winged two of them! I heard a moan, and then the throwing stopped. Game to love. A week later I won a tournament in Barnsley and a month after that I was North of England Champion. Called up for Lancashire, I won both my singles' rubbers against Cheshire and against Derbyshire. I won in the doubles too, but I didn't count that: doubles entailed collaboration and I wasn't by nature a collaborator. Where I was going, a man had to go alone.

The pig episode confirmed my progress. It might not be going too far to say that the pig did even more than ping-pong to bring on that social audacity without which I would never have made it to the Kardomah.

I was working the Bank Holiday fair at Bakewell – home of the Tart – with my father and Sheeny. The summer agricultural fairs were marked with stars in every marketman's diary; you could be lying on your deathbed but you still didn't miss an agricultural fair; and if it happened to be a Bank Holiday agricultural fair, you conjured up the already dead to help you work it. Bakewell was the most fabled Bank Holiday agricultural fair of the lot. At Bakewell you took more money in a single morning than you could count in a week.

I loved the place. Half-timbered tea shops, the smell of warm pastry, a meandering stream, shepherds on the cobbled streets, animals in the pens. And crowds such as you've never seen. Sheeny loved it too. He rang his little dinner bell, clapped his hands, filled the skies with flying plunder, and pulled an edge that extended into the next county. It looked like Judgement Day on the banks of the Eternal River. 'Over here and over there . . . !' By noon there was hardly anything left in the van. That was all right. Things quietened down after lunch. You ran a better-toned pitch for an hour or so, shifting the classier and more expensive swag – the big shticks, as we called them, for size is everything with swag – and looked forward to being loaded and away by four. One of us could take a break at this time, too. I could sit by the stream and think about playing Ogimura for the geisha; Sheeny could walk around town and pull head jockey material; or my father could grab some shut-eye and a cheese sandwich in the van.

It was during this more sedate afternoon pitch – Sheeny and I working it together while my father was out cold – that the pig escaped. There was no mystery about how he made his getaway: Bank Holiday godforbids messing with the gates of the pens and poking the animals with sticks. But why he chose our edge to charge there was no saying. My theory was that Sheeny's gravelly patter attracted him. Who knows, to a pig it may have sounded like love talk. 'I'll tell you what, darling . . .' The music of the heart. Whatever the reason, the pig burst through the crowd, women screamed, Sheeny dropped the bevelled mirror he was holding – 'Who's that in there?' he'd just been asking a punter. 'You? Thank God, I thought it was me!' – and I found myself closer to any animal not a dog than I had been in my life. Strange, how much time you have for stray thoughts in moments of emergency. 'Jesus Christ, look at the size of that pig!' I heard Sheeny exclaim, but I was more struck by the hairs on its snout. Spinster hairs, I thought. Like those that grew on Dolly's upper lip and chin, defying all the hours she put in with her tweezers, S for spinster hairs, only Gershom Finkel didn't seem to mind.

A sweet pinky smell, too, which also reminded me of my aunties. Calamine lotion – that was it. The calamine that used to be brought out whenever there was measles or chicken-pox around, little wet dabs of calamine-drenched cotton wool which somehow always ended up in the sink or on the bathroom floor.

So had this pig had the measles lately?

He began to snuffle me. Sheeny called my father. 'Joel, Joel, there's a fucking pig out here eating your kid.' But no noise on earth could wake my father once he was out, and Sheeny did nothing otherwise to help me. Nor did the punters. They were gone.

What I did next affected Sheeny Waxman so deeply that for years afterwards he couldn't introduce me to anyone without referring to it. 'This is the ice-cream I told you about, the one who forehand-chopped the pig.'

What else was I going to do? Punch it? I'd never punched anything. I did the only thing I knew how to do and played ping-pong on its snout. In Aishky's language, I shmeissed it. In the calmer language of the handbooks, I imparted spin.

Would the pig have gone mad eventually and savaged me, had his owner not turned up when he did? I'm not the one to ask. For a short while I'd confused him, that's all I know. For half a minute or so he had no answer to my game.

This was the turning point of my relations with Sheeny Waxman. When it was all over he lit a cigarette, sat on the side of the van examining his cuffs, and muttered repeatedly, as though the danger were still present, 'Oy a broch! Oy a broch!' He was worried about his collar, too, which had suddenly turned itchy on him; and his tie, which he continued to brush all the way back to Manchester – because you don't go where Sheeny went with pig bristles sticking to your nishmas kol chai.

'I wish I'd seen it!' my father kept repeating. 'I wish I'd been awake to see it! But don't say anything about it to your mother.'

Later, though, whenever our eyes met, over tea and toast in

one of the market cafés, or in the middle of a match at the Akiva, or late on a Saturday night at Laps', Sheeny would jerk his head back, tick with merriment and say, 'Oink! oink!' And I would smile too, and say 'Oink! oink!' back.

Thanks to the pig I could already smell Kardomah coffee.

Also thanks to the pig I began to enjoy the gaffs more. Sheeny's doing. He was prepared to welcome me, now, into that secret confederacy of grafters from which my father had so far protected me. Not the lewd stuff. The old man still stood guard over that. I remember Sheeny introducing a new routine into his spiel one morning in Retford, holding aloft a violently trembling middle finger and begging a buxom woman at the front of the edge to help him stop it shaking. 'What do you want me to do, duckie?' the woman laughed. 'Sit on it,' Sheeny said. It was the nearest my father ever came to sacking him. 'Now, I've told you before, Sheeny,' he warned from the floor, one eye turned to me, 'that's out!' But the close, confidential script which marketmen deploy to communicate under the very noses of the punters, the quick contemptuous code by which you are able to identify nudzhes and shnorrers and nutters, warn against tealeafs, shtum up troublemakers, protect yourself against their cunning while keeping them in complete ignorance of yours – that whole iffy dug-in camaraderie of the gaff which I'd previously been deemed too much of a teapot lid to be trusted with was now thrown open to me.

'Kuk, kuk, the ganov,' Sheeny would say with *sotto voce* urgency, even as he was rising on the balls of his feet, refusing to let one bedspread go if he couldn't move a gross, and I knew to shadow the fat man in the big raincoat to the back of the stall, so that he couldn't fill his pockets with discoloured truffles.

'Na, geshwint, hob saichel, shneid,' I'd mutter to my father between my teeth, so that he'd know to hold the balsa-wood sewing box together and get it in the punter's shopping basket, quick, before it fell apart.

Suddenly I was fly. And I loved it.

Can you be bashful *and* fly? Can you be a kuni-lemele *and* a bit of a wide boy?

I managed.

And I was beginning to say startlingly brilliant things at school. Misogyny, that was my bag. I wrote essays in which I affected to hate women, detailing their imperfections through the ages. Instead of clipping me round the ear and telling me to button my lip until I had steered my fragile bark safely through puberty, my male grammar school teachers, few of whom had come out the other end of puberty themselves, gave me A plus/minuses and started mentioning Cambridge.

Did they play ping-pong at Cambridge? My grandiosity grew a twin. I would be better than anybody at two things. Did Ogimura have a degree? Did Wittgenstein have a drop shot?

Knowing my own nature, I foresaw advantages to myself in the double track approach to success. Should I lose at ping-pong I would be a philosopher. Should I be routed in argument I would be Victor Barna. When you suffer from grandiosity you cannot have too many fall-back positions.

With my distant, not-so distant and immediate prospects bounded by Cambridge, the Kardomah and wherever my bat took me, I finally ventured out of my shell. Not far. All very well multiplying strings to my bow, but there was still the small matter of the in-between to keep me timid. My aunties may have been suffering less mutilation at my hands than they once had, thanks to how busy winning tournaments and writing essays on the woman question I now was, but I continued to brood over terrible in-between related secrets. I hadn't done anything with it. I hadn't put it anywhere. Soon it would be clapped out, yet I still hadn't given it to anybody outside the family to hold. Those are not negatives you want people to find out about when you're nudging towards the age of consent. (Consent? In order for you to consent mustn't somebody first put in a request?) So I stayed within range of my husk, just in case.

But at least I was out. My body temperature was beginning to drop. I was acquiring a measure of control over my skidding mouth. And people no longer said, 'Cheer up, it may never happen,' the minute they clapped eyes on me.

Life was looking rosy.

And then, out of the blue and in quick succession:

Twink Starr was called up to do national service.

Aishky Mistofsky severed the middle two fingers of his playing hand trying to get out of a phone box and then blew off the middle two fingers of his other hand in an explosion.

Gershom Finkel proposed to my aunty, which was a catastrophe however you looked at it, but which would not have been quite the catastrophe it turned out to be had the aunty he proposed to been the aunty he was dating.

And – a not altogether unconnected event, I fear – my adored fatalistic little Polish grandmother lost two thirds of her body weight in six weeks and gave herself up, without a murmur of protest, into the arms of the Almighty.

BOOK II

BOOK II

ONE

Many of the world's best hitters are extremely sensitive . . .

Twenty-One Up, Richard Bergmann

I WAS WITH Twink in Burnley, attending the Ribble District Table Tennis Academy, when he dropped his bombshell. We'd been going to Burnley together, for long weekends of coaching and extensive work-outs, over the course of a year or more, whenever I could escape from the markets and whenever Twink could slip away from his button machine. We caught the bus in Bury and talked tenors all the way to Burnley and all the way back. I say all the way, not because the distance was great but because the journey took a long time in those days, what with stray sheep wandering off the moors and the Ribble flooding and the bus driver running out of diesel or having to stop in the centre of Ramsbottom or Rawtenstall to wait for residents to remove their washing from the main street. We wouldn't have wanted to live a pint of diesel's drive north of Bury ourselves – untamed Shaygetsshire, every inch of it – but we didn't mind the delay: the longer the bus ride took the more opera we could get through. But the moment we arrived at the academy we talked and breathed only ping-pong.

We shared a room and sometimes even a bed, each clinging to the furthest extremity of the mattress (I had to hold on to a mattress button with two fingers one night, so as not to fall off), going through what we'd learnt about our respective games that day. 'You're a more instinctive table tennis spieler *per se* than me,' Twink would say, 'but I'm a more natural all-round sportsman. That gives me the advantage of seeing the ball quicker than you, though you hit it harder.' He reckoned he placed the ball more accurately than I did too, though I didn't believe that was borne out by the first of the day's exercises when we had to try to knock over matchboxes. But I deferred to him because of the difference in our ages.

I was still enjoying the friendship of Twink and Aishky and wished Aishky would sometimes come to Burnley with us. But he laughed at the idea. 'Yeah, that's all I need after a hard week's graft, going marathon running with you two. Why can't we just go to Blackpool to see the illuminations and find some pretty girls to sing Mario Lanza songs to, like normal people?'

Twink and I trained, you see, when we were in Burnley. We changed into our tracksuits after breakfast at the hotel, did twenty-five press-ups in our room, then sprinted to the academy. Before we were allowed on to the tables we had to skip like boxers for fifteen minutes and then do twenty-five more press-ups followed by a further ten minutes of stretching. We drank Lucozade when we were thirsty, chewed glucose tablets when we felt faint, and spent the morning serving into thimbles. After a lunch of light salad and Vimto we returned to the tables and did one hundred forehand smashes followed by one hundred backhand smashes followed by one hundred half-volleys followed by one hundred backhand chops followed by one hundred forehand chops followed by one hundred backhand smashes . . . We filled out cards, noting how many times we'd hit into the net or off the table, then we sat round over tea working out our percentages.

Usually about twenty people turned up for a coaching week-end, though Twink and I were inclined to keep ourselves to ourselves. Most of the others were ferrety Calder or Ribble boys, from Todmorden and Clitheroe and the like, and spoke a different table tennis language. They were greedier in their play, somehow, more pinched and avid, colourless, without flourish or bravura. They'd stamp on the floorboards querulously, I remember; they'd tuck their shorts into themselves like gym knickers and stand with their legs apart, wagging their rumps like mongrels on heat, rubbery and relentless, as dispiriting as rats. I suppose that what I'm trying to say is that they played working-class ping-pong, and brought the cramped back-to-back atmosphere of their living conditions, a moorland narrowness and undernourishment of soul, to the table. Make no mistake, they were not easy to beat. One of them, the hairless chopper Jack Langho from Haslingden, was my chief rival for the number one Lancashire position and probably beat me more often than I beat him. But playing them was dismal, impersonal, ungenerous – they never lit up as Aishky lit up, they never said 'Oy a broch!' when you hit a screamer and laughed that lovely fatalistic laugh which conceded all the power and skill to your opponent, claiming for yourself only the gift to be amused – and when you lost to them you felt you'd been the victim of some petty and pointless felony, as though you'd had your pockets picked by someone you were going to give it all away to anyway.

Am I describing the difference between the amateur and the professional? Was what I liked about Aishky's oy a broch – with its unspoken 'What chance do I have against the shaygets when he hits like that?' – the primacy it claimed in the end for ironic appreciation? When all's said and done you are at liberty to marvel over the shaygets's power of shot because ultimately you value something else more – the right to be amused, the intelligence to register the vanity of all skill and striving at the last. Yes, we were irredeemably amateur, we Akiva boys. Just passing through.

On the way to where?

Ah – to the Almighty, like my grandmother, I guess.

We ended up playing for Lancashire together, Langho and I, alternating the number one spot, forming a formidable doubles partnership which lasted for three seasons, but I am not able to recall a single word he said to me in that time. Maybe he would be similarly blank in his recollections of me. Maybe he doesn't even remember I existed. I hope he doesn't. That will clinch my argument. I was God-bound – not through any choice of my own, but as a matter of cultural necessity; we were all God-bound, we Akiva boys, preparing our souls, via ping-pong, for their final resting place – whereas he just wanted to win. Now I think twice about it, it's not true that I recall nothing he said. I recall him telling me about the state of his elbow, the progress of his wrist strain, the worries he entertained about a calf muscle he'd pulled, the trouble he was having adjusting his grip to the new strapping he'd put around the handle of his bat. 'Played, Jack,' I'd say to him after we'd notched up another easy win in another noiseless hall in Rhyl or Wolverhampton, and he'd take me through the various ailments which had prevented his playing even better. Played, Ollie? Not something it ever occurred to him to say. Who was Ollie? Another person? What's another person? He was lost in the pure egoism of the sportsman. Ask him how he was and he told you – whoever *you* were.

When I asked Twink how he was on our last weekend in Burnley together he immediately changed the subject. There's the difference. We'd had an unusually eventful day. Quite out of nowhere a girl had turned up at the academy, a beautiful all-moving-parts girl in close-fitting brief blue shorts. Lorna Peachley. There were no beautiful girls in table tennis. Strictly speaking there were no girls in table tennis full stop. That was why Aishky favoured us knocking off and going to Blackpool for the weekend, where girls grew like weeds by the roadside. But Lorna Peachley was no Blackpool bog-moss. Lorna Peachley had eyes like Greek olives, a prancing pony-tail of blue-black hair tied with a lovesick purple ribbon, strong even teeth and thighs that fizzed like Lucozade. Those were the incidentals. Where she scored over every other girl either of us had ever seen was in the movement department: somehow or other she was able to set each of her parts (and she had many more parts than other girls, too) in discrete and sometimes incommensurable motion. You didn't know where to look, that's what I remember about her. You couldn't decide where to send your eyes first. If you weren't careful, you'd go dizzy.

'Classy, too,' Twink observed. 'Did you hear her elocution? She says "Deuce" – D . . . D . . . D – not "Juice" the way we do. She's got soft Ds.'

We laughed at that. Soft Ds. That wasn't all she had that was soft, eh Twink, eh Oliver?

Twink had persuaded her to knock up with us. Which wasn't difficult to do given that the Ribble pickpockets weren't offering. We were on an exercise which involved serving, running round the table to retrieve your own serve, and then on to the next person who had to return your return and then run around to return his own, and so on. Three of us running round the table increased the fun without taking away anything from the rigour.

She could play, too. She'd represented Hampshire girls the season before but was in the process of moving house with her parents to Timperley, hence this getting-to-know-you weekend. Yes, she was a player all right, with that all-round game of exaggerated loops and non-stop jigging favoured by southerners. 'She's got one glaring weakness, though,' Twink muttered to me over the Vimto break, 'she's vulnerable against the drop shot.' Then his face splintered into shards of laughter. 'Gevalt!'

So we peppered her with drop shots, driving her from the table with heavy topspin forehands, and then getting her to come charging in with all her parts in motion. I suspect she knew what we were up to. Because in the end she was practising her own drop shots on us. But she was a good sport. She never stopped bouncing on the balls of her feet. Nor did she try to punish us by keeping herself still or just moving in one direction.

Lorna Peachley was the subject to which Twink reverted when we lay at the furthest ends of the mattress that night and I asked him, noticing a change in his mood, if everything was all right. 'Lucky you,' he said. 'She's going to have to play in the Manchester league if she wants to get some decent opposition. You'll get to see a lot of her.'

'So will you,' I said.

He fell silent. Our room gave out on to a busy thoroughfare. A feeble street-lamp sent a yellow poltergeist glare through the torn net curtains. The streets were noisy. Burnley had become the unofficial European capital of rock-and-roll after mill lads in crêpe-soled shoes and kiss-curls had ripped the local cinema apart on the first showing of *Rock Around the Clock*. The town was under a certain obligation now to stay rowdy. Teddy Boys hung around on corners strumming invisible guitars and making electric humming noises with their mouths. The old shrank from them. Where was Lorna Peachley staying, I wondered.

'Not me,' Twink said at last, 'I won't be here.'

I felt frightened. Not of the rockers but of change. 'Why, where will you be?' I asked.

'I've been called up.'

'You're moodying me.'

'It's the emmes. I've been called up. I've got to go to Dorset.'

'Dorset? Why Dorset? Is there a war on in Dorset?'

'I don't think I'll be going to war. But then you never know.'

'Why you?'

Lying on his back, Twink sighed, rattling his lungs. 'My turn,' he said. 'I thought they wouldn't take me with my asthma. But they examined me and said they couldn't find any signs of it. Not real asthma.'

'What's unreal asthma? Surely you've either got it or you haven't. What are they saying – that you've got hysterical asthma?'

He wasn't saying what they were saying.

All at once I felt rage against the system. What about those useless hooligans on the streets of Burnley? They'd make good soldiers. They were born to be soldiers. What else were they doing out there except killing time until they were ordered over the top? And what about Langho? I could see him with a bayonet, standing with his legs apart, stamping the floor, waggling his little proletarian arse, shouting 'Who goes there?' and then telling them how he was. Whereas Twink, who loved opera and ping-pong . . . Where was the justice in putting him in uniform?

The following evening, on the bus home, he asked me back to his house. I'd been there many times, marvelling at his record collection and sitting in the dark with him in his room, comparing Gigli with Björling and di Stefano. 'Name an opera,' he'd challenge me. 'Name an aria.' Then he'd show me that he had ten different versions of it. Ten on LPs *and* ten on 78s. We didn't only do tenors. I remember one or two wonderful Schwarzkopf and Tebaldi nights. And some of the low-down he gave me on Callas went straight into my school essays on women's instability through the ages. But it was the tenors that made our hair stand and our flesh shiver and got us gulping in the darkness.

I could tell, though, that tonight was not going to be just another tenor night. There was an atmosphere of special occasion about tonight. 'I want to spend as little time as possible alone with my mother,' he told me. 'She's going to be a bit broyges with me, and a bit upset.'

No wonder. It turned out that Twink was off to Dorset in the morning. He'd known for months and had said nothing to any of us. His mother was aware he was going, but not when. Tonight, with me acting as emotional lightning conductor, he would have to break it to her.

I felt a bit small still to conduct anything as big as a family rupture. 'Wouldn't Aishky be better?' I asked.

Twink patted me on the shoulder. 'You'll be all right. You don't have to do anything. Just be there. I couldn't ask Aishk. You know his nerves. He'd worry himself too much.'

We went directly to his room where he asked me what I wanted to hear. We both knew it had to be *Figaro* – Cherubino off to the wars. He put on the Lisa della Casa version, and pulled out the Irmgard Seefried so I could make a comparison, then he went downstairs looking for his mother. She was famously emotional, Mrs Starr, a bruised-petal beauty in her time who had been betrayed by so many men you couldn't count them and now imagined that the postman and the milkman and the paper boy were trying to rape and rob her. Sometimes she would sit sobbing on the swirly carpet with her skirts pulled up, showing you the tell-tale bruises on her thighs.

'Why don't you call the police?' I once asked her.

She snorted. 'The police! You know what they'll do . . .'

Mr Starr took no notice of any of this. He occupied an upright wooden chair by the fireplace the whole time, whether there was a fire burning or not, dressed as though to receive company, his thin white hair fastidiously combed, his nails the same unimpeachable pink as his scalp, gold studs in his collar, but never moving and never addressing company when it came. He hadn't left the house or conversed with anyone in it since his brother had embezzled and bankrupted him ten years before. 'His own flesh and blood!' Twink told me. 'My uncle! You couldn't tell them apart. They were like twins, I'm telling you. They started the business together. They put in exactly the same amount of money and took out exactly the same amount of money – and then that! His own brother! Can you imagine?'

I couldn't. I only had sisters.

Everyone in Crumpsall and Prestwich and Higher Broughton had a relation who never left the house or lifted a finger as a consequence of some monumental act of treachery suffered by him at the hands of his own flesh and blood. It was a Bug and Dniester thing: all Jews have to have someone they can't forgive, but Bug and Dniester Jews always have to have someone *in the family* they can't forgive. Usually, though, we were voluble on the subject, took strangers through every detail of the original affection, the closeness, such closeness, and then, with precise reference to dates and hours, the how and the where, the when and the why, the perfidy . . . ! *On my mother's soul, may she rest in peace, I only wish him to burn in hell!* Right down to the particular corner of hell we wished him in. And the exact degree of burn. Mr Starr was the only person I'd come across who wouldn't speak about it. I took that to be a measure of how bad the betrayal had been.

The Starr house itself was forever *in extremis*. An air of desperation clung to every household object. Nothing was confident it was where it should be. Everything was at breaking point. Pictures fell off the walls. Sofas spat their stuffing. Lampshades shattered of their own accord. The china shrieked in the display cabinet. Dresses and blouses and slacks which Mrs Starr took in to re-fashion – for someone had to bring in money – were thrown on every available chair with their seams still unstitched and the pins protruding dangerously, or lay in tangled heaps on the floor like the skins of spent wrestlers from whom the souls had departed. Only Twink's room was in control of itself, every record in alphabetical order according to composer, then cross-referenced on filing cards according to performer; every record sleeve dead-straight on the shelf and dust-free, a card saying *From The Collection Of Theo Starr* glued to each one, though not so that it would interfere with any programme notes.

I turned down the volume of *Figaro*, reckoning that Cherubino was a tasteless choice after all and would only contribute to the emotional scenes to come. After hearing absolutely nothing for about an hour, apart from the spontaneous groaning of boards and the occasional glass exploding in the kitchen, I began to fear heart attacks or a suicide pact. I eased open the door, went out on to the landing, and started to creep down the stairs. I had to be careful: the stair carpet had worked loose from the rods – that's if there had ever been any rods – and if you lost your footing even slightly it would balloon up from the steps and become a forty-five degree slide. This, I suspected, was how Mrs Starr got the bruises on her thighs.

I was only half-way down when I saw Twink – Theo – standing in the centre of the living room holding his mother. I couldn't tell if she was crying, but she was very still in his arms, dressed in nothing but a black slip, her hands clasped about his neck like a lover's, her feet not quite touching the floor. It was almost as if they were smooching.

Mr Starr was erect by the fire, ready to receive guests, squeaky clean, motionless, immovable.

Twink noticed me on the stairs and made a signal with his eyes. 'Leave us,' his look said. 'Everything will be fine. Thanks, Oliver. Leave us now.'

And that was the last I saw of him for forty years.

Whether Aishky fell into bad company as a result of Twink's call-up I was never able to decide. There's the further question of whether he knowingly fell into bad company at all; and even the police weren't able to decide that.

He took Twink's going hard, there's no doubt of that. He pretended it was just a team thing – 'Our mazel, we get to the Second Division for the first time in our history, and now one of our best players decides he wants to become a soldier and defend the country!'; and the truth of it was that without Twink we were indeed seriously weakened and had to resort to fielding both Marks brothers which was never a good idea because they screamed at each other and sometimes resorted to fisticuffs in the middle of a match – but you could see that Aishky was missing Twink's company as well, the teasing, the chipping, the falling-out over competition balls and wet cloths. He was hurt that Twink had gone without telling him, even though Twink left him a note explaining that he hadn't wanted to upset his nerves.

'You see anything of Twink last weekend?' he would sometimes ask me. 'I heard he was home on leave for a few days.'

I hadn't. To my knowledge no one had, except presumably his mother, that's if he'd been in Manchester on leave at all.

No one on the team heard from him or of him. For all we knew he could have been sent to Cyprus or Kenya or some other hot spot and been taken prisoner, or court-martialled, or shot. But it didn't feel like that. What it felt like was that he'd closed a chapter. Made a decision that now he was gone he was gone. Why upset everybody's nerves all over again by re-appearing? Especially with an army haircut. We took partings differently in those days. They were more a matter of course. One day you were there, and then the Cossacks or the SS came through, and that was that.

Not Aishky, though. He took nothing as a matter of course. His game began to deteriorate. His arm stiffened up. He could anticipate the ball all right but it was as if he couldn't bring himself to hit it. He would just stand there, like a man mesmerized, and watch it go past him. 'Hit it, Aishk!' we'd shout out. 'Your ball, shmeiss the gederrim out of it!' But he wouldn't. Couldn't. 'My arm just won't move,' he said. 'I'm playing shots in my head but my head isn't talking to my arm.'

It turned out he was lying. 'I'm not even playing shots in my head,' he confided to me. 'This is the emmes – I can't even *imagine* how to hit the ball any more.'

We tried one of us standing behind him during practice sessions, moving him about as though he were a marionette. Bit by bit we were able to thaw the stiffness out of him, bringing a smile to his face as we bent him forward, swivelled him on his hips, and steered his strong freckled Esau arm through its old satisfying arc. Plock. 'There you are, Aishk, you hit it!'

After about an hour of this he would go loose like a scarecrow, as passive as a baby, happy to abandon his impaired will to ours. The moment we left him to his own devices, however, he seized up again, staring at the ball as though it were an object he'd never seen before and comprehending no possible relation between it and the pimply paddle that lay limp in his hand.

'It's my neshome,' he said to me, at the end of a match from which he'd had to retire after watching five serves go past him without his moving a muscle. 'It's my soul. My soul is saying no to the ball.'

'Maybe you should go to see a hypnotist,' I suggested.

'Or a rabbi,' Selwyn Marks said.

Aishky laughed. 'Maybe I should just see a bird with big bristles.'

He kept trying, though. He kept turning up on match nights, changing into plimsolls and re-adjusting his braces, on the assumption that everything was going to be all right. So when it got to nine o'clock and he still hadn't shown up for a home tie against Prestwich Maccabi – a grudge match if ever there was one – we began to fear for him. I didn't want to ring his home. When you rang home you got mothers and when you got mothers you got trouble, especially if you began by asking, 'You wouldn't by any chance happen to know where . . . ?' And I didn't want to do what the mother would then have done, which was ring the police, the fire brigade, the burial board and every hospital in Manchester. In the end it was a hospital that rung us. Not knowing that you waited for a point to be concluded before you barged into the ping-pong room, Mrs Showman from the front office fell into Louis Marks who was defending twenty feet back from the table, skidded on the highly polished wooden floor, and almost broke her own neck in her urgency to tell us that Aishky was in the Northern Hospital undergoing emergency surgery on his playing hand.

The funny thing was that Aishky had decided not to play against Maccabi even before he had his accident, and it was that decision which caused the accident, not the other way round. He had gone into a phone box on the way home from work to ring me to say he wouldn't be playing. He could tell already that he was not going to be able to raise his bat to the ball that night and he didn't want the Maccabi boys laughing at him. Anderers, it didn't matter. Unserers, well that was different. Verstehes? The only trouble was, the phone didn't work. He struggled with it for a few minutes, looking for different combinations of change and trying to get the operator. All to no avail. The machine swallowed his change and the operator hung up on him. Then his nerves went. He couldn't find the door out. He searched all four sides of the phone box, even the one with the phone attached to it, for a handle, for something to pull, he tried yanking at the window frames, but everything was stuck fast. He thought it might be a good idea to knock on the glass to get attention, but few people were passing and those that were thought he was a meshuggener – who else stood inside a phone box tapping on the windows? Phone boxes you tapped on from the outside. He decided to calm himself by sitting on the floor for a while but then grew afraid that he would fall asleep down there and freeze to death. He had one more go at finding the door, felt his heart make an attempt to get out through his throat, and smashed his hand through a pane of glass. Fortunately, someone saw that the meshuggener with his hand hanging out of the phone box was bleeding profusely, and called an ambulance. When they lifted him from the box, Aishky noted with interest that the door opened outwards.

A couple of days after he was released from hospital, I went to see him in his parents' council flat off Smedley Lane. He was the only one of unserer I knew who lived in a council flat. That he was ashamed of where he lived I guessed because he had never once invited either Twink or me back, and he was most particular, on this occasion, that I should come in the late afternoon when it was dark. Not after six, because then his mother and father would be home, and he clearly didn't want me to see them either. Say five.

When I got there all the lights were out. But behind the fresh medicinal smells I could pick out damp wallpaper and unaired linen.

Emotions, too, leave an odour. Love you can sometimes smell; hate you always can. What I could smell in the Mistofskys' council flat was that Aishky was morbidly devoted to his parents.

He too had a record collection. But they were all 78s and all Mario Lanza. He got me to put 'M'Appari' on the turntable and we sang along with it together. I knew his musical taste wasn't as good as Twink's, and there was no comparison between them when it came to operatic knowledge, but Aishky liked to sing duets with his records, and Twink never did that. Come to think of it, I'm not sure I could have held on to my composure had Twink departed from his customary silent vigil before his record player and suddenly invited me to join him in a singalong. Whereas with Aishky there was somehow never any embarrassment.

All things considered he was remarkably cheerful. He held his bandaged paw out. 'They reckon I won't be able to do much with this,' he said. 'No table tennis, that's for sure.'

I couldn't bear it. First Twink, now Aishky. 'Maybe they're wrong,' I said. My voice was all chocolatey with upset. I felt false too, a kid consoling a man. But I soldiered on. 'Doctors are often wrong,' I said. 'And anyway they don't know your determination.'

He was in far better spirits than I was. He beckoned me to sit on his bed. He wasn't wearing his spectacles, which made him unrecognizable up close, but I could tell that he was amused by something. 'It's a metsia,' he whispered, looking upwards. 'A gift from Elohim. My hand was finished. You saw that. It was oisgeriben. So now I get a chance to learn with the other one – for gornisht – on the National Health.'

And that was what he did. He taught himself to play all over again.

In the meantime, without Twink and Aishky our ping-pong team was looking pretty oisgeriben itself. When you're all playing well you can get away with going into a few matches a man short. But Selwyn and Louis Marks were abusing each other out of any form, Sheeny Waxman was turning up exhausted (oisgemartet, since we're on ois words) as a consequence of his own late nights and the daily detours to transport cafés he was having to make as my father's sidekick, and although I was impregnable, I couldn't win for everybody. So when Gershom Finkel astonished us all by offering to play while Aishky changed hands we were in no position to refuse.

'Only one thing,' he said. 'I play at number one.'

Number one was my spot this season. I couldn't conceal my unhappiness. 'Just humour him,' Aishky said. 'The man used to play for England. What's it to you? Anyway, don't I hear he's going to be your uncle soon?'

As yet that was only a moderately offensive thing to say. Gershom had not so far double-dealt my aunties. Not openly. The only charges one could level against him at this stage were all to do with his demeanour – his general slothfulness, his habit of turning up at our house expecting to be fed, yawning when other people were talking, cheating at canasta and jeering at the idea of me as a table tennis player. Whenever he came round he would pick up one of the cups I'd just won, turn it upside down as though to discover the name of the shop from which I'd bought it, and give a little laugh.

So it didn't please me, although from the point of view of our team's salvation it should have, that his game was several classes above any I'd yet seen with my own eyes. He didn't jump around like the rest of us, he didn't bother to exaggerate a feint or overdo his follow-through, he didn't spend the first five minutes of a game feeling out his opponent, he simply shot out a hand and the point was over. He played as he spoke – rapid sub-machine-gun fire, then the sudden cut-out. Ugly to watch, as it was ugly to listen to, but effective. He was so quick you couldn't always be certain what stroke he'd played. If that was a forehand drive how had he been able to hit it so flat? If that was a flick on the backhand – and the ball reared as though he'd flicked it – how come we hadn't seen him turn his wrist over?

Racket-head speed, if you want an answer. Never mind the before and after – at the moment of impact he was able to generate the most extraordinary speed, the pisher he was.

I understood now why he never took his raincoat off. He didn't need to take his raincoat off. But Aishky, who was still Club Secretary and non-playing captain, insisted he at least strip down to his jacket, by way of showing politeness to the opposing team.

Louis Marks came alive now that Gershom was playing for us. He felt that something of the greatness of the past had returned.

'You can sniff Barna and Szabados on him,' he said. 'Who else plays like that today? You know he was nearly World Champion?'

'Yeah I know, Louis,' I said.

'You know it was only Schiff –'

'Yeah I know, Louis,' I said.

Louis shook his head and rubbed his face. 'It was a terrible thing,' he said. 'What a tragedy.'

'I don't see how it's a tragedy,' I said. 'Everybody gets beaten. If he'd had any bottle he'd have fought back. A lot of people who were beaten by Schiff went on to become World or European champions.'

'Who's talking about being beaten by Schiff? He'd have

recovered from that. He *did* recover from that. He played for England, didn't he? That's the tragedy.'

'*What's* the tragedy?'

'That they stopped him.'

'What do you mean *they stopped him*? If he was good enough, why would they have stopped him? They don't stop you playing for your country just because you're human drek.'

Louis dismissed my rudeness with a click of his tongue, looked around the room, lowered his voice and made a money-counting gesture with his fingers. 'Gelt,' he whispered.

'What are you saying, Louis? That Gershom wasn't rich enough to play for England?'

'Neh! Gelt, gelt!'

'He was too Jewish? Don't give me that. You're beginning to sound like your kid.'

'Who said anything about Jewish? Gelt, gelt. You know Gershom's weakness.'

I didn't. That's to say I knew so many of his weaknesses I wasn't able to single out any one of them for special consideration.

Louis had now become so circumspect he was almost inaudible. He spelt it out, so that no impressionable child within a foot of us would be able to make head or tail of what we were discussing. 'G–a–m–b–l–i–n–g.'

'Since when does being a g–a–m–b–l–e–r disqualify you for playing for your country?'

'Ssh! Saichel, saichel! You're not supposed to gamble on your own results, shmulkie.'

It didn't seem such a crime to me. If Gershom was that confident of himself . . .

'You don't get it, do you?' Louis said. He'd begun to look as wild-eyed as the Ancient Mariner. He even clutched me by the sleeve. 'Gershom bet *against* himself.'

Ah!

With his crossbow, he *shot* the albatross.

'Gershom bet *against* himself?'

'Chochem! Now he understands!'

'You're telling me that Gershom bet on himself to lose when he was playing for England!'

'How many more times?'

'And they found out?'

'Someone squealed. One of the Swedes. That's who we were playing – Sweden. 1946. He lost every match. Not by much, but by enough. You'd have thought the Swedes would have been grateful. But no. Swedes for you! They were good to us in the War, mind you. Anyway, one squealed and Gershom was finished. Never selected again. *That's* the tragedy.'

I fell quiet. Why didn't I run home then and there and tell my aunties what I'd found out? That Gershom was a man who would sin against his own neshome. Who would poison his own soul. Who would betray the only gift he had. What grief I could have saved them!

But consequences take a long time to pan out. Had Gershom Finkel not bet against himself in 1946, had I not kept silent about what I knew about him, had the aunty of mine he finally plumped for been able to have children of her own, who knows whether I would be living today in the circumstances I do.

I live off Gershom Finkel's winnings?

Only in a manner of speaking.

And only indirectly.

And only partly.

And not to any very high standard.

Because he didn't lay that big a bet against himself, the miserable shvontz. He wasn't just a cheat, he was a cheap cheat.

Aishky Mistofsky was back playing for the Akiva in five months. The progress he'd made was so extraordinary that the Manchester League struck a special medal for him, inaugurated a handicap tournament in his honour, and named him inspirational player of the year. Opposing teams clapped him when he went on to the table. Everybody wanted to be the first to lose to him. There seemed to be some superstition in it, as though losing to a new playing hand was in the same category of trespass as touching a humpback, and therefore bound to be lucky. But by week three of the following season he was out again.

This time, though, his nerves weren't to blame. He had simply got caught up in the Bedding Wars.

One way or another, what with the blast shattering our windows, and Cheetham Hill Road being closed to traffic for three days, and the police knocking on our doors asking if we recognized a particular suede shoe which had been blown off in the explosion and presumably belonged to the incendiarist, the Bedding Wars affected just about all of us. But Aishky more than most.

Taking the Copestakes to be the aggrieved party – aggrieved in the sense that it was their bedding shop that was blown up – I could claim some small originating role in their disaccommodation myself. It's just possible that had we not beaten them to the punch for the bomb site between Boots and Woolworths on London Road in Liverpool they wouldn't have opened up their bedding shop in Cheetham Hill in Manchester and ended up a bomb site themselves.

How my father got to hear that there was a plum pitch going begging in the centre of Liverpool, right by Lime Street Station, a handkerchief of waste ground just big enough to back the van on to, unhampered for some reason by any Toby Mush or bye-laws, and yet enjoying all the advantages of a prime retailing position, I don't recall and probably never knew. But the Copestakes, father and son, had got to hear about it as well. Every Saturday morning for six weeks we raced one another down Hilton Lane, over Rainsough Brow, past the Agecroft Collieries, across the Manchester, Bolton and Bury Canal, swinging left on to Bolton Road, sharp right just before Irlams O' Th' Height, and then out like the very devil on to the East Lancs Road, approaching Liverpool through Carr Mill and Knowsley, skirting the West Derby Cemetery ('That's where we'll end up if you don't slow down, Joel' – Sheeny Waxman), the Sugar Brook Sewage Disposal Works ('And that's where you'll end up if you don't take a shtum powder' – my father), and on to the London Road bomb site via Norris Green, Tue Brook and Everton. And every week we won. Sometimes by a whisker, sometimes by a full van's length, but always by enough to thwart them, for once you'd got your front wheels on to the kerb there was no getting past you. Usually we were neck and neck until about three-quarters of the way along the East Lancs. My father liked to keep them just in sight in his rear-view mirror. Then, with seven or eight miles to go, he'd put his foot down. But on the morning of the seventh Saturday we didn't see them at all. It was still pitch black. Week by week the race had been starting earlier, to the point where Sheeny was now going without sleep the night before and wondering whether it wouldn't be easier all round if my father simply picked him up outside the Plaza in his Friday-night jiving and head jockey clobber.

'Any sign of 'em yet?' my father said, as we scorched through Agecroft.

'Don't ask me, Joel,' Sheeny said. 'This is still a Friday night for me. And on Friday nights I don't have eyes for anything except goyishe k'nish.'

My father leaned across me and punched Sheeny's arm. 'Shveigst du,' he said. 'The kinderlech!'

The kinderlech was me – although strictly speaking you have to be more than one child to be kinderlech – sitting up between them on a blanket over the engine. When I was present there was to be no swearing or lewdness of any kind. What Sheeny and I talked about when my father wasn't there was another matter. Similarly what they talked about when I wasn't there. But when we were in each other's company not an immodest word was to be spoken. It was biblical. A word was an event, and for us to have met over an impudicious event would have been tantamount to my uncovering his nakedness. Which is forbidden.

'Like the kinderlech doesn't know from anything!' Sheeny laughed. He was especially hoarse this morning. 'Tell your old man how you've never seen what's between a shikse's polkes, Oliver. Oink! oink!'

I blushed, liking the imputation of wantonness and ashamed because I had done nothing to deserve it.

'Shtum,' my father said. 'And tell me when you see the Copestakes.'

But we didn't see the Copestakes. Not charging out over Rainsough Brow, not anywhere along the East Lancs, not charging into Carr Mill. Not a hair of them. 'Do you know what I think?' my father said as we hit Norris Green. 'I think they've finally had a sickener and packed it in.'

'Alevei!' Sheeny said in his sleep.

'Yep. The grobbers have given up. Bleh, bleh, bleh bleh bleh!'

Had he had an ounce of Saffron superstition in his bones he'd have known never to exult in a victory even after the event, let alone before it. But there's no telling a Walzer. And what of course we saw, as we came rattling up the London Road with the brakes of our yellow Commer smelling like Saudi Arabia and the engine smoking like Gehenna, was the Copestakes' Ford, already on the bomb site, in full and uncontested possession!

Bleh, bleh, bleh bleh bleh!

'How the hell,' my father wanted someone to tell him, 'have they managed that?'

But just a moment . . . There was the Copestakes' Ford right enough, but where were the Copestakes themselves? Were the boot on the other foot, and the boot *had* been on the other foot every Saturday prior to this, the Copestakes would have found us jumping about and clapping our hands to keep them warm, bleary eyed and hungry, but already busy putting up the stall, clanking bars, throwing planks, in other words incontrovertibly *in evidence*.

So why weren't they?

My father got out of our van and went over to theirs. He walked around it a few times, keeping his distance as though he feared it could be boobytrapped, then chancing a closer inspection, peering into the cab, trying the doors. At last, after scratching his head, he felt the radiator. Cold! Ice cold!

'The chazerim must have driven here last night,' he said. He was outraged by this breach of etiquette, hopping mad, like a boxer who has been hit low.

'So what do we do?' I said. It was early in the morning. There was still time for us to drive to one of our old gaffs, shmeer the Toby *and* have a bacon and liver butty prepared for us by one of my father's transport café floozies.

'I'll tell you what we do,' he said. 'We move the van.'

'Our van?'

'Their van.'

'They've left the keys in?'

'Course they haven't left the keys in. We'll have to bump it. Wake Sheeny.'

Sheeny was still asleep, with his head on his chest. It was the only time he was ever still. I shook him gently. 'We're bumping the van,' I said.

'Bumping whose van?'

'Bumping their van.'

'Not me,' he said. 'Not in this whistle. Tell your old man he's off his rocker. You can't go round bumping people's vans.'

But my father was resolute. We hadn't been beaten fair and square. The Copestakes had pulled a fast one. Which meant that we were within our rights, morally, to bump their van out of the way before they got back from wherever they were skulking. If Sheeny wouldn't help, fine. We'd do it together. Father and son. Backs to the bumper, shoulders to the wheel.

It's amazing what you can move when you have right on your side. The Copestakes' Ford wasn't as big as our Commer but it had good brakes and was laden with blankets and pillows and eiderdowns and counterpanes and bolsters and palliasses and sheet-sets and pillowslips and valences in boxes and, from the weight of it, a good few mattresses and bedsteads and quilted headboards as well. Inch by inch, though, heave by heave, we bumped its nose and then half its chassis out into the street. We'd have succeeded completely had my father's 'And one, and two, and three!' not woken the Copestakes, with whom their van also happened to be laden and who had been sleeping the deep sleep of the devious among their wares.

What followed was a fracas of such unseemliness that in the end only the police could restore order. Quickly coming to an understanding of who was up to what, the Copestakes scrambled out through a side door, rubbed the sleep from their eyes and, calculating that they were no match for us physically, began placing bricks, of which there is never any shortage on a bomb site, under the tyres. No sooner did a brick go under one tyre than we removed it from another. And no sooner did we remove it than they replaced it. The quicker they moved, the quicker we did; and the quicker we moved, the quicker they did. 'Front offside!' my father shouted to me. 'You take the front offside. Get that brick away. Offside, *offside*! That's nearside, you tsedraiter!' The chase around and around the van had got so hectic that it was difficult to remember whether you were kicking bricks out or stuffing them in. 'Rear right!' Copestake called to his kid. 'There's nothing under the rear right.' 'But I thought I'd just put one under the rear right.' For a split second we had all the wheels free. 'Geshwint!' my father yelled. 'Push!' But we could never keep all four tyres free for long enough to make any further progress in our bumping.

Even before we had become rivals for the bomb site we hadn't much liked the Copestakes. My father had gone to the same primary school as Copestake Senior and remembered him as a sneak. And funnily enough I had gone to primary school with Copestake Junior and remembered *him* as a sneak. It's possible that neither of them actually sneaked but both just looked as though they did. It was their complexion that gave you the impression of surreptitiousness. They had a dirty shine on them like cockroaches, and they moved furtively like cockroaches too, turning up and vanishing and turning up again you couldn't tell from where, just as they'd appeared from inside the bedding this morning while we were rightfully bumping their van into the road. One other thing I remembered about Copestake Junior from primary school was that he sold tickets to see Reeny Cohen do pee-pees in the garages behind Huxley Avenue. I can't say what his arrangements were with Reeny Cohen, but if she didn't know he was profiting from her water then sneaky was definitely the word for him. Otherwise plain disgusting.

It was this over-and-above dislike for the Copestakes that erupted in the early morning on London Road when, after what had at first been a silent chase around the van – silent as far as our talking to them or their talking to us was concerned – Copestake Senior suddenly took it into his head to start cursing. 'Putz!' he shouted at my father. 'Kaker, yentzer, tochesleker.' In other words: prick, shit-head, fucker, arse-licker.

'Hob saichel,' my father shouted after him, 'mit der kinderlech.'

'Hob saichel! You push my van into the fucking road and you tell me to hob saichel.'

'No swearing. I don't care what you do in front of your own family but I've told you, no swearing in front of *my* kid.'

They were both breathing heavily, both panting, and if you had turned up on the scene innocent of what was afoot you would have been hard pressed to decide which of them was chasing the other.

'You want me to worry about your kid, now? I'll tell you what I think of your kid, Joel Walzer – Ich hob your kid in toches!'

And that was when the police had to be called, otherwise my father would have torn him limb from limb. As I've said, we were biblical.

Spoil it for one, spoil it for all. The police closed London Road to casual traders, and for a number of years not even a barrow boy was allowed to do business there.

It wasn't a serious blow to us. We could, as I've already said, return to one of our old Saturday gaffs. But it set the Copestakes back. It seemed to turn them off the markets too, because suddenly they materialized, cockroach-like, on Cheetham Hill Road as Copestake's Cash 'n' Carry Bedding Emporium – Retail Service At Wholesale Prices. A move that was bound to infuriate Beenstock's Cash 'n' Carry Bedding Emporium – Wholesale Prices With Retail Service, which was only half a block away on the other side of the road.

Ike Beenstock was the brother of Sam Beenstock, otherwise known as Sam Sam the Bedding Man, for whom Sheeny had worked before coming to us. I mention that only because it always seemed to me possible, though I never made enquiries, that it was through Sheeny that Ike Beenstock made the acquaintance of Benny the Pole. But it's also the case, I admit, that anyone who knew anyone who frequented the Kardomah was in a direct chain of hearsay that led ineluctably to Benny the Pole.

How any sort of glamour or intrigue was able to attach itself to the specific fact of Benny's being a Pole, given how many Poles there were among us, is a mystery to me to this day. My mother's mother, as I have already explained, not only came from Poland but made a little Poland around her wherever she went, but we never thought that that lent her fascination or allure. Nor did we once consider referring to her as Granny the Pole. In Benny's case, though, Polishness was all at once transformed into a sinister and shadowy quality, suggestive not of smoked sausages or peasants who stank of their own animals, but brotherhoods and contraband and seduction. Benny the Pole could fix things. Benny the Pole could find things. Benny the Pole could lose things. But above all, Benny the Pole could pull.

Because not everyone dared venture into the Kardomah – and even those who had successfully negotiated Laps' sometimes lacked the nerve to make the transition – Benny the Pole put on a free public pulling demonstration on the footpath outside the Kardomah on Market Street every Saturday lunch-time in good weather. Even in the week, provided it wasn't windy, this was a seething pitch. Need a new watch, cheap? A diamond ring? Tickets to see Manchester City? Tyres for your Jag? Radio for your Jag? The Jag itself? The footpath outside the Market Street Kardomah was the place to go. The talk was good too, if you were of the right age. Burial boards, heart disease, cures for arthritis, facials, tailors, football, horses, cars (especially the rights and wrongs of owning a Mercedes), poker schools, holidays in Rimini, and birds. The facials helped but in the end it was only the birds that kept you young. Tsatskes. Every boy must have his tsatske. Which was why Benny the Pole enjoyed such celebrity. He possessed the secret of eternal youth. And on Saturdays, from about twelve, you could watch him work.

What did he have going for him? Not looks. He was a knobby rather than an aquiline Pole – that's if he was a Pole at all – with scarred, over-sunbrowned skin and tuberous eyes which lacked even the saving Polish grace of expressing sadness. He didn't have much in the way of physical presence either, being more on the tall side of short than the short side of tall; though it was hard to gauge the amount of meat there was on his bones because of the way he wore his coat, loose over his shoulders like a cloak, with the sleeves empty but menacingly mobile, giving him the impression of being a man with four arms. His toupee was among the worst I'd ever seen, both for fit and for colouring; yet because of the success with which it was associated every Kardomah frequenter over fifty wore one just like it. (Hence their reluctance to gather on the footpath on windy days.)

Discussing him once with a woman who'd yielded to his spiel – by which I don't mean to imply that there were any women in Manchester who *hadn't* yielded to his spiel, only that they didn't all discuss him – I learned that he had beautiful violin-like feet, small, curvilinear, harmonious, with an almost feminine instep. He was without doubt conscious of this natural advantage, for he was known to spend a small fortune on pedicures and was always sensationally shod. I cannot say that I vouched with my own eyes for the truth of the rumour that he never wore the same pair of shoes twice; I saw him on too few occasions for my observations to be worth anything on that score. But the three or four pairs of shoes I did see him wear I never forgot. Only on Benny the Pole had I ever seen gold heels. Only on Benny the Pole had I ever seen sneakers made from the cheek pouches of the Komodo dragon. So maybe his secret was in his feet, in the lightness with which he approached his victims.

He was the first man in Manchester to jingle. Before Benny the Pole no man resident in the north of England would ever have thought of wearing a chain around his wrist let alone around his neck. Unlike most fashions, which start among the young and slowly catch on with the more conservative generations, the wearing of gold chains in Manchester took off first among the old. Our grandfathers dared before we did. They gathered outside the Kardomah with too much face on show somehow – barefaced, that's the only word for them, as barefaced as camels – and like camels ready to be mounted, they snorted and showed their brown teeth and jingled. Jingle, jingle, croak: I can still hear the sound of them and see the dust rise as one by one they drew themselves up to their full height – full for them – held on to their toupees, stepped out into the path of a young woman and offered her a shtup. Still shtupping, or at least still offering, at seventy. And for all of that we had to thank Benny the Pole.

The offer of the shtup – the offer of it, not the request for it – was the distinguishing feature of Benny the Pole's technique. I'm not at all sure that there was anything else. Of course there were bound to have been some crushing refusals in the early days. But by the time Benny the Pole was an accomplished fact, any young woman chancing her arm alone in Market Street would have known who it was that was accosting her, and must have felt a tremendous weight fall from her shoulders. For imagine the insult to your person in walking past the Kardomah at a lunch-time on a Saturday and *not* being offered a shtup by Benny the Pole.

That there would have been an admixture of fear in many women's capitulations I didn't doubt. Benny the Pole could easily have been concealing a sawn-off shotgun in one of those empty sleeves. And that it was a willing fear, an impious curiosity as to where else those dragon shoes trod, a self-demeaning half-readiness to trollop it for a season in whichever underworld the Pole was offering them privileged access to, I also didn't doubt. I had a low regard for women based on their low regard for me. Not my aunties, of course, but then my aunties weren't really women. Yes, my sex was responsible for Benny the Pole in the sense that he was made of the same puppy-dog tails as the rest of us. But the all-things-nice sex was still more responsible in the sense that they yielded to him. They could have said no to the shtup. There were other men offering. There were other men too shy to offer. But the women craved the compliment of the insult. In this way what Benny the Pole taught me influenced my misogynistic essays and so helped clear the obstacles between me and Cambridge. And yet – such are the ups and downs of men's fortunes – when I started university Benny the Pole still wasn't through his term at Strangeways.

Even though he was given a few years of his own in Strangeways to think about it, Ike Beenstock never recovered from the surprise of learning that Benny the Pole had undertaken the actual arson himself. He talked to me about it once, during one of my university vacations, when I was hungry for Bug and Dniester conversation, and had turned up at his house to collect his daughter

Sandra on a date. 'I always imagined he'd be farming it out,' he told me. 'Don't get me wrong; to this day I consider it a compliment to me and my family that he looked after us personally. But who'd have expected a gantse macher like him, with his connnections and his dress sense, to go kriching around on his hands and knees with a box of matches?'

Maybe he'd meant to farm it out. Maybe he'd had the very man for the job in mind on the day Sam Beenstock, acting on behalf of his brother, brushed past him on the footpath outside the Kardomah and slipped into his coat pocket the sealed envelope containing the bundle of used flims, the address of Copestake's Bedding Emporium, and the instruction, written in letters cut out of the *Jewish Telegraph*:

I don't *care* whether you bomb it or *burn* it or what you do, just *get* rid of it

Maybe the very man for the job had gone missing at the eleventh hour, or maybe Benny the Pole just wanted to do something for himself that didn't end in a shtup. Whatever the circumstances, alone and without an accomplice Benny the Pole climbed over Copestake's back wall, made free with a can of paraffin, lit the torch and famously lost the shoe by which he was ultimately and irrefutably identified. Who else in Manchester wore two-toned alligator suede slip-ons with built-up mother-of-pearl inlaid heels?

Alone and without an accomplice . . . So to whom did the two fingers, which were also found at the scene of the crime, belong?

That they weren't Benny the Pole's the police were quickly able to ascertain, by virtue of the fact that he still had five on each hand. Not that they'd ever seriously believed they'd come off the same person who'd lost the shoe anyway, since the shoe was found at the rear of the store and the fingers were found at the front and it was unlikely that anyone would have been nutty enough to run through the building once it was alight, either without his fingers or his shoe.

There was only one person the fingers pointed at. Aishky Mistofsky.

On the night Copestake's palace of polyester and foam rubber went up like a volcano, Aishky had returned to the hospital which had looked after him so well the time he'd tried to punch his way out of the phone box. The problem on this occasion related to his other hand. He couldn't feel it. He so couldn't feel it that he feared he might have lost it altogether. He hadn't the courage to look. To be on the safe side, he'd thrust the arm into the front of his shirt, where it pumped blood in time with his heart, then he'd walked to the hospital. He held his nerve admirably until he got to Emergency, where the sight of other people's injuries and the question 'What have you done to yourself this time?' caused him to faint clean away. When he came to in the hospital bed he was sans another couple of fingers and the police were waiting to talk to him. At first they were going to charge him with arson. But once the shoe had led them to Benny the Pole they amended the charge to complicity. Aishky was watching the front of the building for Benny the Pole, that was their theory. Aishky was Benny's look-out. Eventually they dropped that charge as well. Fantastical as was Aishky's claim that he'd been innocently wandering along Cheetham Hill Road at three in the morning trying to get his mind in order, and that he'd only crossed the road to Copestake's bedding warehouse because he'd thought he'd seen smoke, which was the reason he'd pushed open the letter-box in the showroom door – an act of wild impulsiveness that could have lost him a lot more of himself than two fingers, considering the amount of fire that leapt out through the letter-box – they believed him.

'Why were you trying to get your mind in order?' they asked him.

'Because I was worrying. I'm a worrier.'

'And what, on the night in question, were you specifically worrying about?'

Apparently Aishky didn't even hesitate. 'Crimes against the Jewish people,' he said.

Would anyone really have attempted to look through the letter-box of a burning building? It was hard to swallow, but nothing otherwise linked Aishky to the crime. He had no record of wrong-doing. He was not known to the Copestakes. He was not known to be known to the Beenstocks. It was impossible to connect him with Benny the Pole, who for his part contemptuously brushed aside all knowledge of such a person and was especially brusque with the imputation that he, Benny the Pole, was unable to put paid to a shmattie warehouse full of foam chips and duck feathers without an accomplice.

In the end, the only person who thought Aishky Mistofsky could have been implicated in the destruction of Copestake's Bedding Emporium was me. There was a connection which the police hadn't made. Aishky and Benny the Pole via Sheeny Waxman. Sheeny was like a son, as we used to say in the days when being a son was the highest measure of human affection we could imagine – Sheeny was like a son to Benny the Pole. He had modelled himself on Benny and probably enjoyed as much of his confidence as anybody did. He was also harsh in his opinion of Aishky. Assuming Benny the Pole had said, 'Sheeny, find me a shmulke who'll watch the front of the store for gornisht and ask no questions,' I could well imagine Aishky Mistofsky being the first name Sheeny came up with.

Does this say more about me than it says about Aishky Mistofsky or Sheeny Waxman? Was it me who harboured the low opinion of Aishky? I loved Aishky, I hope I have said nothing that could call that into doubt. I thought he was an entirely lovable man. But I loved my aunties, and my mother, and my grandmother too, and look what I did with them. What if the grandiose are in a trap of their own making and cannot respect where they have decided to love? Tsatskes – that's how you see those to whom you give merely your heart. Playthings of the feelings. And how can you have respect for a tsatske?

All that aside, what did anyone's opinions of Aishky have to do with what Aishky himself chose to do or not do? Was there any reason to believe he'd have gone along with such a deal even had it been put to him? None. And yet I still suspected him. I felt I owed it to him not to not suspect him, that's the best I can say. One should never be certain of anyone.

That was the end of the Akiva as a fighting ping-pong force anyway. Aishky joked that he could learn to play pen-hand next, but none of us believed that was ever going to happen. Whether or not the fight had gone out of him, it had gone out of us.

I made an arrangement to go over and see him – after dark, but not so late that his parents would be home from work – in order to deliver the news that Sheeny had decided to play for the Hagganah, that I was thinking of doing likewise, that Selwyn had taken up swimming with the intention of ridding the sport of its rampant anti-Semitism, that Louis was going to Israel to get away from all the talk about Jews, and that nobody cared what happened to Gershom Finkel.

He was less upset than I feared he'd be. 'All good things,' he said.

Then, employing his ruined hands robotically, as though they were cake slices, he put Mario Lanza singing 'I'll Walk with God' on the turntable and we sang along with it, hitting the high notes together.

'So what'll you do?' I asked.

'What do you mean what'll I do?'

What did I mean? Now that you can't use those wonderful strong red Esau forearms for anything, was what I meant, but how could I say that?

'For sport,' I said.

'Sport? Who's been doing sport?'

We both laughed. Of course ping-pong wasn't sport. Football was sport. Cricket was sport. Ping-pong was – But we both knew, without saying, what ping-pong was.

'Anyway, I've got some reading I want to do,' he said. And then he asked me if I knew the *The Scourge of the Swastika* by Lord Russell of Liverpool.

So maybe he *had* been wandering down Cheetham Hill Road at three in the morning worrying about crimes against the Jewish people.

Be that as it may, it was to be forty years before I saw him again, as well.

TWO

The final choice as to who among your club mates and friends would make an ideal partner for you will ultimately rest with your own judgment having due regard to your own particularities of style, methods of playing and weaknesses (which you yourself know better than anybody else).

Twenty-One Up, Richard Bergmann

WHY COULDN'T IT have been Gershom Finkel who saw smoke coming from Copestake's warehouse and thought to verify his suspicions by opening the letter-box and putting his head inside?

Boom!

Much unnecessary suffering might we all have been spared.

But it was too late by then anyway. Both my aunties were already hooked.

Never look a gift-horse in the mouth – that was the worldly wisdom which we subsequently had to pick out of our teeth. Who else was ever going to court my aunty Dolly? For whom else had she ever put on lipstick, straightened the seams in her stockings and learnt dance steps? Gershom Finkel was a one-off, a once-only, a chance in a million. Sure he was freaky, but let's face

it, as my father put it, 'It took one to love one.' On top of that –
and in the fifties these considerations still counted, whether or not
the alternative was ES for eternal spinsterhood – he was one of us,
a Bug and Dniester davener with a covenant from the Almighty
in his pocket and a snipped-off in-between to prove it. Obscene
but true: when the family beheld Dolly on the arm of Gershom
– and when I say the family I mean both sides of the family –
they made the calculation that while no in-between inside her
might have been better than Gershom's in-between inside her,
Gershom's in-between inside her was infinitely to be preferred
to any pale and floppy-prepuced in-between inside her. On such
delicate matters of preference does a kinship system based upon
religion dwell.

But then as I knew better than anyone, this was the trouble with
S for spinsters – by some insalubrious inverse law of non-desire,
you couldn't keep your minds out of their C for cunts.

I don't think I was jealous of Gershom. I was growing up
quickly, even if not quickly enough to satisfy myself, and was
putting my aunties behind me. But it's worth remarking, in
the name of honesty, that while I rarely had recourse to my
perfumed box of mutilated mishpokheh these days, on those
occasions when I did, I excepted, I excused, my aunty Dolly.
Sorry Dolly, you just don't work for me any more. And that
could only have been because I didn't feel she was any longer
mine to cut up, which I suppose is another way of saying that
I was not prepared to share her, even severed, with Gershom.

Not that Gershom was himself possessive. Far from it. So casual
was Gershom in his attentions to Dolly, in fact, that my parents
frequently wondered if his real motive for dating her wasn't
simply access to our house, food, warmth, company, shelter. A
theory which was lent credence, I have to say, by Gershom's
reluctance ever to visit Dolly in her own house.

'I can understand that,' my father said. 'Your father's there.'

'Exactly,' my mother said.

'And it's poky there.'

'Exactly.'

'And it's dark there. Mind you, if I was courting Dolly . . .'

'Joel!'

But he was generous, my father, in the matter of our house being the place where everything social happened for my mother's side, where her mother could escape her husband, where the Violets could bunch together for a *Book at Bedtime* and a crossword and a bit of fussing over me, and now where the oldest of them could do her canoodling. He'd grown up in a big family himself. He knew how fifteen people could live fifteen separate lives in one room. In fact our living area was probably smaller than the one my mother's side fled from every day – for we only had what was called a Sunshine Semi, which meant that the sun came in through the front window and went right out again through the back – but at least it was Heaton Park and not Lower Broughton, at least you could sniff the Pennines instead of Poland, and at least my maternal grandfather wasn't there. Of course it didn't cost my father much to be generous, since he was out of the house himself most of the time; but he could have had thoughts about wear and tear, which he didn't, and he could have played up on Sundays when he was home and the house prickled with spinster embarrassments, but he didn't do that either.

It was the way Gershom Finkel threw himself into Sundays at our place that convinced my father it was us he was after – our food, our company – rather than Dolly. Sunday was bagel day. Now that bagels belong to any-old-place, any-old-time international convenience cuisine, and figure (however uncomfortably) in the vocabulary of the pale and floppy-prepuced, along with chutzpah (with a baby ch for choo-choo train) and shmo (with the open O of the wonder-struck and the unworldly – O gosh! O no!), it may be hard for some people to understand why they once counted for so much. Well, they tasted better in those days, for a start: crisper, nuttier, crunchier, sweeter, saltier, browner, plumper, more burnished, more almondy, more flowery, more boiled, stickier, more elastic; chewier in the dough, sleeker to the touch, more differentiated as to top and bottom, more variegated as to middle and sides, more distinct as to inside and out. The trek to get them was more arduous than it would be now, as well. You had to choose whether you felt like Needhof's bagels or Tobias's bagels or Bookbinder's bagels, then you had to measure that against whether you felt like Needhof's chopped liver or Tobias's chopped liver or Bookbinder's chopped liver, then you had to divide how many they were likely to have left by the time it now was, and get going. They would still be warm when you walked back in with them, too, provided you hadn't over-extended yourself with the extras. But then if you'd under-extended yourself with the extras no one would have been much pleased either. Chopped liver wasn't the half of it. There was chopped herring – old-style chopped herring and new-style chopped herring. (The difference? Sugar, aroma, blind prejudice and who could say what subtle variation of uric content.) There was egg and onion – a yellow baby mash, new-laid and salmonella-free, which the aged and the toothless could suck up through a straw. There were cucumbers: in a tin, in a jar, loose; cucumbers plain, sweet and sour, just sweet, just sour, and new green. There were fish balls, and to give the fish balls taste there was horseradish (chrain, pronounced *ch*rain, an old world ch with a convulsion of the larynx), which we with our soft nursery palates thought was fiery simply because it was red. There were rollmops, not to be confused with Bismark herring. There was Bismark herring, not to be confused with rollmops. There were anchovies. There was smoked salmon. There were latkes. There was pickled meat with a dropped d – pickle meat, as though it was itself in the active business of pickling and might pickle you. And then – the Sunday morning *ne plus ultra* in our cow-mad house – there was smetana and kez – sour cream and cream cheese, this kind of cream and that kind of cream – which no one ever mixed with more dedication, more feeling for texture and consistency, more of an instinct for what looked alike but wasn't, than my father did.

Now does it seem so fanciful of us to have wondered whether Gershom Finkel was stepping out with the most shrinking of the Shrinking Violets solely in order to get at our food?

This much I can say: from the moment he became Dolly's beau Gershom never missed a single one of our Sunday morning bagel fress-ups. He'd arrive early, in no matter what weathers, often well before Dolly got to us, often before any of us were awake ourselves (he thought nothing about knocking us up), so as to be absolutely certain he'd be in position when the bagels turned up warm. 'Have they come yet?' he'd ask, as though they got there under their own steam. Agitation made him louder and more staccato than usual. He fired off bagel-related interrogations. 'Is that them?' 'Where they coming from today?' Otherwise he had nothing to say. He wouldn't even take off his coat and make himself comfortable. He simply sat on the edge of a dining chair, leafing absently through the *News of the World* and *The People*, mouth open, like a fledgling waiting to be fed.

'You'd think,' I remember my father saying, 'he'd have the decency to get the bagels himself just once in a while.'

'Or at least the smetana and kez,' my sisters added.

'Or even just the kez,' I said.

'It's not as though he's pink lint exactly,' my father said.

'Not with three houses,' my sisters said.

'Four,' my father corrected them. He'd heard four. All in Didsbury, all divided into flats, and all bringing in nice rents.

I said nothing. When it came to Gershom Finkel's property I took a shtum powder. I knew where the original funds had come from. Plock plock, I lose, I win.

But I shared in the family censoriousness. We didn't care for landlordism. Nothing we could put our finger on. Just something we'd brought over with us from the Bug. Had we stayed out there we'd have been Marxist-Leninists, or at the very least Bundists.

Which might have been why, over and above the fact that we wouldn't have done anything to hurt Dolly, we put up with her admirer. Landlord or not, there was something of the stray dog, even the mad dog, about him. Reason dictated he be put down. But we couldn't go along with that. There'd been too much putting down. So we took him in. And let him fress our bagels.

Canoodling? Did I say canoodling? There was none of that on his part. Try as I might, I am unable to remember Gershom Finkel ever showing my poor aunty Dolly a single sign of his affection. The snuggling-up, such as it was, was all on her side. She'd drape herself over him while he was idling through the papers as though she couldn't bear not to be reading what he was reading, or she'd suddenly make a dart for him, like a wild impulsive girl, and leap up and kiss him plum in the middle of that born-bald, stayed-bald head of his, or she'd talk about 'we' in a way that seemed simultaneously to give him satisfaction and cause him pain. 'We' weren't taking milk in our tea any more. 'We' had been to hear Perry Como at the Free Trade Hall. 'We' didn't enjoy him as much as 'we'd' enjoyed Sammy Davis Jnr the week before. 'We' believed that while some of the changes were to be welcomed, the Rent Act still favoured tenants at the expense of landlords.

'He's snatched her mind,' I said to my mother.

She sighed. 'Well let's just hope he goes on wanting it,' she said.

'Don't you think that after a certain age it doesn't suit a woman to be in love?' I said.

'No,' she said.

'How old is Aunty Dolly?' I asked.

There'd always been a degree of reticence around the question of my aunties' ages. They were so alike in spinsterliness that I'd been inclined to follow my father's lead, lumping them together as the Shrinking Violets and imagining that they'd shrunk into the world on the same day as one another. Though in the course of cutting them up in the toilet, I must say I'd surprised myself by noticing important differences between them which bore on the athleticism of the poses I was prepared to put them into.

'Not too old,' she said.

'Then maybe I should rephrase my question,' I said. 'Don't you think it's possible she's too young?'

'No,' she said.

It's wise to hold fast to the iceberg analogy when judging the depth of feeling between a man and a woman. Most of what there is you don't see.

As a family, that was how we satisfied ourselves that Gershom was giving Dolly the love she needed. We didn't see it. It was happening somewhere else. In the main, we guessed, it was happening at the Ritz and the Plaza and beneath whichever other spinning ball of slivered mirrors they danced. On the dance floor, at least, Gershom would have to put his hands on her and hold her close.

To the degree that we couldn't imagine Gershom dancing, dancing humanized him. It was so unlikely that it proved we didn't know him, and anything we didn't know about him was bound to be better than anything we did.

As for Dolly, there could be no doubt whatsoever that dancing had made a different woman of her. I myself may not have been a pretty picture, running from the conga eel of romping Walzer women, but my deformity was as nothing compared to Dolly's when some stranger to a family do blundered into the heat-haze of embarrassment around her and asked her to take the floor with him. I'd know when such a thing was happening even if I was taking cover at the other end of the biggest function room in Broughton. I could smell it. Dolly's face I knew I would not be able to look at. To the un-shy, who are the lords and masters of their faces, the word discountenance has only metaphorical applications, but for my mother's side it described transfiguration of the utmost horror. Literally, we were put out of countenance, ousted and exiled from our faces, denied all ascendancy over our features, left helpless as they screwed and twisted and did whatever else they wanted with us. Better to be dead than to be put out of countenance. Dead and done with. Burned. Drowned. Six feet under with the deep snow piled above you. Anything rather than the living death of being buried alive inside your own face and having to look on while it has its way with you. So, no, I couldn't bear to look at Dolly. The expression in the eyes of the birdbrain who'd asked her for a dance was frightful enough. Teach him to think twice the next time. A better and a wiser man, you can bet your life, he woke the morrow morn. He had seen where hell was, and how asking leave for a dance could get you there.

But that was Dolly then, Dolly BGF, Before Gershom Finkel. Now Dolly twirled and spun in a lightsome world of foxtrots and quicksteps and for all I knew to the contrary mambos and black bottoms and boomps-a-daisies as well. She even taught the stuff! Wasn't that typical of S for spinster excess – in six months she'd gone from rank beginner to professor. 'I'm not going to be the one to show you how,' Gershom had said. 'It's like teaching your wife to drive. It can only lead to trouble.' So they'd taken themselves off to a dancing school above a haberdashery shop – I saw that as symbolic – in Moss Side. And now Dolly was their best teacher!

She even tried to teach me, one Sunday afternoon, pushing the twenty or so people who were gathered at our place for bagels back against the walls as though we were at a high school bop, girls on that side, boys on this, except that there were no boys in our house. She got nowhere with me. It was too embarrassing. Her new vitality sent shivers down my spine. It was as if she'd shed her old skin and still hadn't grown a replacement. You didn't dare look for fear of seeing things you shouldn't see, her gederrim, her liver, her kidneys, her pink pulsing heart. And besides, I wasn't able to count out rhythm.

'It's natural,' she said.

Nothing was less likely to reconcile me to nature than the word natural on the lips of one of my aunties.

'I can't,' I said.

She should have had fellow-feeling for my discomfiture, but have I not said that the shy are tyrants of self-engrossment, that they burn alone, leaving their fellow sufferers to be consumed in their own flames? And the ex-shy are more callous still.

'Just find it in yourself,' she said, steering me into the middle of the room. 'One, two, three, and . . . one, two, three . . .'

No use. The only thing in nature One, two, three reminded me of was bumping the Copestakes' van out on to London Road in Liverpool.

'I don't understand it,' Dolly said, 'you must have rhythm for table tennis.'

'He hasn't,' Gershom Finkel answered for me.

She had more success with Dora.

But then so did Gershom.

Cutting up my aunties was an act of love. When I want to bring them back to the front of my memory today, it's to my box of mutilated photographs I go first. My *memory* of my box of mutilated photographs. (The box itself I no longer have. I took it to Cambridge with me, years later, and threw it in a bin behind the cricket pavilion on Parker's Piece, where I calculated that anyone finding it would not know what it was, or at least who *they* were.) In the box I was able to distinguish them more keenly. I paid them greater attention. The reason I am able to recall now that Dora only ever turned her eyes towards you in order to let you know that you were wrong, and that she had a slyer way of smiling than Dolly, as though there was an understanding as to truth which she'd reached only with herself, and that she was more coquettish than Dolly in the quiet as a nun style, and had a slighter and less lumpy bust – not unlumpy just less lumpy – is that I had to make allowances for these things when choosing which prefab kid's mother's body to attach her to. Art – art gets you there every time.

Whether Gershom made similar observations in the course of taking both sisters out dancing I have never been able to decide. It may be that Dora's sly interior smile bears on Gershom's preference only in that it helps explain how come she went along with it, or worse still, encouraged it. 'If you have a choice of two, always go for the quieter one,' Sheeny Waxman once advised me. Among those of us who frequented Laps' it was common knowledge – even I knew it and I knew nothing – that the quiet ones were the best ones, that they asked the least, gave the most, and screamed the loudest. But Sheeny's point was subtler than that. If you have a choice, go for the quieter – the quiet*er*. In other words, where there is competition between two – and when isn't there competition between two? – the less socially confident will be the one to deliver because she is the one who has a score to settle. The mistress is almost always more timid than the wife, but where the mistress is the wife's best friend (let alone her sister) there is no almost about it, she is invariably the more timid. Invariably.

Boo to the goose.

Boo.

Boo.

Boo.

Poor Dolly, having to lose to the only person less confident than her on the planet.

Poor Dora, having to destroy her own sister in order to find some self-worth.

Poor Gershom – No. We could have been wrong, my mother, my father, my sisters, Fay, me, but our sympathies didn't extend that far. Gershom's heart was not engaged. Not in either direction. If his heart had ever been engaged to Dolly, however fleetingly, he would not have been able to drop her off in Lower Broughton after a Wednesday night swirling at the Ritz, mention it to her, as a sort of afterthought, while she was getting out of the car, that he believed Dora made a better partner for him – nothing personal, just a compatibility thing – and then drive away. And if his heart had been engaged to Dora he would not have encouraged her, or allowed her to encourage him to encourage her, to make a stranger of her sister. No. There was no reason to poor-Gershom Gershom. He had nothing much to do with his life, that was all. I knew why but couldn't say, for fear I'd be castigated for not saying earlier. He had nothing much to do with his life because he'd bet against his own gifts when he was young. Plock plock, I lose. He'd fouled his own nest. Serve him right.

But what about when it came to fouling ours? My father was afraid that now he'd got a taste for it he wouldn't stop. Next it would be my mother he'd try. Then Fay. Then my sisters. Because wherever he looked in my family there were sisters, and he specialized in sisters.

My mother made a sound like a death-rattle. 'I think you'll find,' she said, 'that he'll have the brains to stay away from here in the future.'

'What, and miss the bagels?'

It was a black joke. What wasn't black at the moment? The last thing we really expected on the very first Sunday after Black Wednesday was a visit from Gershom Finkel. Dolly had been put to bed in our house. She was given my sisters' room, my sisters moved in with my mother, and my father moved in with me. We crept about, not speaking. Neuralgia had spun its web among us, a black spider that hung where we could see it, but which we didn't dare disturb for fear of its venom. All our heads ached. Nothing and no one was in the right place; every pattern was dislocated, as they are when you take in the dying. Dora remained at home, in an excitable and heightened state, according to Fay, who ferried herself and my grandmother between the two. Fay feared as much for Dora's health as for Dolly's. There was a strange light around her. And she had started to make small talk with my grandfather, which no one had done for years. 'Seeing the man's point of view suddenly,' was my mother's reading of that. My father had a more practical interpretation. 'She's just softening him up,' he reckoned. 'Trying to get him on side for when Gershom moves in.' Fay pulled a face. 'In that event we'll all have to come here,' she said. It was naturally assumed that 'here' would be safe, and that Gershom would move the centre of his operations to Lower Broughton, however poky it was. So, no, we most definitely did not expect him to turn up for bagels as though nothing out of the ordinary had happened.

But turn up he did!

He did. He did. And what is more he came early!

It was my mother who opened the door to him. 'No,' she said. 'Dolly is here.'

'Oh, is she?' He didn't give the slightest sign that seeing her would at all inconvenience him. He made as if to come into the house.

('He was looking over my shoulder,' my mother told us afterwards. 'He was actually trying to look past me to see whether the bagels had come.')

'No,' she said again, 'you can't come in.'

('I actually had to bar his way,' she told us. 'I thought he was going to walk over me.')

He started to laugh. The same broken, rat-a-tat-tat laugh he used when he was pretending to admire my medals and cups, turning them upside down and examining them for price stickers. 'All right,' he said. 'You've taken sides. Fair enough. I thought as Dora's sister that you'd have stuck by her. But fair enough.'

('I could have hit him,' she told us. 'I don't know what stopped me.')

He turned and walked back down the path, airless and loping as when he circumnavigated the ping-pong table at the Akiva, a man not among friends.

My father called him before he got to the gate. 'Gershom, I'd like a word.'

'No, Joel,' I heard my mother say.

'Don't worry, I'm not going to touch him. I just want a word.' He had his coat on. And was jiggling his van keys. 'Let's go for a spin, Gershom,' he said.

'I'm frightened of what he's going to do to him,' my mother said. 'You know your father. He forgets his own strength.'

It's exciting for a boy to have a father who doesn't know his own strength, or at least it is when that strength isn't getting to know itself on him. But my sisters too were stimulated. Boy or girl, we all want a father who will put a bit of justice back into the world. We tried to imagine what he might be doing to Gershom now, twenty, thirty, forty minutes after he'd requested a word. 'That's a hell of a long time for a word,' I said.

'Not if the word's "Die, you bastard",' my sisters said.

'That's three words.'

'Well, you know how Dad always exaggerates.'

'I don't think he'll kill him,' I said. 'I think he's driving him to Miles Platting and is going to dump him there.'

'Why Miles Platting?'

'Because Miles Platting is a good place to dump people who won't collaborate.'

'Isn't the problem that Gershom has been collaborating only too well?'

'That's enough of that,' my mother said. 'How long is it now?'

I looked at my watch. 'An hour and ten minutes. Maybe he's gone to get the bagels.'

'Maybe he's gone to make Gershom get the bagels,' my sisters said.

We all agreed that was the start of the perfect punishment. But only if he was going to get Gershom to buy the bagels every week. And all the extras. None of which Gershom would ever be allowed to eat. He'd have to sit, Sunday after Sunday, tied to a chair with his mouth open, and watch while we wolfed the lot. In Gershom hell.

'Naked,' I said.

But my sisters drew the line at that.

Two hours later my father returned. Carrying the bagels. But otherwise alone. And wet.

'Where have you been?' my mother asked.

'Get the plates out first,' he said. 'And get me a fork for the smetana and kez.'

Only when he'd mixed the cream with the cream, not too much of the one, with not too much of the other, did he tell us where he'd been.

'The lake,' he said. 'Heaton Park Lake.'

'Oh, Joel, you haven't,' my mother said.

He trowelled smetana and kez on to half a bagel, smoothing the surface, taking out all the lumps and bubbles, leaving us to imagine the worst for half a minute more. He was dangerously pleased with himself. I pictured Gershom's sarcastic head bobbing on the water, in the scummy froth around the island, exactly where I'd found that first ping-pong ball which it wasn't too fantastical – was it? – to blame for all this. No doubt my mother pictured something far less cheerful.

'I took him for a little row, that's all,' my father said at last.

'And?'

'He said he didn't need any money.'

'You offered him money?'

'Of course I offered him money. You'd have expected me to offer him money if he'd been a shaygets. I'm not saying I was going to give him any money. He's ongishtopt with gelt. But at least once the offer's made you both know what you're dealing with. He said he didn't want money; I said I didn't want him near my house. He said Dora had her own house; I said I didn't want him near that house either. He said he had plenty of houses of his own to take Dora to; I said he'd better take her to one of them quick smart. He said he'd come to his own decisions in his own time, thank you; I said I'd throw him into the soup and hold him under if he did to Dora what he'd done to Dolly. He said he saw what I was driving at; I said good.'

'And?'

'What and? There is no and. That's it. The End. He'll have Dora out of there by midnight. Who knows, maybe he'll take your old man at the same time. Tomorrow Dolly can go home. The kids can go back to kipping in their own beds. I can go back to kipping in mine. And we can go back to living like a normal family again.'

'Well that's fine,' my mother said. 'A normal family. That's just terrific. And what will Dora go back to living? All you've done is throw her into his arms.'

'I thought she's already in his arms. I thought that's why you've got another sister lying upstairs trying to eat the mattress.'

My mother shook her head. 'If Dora goes in these circumstances it'll kill my mother,' she said. 'I wish you'd think before you act, I wish you wouldn't just rush at things like a bull at a gate.'

'I did this for you,' my father said.

'Well you've done me no favours,' my mother said. 'You've done no one any favours. Except Gershom Finkel.'

My father threw his hands in the air and looked long in my direction. It wasn't hard to understand what he was telling me. 'These are the thanks you get trying to help your wife's family.'

It went straight into my Monday-morning school essay, 'Against Women and Their Matrilineal Kinship Structures'.

My mother was wrong about my father doing Gershom Finkel

a favour. Several years later, in the course of attempting to sort out a delicate matter of family business, I called on him in the Didsbury house to which he'd fled with Dora on pain of being drowned like a rat in Heaton Park Lake. Dora I hadn't lost contact with entirely – funerals kept us in touch – but Gershom I'd seen nothing of. He hadn't aged much. There was nothing to age. After we'd concluded our business I asked him if he played table tennis still. It was a cruel question. I knew he was out of the game. No one had seen him at a tournament. There was no word that he was playing for any club.

He shrugged. 'The game isn't worth a candle any more,' he said. 'The new rubbers have killed it. I wouldn't go to the bottom of the street to watch a match. You?'

'Yes, a bit,' I said. I was captain of my varsity team. Which entitled me to a white blazer with light blue braiding which I wore as a dinner jacket at May Balls, or, with a cravat, to go punting in when the weather was chilly and the company worth impressing. Gershom would have learnt of this from Dora – all my aunties had photographs of me in my Blue blazer – and would have loved me to give him the opportunity to scoff at it. Table tennis at *Cambridge*? What do they play with – rugger balls? My reticence was designed to irk him.

'Want a knock?' he asked.

I laughed. 'Where? The Akiva?'

'Here,' he said. 'I've got a table. Come. I'll show you.'

He led me up three flights of stairs. The house was still subject to those sudden shoebox occlusions you get in old mansions which have been turned into flats. Boarded-up passages, doors where there shouldn't have been any, ceiling decorations vanishing asymmetrically into hollow walls. It's possible he'd never got rid of all his old lodgers. Certainly there was a stale sitting tenancy smell about the place, as though people had recently been cooking in stairwells and using the lavatory on landings.

I could tell from the wallpaper and carpets that the table tennis room had once been an attic studio flat. A serial murderer might have been comfortable here. But the table was new. A new net, too, strong enough to haul in herring. And good overhead lighting.

'So who do you play with on this?' I asked him.

He squinted at me. 'Dora,' he said.

'Dora? Dora plays?'

'Well, she can hold a bat,' he said.

I remembered how Dora held a bat. Downwards, on a droop. As though her wrist was broken and the bat was dead.

'Which is her bat?' I asked.

There were a number of them lying around on the floor, none in very good condition, along with some cheap non-competition balls.

'Whichever one's on the top of the pile,' Gershom told me. 'She's as happy with sandpaper as anything else.'

Yes, she'd been as happy with sandpaper as anything else in the old dining-table days when I used to beat her blindfold with a bookmark.

So that was their life together. Dora standing motionless at the top of the house, looking inwards, smiling slyly, ruthless in her diffidence, a sandpaper ping-pong racket limp in her boneless wrist, while Gershom smashed balls past her on both wings.

And we'd thought Gershom hell was an infinity of bagel-less Sundays.

But about my grandmother, my mother had been right.

She'd been on shpilkes throughout Dolly's courtship, at the mercy of a thousand alarms, afraid it would come to nothing, afraid it would come to something. Now she was ful mit tsores, heart-broken. Heart-broken for Dolly, that she'd lost Gershom. Heart-broken for Dora, that she'd won Gershom. Heart-broken for both Dolly and Dora, that there was a rupture between them.

Heart-broken for us all that we were mortal and knew nothing of what the Almighty intended for us. Yet it wasn't of a broken heart she died.

A lump, what else. In my family we all die of lumps or cheese. Cancer is unheard of. Say cancer and we become deaf suddenly. My grandmother's lump was almost the size she was when they found it, and probably bigger than her when the end came. We watched her grow it like a Polish cucumber.

'Mother, you're killing yourself with worry,' my mother kept telling her. 'There is nothing you can do now. Dora will make out and Dolly will get over it. If you let her.'

'*Let her!*' my grandmother cried. 'If I hadn't *let her* in the first place none of this would have happened.'

Fay too tried. 'Mother, you're only making it worse for Dolly och un veh-ing all the time. Give her time to realize she's better off without him.'

'If she's better off without him, what's Dora?'

We weren't good at comforting. None of us could find it in ourself to tell the lie, 'Better off with him.'

We tried taking her to the seaside, to Blackpool, Southport, Morecambe, St Anne's, New Brighton; but she'd just sit on a bench in the rain in her babushka, staring out at the colourless sea, growing the cucumber inside her.

Among the many foods and other treats the children of Israel missed once they were released from Egypt was the cucumber. To this day it's one of the ways a Jew registers homesickness: he misses cucumber. Lost and weary, my grandmother grew her own inside her body.

'Which way is Sowalki?' she asked me once. 'I'm tsemisht.'

We were on the promenade in Southport, looking at nothing.

'The other way,' I said.

'The other way,' she repeated. She shook her head. What understanding did any of us have of anything? 'Abi gesunt!' As long as I was healthy.

When she was down to five stone we put her in a bed in our living room. My mother and Fay took turns to sleep beside her.

Occasionally Dolly would come over to do the same, but when she wasn't gloomy she was so precariously exultant and brilliant, like a twelve-branched chandelier about to come crashing down from the ceiling, that we feared my grandmother would never survive a night of her nursing.

My mother and Fay supported each other well. Only once do I remember either of them collapsing in the company of the other. And that was when Fay put into words what they'd both known for some time – that my grandmother would never again sleep in her own house.

We could no longer postpone the hour, hateful though it was to everyone, when my grandfather would have to come and look at her. He was whipped now, in the way of all drunken domestic tyrants past their prime – whipped, whopped, a thing of no account whatsoever. He'd put a suit on, tie, waistcoat, in deference to he clearly didn't know what – a formal family visit of some kind? – and seemed to be surprised it was only his wife he was visiting, and that she was lying on a bed in our living room, and that there was only half as much of her to see as there'd been the last time he saw her.

He stood over the bed with his fists clenched in his trouser pockets, not a trace left now of the old sleepily voluptuous Polski princeling, or the bully who used to scare away my mother's friends.

'*E avanti a lui tremava tutta Roma!*' as Callas used to give us goosebumps, exulting on Twink's turntable.

'Sit on the bed, Dad,' Fay said.

He did as he was told. And waited for his next instruction.

'Hold her hand,' Fay said.

My grandmother flickered her eyes at this, and half opened

them, which seemed to frighten him. ''Ello, love,' he said. ''Ow are you?'

Just that.

'Ello, love, 'ow are you? Want a pint?

Shocking.

But why was I shocked? Because that was all he had to say to a woman he'd been married to for almost fifty years? Or because the vocabulary of his feelings, his diction, his demeanour, were that of a man who might as well have been born and brought up in Droylesden? Let's say both, since the culture of alcohol was to blame in either case. But years later, when the pain of his inadequacy as a husband, father, grandfather, has long past, I still shudder over how he traded his birthright, his ancestry, his foreignness, his freedom from proletarian definition, for a lifetime of drinking northern English beer in a northern English public house.

If the alternative was to be ale the colour of the sea at Southport, blowing your wages at the races and tolerating no atheists, better we'd have stayed on the east bank of the Bug or the Vistula, pogroms or no pogroms.

Snobbery? Only if you think I'm talking class. But I'm not talking class, I'm talking self-respect and metaphysics – what you owe your soul. Your neshome, as we used to call it in the days when we talked metaphysics.

Everything was now happening for the last time. My grandmother would never sleep in her own home again. My grandfather would never see her alive again. And I would never again go with glue and scissors into my scented coffret of concupiscence.

Did I feel bad about how I'd disfigured my grandmother for sport, now that death was on the point of disfiguring her in earnest? Yes, but not as bad as I'd feared I'd feel. I'd cared about her, hadn't I? When I was little I'd loved her to distraction. Later I'd entwined her in my most powerful emotions. Entramelled her in jealousy, equivocation, the paradoxes of reserve and shamelessness. It wasn't my fault that the emotions of a boy my age had to be so ugly. Blame nature.

I heard her die. It was about four in the morning. November, when everything dreadful happens in the north of England. I went from deep sleeping to wide waking in a single movement, disturbed not by noise but by the cessation of it. Suddenly the house was quiet. A sound I hadn't realized I'd been listening to for months, the sound of my grandmother tending her tumour, was gone.

She didn't lie for long in the house, but I didn't once have the courage to look at her. Nor could I bear to do more than squint through one eye at the coffin, which was barely bigger than the box I'd kept her in. I stayed in my room. My mother and Fay were no better. My father handled everything. Death was where my father's side came into its own. My mother's side could die competently enough – couldn't wait to die, some of us – but we needed my father's side to take care of everything that happened afterwards.

My aunties were all together again for the moment when the coffin was loaded into the hearse.

'Look how small it is,' I heard my mother cry. I didn't recognize her voice. She seemed to be wailing through water. 'It's too small, it's too small for her.' Otherwise weeping deprived them of words. They held on to one another like the limbs of a sea monster in pain. But I had to be with the men. Into the cars with the men. Off to the cemetery with the men. While the great writhing Laocoön of watery women remained behind to wail in the deep. Religious practice. The women stay and howl. The men go off and do the business.

They even tell jokes.

I knew what was going to happen. I'd watched from my bedroom window as other cortèges had left from our street. I knew that at a certain moment, just before the tailgate of the hearse was closed, the women broke rank, forgot the consolations they'd found in one another's arms, and hurled themselves on the coffin. Husband, child, parent, it didn't matter who was in there, the women clung on as though by force of will alone they could hold back time. Sometimes they had to be prised off, finger by finger; sometimes it seemed as though the only way to proceed with the obsequies would be to bury them with the coffin.

I stood on the front lawn, in a covey of matter-of-fact uncles, waiting for the wild screaming to start. At windows up and down the street, other boys also waited, knowing that one day what was happening to us would happen to them. My cheeks burned with self-consciousness. I couldn't endure anyone seeing me bereaved. Not just crying – though of course I couldn't endure that either – but actually *bereaved*. Afterwards it would be all right. Walzer has lost his grandma. No big shame in that. But at the time, in the very process of *being* bereaved – no, unendurable.

At the same time as my cheeks burned, my heart froze. All morning my insides had been changing places with one another. Nothing was fixed, nothing would stay still. Now I was frozen solid. I knew what was coming and I feared I would be unable to get through it. I didn't believe I had the warm blood necessary to keep me upright. When it started, first Dolly, then Dora, then my mother, then Fay, each one's grief fuelling the others', I felt my stomach cramp, as though I'd been kicked. Whatever blood was not yet frozen in my veins, froze now. Were these the women who had brought me up with such restraint, these furies tearing at the coffin with their nails, making sounds so ghastly it was hard to believe they were human?

Who could I not bear it for most? The tumour that had once been my grandmother? My poor motherless mother? My rapaciously shy aunties, for whom no mortification could ever be keener than their own?

I saw the torn expression on my father's face. Him? Could I not bear it most for him? For what he couldn't bear on behalf of my mother? Or was it me, just me, I most couldn't bear it for?

It was only when I became aware that my uncle Motty had his arm around my shoulder and was giving me his handkerchief and telling me a joke – 'Jewish bloke goes into a restaurant' – that I realized I'd gone down on my knees on the grass and was bawling like a baby, huge uncontrollable baby sobs, except that no baby ever had so much to sob about as I did.

BOOK III

ONE

No. 16: Don't let anything upset you.

Golden Rules to Remember,
Richard Bergmann

REMEMBER LORNA PEACHLEY, the ping-pong player with the soft Hampshire Ds whose all-moving body parts had given Twink and me so much innocent pleasure on our last afternoon practising drop shots together in the Burnley academy? Well, she re-emerges. Not for long, but to devastating effect. Devastating to me. There is a sense in which I am still devastated by Lorna Peachley, though I'm sure it would astonish her to hear me say that, if anything still astonishes her at her age. But that's always the way with devastating forces, isn't it? They pass through, careless of the trouble they cause, looking neither to the left nor to the right of them.

I'm not complaining. I invited her to do her worst. She would not even have known she had a worst in her had I not found it. So maybe it was me who was the devastating force.

But this is to run on ahead. Before we get to Lorna Peachley we have to make a detour through Sabine Weinberger. Which was the order in which I did them. And I'm not sure we can do Sabine Weinberger either without first addressing the issue uppermost in every ping-pong player's mind at the time I first had dealings with her – to sponge or not to sponge. Every day a new spongiform fantasy was coming in from the ocean beds and rubber plantations of the east – a thicker, softer, more silent and more deadly foam; a more deviously flexuous pimple; sandwich, with the sponge outside and the pimples in; sandwich with the sponge inside and the pimples out; sandwich with the sponge inside and the pimples out but *introverted*. A pimple which you couldn't see! – what devils they were out there in China and Japan.

My own inclination was to leave well enough alone, not because I was a purist – how could I be when I'd started off with a Collins Classic? – but because I liked the control conventional rubber gave me, I liked the sound – plock plock, plock plock: like the clatter of high heels on a wet pavement – I liked its associations with my old club and team-mates, and I liked the game as I played it; I liked chopping deep, arresting the ball on my forehand, telling it who was boss, and that you could only do with pimples. No one in their right mind chopped with sponge. With sponge there was no call to chop. If you needed to chop you were using the wrong rubber. And if you were using the wrong rubber you were in the wrong game.

There was the problem. Take a sponge bat in your hand and you felt you were playing with one of the Copestakes' mattresses. Oof plock, oof plock. Bye-bye all associations with high heels. Wet cots, that was what you smelt now. And who wanted to be reminded of those days? But personal preference didn't enter into it. Nor did aesthetics. Technology had taken over ping-pong and if you didn't go along with the new materials you were left behind. Sure, Ogimura lost his title. But who did he lose it to? Tanaka, another Nip. And he won it back from him the next year, anyway. If you were going to have any hope of sneaking their panting little bell-voiced geishas from them there was only one course to take – you had to get yourself re-rubbered.

Had I still been playing for the Akiva I might have hesitated longer before embracing the silent oriental game. Oof plock, oof plock. In the lower divisions you could still make an impression with vellum. But now that I had gone over to the Hagganah with Sheeny I couldn't count on coasting. Every match was hard these days. Harder to win and harder in the sense of less sociable and easeful. There were no more nobbels in the fog. There was no more tcheppehing *sotto voce* so that the shaygets opposition wouldn't understand. No more moodying. No more boxes of broken balls. No more spitting on the floor. No more fun. We were one of the toughest club teams in the country and we didn't get that way by punching our fists through phone box windows or humming 'E lucevan le stelle' at deuce in the final game.

I was with the men now. Phil Radic. Saul Yesner. Sid Mellick. Handsome devils, all of them. Dark, strong, hairy, grizzled like veterans of the Israeli independence wars. If someone had told me that the one thing Phil Radic, Saul Yesner and Sid Mellick had in common apart from playing for the Hagganah ping-pong team was that they'd all killed a man with their bare hands, I'd have believed it. Not any old man – they weren't criminals – but some enemy of the Jewish people.

Don't get me wrong: there was no Selwyn Marks para-noia among the men of the Hagganah. They weren't on the look-out for persecution. Who, after all, would ever have had the balls to persecute Sid Mellick, who could out arm-wrestle anyone in Manchester blindfolded and with his wrong arm? Or Saul Yesner, whose stomach muscles were so well developed that he used to invite all comers to take their turn at using him like a punching bag? But there was a fierce Bug and Dniester patriotism about them. When Phil Radic was selected to represent England he refused on the grounds that he would have to play on a Shabbes. 'What's with you?' his friends asked. 'You don't keep Shabbes. You've never kept Shabbes. You work a Saturday gaff.' 'Not the point,' he told them. 'It's the principle of the thing. If they want to pick Jewish players they have to respect how Jews live. Let them play on a Sunday.'

'Phil, we're talking playing for England, here!'

'It doesn't bother me.'

Easy come, easy go. Everybody agreed Phil Radic had it in him to be the best senior player in the country. He had all the strokes, a lovely open stance, unusual and dare I say uncharacteristic fleetness of foot, and utter confidence in his own gifts. I loved watching him play. He was spring-loaded. He made ping-pong witty. His sudden accelerations of racket-head speed were like explosions of satire. You didn't see the punch-line coming. And he used all the expanses of the table in a sardonic manner, economically, pithily, finding angles you'd never have guessed were there, leaving his opponent flat footed and looking stupid. People smiled when they lost to him, appreciatively, knowing they'd been done over. It was like having the piss taken out of you, but by a master, so you knew it wasn't personal. You weren't the joke, the game was. Maybe.

But what was most disconcerting about Phil Radic, from the point of view of someone who had cut his teeth on the Akiva, was how unfanatical he was. Twink ate and drank ping-pong. In the days when he had both his hands intact, Aishky lived and breathed the game. The Marks brothers talked nothing else. Before he took up swimming, Selwyn used to walk home from school practising his backhand flick. Whoosh, whoosh! Now he swam home, breasting the air and puffing his cheeks, but every now and then he would forget himself and mix a couple of push shots in with his dog paddles. And as for me, well I saw no future for myself except ping-pong. Even my erotic dreams had a ping-pong component. I would be rewarded for playing well. 'So that's your forehand, now show us your in-between,' Jezebels would beseech me. My night-time anxieties too were all played out on the table. If the Jezebels didn't claim me, the devil himself did, invisible, invincible, a disturbance of the darkness at the opposite end of the ping-pong table, returning every shot I played. Sometimes ten, twenty, thirty seconds would go by after I had hit the ball, time for it to disappear thousands of feet into the blackness, but always, in the end, it would come back. Always. I still dream this dream. It's years since I picked up a ping-pong bat, but in the night I am still trying to get the ball past a faceless agitation of shadows at the far end of the table. And not once in however many thousands of nights of struggle, not once have I succeeded.

Will Phil Radic be dreaming this dream? Did he ever? Of course not. Easy come, easy go. He had other things to think about. As did Saul Yesner. As did Sid Mellick. They were men, not nutty kids. There were engaged in serious business. When darkness fell on their moral worlds they were out strangling enemies of the Jewish people with their bare hands.

As for what to do about the new racket, the men of the Hagganah applied a double standard. It was too late for them. 'You can't teach an old dog new tricks,' Phil Radic said. But they believed it behoved me and even Sheeny, as the next generation – the future of the Hagganah, noch – to re-equip. That there was arrogance in this I had no doubt. We don't *need* the ping-pong equivalent of a three-piece suite – that was what they were really saying. We can go on winning fine just as we are. But you kids . . .

Well, some humiliations you just have to swallow. Others, of course, you can't wait to gulp down. But I'm coming to those.

You don't re-rubber lightly. Everyone has heard stories of snooker players whose careers have been halted or ruined because of a broken or mislaid cue. And with snooker we are only talking one stick of wood as against another stick of wood. Imagine if you also had to throw sponge and pimples into the equation. That's how it was with ping-pong. Make a wrong decision as to grip and you could be undone for a season. Make a wrong decision as to surface and you could be finished for life. The best sports shops understood this and were patient with you while you went through their entire stock twice. Some of them took the imaginative step of installing a table so that you could have a long knock-up before you bought. Alec Watson and Mitchell, where Twink and Aishk had taken me to choose my first tracksuit, actually put up two tables on a Saturday morning. And Saturday just happened to be the day that Sabine Weinberger worked at Alec Watson and Mitchell's to earn extra pocket money.

The Weinbergers lived on the same street as us, but on the opposite side and on the bend, so it wasn't easy for either family to see into the other's windows. This may have been one of the reasons we weren't on especially friendly terms. That the Weinbergers were fugitives from Berlin rather than Kiev or Odessa was also significant. We from the Bug did not hit it off with them from the Spree. We didn't like what we saw when we looked at our reflection in their eyes. We saw yokels. Peasants. Shnorrers. People who parked vans in the street. And there lay the prime cause of our strained relations. Mr Weinberger, who ran his jewellery business from his own garage and went everywhere with an eyepiece on his forehead, like a unicorn, was always the first person to sign any petition against my father's vehicles. I can still see the musty Gothic script on the first line of the top sheet of the complainants' submission, entangled and intricately woven like the handwriting of a spider. 𝕰𝖗𝖓𝖘𝖙 𝖂𝖊𝖎𝖓𝖇𝖊𝖗𝖌𝖊𝖗 – 𝕵𝖊𝖜𝖊𝖑𝖑𝖊𝖗. As though being a jeweller settled the matter as to where vans should and shouldn't be parked.

'*She*'s nice,' my mother used to say. Meaning Mrs Weinberger. 'She used to be a Vulvick.'

Being a Vulvick carried weight, because the Vulvicks were one of Manchester's most distinguished rabbinical families. If you'd *been* a Vulvick it stood to reason that you were now fallen socially and spiritually: as a Vulvick there was only one trajectory you could take. Just how far Mrs Weinberger had fallen can be measured by the fact of her daughter's having a Saturday job. No Vulvick who was still a Vulvick had one of those, unless you call being a rabbi a Saturday job.

There were also some questions to be asked about the way Sabine Weinberger deported herself. At fifteen she already had a reputation. 'Eh, eh, here you go!' we would nudge one another and say when she turned up late at Laps' for a bag of chips. Speaking for myself, I had no clear idea what she had a reputation for doing, only that she had a reputation. 'Her bust is too prominent for a girl her age,' I remember my mother observing, and I more or less assumed that her reputation began and ended with that. I'd have taken more interest had I found her more to my liking. But she was too unserer for me, too spiked and tussocky, on the one hand too like Phil Radic to look at, and on the other too much of a Becky in her manner – Becky being the name we gave to girls who reminded us of our mothers or even of our mothers' mothers. I'm not saying she had nothing going for her. If the stone-throwing prefab boys of Heaton Park had been mad for Sabine Weinberger I'd have understood it. It has its adherents, that midnight scaly Lilith look. There are men who love the thought that they might bruise themselves on a woman's scratchy pelt. But you can only be mad for what's different from yourself, and from where I stood Sabine Weinberger was too much the same.

Speaking of stone-throwing prefab boys reminds me that Sabine Weinberger also had a glass eye as a consequence of some gruesome playground accident when she was a little girl. That too may have contributed to her reputation. She looked at you strangely.

Just before my grandmother died Sabine Weinberger posted me an invitation to a party at her house.

'You'll be going to that,' my father said.

I told him that I didn't feel up to a party what with my grandmother dying downstairs and everything.

'It wasn't a question,' my father said. 'I said you'll be going to that.'

He made me wash my hair and oversaw my wardrobe. He made me stand still as a tailor's dummy while he verified that I'd polished my sad never-trodden-upon winkle-pickers and properly buttoned my Italian suit. He even straightened my tie, he who had never in his life known how to decently knot his own. Then he opened the front door and pushed me out.

'Don't be late,' my mother called.

'Don't be early,' my father said.

I never went. I got as far as Sabine Weinberger's front door, heard the music, saw the dancing, saw the size of the girls, and bottled out. It was the dancing that did me every time. Kids with whom I was completely comfortable, kids I knew from school and Laps', kids I regularly made pickle meat of on a ping-pong table, were suddenly transformed into sophisticates the minute I saw them dancing. It was with dancing the way it had been with ball-playing: I'd turned my head away for two minutes and they'd learnt how to do it. With big girls, too. How come? How were they always able to steal an advantage over me? The size of those girls! What use would I be with girls as big as that – I with my rubbery little virgin in-between?

I never went. Never knocked. Never showed my face. I knew I couldn't go back home and suffer my father's wrath so I crept back into our garden and hid in the privet hedge for three hours, listening to my poor grandmother having trouble with her breathing. When I finally asked to be let in I had soil on my suit and twigs in my hair.

'I see someone's been having a good time,' my father said.

I thought he was going to kiss me.

When I next ran into her in the street, Sabine Weinberger gave me one of those strange sideways glass-eyed looks of hers and reproached me for not coming to her party. I blushed and said I'd wanted to, but that my grandmother was dying. When I ran into her after that I no longer had a grandmother.

She knew. She'd seen the hearse leave from our house. Which meant that she'd seen me sobbing like a baby. She touched my shoulder and wished me long life. 'I know how much you loved her,' she said.

I thought she was going to kiss me.

And had she done so, I was suprised to realize, I would not have half minded.

So there was Alec Watson and Mitchell with its stock of oof-plock foam and sponges, and there were the Saturday-morning ping-pong tables up and ready, and there was Sabine Weinberger waiting behind the cash register with her prominent bust and glass eye – and there were we, Sheeny Waxman and me, miles away on a gaff at Worksop. Or there we *should* have been. All very well talking about going to town and re-rubbering, but when do you get the time if you're a gaff worker and a gaff worker's son? 'Do I ever get a Saturday off from this job?' Sheeny had once asked my father. 'Yeah, when pigs fly,' my father had told him. 'Oink, oink!' Sheeny said disconsolately.

And then, out of nowhere, pigs flew!

The van broke down. Five o'clock in the morning we were outside Sheeny's house, ticking over, waiting for his curtains to open, waiting for Sheeny's mother to show herself, distraught, at his window, and then for Sheeny's father to show himself, distraught, at another window, and finally for Sheeny to appear in person, coughing and twitching and complaining – 'Oy a broch, Joel, what time do you call this?' – when the van went into paroxysms of its own, shook, spluttered, convulsed and died.

'Nishtogedacht!' my father said. 'That's all we need.'

'I'm going back in for a kip,' Sheeny croaked. 'Honk me when you've got her going.'

'You're not going anywhere,' my father said. 'You'll sit here and put your foot on the pedal when I tell you to.'

'You're not going to push her?'

'Where am I going to push her? Into your bedroom? Show me a hill, Einstein, and I'll push her.'

'So what are you going to do?'

'Crank her.'

'Joel, don't be meshugge. You'll wake the neighbours. It's Shabbes.'

'And some of us have to work on Shabbes,' my father said.

But there was no cranking the Commer back to life, Shabbes or no Shabbes. My father disappeared under the chassis for an hour. Then he disappeared into the bonnet, just his short Walzer legs sticking out like those of a creature stuck up the anus of another creature in that Bosch picture we had once failed to turn into a commercial enterprise. Then he disappeared into Sheeny's house, covered in oil, but not swearing, never swearing, to make a couple of phone calls. It was nearly nine o'clock before he could get a mechanic over. And gone ten when the tow-truck arrived.

'That's it,' he finally conceded. 'You've got the day off.'

By that time Mrs Waxman was up and about in a cerise nightie, preparing him Welsh rarebit. She seemed to know how he liked it – lots of cheese.

Sheeny had been asleep in the cab the whole time. Snoring heavily but careful, even while comatose, not to crush his whistle or soil his cuffs. I shook him to tell him the good news.

'What, what?' he cried, trying to throw me off. 'I didn't!' Then comprehension returned to his jittery blue eyes. He twitched his head out from his shoulders, a ratchet at a time. I looked away, one tortoise from another. When he was finally free of himself he said, 'Oink, oink! Let's go and get some new bats then I'll take you to the Kardomah.'

'The Kardomah!'

'Geshwint. Before the shops close.'

The Kardomah? *I* was going to the Kardomah! *Me*?

Oink, oink!

But first we had to do the bats. And Sabine Weinberger.

'I wish you long life,' she said when she saw me.

Hadn't she already said that? It was my understanding that you said it once and that was that. On with life, no more references to death – wasn't that the point of it? But then she was the one with the rabbinical background, she was the half-Vulvick, she should know.

She looked different behind a counter. Older. Taller. More assured. Maybe even more desirable. Her hair was up in a beehive, which drew attention to the fixity of her glass eye, though even that had a gleam in it I hadn't seen before. Did she change marbles? One for home, one for school, one for work?

'This is my friend Sheeny Waxman,' I said. As though there was anyone in Manchester who needed to be introduced to Sheeny Waxman. 'We want some help with rubbers.'

Did I see them exchange looks? Or was that just her new glass eye and Sheeny's tic?

We put an hour in on one of Alec Watson and Mitchell's tables, delighting mere sublunary shoppers, even signing a couple of autographs between shots. 'You should pay us for doing this,' Sheeny joked to Sabine Weinberger. 'We're good for business.'

'I'd pay you if the shop was mine,' she said.

'You mean it's not? Oliver, I thought you told me we were going to Weinberger and Mitchell's.'

Sabine Weinberger laughed, putting her prominent bust into it.

'So there's no discount?' Sheeny said.

'I could ask.'

'We don't want it if it's not from you,' Sheeny said.

Sabine Weinberger made an exaggerated curtsy and squeezed us a glimpse of her tongue.

She was oddly kitted out for working a Saturday morning in a sports shop, in fine steel stilettos (that was why she looked taller) and a tight black jumper (that was why she looked more than usually prominent) and stiff petticoats under a black skirt. Just like Sheeny, she looked as though she'd come to work straight from the Plaza. Though in Sheeny's case all creases had miraculously fallen out of his clothes, and there was not a speck of dust on him, whereas Sabine Weinberger was as crumpled as a used paper bag and had a serious lint problem.

What I couldn't decide was what I thought of her legs. Ask me what I think today and I still wouldn't be able to answer. All legs come up better in stilettos, that goes without saying; but a certain sadness attaches to lumpen, stubbly legs in high heels. On the other hand there is something fascinating about them too, by very virtue of the thing that makes you sad. Because in the end, isn't uncouth more rousing than couth?

If you followed the trail of Sabine Weinberger's stubble you were soon on a journey whose reason was a mystery to you, and those journeys are always the best.

But I am getting ahead of myself again. We were here for bats.

In those days shops in the centre of northern English towns closed at lunch-time on a Saturday. Given that you weren't likely to make it to a city store on a Saturday morning before about eleven, by which time the sales staff were already getting agitated about knocking off, it's hard to see why anyone bothered with Saturday opening at all. But northern life was organized around the same principle as desire for Sabine Weinberger. It was the absence of amenities that kept you coming for more.

Being a Saffron, I suffered greater sensitivities to staff impatience than Sheeny did. 'I think they're waiting for us to go,' I said.

'Are you waiting for us to go?' Sheeny asked Sabine Weinberger.

'*I'm* not,' she said.

'So what do you think?' Sheeny said to me.

'I still prefer a bat I can hear,' I said.

'Yeah, but think of it this way,' Sheeny said, 'if you can't hear it then they can't hear it. That's gotta be worth five points a game.'

'Not if they're playing with a silent one too.'

'Shmerel! – then it's worth five points to them if you're *not*.' After which he turned to Sabine Weinberger and asked, 'Am I right or am I right?'

She was nothing if not accommodating. 'I think you're both right,' she said.

Is that what was meant by her having a reputation?

'How can we both be right?'

'By using sandwich. Some people come in here and they feel right playing with sponge immediately. I can see that you two don't. You're not natural sponge players. And the only answer to sponge is sandwich.'

'You think I might be a natural sandwich man?'

'I think you both are.'

'What do you reckon, Oliver?' Sheeny said. 'You a sponge or a sandwich man?'

'I need more time to decide,' I said. 'I'm not sure what sort of man I am.'

'A sandwich just for me, then,' Sheeny said. And while Sabine Weinberger was taking his money he asked, in an unusually croak-free voice for him, 'So what will you be doing when you close?'

She shrugged and looked away, plucking lint from her far too prominent bust.

'Then you're coming to the KD with us,' Sheeny told her.

The KD.

Not K for King and D for David, but K for Kar and D for Domah.

Kar Domah, the ancient Hebrew scholar and socialite who had

urged resistance against the Romans and held out against them for thirteen years, bare-handed and in his tefillin, on an unfortified mountain top in Market Street.

The KD.

I'd be lying if I said I could remember the old Market Street KD with any exactitude, what shape the tables were, what colour the carpet was, whether a waiter or a waitress served us coffee, or a fabled beast that was half horse, half water serpent. I wouldn't have been any clearer on the details at the time. I wasn't really looking. Not with my eyes. You used other senses to experience the Market Street Kardomah. You took it in through your pores.

Of course Benny the Pole wasn't working his pitch on the pavement outside the KD this Saturday afternoon. Benny the Pole was still repaying his debt to society in Strangeways. Other frog-voiced men past their prime were holding on to their toupees and giving their spiel, but none of them interested Sheeny and so none of them interested me. We went deep into the bowels of the KD, I remember that. As far in as you could go. And every time we approached a table the occupants looked up, looked us over, recognized us or didn't, but knew everything there was to know about us – from the quality of the shampoo we used to how long it took us to wear down the heels of our shoes – before we'd passed. It was like being at a Walzer wedding. No, it was like being the bride and groom at a Walzer wedding, making your entrance only after everyone was seated, negotiating your way to high table while the Klutzberg Trio played 'Chossen-kalleh mazeltov' and all your uncles and aunties banged cutlery. So why, all of a sudden, didn't I mind the exposure? Because this was the KD, that's why. The Kingdom of Dreams.

One thing I hadn't expected – how many of *our* women, Bug and Dniester Beckies, the stubble and sparkle gang, I was going to see. You came to the KD looking to form short-term, obligation-free relationships with cory, ladies of other faiths and cultures, that was how I had always understood it. The KD wasn't a social club. Yes, it was a meat market, but a *treife* meat market. Now I saw what I saw it all made perfect sense. Our girls were here looking for the same. A non-kosher beanfeast. A pig-out. We kept ourselves clean for them, and they kept themselves clean for us, by doing whatever it was we had to do outside the nest. We played away and they played away. Fine. I can't say it didn't come as a shock to me to discover that our girls played at all. Other girls yes, but not our girls. I'd been brought up, by precept and example, to believe that virginity was an exclusively Jewish property. Why would a hymen have been called a hymen if it wasn't Jewish? I had cousins called Hymen. We all did. Becky and Shoshanna Hymen. I could no more think of our girls without a hymen than I could their girls *with* one. But if I'd got that wrong I'd got that wrong. That's what you went to the KD for – to learn. Fine. I wasn't sure I liked it, but fine. We played away and they played away. It was practical. It was like wishing the bereaved long life. It acknowledged that life was for the living. That some matters had to be attended to. It accepted harsh realities.

Whether it actually worked, though, is another matter. What you aspired to was a condition of coruscating short-sightedness. When your own walked by you rose and embraced them, but you never thereafter noticed they were there. Even if they took the table next to yours you didn't see them. Stars danced in your eyes, fireflies flickered on the rim of your Kardomah coffee cup, you glimmered brilliantly, but you were aware of nothing beyond the ring of fire which cut your table off from all the others. And when, despite yourself, you saw your sister making out with a shvartzer? Ah, then . . .

Whatever you allowed yourself to see or not see at the Kardomah, the rule that said you didn't hit on your own was religiously observed. Name me one Jewish marriage that started life in the Market Street Kardomah. One *happy* Jewish marriage . . . So what did Sheeny think he was doing actually *bringing* Sabine Weinberger in with us? Deliberately flouting protocol, that's what he was doing. I wasn't aware of it at the time but I found out later that Sheeny's exorbitant and exclusively gentile-centred head-jockeying had been attracting adverse comment from two or three of the KD Becky-ravers who really should have known better. Rules are rules. Zeta Cowan and Hilary Fishbein particularly had been giving him tsorres. Ironic, considering how far out of the nest those two were prepared to lean. Sabine Weinberger was his answer. Sabine Weinberger was there to kraink Zeta Cowan and Hilary Fishbein. I'm up for anderer *and* unserer, Sheeny was telling them. Look! Kuk this! The only thing I'm not up for is *you*.

Poor Sabine Weinberger, in that case? I've never decided. It's just possible that Sabine Weinberger had ulterior motives of her own, not the least of them being to kraink me. And what had I done to her? Nothing. That was her complaint. Nothing. Having observed me weeping over my grandmother, Sabine Weinberger had fallen the tiniest bit in love with me. But all I wanted to talk to her about was ping-pong rubber.

And certainly all I wanted to do now I'd got into the Kardomah was experience it through my skin, not look at her. Was I disappointed? Nothing ever lives up to its reputation, especially when that reputation has brewed and festered inside the shell of a clammy introvert – surely I was a *bit* disappointed? No, no I wasn't. I couldn't do much with it there and then but I reserved it. Not as in reserved judgement but as in reserved seats. I wanted it for later. There would be a time for such a place. Kardomah and Kardomah and Kardomah.

There would be and there would have been. For by the time a clammy introvert is ready there is no more Kardomah.

We took Sabine Weinberger to the pictures, talking of reserved seats; straight from the hot cinnamon breath of the Kardomah into the conditioned Coca Cola chill of the Gaumont, where Mario Lanza was starring in *Serenade*. We paid for half her ticket each, Sheeny and I; by way of showing even-handed gratitude for which she sat in the middle, holding both ours, which should have been exciting for me as no female person not a mother or a grandmother or an aunty had ever held my hand before, but the music made me think of Twink and Aishky and most of the time I wished Sabine Weinberger had been either or both of them.

Once or twice, when Lanza was off the screen, I took the opportunity to wonder if she and Sheeny were up to more than hand holding. No woman has so much individual control over her limbs that she can be innocent with one hand while being guilty with the other. Sometimes her fingers would unlace from mine and she would grind an excrucied little fist into my thigh, or she would squeeze my knee, rhythmically, in time to some music that wasn't Lanza's, or she would slide a couple of nails inside my shirt and describe an agonizingly trembly circle round my navel, all of which I liked but all of which I realized were probably no more than inadvertent mirror-image reverberations of what she was doing to Sheeny.

Then guess where we took her after that.

No, not Miles Platting.

To Benny the Pole's place on Wilmslow Road!

The Benny the Pole?

There was only one.

Sheeny had the key. Sheeny had had the key for as long as Benny had been down. 'But I don't abuse it,' he told us. 'Benny said I could live here, but this place is like a shrine to me.'

Just as Benny the Pole was the first person in Manchester to wear suede and snakeskin shoes, so he was the first person in Manchester to own a luxury flat.

You hear the word luxury and you think of soft textures. Deep-pile carpets. Armchairs that go oof plock. Bubble baths. 'Luxury!' I remember my father pronouncing as he punched the kishkies out of the little round Rexene pouffes he used to flog for flompence from the back of his van. 'Sheer luxury!' My mother's concept, of course. Sheer luxury for my father meant more of something. It didn't much matter what, just more. A cheese sandwich with extra cheese. A lager and lime with extra lime. A liver and onion fry-up with more liver and more onions. My mother was the one forever yearning for softness.

Luxury for Benny the Pole had more in common with my father's meaning. There was a lot of everything here. A Mancunian lot. A very lot. The placed looked like a swag warehouse. Only of a higher quality than the swag we sold. We didn't sell writing desks with tooled green leather inlays, for example. Or antique wooden globes of the world. Or brass sextants. Or padded bars. We sold cheap birthday cards for fathers which showed such articles as these in just this profusion, but not the articles themselves. None of our punters in Oswestry or Wrexham would have shelled out for a brass sextant.

And nothing in Benny the Pole's luxury pad passed the oof-plock test either. Everything squeaked. Eech plock, eech plock. The parquet floor squeaked. The leather settee squeaked. The soda syphon squeaked. The toilet seat squeaked. The water in the taps squeaked. Even the sheets squeaked.

We got to feel the sheets?

Oh yes, we got to feel the sheets.

I married Sabine Weinberger some years later, I might as well come clean on that score here and now. I married her because I was lonely at Cambridge and she was the only woman I knew at the time who was prepared to keep me company. We are not married any longer. We were not married for long. And we were never married happily. Not *ecstatically* happily. (Name me one ecstatically happy Jewish marriage that began at the KD?) But she is the mother of my children. For what that's worth. Channa and Baruch – though those were not the names we gave them.

Was that the only reason I married her? Because I was lonely? Probably not. Maybe I also married her to finish some business we'd started that night in Benny the Pole's squeaky luxury flat on Wilmslow Road.

She lay with us in turn, separately. She was not prepared to have it any other way. No sandwich after all. And she lay with me first. *Lay*. In the lie down rather than the get laid sense. She kept all her clothes on, slipped under the eech-plock sheets, wished me long life and jerked my in-between. End of story. Or should have been end of story.

I fell asleep immediately. It had been a big day for me. No gaff. Kardomah. Benny the Pole's pad. And now this: my in-between pummelled by someone not myself. A very big day. The last day of childhood. Would I ever blush again? I doubted it. What was there to blush about? I no longer nursed a terrible secret. My in-between had finally been handled. Not all that well, but handled. I was now like every other man. Goodbye shame! Goodnight the colour red! Oof plock, oof plock – I'd been milked of all reason for embarrassment at last.

A good sleep, then on with the business of passing my in-between along to the next one. The giant had stirred and the great chain of masculinity had begun to rattle . . .

Two days later I was knocking up with Sheeny at the Hagganah when for no apparent reason he put his bat down, fell into a chair, and started spluttering.

'What?' I said.

He was holding his heart now, and shaking. 'I've just remembered. Give me a minute, I'm platzing myself to death here.'

'About what?'

'Oy a broch! The bint. Whatsername? Weismuller . . .'

'Weinberger.'

I'd started to go tight. I knew Sheeny had had his go after me. That had been part of the deal. First me, then Sheeny. I was cool about it. Sheeny too had his right not to go home unmilked. But what was *funny* about that?

'I'm remembering,' he said. 'It's coming back to me. I'm lying there with my shmeckle down her throat, taking my time, trying to think about something else, telling her about the time you zetzed the pig – "You should have seen the size of that fucking pig," I'm telling her; "Oink, oink!" – when mitten derinnen she starts shaking her head and covering her ears. "Don't say that word," she says. I think that's what she says. It's hard to tell what a person's saying when she's got your shmeckle in her mouth. But I'm kind of picking up the vibrations. If I'd had a microphone strapped to my putz I'd have got everything she was saying. "What word? Fucking?" "Gobble, gobble. No – the other one!" "What other one?" "The *other* one." "There wasn't a fucking other one." "Gobble, gobble. Yes, there was." "What? *Pig*?" "Don't say it, don't say it," she shreis. So I start nobbling. I can't help myself. She's lying there with my shmeckle in her mouth, I've had two fingers up her cunt, she's got a fucking glass eye, and she's covering her ears because I've said the word pig. Is that funny or not?'

'It's hilarious,' I said.

'That's what I thought,' Sheeny said.

I could have saved myself a lot of trouble later on had I attended to what was salient in that story. Sabine Weinberger had not put to sleep the Vulvick in her. She was still as anti-pig as her mother's side had ever been. Therefore there would still be traces of virulent Vulvicitis in any children we conceived together. Had I thought of that I would never have risked it. Because who wants a pious chuntering little frummy for a child? It's some consolation that it's a long time since either of my chuntering little frummies called me father. But I would still rather not have given them the option.

What stopped me attending to the most important element of Sheeny's anecdote was what you might call a side issue. The little matter of his putz in her mouth. She hadn't done that to me. She hadn't invited me to put two fingers in her cunt either, come to that. Was that why she'd insisted on seeing to me first? To whet her appetite for Sheeny? Was I just the appetizer and Sheeny the main course?

What's the expression – out of the frying pan and into the fire? I was out of the shell and into hell. Sexual jealousy in regard to someone you love is a monstrous thing; but sexual jealousy in regard to someone you couldn't give two hoots for is far worse. There are no counterbalancing imaginings; you do not look forwards to the time when she will do the things to you she did to him; your mind does not revel in a futurity of forgivenesses and restitutions. You are left entirely to your own devices. Insulted in your own single self. Unpreferred. Just that. The only other time I had felt washed up in this way was when I lost my first ever ping-pong matches to Cartwright and Battrick of the Allied Jam and Marmalade factory. And if I am to be to true to what was going on inside my sick little head I would have to admit that I was luxuriating in the same rotting sweetness of self-pity that came with those defeats. What was the pleasure in that pain? Why did it feel so good to feel so bad? What was it about losing that I liked so much?

One good thing was that I no longer rummaged in my filthy mutilated-aunty box, otherwise I'd have had Fay out again, in suspenders, kneeling between Sheeny Waxman's knees. The other good thing was that just as a new week in the league brought a new opponent to beat, so a new day in the street brought a new chance to get even with Sabine Weinberger.

She must have been a bit of a glutton for punishment herself, because she was the one who came knocking on my door. To wish me long life, ostensibly. My father answered, therefore it must have been a non-gaff day. I'd like to think it must have been a balmy summer's day too, because he immediately ushered everyone into the back garden so that I could have the house to myself – to myself and Sabine Weinberger – but I know he'd have ordered everybody out even if there'd been ten inches of snow on the ground. Oliver had to have his oats.

In fact he turned quite nasty soon after this when he suspected that I really was getting my oats from Sabine Weinberger. 'Not with a Jewish girl, you tsedraiter,' he told me. 'Not with someone from across the road. Not with a Vulvick.'

'Who with, then, Dad?' I asked him.

But he wasn't going to answer that. He made a gesture with his hands, meaning *them*, out *there*, in the cory-crowded oceans, in the shikse-sheltering streets.

So what did he think I was going to do with Sabine Weinberger once he'd cleared the house for us? Not pop my dick in her mouth, that's for sure. And not demand that I be allowed to insert two fingers in her cunt either.

Neither of which things, as a matter of incidental fact, I did. But I made it clear to her how sore I felt.

'I've been talking to Sheeny Waxman,' I said.

'Oh,' she said.

'You must have known Sheeny would tell me,' I said.

'Tell you what?' she said.

'Oh, come on.'

'I didn't think it would make any difference,' she said.

'Who to?' I said.

'To you,' she said.

'What about to Sheeny?'

'I don't care about Sheeny. I don't care if I never see Sheeny Waxman again in my life.'

'Is that why you sucked his dick?'

'I sucked his dick because he asked me to.'

'What if I'd have asked you to suck my dick?'

'You didn't.'

'No. But what if I had?'

'I wouldn't.'

'Ah!' I said.

'I want to see *you* again.'

'Ah!' I said.

228

'I respect *you*,' she said.

'So I don't get my dick sucked?'

'Not yet. Not right away.'

'Because you respect me?'

'Yes.'

'But if you didn't respect me you would?'

'Yes, because afterwards it wouldn't matter if you didn't respect me.'

'Ah,' I said – and I saw the beginnings of another misogynistic essay for my English teacher here – 'so this is all actually about whether I respect you, not whether you respect me.'

'If I didn't respect you I wouldn't care whether you respected me.'

'Why do you think I wouldn't respect you if you sucked my dick?'

'Because they never do.'

What I wanted to say was in that case stop sucking dicks, but I saw that that might not be the best way to serve my cause.

'There's always a first time,' I said instead.

She fell quiet. Then she said, 'I'd like to . . .'

I detected the but. 'But?'

She shrugged. She'd said it all. 'Later,' she said. Meaning, when we'd settled the question of mutual respect. In other words, when it was too late to matter.

But if she thought we'd sorted things out, I didn't. 'OK,' I said. 'So that's the dick. Now what about the cunt?'

I now see that as it related to sexual relations between ourselves – the Tiskers and the Taskers – Sabine Weinberger's ethical position differed not a jot from my father's. Do unto others what you wouldn't do unto your own. There was a time when I abominated such a system and took it to be monstrous abuse of those who were not us. 'What are they, these shikses and shaygetsim, these yoks and yekeltehs?' I remember shouting at my father, 'scrap paper to practise on?' In fact my indignation could not have been more misplaced. What we were practising was nothing less than charity, which is supposed to begin at home. We were giving the best of ourselves to the gentiles – here, have, swallow – and saving nothing but the left-overs, the lees, the bitter lees, for ourselves.

And now I'm sounding like my children, Baruch and Channa, except that they would never use the language I use.

Regarding the matter of whether Sabine Weinberger was or wasn't going to suck my dick, all speculation came to an end about a week later in her bedroom when I knelt on her shoulders and pushed it in. Here, have, swallow. I didn't like the me whose reflection I saw in her glass eye. I didn't look gentlemanly. I didn't look a mensch. But you have to do what you have to do. Her fault, for doing what she didn't have to do with Sheeny. I couldn't be expected to go through life getting nothing from women because they wanted to see me again. I was prepared to take my chance. I'd settle for them not liking me and just sucking my dick instead. My loss.

As for respecting Sabine Weinberger after she'd sucked my dick, of course I didn't.

TWO

A wonderfully interesting field is open to the young girl
entering into serious table tennis. If she is keen, there is
no lack of teachers. Whereas a man may have to travel
far to find good practice partners, a girl can always find
a stronger man player to practise with.

Modern Table Tennis, Jack Carrington

AND *NOW* LORNA Peachley?
    Listen and you can hear her body parts moving. Shh,
listen. Oof plock, oof plock.

That's her bat you're hearing. She took the sponge route. The
women's game needed a bit of speed and a fat wedge of naked
foam upped the tempo prettily. Her chopping was always suspect
too, so now she could just stick her bat out and half-volley.
Ooof! Even the balls sighed when Lorna Peachley hit them.

Lorna Peachley came into my life – I mean properly came into
my life – at a time when I was in danger of becoming a winner.
Gone, the red face; gone, the existential bashfulness; gone, the
boy with the rubbery little in-between. I habituated the KD
now. I sat on girls' faces. I played table tennis with the game's
equivalent of the Stern Gang. My own grandmother wouldn't
have recognized me.

And Cambridge? A year or two away yet, but in the bag. I already knew which college I was going to. The misogynistic one.

Everything conspired to make me impressive, even the new bats. I'd gone for sandwich in the end, as Sabine Weinberger, who knew nothing about the game except from a retailing point of view, suggested that I should. Though it was Lorna Peachley I listened to. 'If you're ever going to beat me it's not going to be with pimples,' she told me. But who wanted to beat her? Why would any normal man ever want to do anything but lose to Lorna Peachley? I went along with the pretence that I was experimenting with ways to overcome her, but in truth I only plumped for sandwich in order to lose to her more comprehensively.

That it improved my results against absolutely everybody else was merely a side benefit.

And it didn't even do that right away. To begin with I had to sacrifice half my game to the fucking thing. The first shot to go was my forehand chop. With sandwich you either have to chop the ball so late your opponent has in all probability gone home, or you make no allowances at all and hope to blind him. The backhand lingered longer, but soon I discovered it was more economical and certainly more effective to block. The word tells you all you need to know about the stroke. As for example that it isn't a stroke at all, but an afterthought, a stab, at its most athletic, a lunge. Except when Lorna Peachley executed it. Then it was as though everything soft in nature had mustered in a fairy ring. And the sound she made when she struck was like the air going out of a thousand luxury Rexine pouffes. Oooooooof.

Bit by bit there disappeared from my game – and indeed from the game in general – everything I'd originally loved about it. No more retrieving from the back of the room. No more coddling the ball and making it yours. No more giving it so much dig you could hear it changing its mind in mid-air. Thanks to science, in a few short years the game had gone forwards only to go backwards. Now we were all stabbing and zetzing as gracelessly as beginners. Except, of course, for you know who.

Yet out of this evil sprang forth good. The sandwich bat released the backhand flick that had been locked up inside me. Barna had flicked like no one else in the history of the game, using ordinary rubber with modest brown nipples. So far I had played exclusively (excepting my Collins Classic) with a bat that bore his name, but I had never truly been able to let my wrist go. Something inhibited me. I could drive with it. I could get plenty of topspin, and by changing the weight from my right foot to my left and swivelling my hips, I could disguise its direction and pull off a backhand winner where one was least expected. But that final wristy *coup de grâce* always eluded me. Now, liberated by the spring in the sandwich and the sensation, which may or may not have been an illusion, of enjoying an extra picosecond between feeling the ball on my bat and releasing it, I found a flexibility of wrist that made even Phil Radic stop and look.

In the end it was probably the sound that made the difference. We could no longer with any onomatopoeic justification say that we played ping-pong. Just as everything else in the world was growing noisier, our game had fallen quiet. In fact the new bats were not dead silent. What they did was cushion sound. They put a distance, at once uncanny and unsatisfying, between a stroke and its reverberation. I say unsatisfying because it robbed you of a due consciousness of drama to let fly at a ball with all your strength, only to hear a suffocated squelch, like a ripe grape falling on your neighbour's lawn, the least division of a second later. On the other hand, whatever my loyalty to it, the plock of a ping-pong ball on a ping-pong bat had never struck me as subtle or heroic. I winced inwardly at the moment of contact – plock ouch! – and since no stroke is ever finished at the moment of contact, my follow-through was never the smooth ongoing trajectory it should have been. Now that there was no demeaning plock, I felt free to make a ballet of my follow-through.

Flourish – that's what distinguishes the flick. Over goes the wrist, and up and away in impertinent disregard for decorum – like Fonteyn in the arms of Nureyev, like a shooting star, only more dazzling, more bewildering to the naked eye – goes the racket. Prosaic physiology alone applies the brakes. The socket of the arm says no, otherwise the spiritual momentum of the flick would carry you off for ever into the starry immensity. Yes, take me there, yes.

Forget the world in a grain of sand; if you would hold eternity, buy yourself a sandwich bat, study Victor Barna, and do as I did.

Impossible to describe the sensation of abandon which accompanies a perfectly executed backhand flick. Or the liberation. Or the relief.

It was like running away from home.

It was like having your in-between pulled.

It was like running away from home with Lorna Peachley.

It was like having your in-between pulled by Lorna Peachley . . .

Enough. None of those things happened.

I'd become a devil-may-care flicker, let's leave it at that. And I flicked myself into title after title, into the Hagganah averages, into the newspapers, into the national rankings, everywhere except into Lorna Peachley's pants.

This is the all-time loser's great inborn gift – he knows how to ensure that there remains one avenue of opportunity always closed to him, or to be more positive about it, one lane of disappointment forever open.

Let's get a few things clear. Had I wanted Lorna Peachley I could have had her. That's not arrogance, just simple teenage fact. For our age and for the times I was in possession of the necessaries. Girls respected me because there was still a whiff of

234

the shell-shrinker about me, a becoming withdrawal, a delicacy of feeling but without (any longer) the accompanying disfigurements of bashfulness. And thanks to Sabine Weinberger, I now knew that too much respect got you nowhere, that the time always came when you had to squat on their shoulders and insist on your way.

So I was covered for either eventuality.

I don't think it would be too far-fetched, either, to say that I actually did have my way with Lorna Peachley, given that what I wanted more than anything was not to have her. My desire for Lorna Peachley took the form of a yearning to belong to her, to be hers to do with as she chose, to lose and lose and lose and lose to her. And I did.

It was some time before I ran into her again after that first meeting in Burnley on Twink's last afternoon as a civilian. Her family had settled for a while in Timperley and had they been happy there it's unlikely I'd have seen as much of her as I subsequently did. She'd have starred for Cheshire, I'd have starred for Lancashire, we might have played against each other in a mixed doubles a couple of times a year, and that would have been that. Indeed we did play against each other for our respective counties once, in a deciding mixed doubles rubber in a church hall in Macclesfield, and that was when I acquired the taste for losing to her. I can still remember the shot that did it, a disguised angled half-volley that left me with my feet in a tangle, fending at air. It was on a crucial point. She raised her hands in a salute to her partner, sending a vibration through all her moving body parts. Her breasts shuddered, her belly quivered, and I don't think I can bear to describe – even now – what her vulva did. Was it the way she wore her shorts or was she just built differently from other girls? Transfixing, whatever the reason. The deep creviced V for victory of her mons Veneris never not visible, never not distinct, never not grand, never not moving.

Vulvas come and go in ping-pong as in everything else.

See one, some would say, and you've seen them all. But no vulva moved – actually *moved* and spoke to you – as Lorna Peachley's did.

Who can disentangle what from what in such a matrix of consequences? Which of Lorna Peachley's moving body parts, if any, was decisive in fixing me for ever in servitude to her? I can still see how her pony-tail pranced too, and how the light caught the lovesick purple of the ribbons she wore. Heart-breaking for me, ribbons in a lovely girl's hair. Was I touched, rather than stirred, into submission? And what if I'd won that point, what if you'd netted that half-volley and punched the air in frustration not triumph, sending a vibration of defeat not V for victory through your breasts, your belly, your pudendum (though where was your shame, Lorna Peachley)? Would everything have turned out differently in that case? Would I have loved you conventionally? Married you instead of Sabine Weinberger? Outraged my father who wanted me to practise on shikselehs, not marry them, however beautiful and touching and all-moving? Sired a couple of sweet half-Peachley gentile children, Sally and Nigel, instead of the rabid Channa and Baruch? And maybe stayed in touch with where I hailed from, at the intersection of the Irwell and the Bug, joined the Whitefield golf club with you, played bridge with you in Bury, instead of getting out, going as far away as possible, running running running from the tsatskes and the losing?

Doubt it. Seriously doubt it. A gorgeous prospect, but not for me. I had to lose to someone softer than myself. Lorna Peachley was ideal. Made for it. And there would always have been another winning point to set me off, had she not found just the shot to do it that afternoon in Macclesfield. She had more than half-volleys in her armoury.

Unhappy in Timperley, her family moved to Whitefield Heights. That was decisive. Now she could play for Lancashire. Now we could train together. Now I could be invited over to her house, where she had her own table, partly to practise, partly to give her parents, the doctors Peachley, a closer squizz at a Jewish person. They hadn't realized, when they'd shifted to Whitefield, that they were going to be the sole sandy Anglos in a concentration of ex-beetroot farmers from the banks of the River Dniester, recently made good. What they'd constructed their all-moving blue-black olives-in-garlic daughter out of, these lizard-still, cream-coloured Home Counties homoeopaths, I have no idea. It must have been a mystery to them too. And I guess that was another reason they had me round so often: they wanted to understand the manner of beast that had somehow snuck in between great-granny's sheets calling cuckoo! however many full moons ago.

Brian and Mary. Sweet people. I'd catch them staring at me intently when they thought I wasn't looking, trying to fathom my workings. How could an organism so hot still function? How did I see where I was going with all that hair hanging over my eyes? How come I didn't fall over, with such top-heavy brick shithouse shoulders? I should have introduced them to my father. He'd have tested their understanding of the human sciences.

Of course the other thing they were looking to see was what I might be doing to their daughter. The years were advancing, but we still hadn't reached that nadir of moral decline when parents invited you in to cohabit freely with their children. We were of the age of consent, but only just. Wisdom dictated that we shouldn't be given too much free scope. But they would never have had an inkling of what we were really up to. What *I* was really up to. Not Brian and Mary. Morbidities of the sort I favoured were not dreamt of in their philosophy. Else they'd have insisted we get on with regulation shtupping between games, like ordinary well-adjusted kids our age.

I was making their lovely daughter ill.

She wrote to me, asking me not to call on her for a while. She was confused. Upset. Suffering headaches. Feeling – she didn't know what – *peculiar*.

Welcome to the club. I'd upped the ante recently, having lost to her in a charity cup match, in full public view. A humiliation. A male player of my standing was not expected to go out to a woman, however good. And not so comprehensively. I felt the loss in what the Bible calls the bowels. It went straight there, like a low blow. A sort of nausea, but also a lightness, as if I hadn't eaten for a month. Dizzy, too. I could barely stay upright. Or together. I felt I was coming apart in strips. Disintegration of the moral fibre. You could have blown me over and shredded me. Or *she* could. But then she *had*. Losing to her on her home table in Whitefield with only Brian and Mary peeping was one thing, but out in the world, with all the world watching – oh, the horrid sickly beauty of it, like the sweet disgusting death smell of a bat cave. Too high. Too warm. Too naked. Too many. No god.

Think jealousy, if you're not familiar with the vertiginous sensation I'm describing. Think watching the woman you love submitting to another man's embraces where everyone can see. Go on, get into it! Think two fingers up the cunt. Think three if it'll help. Think everything Othello thought when he saw Sheeny Waxman wiping his dick on Desdemona's handkerchief. And now remove the third party. Keep it just between you and her. Except that there is no you. You're shredded. Blown apart. Not just disregarded but dismembered. Skinned until your bones squeak. And now sit back and enjoy.

It's only love you're experiencing, when all is said and done. Love with all the schmaltz removed. The house, the kids, the pension fund. It's only eroticism without the domestic aftermath.

We'd horseplayed, afterwards, back at her place, fallen into a bean-bag, rolled on to the floor. 'Beat you, beat you!' she'd laughed, and I'd manoeuvred myself so that she had her arm round my throat and I could barely breathe. 'Now finish the job,' I'd pleaded. The urgency in my voice surprised even me. 'One little squeeze. That's all it would take. I won't stop you. I *couldn't* stop you. You're too strong. I yield to you utterly. Make me nothing.'

And she'd laughed and squeezed and laughed some more until she realized that I meant it.

Hence the headaches.

She pointed her bat at my temples, like a pistol, some days later. After beating me again. Bang bang, you're dead. 'Not like that,' I'd said. And I'd taken the bat out of her hand and put the handle down my throat. Like that.

Hence the letter.

Don't take the bat metaphor too literally. I did for a while, in later years, when I was trying to make sense of it all. I frequented clubs where you could actually be beaten with an instrument resembling a ping-pong bat, that's if you can imagine a ping-pong bat made of leather and studs and someone in spiked boots wielding it. A paddle, they call it in the business. Fancy a paddling, me duck?

Altogether too literal. They're right to call themselves fetishists. They've lost the meaning in the means. They worship the mere instrumentation. You know the moment you bend over that that's not it, not it at all.

But you go ahead anyway. You slip your wrists into metal rings, consent to a leather strap closing around your throat, shut your eyes and put up with the grinding unimaginativeness of the ritual, so as not to cause offence or distress. For sadists, too, have feelings.

The last thing I wanted Lorna Peachley to do was hang me from the rafters and paddle me with her bat. Not the *very* last thing, but one of the last things. The point of the bat was that she should use me as she used it. I didn't want to suffer the bat, I wanted to *be* the bat. Let's be clear – not the ball, the bat. The bat. A bat has a handle, so does a man. Maybe it's all very simple really and goes back to the days when all those women took turns to hold me out. By the handle.

Had Lorna Peachley just taken me up by my handle and played a few games with me, all might have been well.

But Lorna wanted to be loved the way we all do.

Meanwhile, in the world of the living, that moral infection of triviality to which *both* sides of my family had always been susceptible had turned virulent. Not just tsatskes. Worse than tsatskes.

Machareikes.

My father had discovered battery-operated toys. Nothing wrong with that, if he'd confined his enthusiasm for them as a market line *to* the markets. But he didn't. He was carrying them around in his pockets and interrupting conversations with them, setting them up in the middle of a table at a Walzer wedding, or even in reputable restaurants, little battery-operated drummer bears, marching penguins, dogs that lifted their legs and did pee-pees. 'Joel!' my mother cried. To me she'd say, 'I don't know what to do with him. He's turning into an idiot!' Not that she was in any position to talk. Her own resistance to swag had been stormed long ago. A plastic palm tree now graced the steps to our front door. Not even a convincing plastic palm tree; not even green. The doorbell played the Chinese national anthem. A transistorized fish tank changed colours in the hall. There were no fish in it; they'd died of shock the day the water turned blood red. The phone was in the shape of a banana. When it rang a siren went off in every bedroom, and a toy fireman slid down a pole on the landing. 'I'm sorry but I think that's great,' the first of my older sister's boyfriends said. He supported Manchester City. 'Do you think they do one in City colours?' he asked. My father said he'd find out. My younger sister's boyfriend was a silver wedding and barmitvah crooner, a melter of melodies in the Frankie Vaughan style. Mo Drats was how he liked to be known professionally. Stardom backwards. A variation on those visual run-on names, like Nos Mo King. So why didn't he just call himself Ima Shmuck? He had a smetana and kez smile and a buttery handshake. (Or Smeta Naandkez?) You had to dry yourself on a tea towel after he'd left. He wondered if they did the banana phone in the shape of a microphone. 'I'll find out for you,' my father said. I could tell he enjoyed having my sisters' boyfriends around. They weren't stuck up like me. Though once they stopped being Jewish the temperature changed dramatically. It almost killed him, for all that, having to throw someone out of the house who appreciated his marching bears.

He'd threatened to do the same when Aunty Dolly brought home her shaygets from the dancing school, but the family rallied around her. Was he mad? Did he think Dolly could survive a second blow? What were we preserving her for anyway? Her womb had walked out on her soon after Gershom, so she wasn't going to shame us with flat-nosed babies called Graham like their father. And wasn't it astounding, really, that another chance had come her way? Jesus, Joel, you never expected she'd find one man to take an interest in her, never mind two! Just get her married and off, geshwint, surely that was the priority. He saw the logic of what we were saying. By the time we were through with him a Hottentot could have had Dolly with his blessing, had there been a Hottentot who wanted her.

So that was more triviality – dancing talk. One two three, one two three. And map reading. Dolly's shaygets was a map reader. He never came to our house or left our house, though he only lived in Kersal, without marking his route out on an ordnance survey map. And he never once came or left without getting lost.

'Perhaps you can help me here, Oliver,' he said to me on one occasion. He had about eight maps unfolded on the kitchen table. And a square map-magnifying glass. And a red felt marker. And a pocket compass.

'Why don't you just get a taxi?' I suggested.

He swallowed air. 'No chance of that,' he said brightly. 'Do you know how much I've saved in my life by never getting taxis?'

It goes without saying that *he* did. He went so far as to show me the actual sum in a cash book he carried everywhere with him. We were talking thousands, even then.

And then there was my grandfather, the dinky Polski princeling with the Droylesden larynx, whom we'd taken in after the death of my grandmother and stuck in a little extension we'd built specially for him at the back of the house, somewhere he could pick his toenails, watch television, and be spared the company of atheists. We'd hoped we could leave him locked up in there until the devil came to claim him, in the meantime shoving a tray of the Polski pap he liked to eat under his door, and occasionally a racing newspaper, thereby showing him more consideration than he'd ever shown anybody else; but eventually we had to let him out because he was staring into the neighbours' bedrooms all day and throwing chocolate wrappers out on to their lawns. I thought the sensible solution was to confiscate his spectacles and stop giving him chocolate, or just to board up his windows, but my mother was feeling sorry for him, now that he was no longer just a horrible old man but a hopeless and horrible old man. 'He *is* my father,' she had a crack at wailing, but we all looked at her. 'Well, he's a human being.' But that didn't wash either. We let him out to watch the downstairs television, anyway, which indulgence he repaid by recognizing the personalities aloud – 'There's that Lady Malcolm!' – and finding ways of getting to cop a feel of my sisters' girlfriends' breasts. 'Excuse me, love' – that was the giveaway phrase. 'Excuse me, love,' he'd croak, like a frog with a tracheotomy, and that meant there was an ashtray he needed to reach, a *Radio Times* he wanted to consult, a speck of dust he was unable to tolerate, all of them just, but oh so only just, the wrong side of Maxine Shneck's tit.

It would have been a matter of the finest discrimination, had anyone bothered to put his brain to it, which of them was copping the greater number of feels that year, Sheeny Waxman or my grandfather.

Long term – though I guess you'd need to verify this with Maxine Shneck and others – the only person to suffer any harm from my grandfather's depredations was me. Every time the privilege was granted me to trace with my fingertips the configuration of a breast, whether a loved one's breast or a stranger's, I would hear 'Excuse me, love' and see my grandfather.

Wasn't it enough that I was connected to him by blood? Did I have to be tied to him by desire as well?

It finished me for breasts, however you understand it. To this day I cannot go near them, cannot take the risk of seeing that indolent evacuated face loom up at me from the pillow.

In the end my sisters stopped bringing girlfriends home. That wasn't too much of a sacrifice: they had reached the age of ratting on their girlfriends anyway. My grandfather stood at our front gate for several months, looking out for them and throwing chocolate wrappers into the street, then went back inside and gave himself to television full time.

It was not without its satisfactions, seeing him reduced to the nothingness of telly watching. It made me believe in natural justice. He who lives a worthless life shall die a worthless death.

But until he actually did die he coughed his worthlessness over all of us. 'Isn't that that Eamonn Andrews?'

Which leaves only Aunty Fay. Fay of my perverted cut and paste days. Fay who had watched her spinster sisters slug it out over Gershom Finkel, while no one wondered if it might not be better, on further consideration, to run away with *her*. And yet she had her attractions, Aunty Fay, if you knew where to look for them. She had startled eyes, like a forest creature's. She had a dark covering of down on her arms, which perversely – but then I was a perverse boy – made her very feminine. And she looked good in high heels and suspenders scissored from the right page of *Span*. Some women come up best in filthy boys' imaginations. Fithy boys or filthy men, it doesn't matter much which, for filthy boys grow into filthy men. He was a filthy bastard good and proper, the one who got her on our banana phone one sultry summer's night. She thought it was her own father at first, on account of the gruff breathing. But he had too much curiosity to be her father. He wanted to know what colour she was wearing, so she told him. He meant *under* her dress, so she told him that too. And the material? A tricky question for Aunty Fay. *Was* there more than one sort of material? Not in the S for spinster sections of the stores she shopped at. Sacking, what else? Burlap. Was she saying she didn't own silk? She laughed. Silk? Her? What would she be doing with silk, whatever silk was. So he sent her a pair. Not too saucy either. Bought from Affleck's and folded genteelly in a white box, a message card attached. *With Kind Respects.*

And how did he come to have her address? Why, she gave it to him.

And the size?

She probably gave him that too. Not out of coquettishness. Out of naivety. She had no defences, Fay. She didn't know what from what. She was another one a Hottentot could have carried off.

'How many nights is this?' my father grumbled, staggering in with a cheese and onion pie wrapped in foil for my mother and finding Fay yet again on the blower, one leg curled under her, one stretched out, legs that joined in swishing silk now, Fay skittish, Fay feminine, Fay fey.

'Shush!' my mother said.

A miracle was unfolding. A third spinster was inching towards a husband.

'What's he going to send her this time?' my father said. 'A frontless brassiere?'

'Joel!'

The things my father knew! What was a frontless brassiere?

And had they met yet, Aunty Fay and her obscene caller? No. They were taking it cautiously. A step at a time. And was he still asking her about her underwear? In the main he wasn't. But then he didn't really have to, did he, since he'd chosen it for her. The perfect riposte, this, to the psychopath who rings you up and badgers you to tell him the colour of your scanties. Get him to go out and *buy* you your scanties.

So what were they discussing? Culture. He was a cultured man, her heavy breather. He liked reading, listening to music, going to the theatre and walking. That was when he could. For the last few years, while his late wife was dying of a slow wasting disease, he couldn't. Hence the loneliness, the wretchedness, the desperation, and as night follows day, the filthy phone calls. Now, though, with his new chum Fay Saffron, he could talk H. E. Bates and Terence Rattigan again to his heart's content.

If you could close your eyes to the manner in which he'd introduced himself, he was quite a catch. He even had a house in Alderley Edge.

'Alderley Edge!' my mother repeated. 'And he condenses books for the *Reader's Digest!*'

Yes, the moral infection of swag had taken its toll of us intellectually too. How long was it since any of the women in our house had bought a Collins Classic? Austens, Jane; Brontës, Charlotte; Gaskells, Mrs? – all forgotten. They read magazines now, showbiz gossip, tittle tattle about the Royal Family, and condensed books. And they'd stopped listening to Tchaikovsky. Once upon a time we'd sat in a circle in the dark, oying over the Overture to *Romeo and Juliet*. It had made us all lovesick together. Not any more. I had my own methods for making myself lovesick now and my aunties were getting off on Sammy Davis Jnr and the Melachrino Strings. We were acculturating to a lower class of English person.

Or *they* were. By way of compensation I was going far out in the opposite direction. I wanted nothing of anything that anyone I knew liked. It was a good job Twink had vanished from my life, otherwise I would have set about putting him right. Getting him on to Lieder instead of all that Puccini crap. Schubert, Twink, and not *Lilac Time* either.

Oh no, swag was not going to get me. I would belong to nothing and to no one rather than to swag.

But by God I had to fight against its volubility. The noise our culture made as it ran down! The racket!

We'd been softly spoken when we'd first bundled our belongings over from the Bug. Shush, lie low, keep shtum, and they may not notice we are here. But we'd forgotten our own lessons. Fallen in love with the host culture again, or rather with the lack of it. Even our pronunciation was deteriorating. Boggart Hole Clough, to take an example at random, Boggart Hole Clough where I'd picnicked as a little boy with some of my mother's friends from the International Brigade, hopping on to a bus at the bottom of Blackley New Road, Boggart Hole Clough which you would have thought was characterful enough already, was now Buggart 'Awl Cloof. We didn't hop on to a bus any longer either, we caught t'buzz. Nor did we picnic. We bootered buhns which we shuvelled into our cake'oles in frunt of t'telly. We sooked hoomboohgs. We moonched fuhdge. Soon we'd be throwing stones.

It was no quieter anywhere else in Kamenets Podolski, north Manchester. We were all racketin' down t'plug'ole together. Next door, where the Markses lived, was even worse. For his seventeenth birthday Selwyn Marks had been given a second-hand Morris Minor. His brother Louis flew back from Israel to teach him to drive it. He'd only been away a year but he was a different colour now – no longer dun from the Dniester but

Negev umber – and spoke with a broken accent. He knocked up with me on the table that was still out in their garden, balanced on a couple of dustbins, rotting, bubbling, whitened by the sun and the rain, curled at the corners. 'I cannot play tsis game any more,' he told me. 'I'm musclebound from drrriving jeeps.' He was in training to lift for Israel at the next Olympic Games. Which meant that while he could raise five grown men above his head he'd rupture himself if he had to bend down for a ping-pong ball. Selwyn had given up ping-pong altogether. Swimming too. Now he was going to be a racing driver. The only sport in which there was no anti-Semitism. 'How do you figure that, Selwyn?' I asked him. 'It's the helmets,' he said. 'They can't see how big your nose is.'

He should never have been allowed to sit at the controls of a car, with or without Louis next to him. He panicked too easily. Just reversing out of the path was more than he could manage without it erupting into a shouting match with every member of his family.

'I've *got* my left hand down. I've *got* my left hand down. What do you *think* I've got down.'

'Selwyn, go slower,' his mother called.

'Mother, if I go any slower I'll be going backwards.'

'Meshuggener!' his father shouted. 'You're already going back-wards!'

'I'm meant to be going backwards!'

'So go backwards!'

'But slower, Selwyn. Go slow. Where are you layfing to?'

'Now come up grradually off tse clutch,' you could hear Louis advising, next to him.

'Tse clutch? What's *tse* clutch all of a sudden. My car isn't fitted with tse clutch.'

'Selwyn, if you don't vant my chelp I can go back to Israel.'

'Vant! Chelp! Why are you talking to me like a fucking German?'

'Selwyn, wash your mouth out.'

'Wash my mouth out? What about vash my mouth out! How can I vash my mouth out ven I'm drriving. I'm drriving a fucking car here!'

'Selwyn, don't talk to your brother like that. He's come a hundred thousand miles to teach you.'

'I'm not talking to my brother.'

'Then who are you talking to? Your mother? You're swearing at your mother now!'

'Let him swear at me, let him swear. Just make him go slow.'

Slow? So far the car hadn't moved more than six inches. But it always ended the same way, with Selwyn snagging the gears, coming up too quickly off the clutch, burning the brakes, and slamming into the front wall.

'If you von't listen to me . . .' I heard Louis complaining one afternoon.

It was Friday. The early rush hour where we lived. Shabbes looming. Everywhere people returning home, bearing sweet red wine and milky bread, driving into their paths. Only Selwyn still trying to get out of his.

'I'm listening, I'm listening!' he was shouting. He was revving the engine hard. I could smell oil and burning rubber. The same smell that hung over Cheetham Hill for weeks after Copestake's warehouse had gone up in smoke.

'Then do vot I'm telling you. Always look in your mirror before rrreversing out.'

'How can I look in the mirror? I'm concentrating on my driving. If I look in the mirror I crash the car.'

'You'll crrrash the car anyway. You always crrrash the car.'

'What do you mean I always crash the car? When did I crash the car?'

'Selwyn, look in the mirrror.'

'I'm looking, I'm looking.'

'Now rrelease your chandbrake, slowly. Slowly! Vot gear are you in?'

'I'm in gear, how do *I* know which, I'm looking in my mirror.'

'Rrelease the chandbrake. You're rruining your brrakes. Rrelease your chandbrake, Selwyn!'

'Which is the handbrake?'

And then bang! Into the wall again.

'That's it,' Louis said, jumping out of the passenger seat. 'I cannot teach you! You're unteachable.'

'I wouldn't be unteachable if you were any kind of teacher. I can't understand what you're telling me. Suddenly you're talking to me like a Nazi. Vot's vid de vot? You go to Israel and you come back looking like a shvartzer and talking like Hitler.'

'You're a lunatic,' Louis said. 'You're a total tsedraiter.'

'*I'm* the tsedraiter! Who's the one that's asking me to do a hundred things at vonce? Take tse brake off, put tse brake on, look in tse mirror, change tse gears . . .'

'Lig in drerd, Selwyn! I should never chave tried! I should chave stayed in Eilat. Teach yourself to drrrive!'

And that was what Selwyn did. He looked in his mirror, found reverse, released his handbrake, eased off the clutch, backed into the street, changed into first and then second and then third, easy, sped towards the main road, had no idea what to do next, and plunged into the traffic like the person he had never in his life been, and never again would be, the bravest wildest maddest kid on the funfair dodgems.

Died on his way to hospital. Mangled. Killed by Christians. Was not how the local Jewish papers reported it. Merely: Selwyn Marks, younger son of Ida and Leon Marks. Tragically. Of multiple injuries. Only a few hundred yards from his home. Driving alone on a provisional licence. His car a seventeenth-birthday present from his loving parents.

Selwyn Marks, suddenly, to the grief of his distraught family.

Marks, Selwyn, beloved younger son and brother.

A flower ripped untimely from its stem.

Marks, Louis, stayed out in the garden for the whole of that night, howling like a wolf and pulling branches off the trees. My grandfather commented on his demented appearance the next day. 'Isn't he that wrestler – Jimmy . . . ?'

The noise was so frightening I wouldn't have dared going out to comfort him even if I'd been able to think of anything comforting to say. But I remained awake, watching from my bedroom window, in a sort of second-best vigil. I couldn't cry. Everything stopped at my throat. But it wasn't the stoppage I'd looked for from Lorna Peachley. That was a rapture. A lightness. This was heavy with fascination. Not the unimaginable torpor that followed my grandmother's death, either: the night that never knows the relief of morning; the grey half-lit dawn that never breaks into the colours of day. No, this was more dreadful because more exciting. I knelt at my bedroom window with my nose to the pane watching Louis tearing up the garden, and was exhilarated.

That was a big thing that was happening out there. A major event. Beautiful, as are all catastrophes.

It was only when he'd smashed the ping-pong table and then ripped apart the dustbins it had stood on, one after the other with his bare hands, banging the jagged sections against his chest, making the blood flow, that Louis went inside.

Inside.

Not so beautiful now.

Not so exhilarating suddenly.

And when I thought of what inside must have been like I was ashamed of myself for not crying for Selwyn and for merely playing at life and death with Lorna Peachley.

You should not make a tsatske out of mortality.

If that is not a commandment it ought to be.

So Lorna Peachley, too, through no fault of her own, became associated with that moral infection of triviality which I was determined to escape.

But not just yet.

THREE

It is definitely harmful to your game to take up a racket unless you are in the mood.

Victor Barna

EVERY MORNING AT school assembly, after prayers, the head-master coughed, looked up like a conductor waiting for his orchestra to settle down, put his thumbs into the lapels of his gown, and read out the names of boys who had achieved something – let it be academic, artistic, sporting or simply in the field of personal development – of which the school could be proud. Stuart Grimshaw had won a place to study hairdressing at Sale College of Advanced Education – well done, Stuart. Mick Hargreaves had saved a cat from drowning in the Irwell – step up to collect your medal, Mick. Doug Swindells had kept a clean sheet in goal for Newton-le-Willows Nebbishkeits, including saving a penalty, *and* his mother was in hospital having her varicose veins removed – we're all behind you, Dougie.

Notice anyone missing? Proud of, and behind whom, the school was not, even though he was currently the fourth ranked ping-pong player under eighteen in the country, holder of nine titles, and owner of more silver cups and medals than Stuart Grimshaw, Mick Hargreaves and Dougie Swindells had had hot dinners?

In the six years I was at the school only one truly accomplished and successful athlete emerged, and that was me. The rest were just nochshleppers. And yet not one word of my accomplishments did it breathe. Which is why when the Old Boys' Newsletter arrives, asking for help to build a new gymnasium, I recite a little curse over it and throw it in the bin. Oliver's revenge.

I did once summon up the courage to knock on the headmaster's door, to formally lodge a complaint. 'What's your problem, Mr Horsfield – isn't the game at which I excel shaygets enough for you? Do you have to kick shit out of people before you consider it sport round here? Do you have to roll in mud and shove your face up someone's arse? Is it too much for you to bear, you yiddenfeit, you anti-Semitic piece of crap, that we should be good at a game *and* win scholarships to Oxford and Cambridge? Is that more than an erstwhile fucking Church of England grammar school can swallow? Well prepare to swallow more, shithead. Meet the master race. You're looking at a double starred first *and* the next World Ping-Pong Champion. Won't *that* be something for you to ignore in favour of how Albert Shaygets came last in the All Radcliffe fishing gala with an already dead mackerel measuring a quarter of an inch – we're all proud of you Albert, you dim-witted freckled little snub nose petseleh, you!'

What I actually said, or rather what I found a roundabout way of wondering, was whether the headmaster was apprised of the fact that I had just represented my county at table tennis. Yes, he affirmed, looking me up and down as though I might be dripping something offensive and indelible on his carpet, yes he was, and he congratulated me if I had attained to something I had wanted, but the school, the *school* attached no more value to what I did on a ping-pong table than to what I did on a shove-halfpenny board. Anything else, Walzer?

You plough a lonely furrow as a ping-pong champion, that's my point. I'm not surprised I got high on losing. At least people *like* you when you lose.

But I didn't start losing all at once. It wasn't a matter of going down to Lorna Peachley and her zinging pudendum and immediately dashing out and losing to the whole world. Quite the opposite at first. What worked best was to beat absolutely everybody and *then* lose to Lorna. You have to be rich to be comprehensively fleeced. You have to have something they want to steal. And you can't go from high to low in a single sweet disgusting bat's cave instant if you're flat on your belly when you start.

It was always when I'd just lifted another title that the longing for Lorna Peachley to take me by my handle and wield me was at its strongest. Behold, the conqueror returns – Imperial Caesar, Tamburlaine, Napoleon, wreathed in garlands, god-like, riding in triumph through Persepolis. Now approach, my little soft-limbed silver-throated witch, unbuckle here and make the tyrant tremble at your feet . . .

Pure pornography. The sexual history of slaves. The epic poem, as old as religion itself (and we are good at religion, my people), chanting the exultant longed-for fall from high to low. But all pornography must end in death – so did I mean it? Did I really really mean it?

Of course not. I was tsatskying. Even when I gave her my throat I was only tsatskying. I'd have run a mile had she put a mark on me. But it felt as though I meant it.

At the last I was only answering a challenge buried deep in the social history of the game itself. It was too small. A parlour game. It suffered from too modest a conception of itself. *Ping-pong* – what kind of name was that? Table tennis was hardly any better, with its reminder of all the ways in which it wasn't tennis proper, real tennis, tennis in the open air, tennis under the sun, tennis that bit into your flesh and turned it the colour of maple syrup, big tennis, expansive tennis, jet-set tennis, tennis for grown-ups, tennis which Jezebels rolled up to watch in their thousands, tennis which made heroes and heartthrobs out of tennis players. Name me ten table tennis players for whom your heart throbs. Name me five. Name me one.

Table tennis. Ping-pong. Gossima . . . Think of it, *gossima*! A good name for a condom, what? You won't even know you're wearing it. Whiff Waff was another one they tried. Meaning what? Something insubstantial, piffling, neither here nor there, like swatting at flies. You won't even know you're playing it. Why didn't they just call it that – *Something Piffling* – and have done?

And what do you do, Mr Walzer? I excel at Something Piffling.

Doesn't it make perfect sense to choose to lose, finally, at such a game?

And what do you do, Mr Walzer? I fail to make an impression at Something Piffling.

Choose to lose at something small and don't you as a consequence win at something big? Was that not the paradox embraced by Jesus Christ our Lord? Forgo the whole world and thereby gain eternity? (I've said we are good at religion, my people.)

This is not a rationalization, though I see that it may appear that way. Grandiose in my ambitions I may have been, but in the final analysis I was never comfortable winning. I didn't like the way it made me feel. And I never liked the way it made other people look. I remain a devoted student of the subject to this day – the illness of winning. I watch it day in and day out on television. I know the personalities – just like my grandfather did. Nastase, McEnroe, Navratilova, Coe, Christie, Lewis, Budd, Klinsmann, Cantona, every member of every Australian cricket team, Tyson, Eubank, Ballesteros, Norman, Hill, Schumacher, Curry, Cousins, Torvill, Dean. A roll call of the psychotic. It's like having television cameras running day and night in an asylum. Me me me me me me me me me me me me. And I am as transfixed by it as anybody. I can't get enough. It's like seeing your own soul out there, your own pumping heart, blood-red like meat in a butcher's shop, charging around in shorts and running shoes. It's like watching your own steak and kidney kishkies punching the air.

The ultimate B-movie. *The Horror of the Human Will.* Forget the Creature from the Black Lagoon. Forget the Fly. This one's really sticky. This one's come out of soup too disgusting to describe. And the telly commentators call it character.

So am I the only Christian around here? Am I the only one who believes that character is letting the other sinner win?

Here, have. You want it? You want it *that* much? Then have it, you sick fuck.

Geh gesunterhait, as Jesus would have said.

In an actual life, of course, these things have their own vicissitudinous way of working themselves out; they have a chronology, a history of apparent accidentality, they come off other people like balls off the walls of a squash court. I was destined to throw matches, to give up, to walk away, to storm off the table because my opponent was trying too hard – such an eventuality was written in my blood, it was always going to happen – but it took Lorna Peachley to get me started.

We were seeing each other again. I'd kept away, after her note, respecting her right not to be given headaches or otherwise made to feel peculiar by me. Up to her to decide what next, if anything. And when. I missed her, but I had no desire to ruin the poor girl's life.

She kept me waiting for about a fortnight, then she phoned, her voice slightly chilly, but not downright freezing, reminding me that a match against Hampshire, her old county, was coming up – a needle match for which she was eager to be on the top of her form – and wondering therefore if we oughtn't to get some serious practice in. We didn't discuss what had passed between us. We just knocked up for hours, careful never to play an actual game, for fear that I'd lose it and the whole thing would start all over. She kept her tracksuit bottoms on the whole time, too, just in case – I presumed this was her reasoning – just *in case* the sight of her prancing pudendum got me thinking about death again.

As if.

I'm sorry for Lorna Peachley. I'm sorry for all lovely girls. They fear they are the cause of their own troubles, but are never quite sure why. If they cover up a little – if they hide this bit or that bit – will it save them? Will someone then love them the way they long to be loved, without complications, without giving them headaches, just for themselves?

We won handsomely against Hampshire, paired exquisitely and chastely in the mixed doubles, saying excuse me if our shoulders brushed, and then contrived to stay over in Winchester an extra night. I was driving now. My father had lent me his back-up van, the Bedford dormobile with the sliding doors, on the understanding that I'd pick up a gross of two-pound sugar bags for him on my way out of town and on my way back in. Sugar was his new plunder line. Out they go and out they go! It was part of our war against the food boys. They'd taken to introducing swag lines, so we'd taken to introducing food. Tins of pink salmon at first. Then ham in triangular tins. Then tea. Now sugar. Knocked out at cost, sometimes below cost. Loss-leaders. And we led at losing, we Walzers. We got through mountains of the stuff. The trouble was the food boys had ordered the cash and carries to stop serving my father. As yet they didn't all know who I was. They didn't make the connection. So I was the sugar shlepper. Provided I picked up as many two-pound bags of sugar as they'd serve me every time I drove it, I could have the van. Which was fine by me now that I'd learnt from Sheeny the trick of criss-crossing the bags in the aisle between the rear seats so that they made a bed. A sugar bed. A bed of pure sweetness. On which, in a lay-by outside Winchester, Lorna Peachley stretched out all her moving body parts, exhausted from their exertions against her old county, and went to sleep in my arms.

We woke in the middle of the night, laughing, with granules squirting into us from underneath.

'Great idea, Sheeny,' I said later. 'That's got to be the worst bed I ever slept on.'

'Did you get what you were after or not?' he asked me.

A tough question. 'Yes,' I said. 'I got what I was after.'

'Then don't complain,' Sheeny said.

Did I get what I was after?

She was beautiful to hold, granulated or not. She melted in my arms. She had that gift. The moving body parts. She fitted everywhere. Her bones folded. She flowed into you like hot wax. And she was more fragrant than a field of flowers. And more flavoursome. Lucozadey, minty, malted milkshakey. Not olivey, as you'd have expected. Not sun ripened. Not sun dark. But sun yellowed. All things white and golden. Honey and yoghurt. I could have drunk her perspiration. I *did* drink her perspiration. I rolled on top of her and licked it from her neck. Then she opened her mouth, and I was gone, vanished, a sea creature that lived a life of complete happiness, wanting for nothing, in the spaces between her syrup gums. And the one luxury item I am allowed to have with me on my Desert Island, to go with the Bible and the eight records of Schubert Lieder? Lorna Peachley's mouth.

And don't come looking for me, please.

The gift. Some have it, some don't. And there's never any way of knowing until you get in there and find out. The gift of bodily mellifluousness. It's more than physical. The body alone cannot generate such music. In Lorna's case it felt ethical. She had a daily beauty in her life.

So you could say she was my big chance.

'Hold me,' she said.

But I couldn't.

I could *take* hold. And of course I could *be* held. But I couldn't *give* hold.

'Love me,' she said.

But I couldn't.

I could *make* love. And of course I could *be* loved. But I couldn't *give* love.

She clutched at me as though she was drowning. I had fucked her head, punched holes in her, and now she was drowning, wouldn't I save her? If I could have, I would have.

She sat up, and brushed sugar from herself. 'Why did you bring me here?' she asked.

I shrugged in the dark. 'Because I wanted to be with you.'

'No, you didn't.'

Didn't I? I shrugged some more.

'I don't think you know what you want,' she said.

She sounded very bitter, weary and without hope, just as my grandmother used to sound.

I said nothing. I sat with my head between my knees and spun in the blackness like a satellite.

'I think you're too complicated for me,' she said. 'I don't understand what you're up to half the time. I can never tell what you want. You make me feel stupid.'

'I'm sorry,' I said, still spinning between my knees. 'I don't mean to do that. I don't think you're stupid. I think you're lovely.'

'Lovely isn't the opposite of stupid,' she said.

'I don't think you're stupid.'

'Well that's how you make me feel. Stupid and useless. Do you think I don't know that you lose to me on purpose? Why are you trying to make a fool of me?'

'I don't lose to you on purpose. And I'm not trying to make a fool of you. I like losing to you.'

'There you are! You *like* losing to me. You do it on purpose.

What for? Why are you making me ill? Why do you bring me out here in this horrible van and then go all touch-me-not on me? What are all these games, Oliver?'

'Believe me, Lorna, I have not gone touch-me-not on you. I have never wanted to touch anyone more.'

'You're not there, Oliver. You're just not there.'

'I'm here,' I said.

'Yes, *you're* here. But your heart isn't. That's if you've got a heart.'

'I've got a heart . . .'

'You just don't feel anything with it.'

'I do.'

'What do you feel?'

I paused. 'Love for you.'

No good. I heard it myself. No good. No bass in it. No weight. No heart. Just Whiff Waff. And you don't get a second go.

'Take me home, Oliver,' she said. 'And then please leave me alone. Go and lose to someone else.'

So I did.

No reason to do otherwise now. Why win? If there was no eel-slick little witch waiting to unbuckle, and take it all away from me again, why bother to ride in triumph through Persepolis in the first place?

No more interest in winning for its own sake?

Couldn't do it. Now that I was entering the men's game, putting away childish things, I couldn't do it. Winning is a test of character, as every sporting commentator will tell you, and I didn't have any character. Grandiosity, yes. Skills, yes. But character? Bottle? Creature from the Black Lagoon determination, knowing what you want and allowing nothing and nobody to stand in your way? Forget it.

I dropped myself from the county team so that Lorna could go on playing uncompromised. I suppose you could say that that showed character of sorts. But I was only getting in before they did. My form was shot. I went for six weeks without winning a game for the Hagganah. And serious questions were being asked about my temperament. Even about my manners.

Things came to a head the night we played the Railways, away. This was never a fixture I'd enjoyed. Even allowing for how little I enjoyed any fixture these days, in the company of the unfanatics, the otherwise engaged who were now my team-mates, the Railways stood out as dismal. The playing conditions were partly to blame. The Railways Social Club was a single room, painted glossy St Onan's Church of England Grammar cream, through which ran more pipes than I had ever seen and which also housed the staff lockers, banks upon banks of them in pitted tin, like a mausoleum for lunch boxes, each one individually defaced with purple marker for identification purposes. This meant that at any time some sooty engine driver would barge in, regardless of the state of play, in order to change into a clean singlet. And you don't argue with an engine driver, or with a guard come to that, when he's just come in off his shift. In an earlier confrontation with the railways I'd hit a ball which landed in a guard's locker just as he was closing it. 'I won't be opening that again, flower,' he informed me, 'until I'm back from Doncaster.' To make things worse the tannoy system had to be on at all times, so that everyone could be made aware of any emergencies, derailments, late arrivals and departures, changes to the roster and so on. And you know what it's like trying to make sense of anything anybody says into a railway microphone. 'Is that me they're calling?' your opponent would suddenly wonder, if you happened to be playing well; and he'd be off to find out, leaving you standing there like a coitus interruptus, going off the boil.

Have I said that there were showers in here as well, behind the highest and most precarious burial pyre of lunch boxes? You could hear them singing as they lathered, drivers, guards, porters, furnace men, getting up steam. 'When your swer-her-heetheart, sends a leh–heh–letter, of goo-hoo-hoodbye . . .' You felt close enough to soap their backs.

'Shut up!' one of the ping-pong players would always shout, feebly, without any expectation of success. 'We're trying to concentrate here. It's match night!'

Came the invariable reply: 'Get fucked – this is a play area!'

The real Hagganah men handled it better than I did. Another night, another fixture, another win.

But *they* weren't in decline. They weren't terminal either/or merchants. They were just taking a break from what else interested them in life. So it was no skin off their noses how distracting the conditions at the Railways were, or what manner of beast you had to play when you got there. Whereas I was personally affronted by every single member of the Railways team, the thin streaks of piss that they were, with their dowager humps and their ruched reptilian necks and their shorts always too brief and their self-castigations – 'Rubbish, you clown!' – and their self-exhortations – 'Come on, these five! come on, these four! come on, these three!' – and their cute nicknames for themselves – Royboy, Stanley Roylance called himself, 'That's it, Royboy, let's go, that's it now' – lanky, loping, leaping, undernourished, their thin hair stuck up as though electrocuted, their little all-bone tocheses stuck out indomitable as goitres, creatures from the black lagoon of the blind will. What were they doing anywhere near my game, whose subtleties were first revealed by moon-faced pessimistic lugubrious men from Hungary and Czechoslovakia – Barna, Vana, Farkas, Boros, Tsorres – witty hangdog Bug and Dniester losers who played in long trousers and collars and ties?

'I don't know about you . . .' Sheeny whispered as we took our seats.

'Me neither . . .' I said.

'They're so . . .'

'I couldn't agree more . . .' I said.

'Where do they . . . ?'

'Say no more,' I said.

We both knew where they . . . The black lagoon.

'Soft hands, let's go!' Roylance urged himself. He was a game down against Saul Yesner, and not liking it. 'What am I doing losing to this twat?' I heard him asking himself as he towelled off. Icy beads of perspiration ran down his throat, as slippery as mercury, not the tropic springs that burst boiling from our pores. 'Come on, Royboy, come on now!'

It sometimes happens that one player has all the luck that's going. You're meant to live with it. Your turn tomorrow. Tonight, fortune favoured Saul. First an edge. Then the top of the net. Then another edge. And then another. Roylance couldn't live with it. 'How many's that?' he exploded. 'Not again!' And then under his breath, 'You jammy twat!'

Saul Yesner raised his hand in apology each time, but otherwise let nothing disturb his concentration. He played like the three wise monkeys. A model of shrewd discretion three times over. He seemed to inhabit some other sphere, like a holy man. It was as though the god of ping-pong played through him. He merely interpreted, making the word flesh. So don't blame him for the flukes – he was just the messenger.

He won easily, without the slightest sign that his victory mattered or came as any surprise to him. Of course he won easily! He no more expected to lose than to feel any of the punches we threw at his stomach.

Royboy could barely find it in himself to shake hands. I could see his lips forming the word twat over and over again.

So when it came to my turn against him it was already a grudge match in my heart if not in his. I murdered him, therefore – is that what you expect to hear? I tore him limb from fleshless limb? I made lean mincemeat of him? I feasted on his kishkies?

It was my match to win, let's put it that way. I held a five-point lead over him when we changed ends in the final game. On my serve. The first of which, a backhand topspin corner to corner sandwich special, I over-hit. Not by much but by enough. It gave him confidence. He hitched his shorts, stuck his toches out and decided to make a fight of it. 'Come on Royboy, these four. These three.' He sweated over every point, pilules of ice-cold mercury, lifted his hand to call a let if there was the slightest distraction – and when wasn't there? – and glowered at me from the other end of the table, as though it mattered, in the end, who won and who didn't.

My lead narrowed but I held on to it. 19–16, with me to serve. He caught me at 19 all.

At which moment someone in overalls walked in to use the phone. Have I said that there was a public phone with an acoustic hood over it in the ping-pong room? This caller was at least aware that he'd chosen a bad moment. 'I'll just *dial* in here,' he said, disappearing behind the door when his number rang, tugging at the phone lead to get as far away from us as was possible. But we could still hear him describing what he wanted for supper.

'Jesus, Joseph and fucking Mary,' Roylance said.

'Let!' called the referee.

I said nothing. Just bounced the ball on the linoleum floor seventeen or eighteen times.

Roylance took up his feral crouch. 'These two, Royboy. Come on, soft hands. These two.'

And that was when my nerve snapped. If he wanted it that badly then he could have it. If I'd been any kind of fighter I'd have made the opposite resolution. If you want it that badly, you sick fuck, you deranged twat-caller, then I'm going to be the one who sees to it you're never going to get it. But that would have entailed my sticking out my toches and mixing it with him. Accepting that we inhabited an identical universe of desire and will. And that I couldn't do. Didn't have what it took. No character. No bottle. Never was a mixer, as my father would have told you.

264

So I did the next best thing. I gave it to him as a gift. I had neither the character to win nor the character to consent graciously to his winning. So I gave it to him. You want it that much? Here, have! Geh gesunterhait, go with god's blessing. And I very obviously served off the table, two preposterously over-hit forehand topspin serves that missed the table by a half-room's length, sending the ball soaring high over the lunch boxes into the railwaymen's showers.

Now no one had won, except on paper.

I can't speak for other sports, but this is not something you do in ping-pong. It's against the spirit of the game. It's ungenerous. It creates bad feelings.

Royboy didn't so much shake my hand as slap it. 'A win's a win,' I heard him saying to his team-mates. 'I don't care how I beat the twat.' But their captain came over to our captain, and our captain had to make a formal apology.

He said nothing to me that night, but he was on the phone to me early the next morning. 'Phil Radic here, Oliver. I've been talking things over with the boys, and we're wondering if you need a few weeks off.'

'Is that a nice way of saying you're dropping me, Phil?'

'You're wrong, Oliver. I'm the team captain. I don't have to find a nice way of doing anything. I think you've been playing too much, that's all. I think you should rest yourself for a match or two.'

'Look, Phil,' I was surprised to hear myself saying, 'why don't you just admit you're dropping me and call it a day at that?' I remember being pleased that I had found the social confidence to take no shit. Once you've been in a shell, you are never free of it. You are always map reading, measuring how far you've ventured out.

'Do you want to come over to the club tonight to discuss it?' Phil Radic asked.

Language traps you every time. A different question might

have elicited a different answer. But, 'I don't really think there's anything to discuss, Phil,' just seemed irresistible, somehow.

And then I put the phone down.

And never played a game of ping-pong in Manchester again.

FOUR

B UT THAT STILL left Cambridge.
And come to that, as far as warm life went, it still left the Kardomah.

My two fall-back positions. You cover yourself if you're grandiose. You can forgo being the best at one thing if you're confident you can be the best at another.

Royboy Roylance wouldn't have been able to find his way to the Kardomah in a blue fit. Point to me. Phil Radic would, but where's Cambridge, Phil? Another point to me.

See how it works.

But it meant that I was necessarily a faithless bastard. Ping-pong? What's that when it's at home?

And what's *home*?

It's a dangerous game to play. You can run out of fall-back positions in the end. You can be left with nothing to beat anybody with. And then where are you?

BOOK IV

ONE

'Ping-pong, Pnin?'
'I don't any more play at games of infants.'

Pnin, Vladimir Nabokov

T HE KARDOMAH WAS my last throw of the tsatske dice, my last spin of the draidle.

On a crunching colourless December morning my mother came into my room with a telegram from Cambridge in her hand. I was lying on my bed, looking out of the window, staring into the grim grey space where a sky should have been, waiting. 'I haven't opened this, darling,' she said. 'But don't be too downhearted. There's still Aberystwyth.'

I grabbed it from her. 'They're not going to be sending me a telegram,' I said, 'to tell me that I've *not* got in. Are they?'

'They could have made a mistake,' she said. And she fled from me, unable to bear the sight of disappointment dawning in my eyes.

They hadn't made a mistake. Not in her sense, anyway.

Later, when I got there and discovered what an exclusively muscular college Golem was, it was brought home to me that I'd been given a place chiefly on the strength of my ping-pong. Golem College boasted more rugby blues than any other college,

271

more cricket blues, more hockey blues, more soccer blues; it fielded the entire Cambridge real and lawn tennis teams; half the Cambridge Hunt; and it had been Head of the River since there was a river. Its only shortcoming was in the sphere of table sports: billiards, bridge, brag, shove halfpenny, ping-pong – anything for which you didn't need to wear a jock. Hence me.

And I'd thought it was my misogyny that had got me in.

But a place is still a place.

What I'd have done had I not got into Golem College I don't know. It wasn't just to get me over ping-pong that I'd fallen back on Cambridge in advance; it was also to get me over Lorna Peachley. I don't recall taking her attack on me as an absent person too much to heart. I knew things about me that she didn't know. But I missed her. I missed our practice sessions. I missed looking at her across the net. I hadn't loved her. I'd messed around with my feelings for her too much to be left with anything as clean as love. I was conscious of a lack, though, and I gave it her name. I kept thinking I saw her in the street. Several times I actually ran after and accosted her, only to find it was someone else. And that's almost love, isn't it? The KD could compensate, as far as mere animal company went, but it couldn't replace her. Whereas Cambridge, I fancied, would give me another crack at her, or at least at someone like her. Someone who had a daily beauty in her life.

In the meantime I had to decide what I was going to do with myself between now and next October, when Cambridge started up for me. I was damned if I was going to stay on at school as a sort of living treasure. Oh yes, Horsey Horsfield was proud of me now – Walzer this and Walzer that – but Horsfield could go to the knacker's yard as far as I was concerned. Love me, love my bat. Except that I could no longer remember where my bat was. And no longer cared. 'What you could do,' my father said, 'is work with me for the next six or seven months.' But the gaffs were going down the tubes, as a consequence of the amount of loss-leading we were doing, and I knew my father would have had trouble paying me. There was even a growing feeling that it wouldn't hurt if I started paying *him*. So I took a job driving a stop-me-and-buy-one ice-cream van in the hope that there'd be a few shillings left over to help the Walzer family finances after tax and whatever I emptied into the cash registers of the Kardomah.

In the winter? Well there's the funny thing about ice-cream. People eat more of it when it's cold and wet than when it's hot and dry. They did in the part of Manchester I serviced, anyway. It's a boredom thing. What else are you going to do in Middleton and Radcliffe when it rains? You stay in, watch the telly, scratch your parts and lick a lolly. This is evening psychology I'm describing. I chose the evening shift. That way I could spend all day at the Kardomah. And afterwards nip into Laps' so that the younger kids could get a gander at me – one-time flicker and chopper extraordinaire, spieler emeritus, now Cambridge double starred misogynist elect.

I wore a yellow nylon coat with deep pockets, played 'Greensleeves' on my chimes, and had to hop out to serve from the side of the vehicle every time I had a customer. Van? Vehicle? It was barely a car let alone a van. A cut-down mini with a cool-box at the back. A fridge on wheels. But the exercise kept me trim. And there was more intimacy in the contact than you get in the conventional stand-up soft-serve Monteverdi van. It was good for pulling, that's what I'm getting at. Women like a nice fresh-faced broad-shouldered young matriculant in a yellow nylon coat, who gives them free ice-creams. They did in the part of Manchester I serviced, anyway.

Make no mistake, those were heady days to be selling ice-cream. Advances in refrigeration and freezing techniques, to say nothing of innovations in artificial flavouring, meant that there was always some new line to introduce the public to. We would be introduced to them ourselves in the depot every

Monday morning, all twenty-four of us, the entire retail sales staff, standing shoulder to shoulder in our deep-pocketed nylon coats, heads down like recaptured truants, waiting for the manager to come out of his office carrying his refrigerated briefcase from which he would draw out, one at a time, one for each of us, the latest wafer, lolly, cornet, ice-pop, tub. Only when we were all provided, and on a signal from the manager, a lordly nod of the head – 'Now!' – would we unwrap in unison, and taste. 'Well, Walzer?' 'Extremely good, sir. I especially like the suggestion of caramel, and the contrast between the soft ice-cream and the hard biscuit. It's like a split with an extra surprise thrown in. I think they're going to take to it, yes, yes I do. And if I may add one more word – (let Rushdie tell you what he likes: I thought of it first) – 'naughty, sir, but nice.' He was an Oxford man himself, our depot manager, but he still admired fluency. 'Excellent, Walzer. Couldn't have put it better. The target for this depot is twenty thousand pieces a week. I believe we can beat that. What say you men?'

'We can beat it easy, sir. We can thrash the living daylights out of it. We can have it for dinner.'

'Exactly what I think.' He kept his refrigerated briefcase open on the desk, so that we should have somewhere to deposit the wrappers and the sticks, when there were sticks. The moment we were all finished he'd snap it shut. The briefing was over. 'Now let's get out there and move them!'

A lady over here and a lady over there.

I did well. I was salesman of the month three months running.

But then when all is said and done, I'd had the training.

And I liked where the driving took me: the wet melancholy lanes and culs-de-sac, many of them still cobbled, reflecting the bile-yellow end-of-humanity phosphorescence of the street-lamps; the back-to-back and front-to-front workers' cottages built in the same sickly pink you'd get in our Neapolitan wafers;

the swag vases in the windows; the swag ornaments; the swag doorknockers and doormats; and the sallow northern women coming out with the telly still flickering in their eyes and their purses chinking. And I say I *liked* this? Yes. What I liked was that I was saying goodbye to it; that soon I would never see it again. No more North, no more poverty, no more wet, no more tsatskes – a few more months and then gone for ever!

The best of them, the more presentable of the tsatskes, I took to the Kardomah to be seen with. They scrubbed up well. They could have done with work putting into their pronunciation of the mother tongue, but I was hardly one to talk. I was Boogart' Awl Cloofin' it with the best of them now, despite all my efforts to stay clear of the infection, and anyway, as Sheeny said, in an interesting inversion of one of Jesus's more controversial aphorisms, it wasn't for what came *out* of their mouths that we valued them.

Sheeny had changed in the time I'd known him. He rarely head-jockeyed now. Whether this had anything to do with Sabine Weinberger, whether she'd converted him to passivity, I cannot say, but ever since that evening in Benny the Pole's squeaking pad he had become lazy and quiescent, looking to be done to rather than to do. I'd collect him sometimes, in my father's van, and drive him to one of the streets on my ice-cream round where a couple of tsatskes would be waiting. He never got out of the van or even made an effort to be introduced; he'd just lie there on the sugar bags like a sheikh, with his flaming putz out, engorged and ticking – for his putz too suffered from the same nervous twitch as the rest of him – waiting to be fellated.

'Couldn't you at least have kept it in your hasen until we drove away from their front door?' I'd expostulate with him, afterwards.

'Did *they* complain?'

'That's not the point, Sheeny.'

'So what's the point?'

'This is my round. This is where I sell ice-creams. They know me here.'

'So you should thank me.'

'Why should I thank you?'

'For giving them a thirst. Oink, oink!'

I wouldn't reply.

'Oink, oink?'

'OK, Sheeny. Oink, oink. Now put it away.'

'What for? Aren't we going to Laps' now?'

He was right. Not about my needing to thank him, but that they didn't complain. I've always been surprised about that – just how compliant women are when it comes to the putz. No one tells you that when you're cowering in your shell. You drag the ocean bottom of your imagination and come up with the insane idea that it might be something to slide your in-between between a lady's painted lips and then suffer months of shame for sinking to such depths. And all along the ladies are thinking the same thought. Not every one of them gave Sheeny what he wanted straight away. Some of them felt as I did, that it was preferable to wait until we'd driven fifty yards down the street. But none ever said, 'How dare you assume that I'll suck on that thing just because you've got the chutzpah to have it hanging out?'

This is not sour-grapes misogyny. I got my share. But I was an incorrigible foreplay man. I liked to know their names. I liked to talk about the weather. I liked to know what they were reading. *Then* I liked to fish my putz out.

And it upset me that all women weren't insistent on these necessary little social rituals themselves.

Partly I felt this out of respect for the women who had brought me up. I wouldn't have wanted to think that any aunty of mine, or any sister come to that, would have woodpecked Sheeny the way those Middleton women did, without a by your leave. But my relative squeamishness proved something else, too. I wasn't the real thing. I wasn't Kardomah to my soul. As far as tsatskying went I was merely a tourist.

I tried the Waxman method just once. I interrupted my ice-cream round one wet bile-yellow but still somehow sticky April evening to pick up a bull-necked choc-ice fresser who'd been giving me the nod every night for a week. 'Get in,' I said. I didn't even open the passenger door of my stop-me-and-buy-one for her. I let her walk around of her own volition and climb in. Then I parted my yellow nylon coat and pulled out my putz. Then I drove up into the fields behind the brickworks, turned the engine off, and sat back the way I'd seen Sheeny do. Sat back and looked down over the shot-towers and chimneys of Middleton. She couldn't reach me. Her neck was not flexible enough. And the mini was not coach-built with Sheeny Waxman ask-no-questions fellatio in mind. 'Out,' I said. Then I lay down in the clammy field and waited for her to do me there. No, warm for the time of year, isn't it. No, I'm going to Cambridge at the end of the year, and what do you do for a crust. No, read any good books lately. And it worked. Sheeny was right. She didn't complain. It's even possible she was grateful not to be harassed with small talk. The only one experiencing difficulties was me. I had been too well brought up. It had always seemed to me that politeness demanded a big come. Astounded expression, rolling eyes, spasming shoulders, quivering feet, ten-minute howl – the works. But half-way through Act IV Scene v I over-convulsed and spilled the change from the pockets of my nylon coat. The evening's takings, all of it in threepenny bits and sixpenny pieces, flung far and wide across the meadow of old bricks and weeds. I finished coming then got her to help me gather in the dosh. Anyone watching would have thought we were lovers in the grass, looking for four-leaf clovers and daisies to chain around each other's necks. We fell to talking as we searched, whatever we were, which I suppose you could say was a sort of foreplay after the event. Also not something Sheeny expended any energy on. So I still wasn't able to feel I'd succeeded in being a callous carefree fellatee.

I didn't find all the takings either. And that wasn't the end of my problems. So little was I a callous carefree fellatee that I'd taken the keys out of the ignition when I lay me on the grass – don't ask me why: just to be on the safe side, I suppose, just in case she decided to swallow those as well, just in case she had a mind to make off with the vehicle while I was coming – and these too had rolled out with the change. And were gone.

We searched for an hour. Then I walked back down with her in the warm rain and rang up the depot from her house. There were questions to be answered in the matter of what I was doing parked in the middle of a hill field when I was supposed to be out selling ice-cream. And what I was doing throwing away the keys. But the real trouble came when I was towed back into the depot with melted ice-cream pouring out from the back of the mini-van. For if you lost your keys you lost your freezer.

'Every night,' the manager said to me the next day, 'I have to remember to plug in my briefcase. Do you know why?'

Of course I knew why. Because he was a loser, that's why. But what I said was, 'To keep it cold, sir.'

He showed me the palms of his hands. 'Exactly. To keep it cold. And do you know what would happen if I forgot?'

Of course I knew what would happen. His life would improve. But what I said was, 'You'd have a wet briefcase, sir.'

So far he seemed pleased with me. 'Exactly. And if I have a wet briefcase . . . But you know the rest. You're a smart lad.'

'Thank you, sir.'

'Look, Walzer,' he said, changing his position in his chair, and changing his tone, too. Confidentiality, that was what he was trying for. Smart lad to smart lad. 'Look, Walzer, I can do one of two things. I can take the cost of the ruined pieces out of your next pay-packet.' (Pieces, we called them. Christian for shticks.) 'Or I can sack you.'

He was Oxford, as I've said. Balliol. Handsome, with shadow-grey jowls. And sad. It couldn't have been what he had ever anticipated for himself, having to remember to plug a refrigerated briefcase in every night. But you start with reading economics – and the next thing . . . That's the way with tsatskes – they imperceptibly creep up on a man.

Maybe I saw myself in him, my own future. Maybe I was just losing my bottle again, the way I had against that limber foul-mouth Royboy Roylance. Or maybe I was once more the gull of language, as I'd been when talking on the phone to Phil Radic, and couldn't resist the answer hidden in the question. I wasn't much good at protecting my own interests, whichever way you read it.

'Why don't you just do both, Mr Lightbowne,' I said, removing my yellow nylon coat without even bothering to check for personals, and flouncing out like someone failing an audition for a chorus line.

So I got to put in a few months with my father after all. And was there, in the middle, when the gantse geshecht came falling down.

The times were partly to blame. Swag wasn't what it had been. People were spending their money on different things. The technological revolution hadn't yet happened – no one had a computer or a facsimile or even an answering machine in those days – but transistor radios were coming in, and tape recorders were turning into cassette players, and when they weren't jigging to a monotonous beat the poor were going to the Costa Brava and returning with more sophisticated attitudes to domestic ornamentation. Why have a love-in-a-cottage chalk wall plaque over your fire when you could load the mantelpiece with dying bulls and flamenco dancers whose satin skirts twirled in the updraught? Swag itself was changing – that's what I'm saying. Swag was becoming internationalized, fulfilling grander dreams.

And my father didn't notice, was that the problem? He was yesterday's swagman?

Partly yes and partly no. He was slow to perceive the transformation, that's undeniable, but I believe he would have got there in the end. Swag was in his blood. Eventually he would have heard it crying to him in the night. Were he alive and in business today he'd be doing well with mobile phones. That's what an eye for useless crap he had. So no. The real reason everything came tumbling down around his ears was that he'd never had the slightest idea how much money he had to spend or what anything was costing him and therefore what anything should sell for. Mike Sieff had been right all along when he'd clapped his hands and yelled and screamed and wondered if my father had been out in the sun too long, knocking the gear out at that price. It was no surprise that he was going bust. The surprise was that it hadn't happened years ago.

He never opened his bank statements. He never took them out of their envelopes. He didn't want to see. So long as he hadn't seen in black and white how little money he had in the bank he could legitimately proceed on the assumption that he had plenty.

He could never find his invoices.

My mother would tear her hair out. 'Joel, how can you price anything if you haven't got your invoices?'

'I can remember.'

'So how much were the bathroom cabinets?'

'The ones with no shelves?'

'Yes.'

'And the broken mirrors?'

'Yes.'

'I got those at a special price.'

'And what was that?'

'Oh, I don't know, about a funt.'

'What do you mean *about*?'

'About a funt, I don't know.'

'Each? A pound each? A pound for the lot? Which, Joel?'

'*Each. Each.* A funt each. Or was it two funt? Something like that. Stop hacking me on a kop.'

Who cares? That's what he wanted to say. Who cares? As long as we move the stuff out. Over there and over there. And again. And another. Last one. Who's a liar?

If she really kept on at him he'd lose his temper and say, 'It's a loss-leader, now can we leave it at that!'

I don't know how many times my mother, let alone his accountant, let alone his accountant's mother, took him through the principle of losing a little in order to win a lot. But he was always bored by it. 'Yeah, yeah,' he'd say. 'Loz me ein. Don't make me oisgemisht. We're shifting gear, that's all that matters.'

The rest of us fared no better. 'What are you lot complaining about?' he'd say. 'You've got a roof over your head, haven't you?'

In the end we very nearly didn't.

Even he realized, before the end finally came, that he had to make a show of looking like a man in control. 'Now what have I done with that invoice?' he'd say, just as we were about to sit down to supper, frisking himself with the astonished look of a person who had never mislaid a thing in his life. Then the hunt began. Every pocket. The turn-ups of his trousers. The back of every chair. Under the table. Under the bed. Under the mattress. The bin. The garage. The van. Wherever he'd been. Where *had* he been? And if we were lucky we would find it, still at the warehouse, lying in a pool of diesel at the local garage, floating like a lily in the gutter outside Sheeny's house, left on the counter of some transport café, or just in an extreme corner of his back pocket all along. He didn't own a wallet. Never had owned a wallet. He *was* his wallet, that was the idea. If he had a wallet he would lose it, so he stuffed papers into whichever part of himself happened to be to handiest. We'd all seen him throw five-pound notes on the ground, imagining that he was scrunching them into his trousers. Sometimes we'd have to go out searching for cash, never mind an invoice, the day's takings, hundreds and hundreds of pounds which he'd put *somewhere*. I recovered seventy smackers once, out of a lost sum of four hundred, just by following a trail of fivers to a phone box. Someone was using the phone when I got there so I knocked on the glass and reached in, retrieving another fifty wrapped in a brown paper bag.

When I told him what had happened to my ice-cream job he had the decency to see the joke. Like father like son. We both couldn't keep a shilling in our pockets.

And then one day it wasn't funny any more.

The house went from noisy to quiet in a single instant, and then went from quiet to noisy just as abruptly, but now at all the wrong times. People I had never seen before arrived in the early morning carrying boxes, then more people I had never seen before arrived in the dead of night to carry them away. There were constant phone calls out of business hours, some of them confidential and rueful – shushkehing phone calls: mutter mutter, ech ech – some of them wheedling, many of them angry, all of them futile. The phrase 'You soon know who your friends are' was forever on my father's lips. He lost stature. His brick shithouse shoulders looked as though they'd been hit by a semi-trailer. He slumped and lost weight. He lost his appetite. One by one, my mother lost the rings from her fingers. Pawned. Reduced to pawnage – us! *Us!* Who until now had never known what or where a pawn shop was. But we were learning quickly. We were helpless in the arms of a process which I thought only attacked the families of crooked financiers or ne'er-do-wells: we were going mechullah.

'If it wasn't for you kids,' my mother said, 'I'd put my head in the oven.'

To my sisters she said, 'Let this be a lesson to you. Never marry a man who doesn't know where his invoices are. However much he makes you laugh.'

She had become like the Lady of Shalott. She wouldn't look out of windows or answer the door or telephone. Thro' the noises of the night she hid in shadows. The curse had come upon her.

There was only one consolation. The tower was in her name.

I've been told by other bankrupts that when it finally happens, when you go from *going* mechullah to *being* mechullah, there is a wonderful sense of relief. It wasn't like that with us. The final blow was the bitterest blow. Because it was delivered not by any impersonal system of justice or retribution, but by a mortal enemy. Copestake.

Yes, *that* Copestake! Cockroach and fatherer of cockroaches.

Come the hour when the forests are all gone and the ice has all melted and the hole in the firmament is big enough to drop a hundred moons through, one creature will still be crawling across the face of the ruined earth, the copestake, inexpungible, impervious to all extremes of climate, proof against insult and obloquy, resistant to fire itself.

Yes, he had done well out of the insurance on the charred Cheetham Hill Road emporium. So well that for a while people wondered whether Benny the Pole mightn't have been working for him and not the Beenstocks all along. Though it wasn't beyond Benny, his old Kardomah chinas chipped in, to have been in the employ of them both. Against either of these theories was the condition of Mrs Copestake, who had begun to shake on the day after the fire and hadn't stopped shaking since. Why would she be shaking if she'd got what she wanted to get – assuming she wanted what her husband wanted, that's if he had ever wanted it (and conspired to get it) in the first place? Of course there could have been discussions between Copestake and Benny the Pole without Mrs Copestake being party to them; men who love their wives frequently keep them in the dark. But in that case Mr Copestake would surely be at the mercy of some pretty mixed emotions right now, seeing his wife quivering like an aspen, and by all accounts he wasn't.

The only thing mixed about Copestake was the business he was doing, swallowing up every import warehouse and factory, every betting shop and flop house he could get his hands on in a rough square bounded by Cheetham Hill Road, Waterloo Road, Derby Street, and Strangeways. He'd grown up there, poor and unloved – for who can love a cockroach? Not even another cockroach can love a cockroach – and now was systematically making himself sole landlord of the place. Copestake returns! Deny me this time!

Another psychotic winner riding in triumph through Persepolis.

Among the warehouses he had most recently gobbled down was Patkin Bros, importers of chipped tsatskes from Taiwan, every one a shneid – my father's biggest creditor. If Patkin Bros called in then that was that. And why wouldn't they, now they were Patkin Bros only in name, in reality Cockroach and Son?

For two whole weeks my father went about klopping the side of his head. 'How do you like it! Of all people! Him, of all people! What are the chances of that happening? Copestake! A klog oyf im! How many million people are there in Manchester? Two million? Three million? And it has to be Copestake. What are the chances of that? You're the mathematician, Oliver – what are the chances of that?'

'Between two and three million to one,' I said.

Knowing the cold figures only made it worse. 'Three million to one! Three million to one and it has to be that farbissener! My mazel!'

'You could try talking to him,' my mother said, from the shadows. She was lying down with a cold compress on her head. Migraine. We all had one. A migraine each. All except my father who could go on and on klopping the side of his head and never even get a headache.

'I've tried talking to him.'

'Recently?'

'What's recently? I've tried talking to him. He doesn't talk. He puts bricks under vans. And he swears like a yok.'

'I could try talking to *her*.'

'Why bother talking to her? She's tsedrait. She shakes all day.'

'She's got St Vitus's. You should be sorry for her. She didn't shake before she married him. She was a Fingerhutt before she married him.'

'I know she was a Fingerhutt. What's that got to do with anything?'

'I went to school with her.'

'I went to school with *him*.'

'They were nice people, the Fingerhutts. Her father was a lovely man. Very gentle. I could talk to her.'

'What about? Her father? They may be very nice people, the Fingerhutts, they may be the nicest people in Manchester. But they'll still want their money.'

'I thought you said it's not their money. I thought you said it's Morris and Henry Patkin's money.'

He threw his hands in the air. 'Just leave it to me,' he said. 'You've never understood money.'

And a month later he was mechullah.

All very well having everything we owned in my mother's name, we still had to upkeep it. And we still had to eat.

My sisters were working, but they had flibbertigibbet jobs like demonstrating in Kendalls or giving away cigarettes at car shows, and they spent more on vanity bags and false eyelashes than they earned. Their long-term prospects were good – you never heard of a demonstrator at Kendalls who didn't ultimately marry well – but until then we couldn't look to them to do much more than buy their own bagels every Sunday. And not give my father the platz in these trying times by being seen out on the arm of a shvartzer.

As for me, I'd be off to Golem College any day now, and there was no question of my putting that off to help out. I was the future. Our hedge against ever having to be sent back to the Bug.

'I could try the buses again,' my father said.

'Over my dead body,' my mother told him.

Shtuck, that's what we were in. Serious shtuck.

Then, out of the blue, mitten derinnen, Sheeny turned up with a suggestion. Lancelot Waxman, his armour ringing as he rode between the barley sheaves. Singing tirra lirra, instead of oink oink.

Giving Sheeny his cards hadn't been easy for my father. Despite their age difference, they had grown fond of each other. Sheeny was like a little old man half the time, anyway. And my father was more of a boy than I had ever succeeded in being. So they met each other coming the other way. They had good times together. Better times, I suspect, than they ever let on. And no doubt better times than Sheeny and I had ever had. They were on a similar wavelength. They were both pleasure opportunists. They didn't think there was anything wrong with tsatskying if it made you happy. And they worked well as a team. As my father said, they shifted a lot of gear between them.

'It won't be the same without you revving up the Commer outside my lettee in the shvitzing cold, Joel,' Sheeny told him. 'I won't know what to do with myself Shabbes mornings.'

'You could try going to shool,' my father said.

'Only if you pick me up and take me, Joel.'

I wasn't there when they shook hands and called it quits, but my father described the farewells to us. 'I don't know what the kid's going to do now,' he said. 'He took it hard.'

He was taking it hard himself.

'He's not a kid,' I said. 'He's five years older than me. And every grafter in Manchester will be after him once the word's out that you've sacked him.'

'I haven't sacked him. That farbissener Copestake's sacked him.'

A couple of afternoons later, sitting over keife and coffee in the KD, Sheeny said, 'I'm worried about your old man. He's getting on. What's he going to do now?'

That was the nice thing about the KD. You had to have skirt with you but you weren't obliged to address it. You just talked normally, as though it wasn't there.

'He isn't getting on,' I said. 'He's only about five years older than me. He'll be all right. He's a good grafter.'

'You're telling *me* he's a good grafter? Listen to me, Oliver – he's the best grafter there is, your old man.'

'Then he'll be all right. He'll find something. Another coffee, girls?'

But no one is in too much of a hurry to employ a person who's just gone mechullah, good grafter or not. It's bad karma, apart from anything else. Shit sticks. And you're always wondering – did he go bust because he's a shmuck or because he's a villain?

Of course your old enemies are quick to offer you something demeaning. Copestake himself put it about, for example, that he was prepared to let bygones be bygones and rustle my father up a warehouseman's job or the like provided he came crawling on his belly to ask for it.

'I'd rather beg on the streets,' my father said.

Which, week by week, was looking more and more like his only option. Until – tirra lirra – Lancelot Waxman came riding out of the shtuck-mist.

I was surprised to see him at the door. I wasn't aware we were going out that night. I was also surprised not to see him in a whistle and flute (which meant we definitely *weren't* going out that night). He was wearing jeans, which I'd never suspected him of owning, and a turtleneck sweater, ditto. Casual didn't suit him. It diminished him. It took away from his seriousness. Especially the roll neck, which chafed his skin and exacerbated the twitching.

But I now understand that his choice of wardrobe was dictated by exquisite tact. He didn't want to look prosperous. He didn't want to appear up while my father was down. He didn't want to look like the boss. For that was the proposition he had come to put. That he should now employ my father!

'This is the emmes, Joel. I'm offering you the job you gave me, except that I'll still be pitching and you'll still be working the edge. It'll be no different. You can even pick me up in the shvitzing cold. But half an hour later.'

'This is very, very nice of you,' my father said. 'I really appreciate it. But I don't think it's on.'

'Why not? Have you got a better offer?'

'I'll be straight with you, Sheeny – I don't have any offer. So I'm grateful to you. But I don't see it.'

'What don't you see? It'll be the same as before. I'll sleep, you'll graft.'

'It can't be the same, Sheeny. I've lost the gaffs, for a start.'

'We'll get new gaffs. We'll get better gaffs. That was half the trouble. Your gaffs were no bottle, Joel.'

Tough words. No gaff worker wants to be told his gaffs were no bottle. Not when you've put as much work into greasing up the Tobies as my father had. But he had to take it. That's what going mechullah means. You have to accept the world's retrospective judgement on you.

'No gaffs are any bottle these days. The gaffs are over.'

'We'll find. We'll find. You leave that to me. The gaffs are my deigeh.'

'I don't think I've got the stomach left for it, Sheeny.'

'You've got a stomach left for eating, Joel.'

My father patted himself. 'Well it won't do any harm to eat a little less,' he said.

'Who's talking less? If you're not working soon you'll be eating gornisht. Am I right? Say you'll think about it, at least.'

'I'll think about it.'

'No. Reem. Say you'll seriously think about it.'

'I'll seriously think about it.'

'Good. Don't take too long, that's all I ask. I'll ring you later tonight.'

'That's a bit soon, Sheeny. Ring me tomorrow. But you know now what the answer's going to be.'

'I'll ring you in the morning, Joel. Not too early. Sleep on it.' And he went off, goaded to madness by his turtleneck, jerking and twitching like Houdini in a straitjacket that was finally too much for him.

My father, too, was exercising tact. He hadn't said, 'Sheeny, it takes money to start a business. I know how much I've been paying you. And I know how much you spend on cuff-links. Forgive me, but you're dreaming.'

They had to get to that, in the end. 'I know it's none of my business,' my father finally said, 'but how are you . . . ?'

'That's a fair question, Joel. I've got a backer. And if you're worried, I'll pay you three months' greens in advance. How's that?'

How else could it be?

And the backer? Well, as my father said, it was none of our business. But you can't help being curious. And our curiosity stopped at the door of Sheeny's father. Who else? Of course Sheeny was being mysterious. He didn't want to say, 'My dad. That's who.' Whereas *a backer* had the ring of high finance about it.

But he let the cat out of the bag to me, one night, having got himself uncharacteristically drunk. One thimbleful of sweet red Israeli wine from a squeaky padded bar had done it. Another way in which he was like my father. Shicker at the sight of a corkscrew. We were with keife in Benny the Pole's pad. Our last night there for the time being. Because in the morning Benny would be out of cheder. Not free, just on highly conditional parole – which, wouldn't you know, the meshuggener blew, but free enough to stand on the pavement outside the Kardomah again and waylay young women. I made some denigrating reference to criminals and society's responsibility to lock 'em all up for life, especially arsonists who fuck up to the extent of making millionaires out of their victims. 'Well, let's hope he ends up making millionaires out of us, Oliver,' he said. I said that I didn't see how Benny the Pole was ever likely to make anything out of me, and that was when Sheeny blurted out that he'd already made an employed man out of my father.

'Benny the Pole?'

Benny the Pole.

'You're not saying . . . ?'

He was saying.

'*The* Benny the Pole?'

'The geezer whose let you've been shtupping in for years, Oliver, yes. *The* Benny the Pole. The *only* fucking Benny the Pole.'

There were things about finance and the justice system I didn't understand. For example that you could give somebody money when you were in cheder. For example that you were allowed to *have* money when you were in cheder. Didn't they take it all away from you? Wasn't that its point as a deterrent?

There was a differece, Sheeny explained, between a bankrupt and a lag. Benny the Pole had never gone bankrupt.

Cheder yes, mechullah no.

It felt like a value judgement. Against my father.

I couldn't believe it. Hauled out of the shtuck, snatched from penury and starvation, pulled off the cross, by Benny the Pole. A spiv in a toupee. An arsonist. A croaker into the ears of young women. A croaker into the ears of young women, what is more, on behalf of other croakers. What did that make him? What did that make *us*?

I felt quite sick.

'Just don't ever tell my father,' I said.

But Sheeny only threw me a long strange look.

★　　★　　★

Funny the way life works. Thanks to Benny the Pole there was smetana and kez on our table again. And thanks to Gershom Finkel there is bread on mine.

Only partly thanks to, in both instances, but still. And not that much smetana and kez, or bread, but again, still. You don't look a gift-horse.

They do what they do, these ganovim. They do their best for you. It's not Gershom's fault if I don't live to the standard I would like. And you can hardly blame Benny the Pole for the dejection that settled on my father once he went to work for Sheeny. You can't be employed by someone who was once employed by you and be happy about it. You can't fall from high to low and be expected to enjoy it. Unless you happen to be a glutton for punishment. Which my father wasn't.

One in a family is enough.

TWO

I seemed to be forever shrinking into myself, while others
around me were forever sliding away.

*The Money Player: The Confessions of America's Greatest
Table Tennis Champion and Hustler*, Marty Reismann

W E NOW ENTER an embarrassing phase even by the standards
of this history of embarrassments.

You've heard me make that claim before. But then I was
preparing the ground for nothing more embarrassing than the
years I spent locked away in the lavatory cutting up and otherwise
defaming loved ones. Pish! What I am about to describe is
embarrassment big time. Mortification Grandiflora. First Degree
Humiliation with Aggravated Abasement.

We now enter Cambridge.

As a fall-back position for someone of my grandiosity, Cambridge
had this and this alone going for it – you had to be there to know
how bad it was.

Back home in the Kardomah no one knew from nothing.
Cambridge? Gevalt! They stared when I walked in, broke the
house rules in the excitement, looked me over with hymeneal
eyes. Which in the end was all you could ask.

I remember Alex Libstein, the estate agent's son, trying to put me down when I was back in Manchester one vacation being seen at Laps', where they also knew from nothing. We were in the pickle meat queue together. 'Isn't Oxford supposed to better than Cambridge?' he wondered in a loud voice.

'Depends on the subject, Alex,' I told him. 'For economics, languages and law, maybe, but not for spying or any of the moral sciences.'

That's grandiosity – dropping the phrase moral sciences in Laps' on a Saturday night.

Grandiosity tinged with sadness though, because *I* knew even if they didn't.

So was that what Oliver the Ripper was reading at Cambridge – Moral Sciences? Was that to be my antidote to tsatskying? Hobbes's *Leviathan*? Yes and no. What you read at Cambridge, and certainly *how* you read it, has a lot to do with the college you wind up in. Left to its own devices, Golem College would have preferred its undergraduates not to read anything at all. Sanctuary – that was what Golem provided. A quiet out of the way place by the river for rugby backs and javelin throwers to while their best years away in, undisturbed by thought. As for me, yes, I'm sure of it – they wanted me for my ping-pong and wouldn't have minded if I'd never written an essay the whole time I was there, so long as I led them to the top of the UCTTC ping-pong ladder at the end of the year and was instrumental, as a Golem man, in turning the tables on Oxford who to date had the wood on us when it came to table games. But every Cambridge college must present a *semblance* of academic activity. The college had a library; someone had to go in it once in a while and at least *pretend* to be interested in a book. So Golem wasn't exactly going to stand in my way, academically. Fine, Walzer, become a farkrimter sour-puss under Yorath and Rubella, if you must have a fall-back position. Just

don't become fanatical. And don't allow it to interfere with your
ping-pong.

Yorath and Rubella, joint Directors of Studies at Golem –
inspirational figures at the time, though scarcely remembered
today. Except by me, except by me, except by me . . . Dr Iaoin
Yorath, author of *The Bleeding Wound: Women and Anguish in
the Nineteenth-Century Novel* and its sequel, *The Wound Staunched:
Suffering and Redemption in the Woman's Novel of the Nineteenth
Century*. And Howard Rubella (Ph.D. pending) – still is, by the
way – author of nothing, but a renowned teacher and expert
on marriage and parturition in literature, though he himself was
single and childless. My mentors.

So, no, not Moral Sciences strictly speaking. Not Hobbes or
Hume. What I was actually majoring in was Collins Classics.
Somewhere along the line I had ditched misogyny (it was
only ever a growing pain anyway) and returned to the faith
of my aunties. Austens, Jane; Brontës, Anne; Brontës, Charlotte;
Brontës, Emily; Burneys, Fanny; Eliots, George; Gaskells, Mrs;
Mitfords, Miss. I had even brought the original green volumes
of my boyhood down from Manchester, concealing them under
my bed at first, imagining I would need to buy more grown-up-
looking versions from Heffers when my grant came through. But
that turned out to be an unnecessary compunction; every one of
my fellow students owned the same leatherette editions I did, so
I felt free to arrange them on my shelves in alphabetical order.
Austens, Jane, etc.

I did, though, decide against bringing out *Dr Jekyll and Mr
Hyde*. It was a wise decision. Not because it was bashed after
the years it had served as my *de facto* ping-pong bat, but because
it was written by a man. Books written by men were frowned
upon by Yorath and Rubella. We were here to study literature,
and literature was written by women.

I remember my first week in Cambridge, and I remember my

last, otherwise it's a blur. Necrosis of the memory. Nature's way of being kind. It's not reality man cannot bear too much of, it's shame. It's Cambridge.

And of my first week it's the first day I remember most clearly. Everything that was ever going to happen to me in Cambridge, happened that day. Everybody I was ever going to meet, I met then. And everything I was ever going to feel − but let's leave feeling out of this or hysterical amnesia will swallow up even day one.

Day One. It Happened On Day One.

For all the difference the other years made, I might just as well have gone home in the morning.

I arrived off the Manchester train in the early afternoon, and was immediately suspicious of how everyone appeared to know one another. Not only the returnees, but new boys like me. Where had they met? Was this another of those party situations where you turn your back for two minutes and when you next look around everyone is intimate, in love, and skilful on the ball?

The taxi driver laughed when he saw my matching suitcases − though even I had thought the compressed cardboard a tolerable imitation of bruised leather, and the polka-dot pattern not lacking in traveller's chic. When I told him which college I was going to he laughed again.

'Are those dogs or bags, sir?' the college porter asked me. 'Because if they're dogs they're not allowed in your room.'

Then he laughed too.

They could smell swag on me.

There were three invitations in crested college envelopes waiting for me in my pigeon hole. An invitation to sherry from Lord Neville-Hacket, the Master. An invitation to sherry from the President of GCQ, the Golem College Quaffers, the college sporting club. (This was the moment I realized my reputation as a spieler of distinction had come before me.) And an invitation to sherry from Yorath and Rubella. All three were for 7.30, after hall, that night.

I succumbed to an immediate migraine. How do you go to three sherry parties simultaneously? For a grandiose emergency-recourse man there can be nothing worse — all your fall-back positions falling at once.

Rather than think about ordering preferences, I forwent the luxury of taking slow possession of my oak-panelled room and spent what was left of the afternoon at Woolworths instead, choosing a teapot, a toasting fork, two willow-patterned sideplates, and a tea cloth with the University arms on it. I also had to see to personal stationery, decide on a ring-binder, and organize to have one of the old coffee-table Bosch prints framed. Returning along Jesus Lane, absorbed in perturbations not of my own making, I knocked a small elderly gentleman, who on a second glance proved to be E. M. Forster, into the gutter. Too overawed to apologize, I backed into the road and was hit by C. S. Lewis on a bicycle. In the course of neither of these collisions did any party say a word or otherwise signal awareness that anything had happened. For the however many semi-amnesic years I was there — if I was there — this remained the Cambridge way. You didn't see, you didn't allude, you didn't acknowledge. You went everywhere with your eyes down, and if that meant that you rode over your own tutor neither you nor he was going to be uncouth enough to mention it. Practicality lay behind this, partly. I see that. In a small town you can't keep saying hello to the same person. Nor can you go on apologizing — 'Whoops! There I go again' — every time you inadvertently barge him into the river. But shyness had a lot to do with it as well. And shyness, as I knew from my own family, is catching. Already, after only an hour of Cambridge, I could feel the red rush of awkwardness returning to my cheeks. If I wasn't careful I would soon have a shell on my back again. And it would be no consolation that every other person in Cambridge was carrying one too.

Not wanting to make anyone's acquaintance in this condition, I didn't linger in the main Golem quadrangle – an ugly open-plan classical rehash, like Old Trafford with Doric columns, at present littered with trunks and *real* leather suitcases which no porter found funny – but returned quickly to my aerie, opened first the first and second the second door, turned on the gas fire, and stretched out on my bed.

Ah, Cambridge! My Alma Mater. My foster-mother-in-waiting – at last!

Back home, my real mother and my aunties would be thinking about me. Oliver gone where none of them had ever been or ever dreamt of going. Oliver collegiate. Oliver become a man. Oliver receiving invitations from *Lords* noch. Oliver confronting his destiny.

Swish! went the Lady Ogimura's kimono. From a willow-patterned sideplate she helped herself with dainty fingers to a toasted teacake dripping butter. Snap! went her suspenders.

At about five someone knocked. I had dozed off, overcome by gas fumes. I wasn't sure whether to shout 'Come in!' or to answer the door formally, so I did both, colliding with my visitor in the airlock between the inner door and the outer.

'Sorry,' I said.

'Sorry,' he said.

He was a black white man. That's to say he was white but appeared to carry a black shadow of himself around with him. He saw me mystified by his penumbra. Staring.

'Sorry,' I said.

'I knocked,' he said, 'because your oak wasn't sported.'

'Wasn't it?' I said.

'Sorry,' he said. 'I've disturbed you. You should sport your oak.'

He had a thick throaty voice which seemed to be a burden to him, like a heavy shopping bag. And a surprise to him too, as though he suspected it belonged to someone else. Maybe even wished it to belong to someone else, since he looked mightily uncomfortable as himself. He had a deep dark cleft in his chin, of the sort my sisters considered manly, which he sawed away at with the side of his thumb, making it ever deeper.

'No, no,' I said, 'I want to be disturbed.'

'So I *have* disturbed you. Sorry.'

'No you haven't,' I said. 'Please come in.'

'Thank you,' he said. He fell into my room. Sideways. 'I'll have dry.'

I looked at him.

'. . . Sherry.'

Damn! Sherry! I had the teapot, I had the toasting fork, but where was the sherry? 'Sorry,' I said, 'I only got in a couple of hours ago. I'll nip out . . .'

'No, no. Buttery's closed. Anyway, look, why don't you come to my room.'

He looked around to be certain it really was him who was talking.

'I could make tea,' I said.

Through a thicket of black wrist hairs he consulted his watch. Charily, as though he feared it might jump him. 'Too late for tea for me,' he said. 'Do you have port?'

'Sorry,' I said. 'Port ditto.'

'How do you mean?'

'As with sherry, so with port . . .'

'Is that a northern expression?'

'No. Just as I don't have sherry, I don't have port.'

'Oh, sorry,' he said. 'I thought it might be an expression. *As with sherry, so with port.* Like *plus ça change.*'

'Sorry?'

'*Plus ça change, plus c'est la même chose.*'

'Oh, that.'

'*As with sherry, so with port. Plus ça change . . .*'

'I see it,' I said.

'So have you got any?'

'No,' I said.

He looked relieved. Now he could gracefully leave. He'd only just entered but being here was a torment to him. And to me. 'Then come to my room,' he said. 'I've got bottles of the stuff.'

'By the way,' I said as we clattered down a flight, 'I'm Walzer.'

'I know,' he said. 'It's on your door. I'm Rivers.'

'Not St John,' I laughed, giving him my hand.

'I am actually, yes. My brother's Rochester.'

'Rochester Rivers?'

'No. Edward Rochester. He's my half-brother.'

'The next thing you'll be telling me,' I said, 'is that your mother's locked away in an attic.'

He shot me an intense look from his whiteless eyes. A black bolt. 'How did you know that?' he said.

I tried for a joke. It was either that or die. 'As with sherry, so with port,' I said.

'Sorry?'

'As with sherry – look, it doesn't matter.'

I didn't have a chance. I saw it at that moment, once and for all. Not a hope. I'd never hold out against them. Once a turtle, always a turtle. And I'd come to a turtle farm.

We were now in his room. He told me he'd come up only yesterday, yet already the room bore the stamp of the man. Dark. Confined. Over-charged. Ominous. Fucking deranged. How had he done it in a day? I looked at his shelves. Austens, Jane. Burneys, Fanny. Brontës, All Of Them. But also Dostoevskys, Fyodor. And Gogols, Nikolai. And Pushkins, Alexander. Not in translation, either.

'You read Russian?' he asked me. 'You look as though you read Russian.'

'No,' I said. 'Though I come from there, partly, sort of, a long time ago. You?'

'Do I come from there?'

'Do you *read* it?'

'Read it, speak it, breathe it,' he said.

Then he directed my attention to the mantelpiece on which were a number of heavily ornate icon-like frames all containing photographs of the same woman. Plump and peevish and over-painted.

'Yasmin,' he said.

'She's very beautiful,' I lied. No more attic jokes.

'My wife,' he said.

'You're married?'

'Not yet.'

'But you're about to be?'

'Soon. The moment she agrees.'

'She hasn't agreed yet?'

'She hasn't met me yet.'

His hands shook when he poured me port. Mine shook when I lit his cigarette. We affected each other badly. We set each other jumping, like a pair of back to back magnets.

'Not that I've got much time to play with,' he went on. 'I'm not expecting to live all that long.'

'Sorry?'

'It has to be soon because I've been told I'm not going to live long. Look,' he said, showing me his palm.

There were no lights on in his room, and only the smallest turret window, giving out on to a shaded service yard. So it wasn't easy to see much. But even in the dark I could make out that he had no life line to speak of. *To speak of*? Let's not beat about the bush – he had none. As far as his palm was concerned he was already a dead man.

'How do you mean you've been *told* you're not going to live long?' I said, which in the circumstances was as good as changing the subject.

'Fifty years ago my grandfather met a Kazakh fortune-teller on

300

a train from Uzbekistan to Tientsin. The fortune-teller tried to leap from the carriage when he saw my grandfather's palm, but my grandfather insisted on knowing the worst. "If it's to be, it's to be," he said. "On your own head and the heads of your progeny be it," the fortune-teller replied, and proceeded to tell him that neither he, nor his youngest son, nor his youngest son's youngest son, would survive past the age of forty. My grandfather died in his thirty-ninth year. My father died when he was twenty-eight. I am the youngest son of the youngest son.'

What do you say to that on your first day in Cambridge?

I wished Sheeny were here. 'Oy a broch!'

Without him the best I could manage was, 'I'm not sure how much trust I would want to repose in a fortune-teller I met on a train in that part of the world.'

Cambridge prim. And I hadn't even had my first tutorial with Yorath or Rubella yet.

'Aren't you?' St John Rivers said. He'd turned shirty on me. Suddenly he wasn't two people. Shirty, he was entirely himself. 'Aren't you? It would be interesting to hear what my father and grandfather would have to say to that.'

Whereupon he walked out. Walked out of his own room and left me there in the gloom, to finish my port, gaze on Yasmin and sport his oak for him. When I next saw him he was at the Master's sherry party, showing his palm around. He affected not to know me.

I would soon learn that by Cambridge and especially by Golem College standards there was nothing especially untoward in any of this – people were always walking out without a word. Tutors did it as a matter of course. One second you were rehearsing your weekly essay before the sternest of judges, the next you were reading to an empty room. Often you didn't even see them go. Lecturers practised it too, turning on their heel mid-sentence, their gowns billowing, leaving three hundred of us with our pens in the air. All perfectly commonplace. Not rudeness, shyness.

They weren't up to saying, 'Excuse me.' As for affecting not to know you, that was a Golem College speciality. Iaoin Yorath would wonder who you were in the middle of a conversation. I have a dim memory of him dismissing me from his presence on at least two occasions on the grounds that I was an interloper and that he only supervised members of the college.

'Dr Yorath, I am here in your room at your invitation,' I can just about remember telling him.

'The more fool me!' was his reply.

I mention this by way of protecting St John Rivers's good name. Yes, he was fucking deranged, but they all were. Taken all round he was probably less deranged than the rest of them. At least he wasn't a fantasist. In the matter of his prognostications about his marriage to Yasmin, for example, he was proved dead right. He'd seen her photograph in a Leningrad paper originally and had tracked her down from that. He was writing to her every few days at the time I encountered him and she was replying with a weekly photo. Finally he went to collect her. Married her in the Christmas vacation with the blessing of her family, posed for a rigor mortis wedding photograph on a bridge on Nevsky Prospekt – the Venice of the East, my arse, St John! – then brought her back to Cambridge. This was in his third year as an undergraduate. Two months later she ran off with the captain of the Golem College croquet team. Not a word. Just wasn't there any more. The ethos had got to her, too, you see. Didn't even leave him a photograph.

Shortly before his finals, St John Rivers threw himself out of his little turret window.

So he was right about his life prospects as well.

But I didn't yet know what was in store for either of us. For Day One, Person One, he was fucking deranged enough.

By the time I got to the Master's sherry party, which I reckoned had to be number one priority whatever I did next, I was on shpilkes. If my suitcases were wrong then my Kardomah suit was bound to be wrong. St John Rivers had not understood most of what I'd said to him, thinking I was speaking in Manchester tongues – what if the Master asked me to pronounce Boggart Hole Clough? What if he wasn't looking where he was going and walked into me? What if I walked into *him*? What if I made an allusion to a mad wife in the attic and he *had* a mad wife in the attic?

I've said it's catching, embarrassment. And I'd caught it. I was in a fever of it.

We stood in a line and the Master inspected us, like troops. I remember thinking he was going to check behind our ears. We were all freshmen. Welcome to Golem College, that was his message to us. Welcome, men.

Men? I'd become a man all of a sudden. If I was a man why didn't I *feel* like a man? And why didn't the others *look* like men?

Why didn't the Master look like a man, come to that?

He didn't have a young face exactly. In fact, when you got close, you could see that it was coming apart, the jaw precarious, the cheeks dropping, the eyes loose enough to be shaken out of their sockets. But he bore no signs of wear and tear. It wasn't dilapidation that was at work on him, it was disparity. No two features agreed. His face had simply fallen out with itself.

He walked along the line, asking names and shaking hands. When he came to me something extraordinary happened. He said, 'Don't tell me.' Then he lowered his head, showing me his baldness. Was I meant to kiss it? Was that what you did when you met a Lord? 'Don't tell me, don't tell me,' he said again, tapping his temples. Then he came back up smiling. Not one tooth alike unto any other, except in the matter of looseness. 'Walzer!' he said. And he played an imaginary ping-pong shot, a scooping backhand drive that would have missed the table by a mile.

'Yes, sir,' I said. 'That's me.'

'Well?' he waited. 'What's your response?' And when he saw that I was nonplussed he played the shot again, this time from a less cramped position and with more topspin. 'Well, Mr Walzer?'

Was I really expected to pretend to hit it back? Were we really going to play a game of shadow ping-pong with everybody watching? And was I required to let him win?

I chopped. Deep and low. My classy forehand chop from before the days of sponge and sandwich.

'Good man,' he laughed, moving on. 'You'll do.'

Not keeping it simple, that was always my trouble. Just like my father with his Yo-Yo. 'Point to you actually, Master,' I said. 'I've netted my return.'

He was polite enough to nod. But I could see that already I bored him. Prolix. Pity.

For my part I was chuffed that he knew my name almost alone of all the line of freshmen, but I had mixed feelings about being here on the strength of my ping-pong. I thought I'd put all that behind me with the swag and tsatskes. To be resurrected, as a fall-back position, only if I flunked Collins Classics. That's assuming I *could* resurrect it.

'What was all that about?' St John Rivers asked. He seemed to know who I was again.

But he walked away while I was telling him.

An improbably tall person, neither man nor boy, surveyed me through what, from that distance, looked like an airman's helmet, but was in fact nothing other than a pair of very square spectacles on a very square face. 'You're not a bloody hearty, are you?' he demanded.

I wasn't confident I could get words to carry to his height. So I lobbed him up a Bug and Dniester shrug. Meaning, if you look at it this way, but then again if you look at it that way . . .

'Well are you or aren't you?'

It was actually a reprimand. If I stayed talking to him any longer he'd be telling me to make my bloody mind up. And he was no less of a freshman than I was. I'd seen him in the line, inclining extravagantly to the Master who himself was no short-arse. So I put into practice the one lesson in Cambridge etiquette I'd already learnt and left him to his ire. But it embarrassed me to do it. It wasn't how I'd been brought up to behave. It contravened the convention of tcheppehing.

'Can't say I blame you,' someone whispered in my ear.

I turned around in surprise. And found myself looking into an open face, clear blue eyes, a broad smile, a slightly dizzy quiff of blond hair, relaxed stance, easy demeanour – someone like myself, at last!

'Oliver Walzer,' I said, holding out my hand.

'Robin Clarke,' he said pleasantly, holding out his.

'Bit of a brute for someone who offers not to approve of hearties, isn't he?' I said.

'Yes, isn't he. Name's Marcus Whiting, I'm told. Classics scholar. They say very brilliant.'

I pooh-poohed that. 'We're all very brilliant,' I said.

'Oh, I'm not. I'm not brilliant at all.'

'You wouldn't be here, else,' I said. Already I liked him. Maybe he wasn't very brilliant but I liked him. The goyishe friend – could this one be *the goyishe friend*? Whose sister I would marry in a little country church in Gloucestershire? Where we would raise horses and soft-voiced goyishe children called Christopher and Amelia? And only ever have cheese *after* dinner?

He laughed. 'Trust me I'm not,' he said. 'I'm not even clever. But I can see you are.'

'Brilliant or clever?'

'Brilliant.'

I smiled and shook my head.

'Yes, you are,' he said. 'All Jews are brilliant.'

I swallowed hard. I could have walked away but I foresaw an element of farce in that. Ricocheting from one to the other like a steel ball on a bagatelle board.

'Not *all* Jews,' I said. 'Just as not all gentiles.'

He was still shining his countenance upon me. 'I'm glad you said gentiles and not Christians,' he said. 'It's a common mistake. As a Christian myself I feel that there is a great deal of the Jew in me. Where would we Christians be without the Jews after all?'

'Where indeed,' I said.

'Which is why it's so important to Christians like myself to try to win Jews back to their original faith . . .'

I held up a hand. 'No,' I said.

'You don't even know what you're saying no to yet.'

'I do,' I said. 'I'm saying no to everything.'

'Couldn't we meet over a beer, to talk about it.'

'Jews don't drink beer,' I said. 'It interferes with their brain cells.'

He fell quiet for a moment or two. Then he said, 'I see that I've hurt your feelings. I'm sorry. I didn't want to do that. I love all Jews.'

'Well that's more than I do,' I said.

Now that he'd said he'd hurt my feelings I needed to escape him. As long as he'd only hurt my feelings I was no more than annoyed by him. But once he'd said he'd hurt my feelings, he'd hurt my feelings.

So stuff his sister.

'I have another party to go to,' I said.

'Quaffers? I'm off to that. I'm a bit of a hearty myself, I have to confess. Hockey. You're ping-pong, I gather. I'll walk over with you.'

'No need,' I said. 'I'm going to Yorath and Rubella's.'

On such pin heads do major life decisions turn.

Although I didn't of course know this at the time, the distinguishing feature of a Yorath and Rubella party was that neither Yorath nor Rubella was ever at it. At least not until it was over. Too shy. In Yorath's case too shy and too angry and too domestically intricated. In Rubella's case, just too shy.

You were meant to back blindly in, bang into a sherry, inveigle a book off the shelf or better still a faded cyclostyled sheet with extracts of books on it, keep your head down, and not address a soul. The silence of the grave – that was the other distinguishing feature of a Yorath and Rubella party, though I didn't know that at the time either.

But I am ashamed to say I took to it as a whelk takes to brine. There must have been twenty Collins Classics men in Yorath's room when I turned up, all absorbed into paper, all with their eyes occluded. *Dido and Aeneas* was on the turntable. But very low. 'When I am lai-aid, lai-ai-ai-ai-ai-ai-d in earth . . .' Woman's grief. Isolde next. An instinct for staidness, no less than embarrassment to the bone, told me not to break into the solemnities by introducing myself. Nobody was curious anyway. Besides, we were bound each to each at a level below the mere naming of names. We were a species unto ourselves. The Unmanned.

I picked my way through the strewn cyclostyled sheets – practical criticism exercises designed to demonstrate the ways in which Oliphant Mrs had the writerly wood on Hemingway Ernest, or Behn Aphra the intellectual, emotional and every other sort of beating of Pinter Harold – and found myself a corner. Unless a hand came through the bookcases, no one could get me here.

Every now and then someone would laugh, the demented laugh of the solitary, the laughter of the hermit bookman occasioned not by happy accident but a perceived inferiority in a male writer of no merit. Not surprise, but confirmation. The laugh rippled through us like a cold breeze, invigorating our brave marginality, binding us in our contempt for those whose heads did not grow below their shoulders. Conjoining us in chill. For those we laughed at most were the hot. Not hot as in shell-bound, not hot with the celerity of one's introversion, but hot as in rash, nimble, impetuous.

And this was my chosen world for however many years?

Still is. Open me up and you will find that my blood runs Collins Classics green.

It shouldn't be that much of a surprise that I joined the Unmanned. The shy, too, must have their day. And ours was an Elect of the Shy. Just because our eyes were lowered and the laughter froze like hailstones in our throats, it didn't mean that we too didn't find it passing brave to be a king and ride in triumph through Persepolis. It's possible we were the cruellest conquerors of them all. Certainly we were the most supercilious. The lowest in the saddle but the most high and mighty in our hearts.

But the die was not cast yet. It was still only Day One, hard as that was to believe, and before midnight struck I could yet go over to the hearties.

No, I had not given up entirely on the Quaffers' bash. Try everything, wasn't that my father's motto? Try nothing spoke every bit as persuasively from my mother's side, but I was *already* trying nothing, wasn't I?

The Yorath and Rubella party broke up just after nine. How could I tell? Because that was when Yorath and Rubella arrived. Yorath in a rage, curled around and around himself like a small unexploded firework, a rip-rap, smelling of saltpetre and powdered milk and Milton and uncut pages of forgotten novels; Rubella a step or two behind, a slothful Yakipak with voluptuous charcoal eyelids and the curly carmine lips of a led-astray cherub. I expected some secret nod of Laps' or KD acknowledgement from Rubella, unserer to unserer even though the Bug and the Guadalquivir were a continent apart. But I got nothing. And never did, not in three long years as an undergraduate and another five, ten – God knows how long I was there – as a research student. Just once, towards the end of a tutorial excruciating even by Rubella standards, he stuttered out something about my judgement being impaired by the ethic of first-past-the-post commercial individualism into which I'd been born, and our eyes met over that right enough. But it was hardly a meeting of the sympathetic. Later I learned that the two-faced trumbenik was able to indulge his lifestyle of superior last-past-the-post unpublishedness on the back of a family of wholesale haberdashers. From the North! His embroideries, his hand-woven rugs, his exquisite one-off Judith and Holofernes curtains, his Angelica Kaufmann wallpaper, his little wilting Gwen John self-portraits – all paid for by my aunties in yards of spiritless elastic!

He stood on the stairs as we squeezed past him. We careful not to touch, he careful not to be touched. 'Cho',' he said to each of us in turn. It was the best approximation to Cheerio he could manage. Too shy to essay so many syllables with a single breath. And too fucking fastidious ever to be caught forming a word that had Cheer in it.

Yorath didn't even bother with Cho'. He hopped from leg to leg with the key to his door in his hand, desperate for us to leave, his narrow body vibrating with the myriad cares of a principled marriage. Hold Yorath to your ear and you would hear the roar of his wife's bleeding. But you wouldn't want to hold Yorath to your ear.

While he used his college room for seminars – hence the practical criticism sheets – Iaoin Yorath conducted all his one-to-one teaching, the only sort that really mattered in Golem College, in the parlour of a cramped worker's cottage off Parker's Piece where he was otherwise dragging up his sprawling family. Thanks be to God for the kindly necrosis of memory. I cannot now remember the architecture of the room in which I spent so many miserable and ungenerous hours, arguing for comedy though we never found anything funny, stressing the importance of narrative though in our conversation we frowned on anything approaching an anecdote, invoking life as the final arbiter of art, *life*, though we leapt from the living as from the leprous. But it falls to no man to be so fortunate as to forget *everything*. I still see the angel of the house, Yorath Mrs Herself, aflutter at the door in her slip in the cold Cambridge morning, big with yet one more, so white she was yellow, her large wet exhausted eyes imploring you to be gone although you'd only just arrived. And I still see that other angel, the angel of domestic desperation, pass over Her Husband when the babies began to cry – not a normal cry, a harrowing unending wail, as though a bear had crossed Parker's Piece and got into their house and was dismembering them a joint at a time – at the very moment that he, the doctor not the bear, was coiled to explode like a rip-rap, enraged that you had gone out on a limb and found interest in something that wasn't available as a Collins Classic.

He screamed at me once. 'I don't have time, I don't have time, Walzer, to go combing the back streets of Cambridge for some lurid continental paperback romance that you've taken it into your head to write about.'

'You can borrow mine,' I suggested.

'I don't want to borrow yours. I don't want to read it. Do you understand that? Nothing you've said makes me want to read a word of it. You've failed to engage me. You've failed to persuade me that there's anything behind your interest except fashionable prurience. If you *must* read something foreign read *Adolphe*.'

I took a note. 'Is that by Benjamin Constant?'

'By? *By*? Who is a novel ever *by*? Without Madame de Staël *Adolphe* would not have existed. Without her desolation – but read it, read it, Mr Walzer, and don't bother with who it's by.'

And then the bear got in and the babies started. All of them at once. And a bottle exploded in the kitchen. And the phone rang. And soot fell down the chimney, blackening my essay. And the gas meter ran out of shillings. And the next student rang at the door. And Mrs Yorath went into labour.

The lurid continental fashionably prurient paperback romance, by the way, was *The Castle* by Franz Kafka. A Man.

Unless it was by Milena Jesenská Pollak.

★   ★   ★

I couldn't have been given more clues. Rubella was unable to put his fallen cherub's lips around any word that had a Cheer in it, and the hearties were unable to get their mouths around anything else.

'Cheers, Oliver.'

'Cheers, Oliver.'

'Cheers, Oliver.'

Friends!

Friends who weren't silent, or lofty, or doomed, or bashful as a matter of intellectual and moral principle, or who didn't walk off in the middle of a conversation.

Cheerful friends!

'Cheers, Ollie! Cheers, cheers, cheers, cheers . . .'

But they were the wrong sort of friends.

They were already rampaging when I caught up with them, leaving the college by the rear gate and heading for the Market Tavern. Singing songs. Rugby songs. Rowing songs. What did I know what songs?

Someone recognized me. 'Here's Ollie Walzer!'

A few of them looked around. A name to conjure with in sporting circles, Ollie Walzer.

'Ping-pongers Walzer?'

'None other,' I said.

And I let myself be swept up by them.

'What about a ping-pongers song, Ollie?'

'There aren't any,' I said.

And then suddenly, I had no idea how, but without doubt emboldened by sherry, I thought of one. Or rather I saw my way to one, since first of all I had to write it. Adapt it, at any rate. 'Ilkley Moor Bah't 'At', I gave them, changing the refrain to 'Ilkley Moor Bah't Bat', which struck them as demonstrating so much inventiveness and cunning, so astounded and bedazzled them each time the refrain came around, that had it not been for the presence of bulldogs in their bowler hats on the opposite side of the street I might well have been chaired into the Market Tavern as a hero.

The dimness of recollection that makes a waste of the ensuing years begins about now. That we drank a lot in the Market Tavern, my new hearty friends and I, drank a lot and drank it noisily and quickly, I have no doubt. That they asked for further proof of my lyric genius and that I obliged them, I also have no reason to disbelieve. A bastard version of 'The Good Ship Venus', to wit 'The Good Ship Golem', lingers with me still, though I retain no more than the opening lines, which in all conscience write themselves –

> *'Twas on the good ship Golem*
> *That all our balls got swollen;*
> *We cooled 'em down*
> *In Newcastle Brown*
> *And still no one would hold 'em –*

and a couplet from a later stanza –

> *The Master Neville-Hacket,*
> *A devil with a racket*

which had the merit not only of naming names – a strategy which never fails with hearties – but also of bringing us full circle back to sport.

Otherwise I remember only that we spilled beerily out into the market at closing time, shouting Olly! Olly! which is Cambridge rowing hearty for 'Come on, the next five, the next four' – a chant modified, once someone saw the possibility, to 'Olly, Olly, Ollie!'; joked ungraciously about totty and I fear abused one or two; frolicked around the fountain; fell in; pissed against a college wall (not ours); ran back pursued by proctors; and returned by the gate we'd left by, only this time up it rather than through it.

At thirty seconds past twelve I was back in my room. Day One – the last day of verdant boyhood – was finally over.

★   ★   ★

When I woke sadder but no wiser on day two I was still in my clothes and still wet from the fountain. I had ruined a good Kardomah suit. I had ripped my gown climbing in. I had a thumping headache. And my throat was sore.

Why would my throat be sore? Ah, yes. Olly! Olly! Oh, God! I'd been showing off, hadn't I, bawling plebeian roundelays for the behoof of public school Yahoos, composing ditties which lacked even the merit of rude invention, proving I could piss higher up the walls of Peterhouse than any soft sod from the South.

I'd never pissed up a wall in my life. What gave me the idea that I might be good at it?

Olly, Olly, Ollie!

I had been tsatskying again, hadn't I?

I had hit the town footling.

And what's more I had run the risk of being picked up and arrested by the University Police. On Day One! Some way of saying thank you to my family that would have been. He goes to Cambridge and he's arrested! For five thousand years we had managed to stay out of trouble. Five thousand years in five hundred countries and not a single violation of the civil code. Not even a parking ticket. And now this one goes to Cambridge and ends up behind bars!

Yes, I had hit the town footling. Footling with intent.

In a fit of self-disgust I opted for Yorath and Rubella.

THREE

'Do you think because I am poor, obscure, plain, and little, I am soulless and heartless?'

Jane Eyre, Brontë Charlotte

'Yes.'

Walzer, Oliver

Notice anything, notice any*one*, missing from the preceding?

Totty.

We had the word. We loved the word. We wrapped our tongues around the word. 'Nice piece of totty, that, what!' We even had *their* words. Shelves upon shelves of them. For what were Austen Jane and Eliot George if not totty?

What was Dido? What was Isolde?

But the flesh and blood thing, that which the word denotes – not to be seen.

Yes, there were colleges *for* totty. Totty-only colleges. But somehow it was never really totty that you got there. It was something else. Not everybody felt as I did. There were some, among the hearties and even among the Unmanned, who had no complaints whatsoever about the contents of these totty-only colleges. They wooed them, fell in love with them, married them, betrayed them, just as if they were perfectly normal totty. But they didn't look like perfectly normal totty to me. I was spoilt, I'll admit that: I'd slept on a bed of sugar bags with my arms around Lorna Peachley, I'd habituated the KD, I'd eyed off the best there was; but all KD comparisons apart, who they most reminded me of were my aunties.

Not in appearance, of course. They weren't Sowalki drowsy with little fish-ball cheeks. In appearance they resembled the Brontës. They had that distrait look about them, that air of affecting not to hear the agonizing cries, the sound of souls rending, coming from the other room. In the face of the mayhem they tied back their hair and stared sideways. Governesses fallen from high estate – that was who they looked like. Governesses with family secrets, whose voices wobbled and sawed like silk tearing. But in matters of simple social adeptness they reminded me of my aunties. There was that same fear of dogs and shadows. That same alarm when anything moved suddenly. And that same incompetence with respect to brassieres.

I actually taught one how to dance once. Imagine that. Imagine the measure of the ineptitude that could make me feel relaxed enough to show the way on a dance floor. True, it was only a small dance floor at a small party. And true the dance was only the twist. But even so!

'Now come down,' I remember saying. 'That's it, but keep revolving. Good. Now come up again. Yes, but still revolving.'

My aunty Dolly would have been proud of me.

I must have put a hand out to help with the angle of torsion, a light touch of encouragement on the hip, because I remember leaping back from the lumpiness as though I'd hit a tumour. Haberdasher's swelling. Did they shoplift, these S for spinster, T for totties? Were they thread and tape kleptomaniacs? Was that what my aunties had been up to for all those years, was *that* why they'd feared shop assistants – because they'd dreaded someone discovering the half mile of elastic they'd stuffed inside their bloomers?

The twist was the beginning and the end of it, anyway. I kept a shy distance, and the lumpy mattresses of Totty Hall knew not my impression.

When the touchy silence of existence among the Yorath and Rubella head shrinkers of Golem got too lonely to bear I frequented those back streets of Cambridge to which Yorath had mysteriously alluded in relation to Kafka. I led a secret life. So secret that I kept it from myself. Was that me sitting reading the *Daily Mirror* over bacon sandwich breakfasts in a transport café off the Newmarket Road? A chip off the old block? Couldn't have been. Me holding hands behind the laundromat dryers with a woman old enough to be my mother? Impossible. So how come I am able to remember her name? Rose. The laundromat belonged to her. *Rose's Launderette*. How come I am able to remember that? I took my shirts there for a service wash, that was all. We fell to talking, that was all. She did my ironing for me and I stroked her ruined hands. And once in a while took her to the pictures. Where we may have kissed. Who can say?

My Cambridge.

Brideshead for some. Rose's Launderette for others.

Don't mistake me – I count my blessings; I know I was lucky to have had her.

And then there was ping-pong. Also something I did furtively.

I'd said no at first when the invitation from the college team and then from the UCTTC itself appeared in my pigeon hole. Thank you for asking but I no longer play. But I ran into the Master outside the porter's lodge shortly after that, and I thought I detected a hint of remonstration in the way he feinted his backhand drive at me. 'Eh, Walzer?' If Golem had given me a place on the understanding that I'd raise its ping-pong profile, then I was obliged, was I not?

No doubt there was even something in my contract.

It goes without saying that nobody at Golem College could touch me, out of practice though I was. Nobody anywhere else in the university either, with one exception. An imperious Sri Lankan. Elongated, fine and prickly like a pandanus palm. Somebody da Silva. I am not being impolite. I have genuinely forgotten. But I admit that had I not genuinely forgotten I would have faked it, because he stole from my glory and got on my nerves.

As long as he was out of the way, though, playing for his college and not mine, I was able to recapture some of the old satisfactions. It was fun winning again. A blood sport given the calibre of my opponents, but the more fun for that. At the beginning. Do you know, I was able to bamboozle half of them with spin. Not complex spin – just spin. Side. Old-fashioned dining-room table side. They hadn't come across it before. They stared in astonishment, immobilized, as the ball landed on one spot and then slewed to another. How did I do that?

One of my opponents, a King's man, even complained to the referee. 'He's *spinning* the ball,' he said.

And the referee had to check the rules to see if spinning the ball was allowed.

That was the standard we played to.

So the fun I'm describing had its limits. It was like picking off rabbits with a howitzer. After a while you start to feel ashamed. What would Sheeny have said had he seen me tormenting some nebbish from Queen's who wasn't even sure which part of the bat was the handle? How would Phil Radic have greeted the return of my will to win? 'King of the kids, eh, Ollie. Didn't I say that all you needed was a rest?'

So here I was again, entrammelled in humiliations. Mortifying to lose, mortifying to win.

No wonder I kept it furtive, slipping out of my room with my bat and plimsolls rolled inside my undergraduate gown, and my shorts on under my trousers, hoping that no fellow Yorath and Rubella man would see me go or guess the nature of my errand. I'd raised the question of sport just once in an essay. *Vis-à-vis* the archery scene in *Daniel Deronda*. Nothing more than an admiring reference, in passing, to the strength of Gwendolen Harleth's arm. It drew a gasp and a circle of red ink from Yorath. On the road to womanly wisdom, Walzer, Gwendolen Harleth's vaingloriousness was the first welcome casualty. Or had I misread?

A *locus classicus* for us was the scene in *Persuasion* where Louisa Musgrove is punished for her vulgar mettlesomeness by being thrown from the Cobb in Lyme Regis. More than a *locus classicus*, actually a sacred site. Rubella once hired a minibus to take us all down there for the weekend, to see with our own eyes the place where the only athlete in the *oeuvre* of Austen Jane – for she was to all intents and purposes a gymnast, Louisa Musgrove – symbolically paid for her impetuosity with her life.

Yorath came to join us later, driving down separately with his family. I'd never before seen him, and never again saw him, in such high spirits. 'This is where she jumped,' I heard him pointing out to his little ones. 'Right here. And over there is where she landed. As though dead. Not because she was lively – you mustn't make that mistake. Jane Austen never punished vivacity. But because her mind was poor.'

A shudder ran through us all. A poor mind was a charge we may have laid frequently, but we never laid it lightly.

One by one we trooped off the Cobb with our heads lowered, knowing what we knew.

It didn't take much imagination on my part, therefore, to work out what they'd have thought about someone who put his mind to *ping-pong*. Better that they never found out. Better that I kept it a secret from them, along with Rose's Launderette.

As for my Golem team-mates, none of whom of course was a Yorath and Rubella man, they have melted from my recollection. All I remember is that they easily ran out of breath, wore elasticated shorts and were inordinately impressed by my skills. Shot, Ollie! Beautiful shot, Ollie! Olly, olly, Ollie!

All hearties are slavish – I learned that on Day One. You can twist a man-mountain head-butter from Bucks around your little finger with the lamest limerick. Make him up a dirty song that rhymes and he's yours for life. Tongue out, following you down King's Parade panting, like a poodle. But my ping-pongers team-mates weren't even the real thing. Podgy would-be hearties from Shropshire and the Borders, they followed behind what was following behind. Poodles' poodles. And on such I squandered my gifts.

Playing for the university provided slightly stiffer opposition, and gave me back a bit of pride, but I was still keeping company with minor-counties over-appreciators who wore elasticated shorts. All except Question-Mark da Silva. A class act, da Silva, I'll give him that. And not just because *his* shorts were belted and pressed. He was the only non-Bug and Dniester ping-pong player I'd ever come across who had wit in his game. Maybe not wit as Phil Radic employed it. It was colder than that. Phil Radic's game was for everybody to enjoy, not least the person on the receiving end of the joke. Da Silva played derision ping-pong and when he was finished with you you were dead. I never faced him competitively. I was careful not to let that happen. But we were the first-string doubles pair against Oxford, in my only representative year, and that was killing enough. He called me away from the table half-way through the second game – we'd fumbled the first – to tell me what I was doing wrong.

'You play your game,' I said, 'I'll play mine.'

'That's not how you play doubles,' he said.

'That's how *I* play doubles,' I said.

He looked down upon me using the full length of his nose.

He had a very fine nose. 'Precisely,' he said. 'That's how *you* play.'

'You play how you play,' I said. 'I'll play how I play.'

'That's the whole fucking trouble,' he said. 'The way you're playing I can't play my fucking game.'

How they swore, those Sri Lankans.

In Fenners too, with people watching. Dignitaries. For it's not nothing, a Varsity match.

No wonder we lost.

I lost my singles as well. The old trouble. The sick fucks wanted to win too badly. And they'd seen spin before, too, the chazerim.

Oxford 10, Cambridge 0? Probably not. Da Silva must have won his singles. Oxford 8, Cambridge 2 sounds more like it.

After which I gave it away. This time there really was no more ping-pong, let the Master think what the Master liked. Disapprobation – that was where I sought superiority henceforth – in prim disapprovals and disavowals. I became a head-shaker. A nay-sayer. World champion in not having any.

But at least I'd earnt the right to buy a white blazer with light-blue braiding around it. A half-blue – that was all they gave you for ping-pong. For a full blue you had to roll in mud and put your face in another man's arse. My usual complaint. It's not sport for the shaygetsim unless there's toches in it.

Still, a half-blue is better than no blue. And it cut ice in the Kardomah, that's for sure.

A funny thing, though. Years later, coming out of Harry's Bar, I ran into a person going into the Hotel Monaco and Grand Canal of whom I had no recollection whatsoever, but who was adamant he had played against me, for Oxford, on the night I had fallen out with da Silva. 'A thrashing,' he said.

I hadn't remembered it as that bad. ''Fraid I've lost it in the mists of time,' I said, 'but didn't I take you to a final game?'

'Didn't *you* take *me*? Ha! I didn't get ten points in either game. You destroyed me. The spin you put on!'

'Hang on,' I said. 'I never destroyed anyone that night. I lost every match I played.'

He shook his head. Bought me a Bellini on the strength of it. I'd been unplayable, he reckoned. Tougher even than that Pakistani chappie. Oxford's worst defeat by Cambridge in a decade.

'You've got the wrong year,' I told him. 'You've got the wrong person. I was on the team that went down to Oxford.'

But he insisted on his version of events. Maybe he was drunk. I agreed to giving him my address, at any rate, so he could send me the relevant cuttings. We drank another Bellini to that, watched the Canal plash and the scabby gondoliers toss lira for passing boys, and speaking for myself at least, forgot all about it. A couple of weeks later I heard from him. A nice note. On legal practice notepaper. Lovely to see me again, blah blah. After all these years, blah blah. Still spinning, he observed. Ho ho. Together with copies of the match reports from the *Cambridge Evening News* and the *Oxford Mail*. Confirming his impression of the result in black and white. Cambridge 7, Oxford 3. Ex-Lancashire wiz Walzer and classy Colombo hitter da Silva too much for Oxford. Team of Walzer and da Silva a delight to cognoscenti of the game.

Explain that.

Can a person be so wedded to defeat that he remembers it even where it wasn't?

And does that mean I can expect somebody to hail me outside Harry's Bar one of these days and tell me that my life has been one long success story after all?

Sabine Weinberger came to live with me in my final under-graduate year in Cambridge after I'd met up with her again at a silver wedding. My family, her cake decorations. She had become a silversmith, a fashion jeweller and fabricator of table tsatskes much in demand in north Manchester. Like her father she wore a unicorn micrometer on her forehead which she lowered over her bad eye when she wasn't working.

Relations had not been good between us following the night I'd forced my disrespect down her throat at her place. That indecorum belonged to another age, but the hurt was still palpable on the occasions I was back in town and we happened to run into each other. When she saw me at a party she'd hurl herself into the arms of the nearest man, gyrating lewdly if there was music playing, throwing her head back and laughing like a gypsy if there wasn't. See what you've lost, that was what she was saying. Everybody wants, and everybody can have – except you! I opened a cupboard at a Christmas bash once, looking for my coat, and found her with her pants off in the company of two Italian waiters from the Mogambo. I've never seen anyone more pleased to be disturbed.

Just because you can see through a ploy doesn't mean it isn't working. If anything, the transparency made it the more transfixing. And I came to be excited by the idea that my very presence assured her unchastity. Yes, it was a sort of jealousy, but a greedily slow and curious jealousy, biding its time, wondering what lasciviousness next. Was there nothing I couldn't make her do?

It suited her to be a silversmith. She found herself in her occupation. The micrometer alone was alluring. A marvellous deformity, like a single jewelled eye in the head of a minotaur. All the ornamentation she designed for her own use drew on some monstrous, mythical creature theme or another. I saw her encased from head to toe in a rippling tin foil sheath once, finned like a mermaid. She attached raking witches' claws to her fingers, ten silver killer-thimbles, and buckled a spiked hell-cat collar around her neck. Long before they became a routine fashion item she was dragging manacles and shackles behind her. But it was Old Testament she did best. Great clanking Bathsheba bangles, gleaming Esther hair-combs, wives of Solomon necklaces coiled as dangerously as snakes, slithering towards her bosom. She clashed like cymbals. I loved that. When she saw me enter a room she fell ringing into the arms of other men.

Slut Jewess, I guess that was what she was doing. The Slut Jew*ess*. The contents of my old box of family mutilations made flesh. She was plain, she was stubbly, she was local (as good as family, almost); but I didn't have to cut her up to make her lewd. Lewd she could do herself. The Slut Jew*ess*.

Funny how the second syllable of that word changes the first. Say Jew and you think of someone bent and bookish; say Jewess and the desert is suddenly alive with swarthy bangled whores writhing around a golden calf with their brazen tits perspiring.

A silver calf, in this instance.

It's the ess that does it. It's the ess that gives it the juice. Jew*ess*.

Ess. Ess for Sarah. Ess for Sahara. Ess for So Who Needs a Shikse. Ess for Slut.

And lonely mid the mirthless and the silent of Golem College, bereft of all totty as I'd been, I finally had no defence against her clanking.

She had the smell of other men on her when I backed her into a cupboard under the stairs at the Broughton Assembly Rooms, attacked her silver clustered pendants like a bell-ringer, and told her I had ears for no one else.

'You don't respect me,' she laughed.

'*They* don't respect you,' I said.

'I don't respect them.'

'And that's why you fuck them?'

'Who said I fuck them?'

'I can hear you fucking them.'

'And what does it sound like?'

'Silver bells.'

'And that's why you want to fuck me?'

'Who said I want to fuck you?'

'So what do you want?'

'Your disrespect.'

'In that case you do want to fuck me.'

'How so?'

'Because that's how I show my disrespect. I let them fuck me.'

'You must disrespect a lot of men.'

'I do.'

'I know.'

'And that's why you want me?'

'That's why I want you.'

And a year later, reader, in a little uncivil ceremony on the lawn of Golem College, with our bemused families in attendance, I married her.

This isn't a marriage story. Everybody knows what happens in a marriage and it happened in ours.

She was an act of recidivism on my part, but I have no regrets or complaints. She may not say the same about me, but I charge her with nothing. She kept her part of the bargain. She was as dirty as I wanted her to be, the Slut Jewess of Cambridge, the totty to end totty, and then when she thought that was enough she had the strength of mind to say so. 'Now we'll have children,' were her exact words.

I cannot even claim that she jeopardized my career as a Collins Classics academic. Rubella liked her, believed he understood her, and even explained her to me sometimes. 'She's actually a very shy person,' he dared to tell me once. What Yorath thought I have no idea. Yorath never talked to actual women. But Yorath

Mrs became a friend of Sabine's through kindergarten, and that was enough. The kinder spoke.

There were no money worries either. Sabine opened a jewellery studio in Kettle's Yard where she made enough for me to go on with my research and father a hundred Walzers. And then did the same in Bristol when it was time for my researches to continue there. She was the perfect wife. She travelled well. She fitted in. She earned.

So what was the problem? The connection. In the end I couldn't take the connection. *Only connect.* Well, I'd knocked *him* into the gutter on Day One. That should have been a warning. I couldn't connect. I was ashamed of her. Not because of her glass eye. Not because she'd done slut. Not because she was now doing non-slut. And not even because she was a mother, although mother is a serious charge to lay against any woman. No, what I couldn't hack was that she was unserer. What was I doing with one of ours, one of us? Now that the tarantella fever of the gypsy Jewess music had cooled, now that I no longer listened to her bejewelled thighs clanking faithlessly in the night, I couldn't see the point of her as a companion for me. She was a backward step. The children were a backward step. We had two. She wanted a third. She'd worked it all out. There was time for a fourth. Maybe a fifth. How many backward steps could I take before I fell?

What is the meaning of life if it is not escape through ascent? Up out of the dirt, out of the filth, out of the shell, out of the suck and pull of the swag and the tsatskes, up and away into the clear uncluttered blue. Shaygets blue? No, I never wanted to be a shaygets. Just a tree, a good strong healthy Bug and Dniester tree, re-planted in a more clement soil, showing its branches above the others.

Otherwise I might as well have stayed in Manchester and gone on playing ping-pong.

So, goodnight Sabine Walzer *née* Weinberger.

And the children? Baruch and Channa as they were not as yet called?

Oh, yes, the children.

I affect a hardness of heart in relation to my children for reasons that are only partially clear to me. I don't trust people who are pious about children. I'd go further: it's my experience that people who are pious about children nurse a malevolence towards the rest of humanity that would make the devil reel. They only have to begin the sentence – 'The last thing I want to see while I'm sitting watching television with my children . . .' – and I know I'm in the presence of unadulterated evil. But that's not it; that's not the reason I affect a hardness of heart in relation to my own.

Somebody has said that you cannot love a child unless you once loved the child in yourself. What do I mean *somebody* has said it? *Everybody* has said it! Well, the child in myself was no great shakes. I couldn't wait to see the back of him.

And I knew what remained of me well enough, now that I *had* seen the back of him, to be reasonably confident I wouldn't terribly miss being a father. But that didn't mean I couldn't wait to see the back of *them*.

I walked them to school in Clifton on my farewell morning, the three of us enjoying the nip of cold in the air, kicking leaves, smelling the buildings. It was the eternal autumnal school morning. I could taste the leather strap of my old school satchel on my teeth.

But their satchels weren't made of leather. Brightly coloured nylon, that was what they carried their books and pencil cases in, because schooldays were meant to be happier now.

I held each of them by the hand, to stop them skipping into the road. It was like being plugged into two separate sources of warmth. I am deriving pleasure today, I thought, doing for the last time a thing I have never enjoyed doing before. That's how important pain is to pleasure.

They were too small still to understand what it meant when I knelt between them at the school gate and said, 'Now Daddy is going away for quite a long time, but I'll write to you and send you presents.'

What's 'quite a long time' when you don't add up to ten between you?

They weren't distressed. They didn't know to be distressed. As for me, I couldn't hold my face together, but I wasn't sure who I was the more distressed for, them or me. At the moment of taking permanent farewell of your children it's difficult to make those sorts of distinctions: you are more them than you are yourself.

And then they were gone, swept up into the noise of the playground. The noise I never liked when I was in the midst of it; the noise I now love with a passion when I pass it on the other side of the railings.

I made it half-way home, my jaw disconnected from my face, my head going from one side to the other, struggling for air like a fading swimmer, until the waters crashed over me and I found myself, I didn't know how much later, cowering in somebody's front garden, hiding from the world just as I had when I'd lacked the courage to front up to my children's mother's party a thousand years before.

What's the opposite to a presentiment? What do you call the sensation – infinitely less spectral than *déjà vu*, infinitely more behavioural and normalized – of having done a deed a hundred times before, although you never knew you had until now? That was how I felt about this morning's leave-taking of my children. I knew the scene backwards. It was as if I'd been practising it all my life.

So, yes, goodnight to them too.

They were better off without me. The grandiose have no business fathering children. Especially the grandiose who like to lose big.

That's no example to set a child.

FOUR

There is no such thing as an ex ping-pong player. Years after your last game you go on wondering why you lost, or why you couldn't have won more comfortably.

You are never free, no, not even in the grave. As your flesh rots around you in the blackness, you will still be trying to hit the ball past an opponent you cannot see. One thousand, two thousand, three thousand years of striving . . . and still, through the silent night, the ball coming back . . .

Ping-Pong Under the Roman Occupation, Kar Domah
(Reprinted in *Ping-Pong: A Guide to the Perplexed*,
Oliver Walzer)

I LEFT THE country. Cleaner that way. Let them hear the twig break. Besides, there were more jobs for Collins Classics men out of the country. Colonies especially good. There was so much interest in the Brontës – any of them, didn't matter which – that you only had to say you'd read one and the job was yours. Embarrassing, the number of offers that rolled in. But those were simpler times. The women hadn't yet re-appropriated the women. And French theory hadn't yet cowed the glorious pragmatism of the Anglo-Saxon mind. You read a book and extrapolated its moral, that was all there was to teaching in those days. You read the novel, you told the story, you animadverted on its adequacy to experience. Full stop.

Our subject was the book, not the sociology of the study of the book. Babies that we were.

I should have seen the writing on the wall when my own Ph.D. thesis – *The Wound Re-Opened: A Comparative Study of Shyness and Other Social Excruciations in the Novels of Edith Wharton and Virginia Woolf* – was knocked back comprehensively not only by the Syndics of the Cambridge University Press but by every academic publisher in Britain and America. A methodological problem. I was too old fashioned. I was no good on words as signs. Arkansas University Press liked my prose style and wondered if I had anything more up to the minute in the pipeline. Hence my ping-pong manual. But by the time they got that out into the shops in a language which Americans could understand it too was obsolete.

Now I hang on by my fingertips. Independently funded colleges, shonky private universities, non-Italian language speaking institutions with the occasional extra-mural this and that for visiting foreigners – I take what I can get. I am yesterday's man.

It's amazing how long you can go on being yesterday's man and still draw breath. It helps, of course, if you have a little something from Gershom and Dora Finkel to ease the pain. It means you can rent a very small room not quite overlooking the Grand or even one of the Not So Grand Canals, but looking over something every bit as smelly, and afford a sufficiency of pasta and cheap Venetian wine and free light. And it means you can believe you've attained the clear uncluttered blue.

For the Brontës as understood by a man there is now little or no call, but people do want to know what Byron and Ruskin and Henry James did when they were here, to say nothing of Casanova. And I can give them that, not exactly from the woman's point of view, but as it *impinged* on women, so to speak.

It's not impossible you've seen me on your summer holidays, or in the course of one of those lightning weekend breaks designed to relieve you of your air miles, holding aloft a black umbrella, leading my Asian and American charges from one culture-drenched palazzo to the next, on and off those magnificently unfillable and not at all vaporous pontoons, the vaporetti, halting on this bridge or on that to tell them of murders and seductions and other art-associated gossip. Most of it invented by me.

The Moody-Merchant of Venice.

But at least it's not the Irwell.

And at least it's not swag.

Correction: at least it's not Walzer swag.

And the death thing doesn't worry me? The coffined gondolas, the sudden closures of vista, the menacing shadows, the floods, the fires, the sinking stucco, the feeling you have that the malaria has never really gone away?

It's someone else's death – that always helps. I see or hear one drop almost every week. Sometimes it's just the sound of one going into the canal you hear. Not a splash, more a thud. Like someone falling on to a sheet of Copestake's foam. Ooch plock! But you can also get the whole melodrama, such as when I had to lead a group of my charges away from an outdoor restaurant in San Stefano recently, where a gentleman no older than me was springing blood from both nostrils, a pair of crimson jets flooding his basket of bread, his plate of *coda di ròspo*, stealing over the starched white tablecloth as though from underneath, as though the table itself had been wounded and meant to bleed for ever. It's a deeper red when it's more than just a nose bleed. And a heavier downpour. When the brain is bleeding you don't even try to save the fish.

But of course for a moment it looked beautiful, like another proof of the ancient Venetian gift for decoration. A bold aesthetic coup – red on white, liquid on cloth, flesh on stone.

I suppose I ought not to have walked my party in the other direction. Isn't death in Venice what they have come to see? For certainly no one does it better.

So no, except in so far as everything worries me now, the death part of Venice doesn't worry me unduly. There's been more of it in Manchester. Too much death in Manchester for me ever to go back willingly to the place. The city itself had the heart ripped out of it long before the IRA did its bit. Torn apart to make room for tsatske precincts for the post-industrial poor. Tickle the poor into town with tsatskes and they take over the town. Mate, multiply, bebop, stick needles into themselves, put pistols to your head. Try Manchester after midnight today and you'll think you've walked into the Book of Revelation. I'd say wall it up and forget it exists if there weren't some of my own still in there. Not many. Not as many as there used to be. The heart has been ripped out of the Walzers and the Saffrons as well. And that's the only reason I ever return: to bury another of us.

Fay was the first. Suddenly and in her sleep. Of fright.

Routine check-up, routine recommendation that she come back in for a second opinion. Just in case what they'd found was a tumour. They named it, you see. They spoke the word. Only *just in case*, but the word was out and once the word's out there's no taking it back.

She died dreading.

The old Saffron fear of sphericality – whatever was round and incalculable.

And the old Saffron horror of our own insides.

Poor Fay. I know how she must have felt. If only we'd been born hollow. With our giblets in a removable plastic bag.

I flew back from a conference for her funeral. It was November, as it always is when we bury our northern dead. The ground cold but not yet hard. We die soggy in the North. We come apart like cardboard.

My mother was scarcely alive herself. She had wept for

thirty-six hours. No sleep, no food, just tears and telephone calls.

'I feel as if I'll cry for ever,' she told me. 'Poor Fay. She was just a kid. She was barely older than my own children. She hadn't started to live yet. I won't ever get over it.'

Too cruel when it's the youngest who goes first. But there was an over-and-above cruelty which no one could bear to put into words. No, she hadn't lived, but she *was* just starting to. She died, as though to satisfy some spite at the very core of things, just as she was putting a life together. She was in love, skippingly in love with her nuisance caller and engaged to marry him. For years she'd rejected every suggestion of a face to face encounter, content to go on talking over the blower, afraid of what he would be like in the flesh, afraid of what *she* would be like in the flesh. Then finally they did it, met for tea and cucumber sandwiches at the Midland Hotel, pink carnations in their buttonholes, a palm court orchestra playing, and my father hiding behind the palms in case of trouble. There was no trouble. How could there be? They were already good friends, knew everything there was to know about each other – favourite book, favourite walk, favourite short piece of music, favourite long piece of music, favourite colour, favourite smell, favourite fear – and had learnt to understand the meaning of every hesitation and intake of breath. The telephone teaches you to listen if nothing else. And they'd been on the telephone a long time.

Had she lived, she would have changed her name to Fenwick, moved into a house with verandahs on Alderley Edge, woken to the sound of birdsong, and become a stepmother, maybe a mother in her own right. It was all just beginning for her. She wasn't even forty yet.

We had to tear my grandfather away from the television for the funeral. Put a suit on him, empty his pockets of sweet wrappers, brush his hair and shove him into the hearse. For a brief moment all sides of our family thought as one: it should have been him we were removing from our sight.

That we were changed by Fay's death goes without saying. But what changed us most was the depth of Duncan Fenwick's grief. He was inconsolable. He hung on to my mother when the coffin was carried out of the house, and then joined the remaining Saffron women when the time came for them to throw themselves upon it. He called her name over and over – 'Fay, Fay, oh Fay!' – a bloodcurdling lament which made her unrecognizable to us, not ours at all in death, because at the last she had not been ours but someone else's in life. We made room for him, even Fay's sisters parted, so that the last kiss on the coffin could be his.

We let him have her.

No one could have looked less like us, less like either side of us. From the way he dressed and carried himself you would have picked him for a market gardener, a small landowner in corduroys and green waterproofs, smelling of turnips and rabbit fur. But there was something of the New World pioneer about him too, an optimism in the way he took his time and moved his stringy joints, deceptively pared down, like a nutcracker. He was lightly freckled, with a tumble of pale orange hair and piercing powder-blue eyes. He spoke slowly, and nicely. A Manchester distinction. *Doesn't he speak nice!* It was his gentle well-spokenness that had attracted Fay to him in the first place when he'd rung at random to ask the colour of her pants. None of us bore such confident leisureliness in our voices, as though there weren't a thousand other things happening that you had to be heard over, as though there was no reason in the world to rush your words, because where you lived everything had stayed the same for centuries, and marauding Cossacks were few and far between. And yet here he was, among us, grieving with us, sorrowing *for* one of us. Forever to miss Fay as much as we would. Maybe more.

And maybe with more reason. Because Fay's queer unaccustomedness, her absence of all worldly competence, had saved him from God knows what fate. Who else but Fay would have kept the phone to her ear and listened to all that filth in the first place?

So we let him have her, and more to the point, we let her have him. There was the change: we conceded they'd been lucky in each other.

Whenever one of my sisters next took home a floppy-prepuced white man the name of Duncan Fenwick would be invoked to prevent either my father or my mother – depending on whose turn it was – getting the platz. Hadn't Duncan Fenwick, against all the odds, turned out to be a shtik naches? Hadn't he shown himself to be a mensch, a gentleman, a person of the deepest feelings, capable of a loyalty to one of us that maybe none of us could match? So why shouldn't this latest treife gatecrasher turn out to be the same? Duncan Fenwick had adored our Fay, alav ha-shalom, and would have made her deliriously happy: why shouldn't Gordon le Goy do likewise with our Hetty? And in the end, as though we'd gradually stopped noticing the difference, as though it had ceased at the last to matter, that was precisely who we welcomed into the family – Gordon le Goy. Followed by Benedict von Baitsimmer. My brothers-in-law.

I say 'welcomed', but you know what I mean. Didn't offer a thousand pounds in used flims to vanish out of sight. Didn't set about with an axe. Didn't say prayers for the dead over Hetty and Sandra as a consequence.

You know – *welcomed*.

But even that would have been a welcome too far in the eyes of some. All very well being accommodating, but wasn't our neighbourliness bound to spell the beginning of the end of the Saffrons and the Walzers?

You know the game: change Walzer to le Goy in four moves, altering only one letter at a time. You have twenty seconds.

Baruch and Channa Weinberger *née* Walzer's view exactly. In fact in their view the twenty seconds were already up. The dreaded thing had happened. What Hitler hadn't achieved in Auschwitz – I know, I know: there's no bottom to the vulgarity of the Orthodox – we Walzers had done to ourselves in north Manchester.

Well I'm their father and it's my duty to tell them what I think. Shem zikh in dayn vaytn haldz. You should be ashamed to the depths of your throat.

To be humane means to stay calm and wait your turn. What goes around comes around. The goyim thicken our soup, we thicken theirs.

That's always been the way of it. How otherwise do you explain the tristful warrior aspect of the Kazakh which you've inherited from my side of the family, and that inane insensate Junker expression which you've been cursed with from your mother's? Why do you think you still don't look like fucking Abraham?

I don't mind admitting, though, that I'd have liked to see Gordon le Goy married to my Channa, thereby signalling the beginning of the end of the Weinbergers. But what father ever gets to live to see his fondest hopes realized? My little Channa returned full circle whence she'd came and married a Vulvick. I flew in to Manchester from Venice especially for the wedding. The full frummie monty. Bride waiting on the chuppah in her new sheitel, just come from a vaginal scrutiny in the ritual baths, hopeful as a morning flower with all her petals open. Bridegroom wrestled to her side, his fringes flying, putting up a fight – Don't make me, don't make me! – the one with everything to lose. How's a father meant to feel when he sees that? You're lucky to have her, you kuni-lemele. A boy with pin wheels stuck to his ears is lucky to have anyone, never mind my lovely Channaleh. But then I was lucky to be invited. The whole shlemozzle at the party after, too. Some party! Men on one side of the screen, women on the other, for the women must not be inflamed by the sight of the black hats dancing. But I'm coming to all that. And in mitigation of the horror of it, I must say that if I hadn't flown to Manchester for Channa's wedding to Shmuelly, I wouldn't have known about the Ninth World Veterans' Ping-Pong Championships, in town at the very same time I was.

But I'm coming to that too.

After Fay, they were lining up to drop.

My grandfather went next, of an infection brought on by ingrowing toe-nails. He had stopped cutting them and was bending them over and pushing them back inside instead. We laughed about it at the funeral.

And a few years after that, Gershom of bowel we don't say what, quickly followed by poor Dora of loneliness. She'd got to know no one in south Manchester. Gershom had kept her locked up in his ex-boarding house, made her butter bagels and cook lokshen soup for him, made her play ping-pong with him, and once in a blue moon took her out to bingo. Her body wasn't found until about five days after her death. Still relatively fragrant, apparently, because of how cold her bed was. Gershom had forbidden her to use the heating, except for an hour on the most freezing mornings, and she was still obeying orders.

But then I have reason to be grateful she wasn't splashing his hard-earned spondulicks about.

Dolly died of fright, like Fay. The t word again. She too didn't make old bones, but her passing was somehow less upsetting than the others'. Perhaps because we had mourned for her already. 'I take consolation in this,' my mother said, 'she did better than any of us ever expected she would. At least she had a life.'

She had a life. She started her own dancing school in Rusholme in partnership with her shlemiel map-reading husband and was engrossed in Old Tyme every day she was alive thereafter. 'I'm never bored,' she told me on one of my visits home. Her voice

337

was like a needle skidding across vinyl. 'I don't know what people mean when they say they're bored. I think boredom is a betrayal of life.' By life she meant ballroom dancing. Boredom is a betrayal of ballroom dancing. And when my mother said at least Dolly had a life she meant at least she had ballroom dancing. Whether she ever got over Dora's betrayal of her we never knew. But Dora stopped dancing once Gershom took her south, never swirled under a spinning ball of light again, and that must have made it easier for Dolly.

So they were all gone, all the Shrinking Violets, and my box was empty now. Not an S for spinster Saffron left for me to cut to pieces even in my imagination.

My mother took the passing of her sisters hard. It was an accumulation of grief. With the death of each sister she had to mourn afresh the death of the sister previous, and the death of her mother in all of them. She carried her head slightly aback, like a boxer, knowing only too well where the next blow was coming from, but not knowing when. 'Aloof,' some members of my father's family called her, but no one could have been less aloof. She was punch-drunk.

My father's side lasted longer, as they were built to do. And when they did go they were so old you scarcely noticed. The first exception to this was uncle Motty who passed away in the lavatory, no doubt still trying to bang the last drop out of his penis. And then, before anyone could recover from the shock of Motty, my father himself.

The fight had gone out of him after he went mechullah. You might not have known that had you never met him in earlier days. On the face of it he was still a great pleaser, still carried toys around in his pockets, was still waiting for the big something, still parked his van – that's to say Sheeny's van – in some odd places, still had ants in his pants. But he wasn't the same man. He'd lost his cheyshik for life. His will for it, his desire. The big thing wasn't going to happen; he knew that even though he still waited. He kept his ear cocked, just in case, but it was force of habit more than anything else. The big thing had passed him by.

He worked for Sheeny Waxman for two or three years, then they parted amicably. Enough. Enough, for both of them. In the end it was Sheeny who called it a day. Medical reasons. Pitching was wearing out his throat. He kept losing his voice. If he went on going berserk from the back of a lorry much longer he would lose his voice and not get it back. I heard rumours that he had bought a car showroom with a Jaguar concession in a partnership of the hoarse with Benny the Pole, but by then I'd lost contact with him. Cambridge and Sheeny didn't mix. For his part my father was relieved to be out of it. He hadn't been able to bear not being his own boss. Yes, yes he could just about accept the idea of working for my mother – since no one would believe he really *was* working for her anyway – so yes, a little swag shop on Victoria Avenue was just the ticket; but it turned out he didn't have a lot of heart left for swag either. As his only biographer, I designate these his Wilderness Years. He just wandered around. He shmied arum. He patshkied. He'd knock up a set of shelves for my mother, then he'd go for a wander. He'd install a new security grille, then he'd be off shmying again. The grille was one thing but the lock, the lock . . . Looking for just the right lock with just the right barrel, inspecting the stock of every locksmith in Manchester, could take a week, a fortnight, a month. You never knew where he was going to turn up. You never knew where you would see him next. I was hardly ever at home but the few times I did come back I had to organize search parties to find him. Salford was where we always started. He seemed to like it there. Salford suited him. The junction of Great Cheetham Street and Bury New Road, past the Rialto, down through Albert Park to Pendleton, taking Cromwell Road between the Racecourse and the Greyhound Track, neither of which held the slightest intrinsic interest for him, turning right at Brindle

Heath for Irlams O' Th' Height or left to Seedley and Eccles and all points west. The functional part of town. The hinterland of the city. But also the way out. Definitely not warehouse or cash-and-carry territory, and not the nest-hot Salford of his birth either. It was unassociational Salford he liked. Big barren spaces. Wide roads. Colliery views. Places where he could buy timber. Weigh out nails. Pick through locks. Measure lengths of iron. Test alarm systems. Stop for a toasted cheese sandwich. Patshky about. Shmy arum.

But at least he no longer had any invoices to lose.

For twenty-five, thirty years he tsatskied. It was his revenge on the big thing that never happened. You won't approach me, I won't approach you. If the mountain won't come to Mahomet, then Mahomet will just have to shmy around.

Big Thing 5. Joel Walzer 21.

Well done, Joel. Except that when you whop Big Thing, no one's watching.

For twenty-five, thirty years he tsatskied, filled his arteries with cheese, and then he died.

I took my turn to sit up with him during some of his last nights in hospital, sat at his bedside holding his hand, while the other old men with blockages trailed hopelessly from their beds to the lavatories and back again, shaking their heads, carrying their cardboard chamber-pots in front of them, empty, empty, always empty.

One night while he was dozing he suddenly tapped himself on the forehead and said, 'Well that's that sorted.'

'What is, Dad?'

'What?'

'What's sorted?'

'Oh, hello Oliver, where are you now?'

'I'm here, Dad, with you.'

'Tsedraiter! I mean where are you living now?'

'Venice.'

'Venice? Very nice.' He changed his position in the bed, agonizingly slowly, using his elbows. He didn't like it when anybody tried to help him. 'Where's Venice again?'

'Italy. It's the one with all the gondolas and canals. We used to do a coffee table with Venice on, remember.'

'Don't talk to me about coffee tables.'

'Sorry.'

'No, I remember. Lots of water. I didn't know you liked water. You can't even swim, can you? You'd better not tell your mother you're near water.'

The things he knew about me, my father. The things he'd had time to notice, after all.

'I'm not there for the water,' I said.

'So what are you there for?' Father to son. It's all right, Oliver, you can tell me. Nekaiveh, eh? Bad boy. Tell me, tell me. Remind me of what it's like to be somewhere you're not supposed to be, with your eyes black and your heart thumping.

But I was, as I'd always been, a failure to him. A nebbish, primmed up by my aunties, prigged and prissified by Yorath and Rubella. A milksop.

'I suppose I'm there for the light,' I said. Just what he wanted to hear. 'And the buildings. And my work.'

He nodded. Ah yes, work.

'And I'm like you,' I said. 'I enjoy shmying arum. It's easy to get lost in Venice. In that regard it's like Salford.'

'Is it?' He seemed impressed. 'Is there a gaff there?'

'It's all gaff,' I said. 'It's just one big gaff.'

'So what are you doing in a place like that? You always hated the gaffs. You're like your mother. She always hated the gaffs.'

'Not always, Dad.'

'She did. Always. Too sensitive. Wouldn't say boo to a goose. Still won't.'

'I meant me. I didn't always hate them.'

'You did. You couldn't wait to get away.'

341

'It's not true. I had some good times on the gaffs.'

'Name one.'

'Dad!'

'Go on, name one.'

'What about when the pig attacked us at Bakewell.'

'Oh yes, the pig. Oink, oink! I'm sorry I missed that.' He smiled at the recollection, tried to laugh, but ended up in a tangle with his tubes, having to bang the phlegm out of his chest.

'And London Road,' I said. 'The day we found the Copestakes' van on the bomb site before us and you decided we'd push it out of the way . . .'

This time he had to laugh, phlegm or no phlegm. 'The look on your ponim,' he said. 'I can still see the look on your face when the side door opened and those nutters fell out.'

'And what about the bricks?' I said. 'What about when they put bricks under the wheels to stop us pushing, so we had to run round taking them out, and they had to run round putting them back under, and we had to run around taking them out again . . .'

He held his hand up to get me to stop. Otherwise he would die laughing. I noticed the see-through plastic dog tag round his wrist. What was that for? Identification in case he got lost wandering from his bed to the lavatory? He used to have wrists like Victor Mature. He could have pulled a temple down with those wrists once upon a time. Even when I'd last seen him he could have shaken a small synagogue. Now, in a matter of a few months, they had become a little old man's wrists, a frail tracery of sunspots and chicken bones, incapable of trembling a lulav.

Enough, Oliver, stop, you'll make me die laughing. Well, why not. Better that way. Die choking on your own laughter, Dad. Die grinning that big daft boyish shmerkle with which you won the heart of my mother, the one you employed to wow them at the World Machareike Championships that sultry Saturday afternoon in 1933 when you felt that something big was still within your grasp.

The one I didn't inherit.

So no, I wouldn't stop.

'And what about the look on *your* face,' I went on, 'when Copestake called me a you-know-what? And the cops had to come to pull you off him? And what about the time you let me roast at the back of the edge with a nest of suitcases under my jumper? And what about Sheeny's mad antics when he'd plunder everything and you'd get furious with him . . .'

But he was asleep now, haggard, ravaged, his breath troubled and uncertain, his cheeks wet.

And now my mother sits alone, surrounded by swag, with her head set further back on her shoulders than ever, tensed, blind-eyed and all-seeing like Tiresias. Yes, she knows where the blow will come from. It will come from us, the children or the children's children, the only ones she has left. She has the air of someone who now does not expect to die herself. She will be here until we have all gone. It's her job to be here until we have all gone, to shepherd us out, as she shepherded us in. To bear the scars left by the going of every one of us. So she sits and waits. And counts.

The last time I saw her she apologized for having given me life.

That's how grave we have become, what's left of us.

'Don't be foolish,' I said. 'What can you possibly suppose you have to apologize for? I have loved, I *am loving*, my life. I would not have been without it. I thank you for it.'

'Do you?'

'Of course I do.'

'That makes me feel better,' she said. 'But I know how hard it's been for you.'

I shrugged, as if hard was nothing. 'That's part of it,' I said.

But then suddenly rebelled against the idea that I'd had it hard at all. 'Not that I'm sure I know what you mean,' I added.

She looked at me long and evenly, my mother Tiresias. What did she know? I found my colour changing beneath her scrutiny. A phenomenon that had not occurred for forty years. Did she know about my box? Did she know what I'd done to Grandma, and to Aunty Dora and to Aunty Dolly and to Aunty Fay? Did she know about Lorna Peachley and what I'd wanted her to do to me? Some things a mother should not know about her son. Some things a son should not know his mother knows.

But if she did know she kept the details to herself. 'You've had your disappointments,' she said.

I wasn't sure I even wanted to concede that. Doesn't I've had my disappointments usually mean I've had *only* disappointments. Whereas I –

'You've nothing to apologize for,' I said again, backing off. This was all too elemental for me. Another reason I was holed up in Venice – to escape the final act of Families.

'Well I hope you're telling me the truth,' she said.

And that was that.

In fairness to her, it's hardly surprising her mood was grave. I was over for Channa's wedding, and a lot of unanswered family questions were suddenly back buzzing around our heads.

Sabine had returned to Manchester with the children immediately we split up. No point hanging around the Christian world once Mr Shaygets himself had pissed off. From a fatherly point of view there was some advantage in this since it meant I could see my children whenever I was home for a funeral. But I suppose that from a filial point of view that was hardly well calculated to give me a good press. How come Daddy only ever comes to see us when someone's died? Eventually Sabine would have had to tell them. Daddy isn't a good man.

Herself, the moment she took up her Manchester matronage Sabine reverted to being the good woman it was always in her

Vulvick genes to be. No more hiding in cupboards with waiters from the Mogambo whom she was unable to respect. She let it be known that she had her one good eye fixed on an Orthodox marriage the second time around, but there was nothing doing. The Orthodox don't give second time around. She settled in the end for quasi-mystical Zionist folksie, a freckled Canadian/Israeli who'd seen God at the Wailing Wall and now ran a travel agency on Bury Old Road, specializing in holidays for people desirous of doing likewise, and this was enough to direct my children into a course I would never have chosen for them. By the age of six, Channa (at this time still Charlotte) knew the words of every new Israeli folk song, was starting to be kitted out in those long, ill, shapeless you-can't-see-my-cunt dresses to which all eerie cults are partial, had turned cross-eyed on account of the amount of Torah reading she was doing, and looked like the mother of ten children herself. Only two years her senior, though he was already more bent and crooked than his great-grandfathers on both sides, little Baruch (at this time still known as Marvin) was as fringed as a sultan's tent, and as white and furry as a moth. When I lifted him up in my arms I felt I was holding cushion stuffing.

'This isn't my wish for them, you know,' I told Sabine. But there is no repeating her reply.

It was getting time for me to back off anyway. Sabine's new husband was wanting Marvin and Charlotte to call him daddy, and that's the point at which you either stand and fight or quit the scene once and for all.

And we all know what a fighter I am.

If I found it undignified to battle for the points at deuce in a game of ping-pong, imagine how I relished the prospect of brawling over who had the right to have my children call him daddy. You want? You want that badly? Here, have, you sick fuck!

I consoled myself, in so far as I allowed myself to think about it once I was back in Saskatchewan or Wellington or wherever, by imagining a time when they would rebel and come to me. I will be in the middle of a class on *Silas Marner*; there will be an unexpected knock on my office door; I will shock my students by my trembling; I will rise and go to see who it is who's knocking, and I will find – yes, them, them, who else, no longer moth white, no longer cross-eyed, no longer flocked and frocked and fringed, two of the fairest and most secular children you have ever seen, bouncing up and down on the balls of their bold bare brown feet, crying, 'Daddy, Daddy, look at us, we have run away from Yahweh!' And I will take them in and smother them in kisses.

Well, I was almost right. They did rebel. They did reject their mother and their visionary second daddy. But not for the reasons I'd have liked. They rejected them for not being fervid enough. 'But Mummy, Mummy, Moshiach is coming!' they cried, changing their names to you-know-what and flinging themselves down that black well of messianic Hasidism of which Manchester is today as much a thriving battery farm as it once was of Yo-Yoists and Mosley's Black Shirts. I suppose I should have been flattered. What are Hasids after all but mental orgiasts from our side of the Bug? In their own way Channa and Baruch were turning tail on their cold maternal Junker ancestry in favour of their daddy's (their real daddy's) bunch – the whirling Russki Walzers. A compliment to me, n'est çe pas?

Maybe that was why I got my invitation. The bride and groom must have wanted their union enriched by one drop of genuine Ukrainian peasant blood.

I've told you what I thought of the wedding. It turned my stomach. I watched my mother ratchet back her head another couple of degrees, then dab her eyes in the fashion of all grandmas; a marriage is a marriage is a marriage. I watched her lose herself in ceremony, shuffle back and forth in time, remember hers, remember mine, remember Fay's that never was, but in the end I suspect the masculinism must have turned her stomach too. Not that I was able to find out. We weren't allowed to sit together.

One consolation though: later I was allowed to dance with my new son-in-law.

If I had to compress all my objections into one objection then what I couldn't forgive most about the thing Channa had done was the colour of her husband's mouth. No daughter of mine should ever have wanted to put her lips to something as red and wet and unformed as that. That's if they were ever intending to touch lips.

Not a subject a father should be putting his mind to? You bet it isn't! But who were the ones making it impossible for me to do anything else? Who were the exhibitionists inviting me, by that hideous inverse law of demonstrative modesty, to imagine every immodesty known to man?

As with kindness so with chastity: it only becomes you when you keep the evidence of it to yourself.

They could of course – and this is their justification, my little ones – have me for dinner morally. They could argue that someone has to respect distance in a family; that my form of shrinking was hardly superior to theirs; that they at least don't cut one another's heads off in order to see how they would look on the bodies of trollops. And that they are not intending to abandon their children.

And they would have a point.

But then I could just as easily make plain to Channa that her refusal to invite my sisters – her own aunties – to her day of days, put her (as indeed it put Baruch, who should have counselled otherwise) for ever beyond the moral pale.

I learnt of this omission first on one of my mother's absorbent sheets of Albanian notepaper. She was deeply wounded on my sisters' behalf, but she sought as always a practical solution. We wouldn't tell them.

'T-G they're not likely to hear of it where they're living.'

I wrote back and said that under no circumstances would I dream of attending a wedding, even my own daughter's, that excluded my sisters on the grounds that they were married to untouchables.

I also reminded her that my sisters were only living in Bury.

Back came the Albanian reply – 'Try looking at it from Channa's point of view. She's marrying into a very devout and very well-respected family. If you were in Manchester more you would have a better sense of how well she's done, and you would be more proud of her. You already have very little to do with her. If you don't go to her wedding you will end up losing all contact with her completely, G–d forbid.'

'Which won't unduly worry me,' I replied by return.

'But it will me,' my mother answered. 'I'm her grandmother.'

So that was how your father came to be there for your noxious nuptials, Channaleh, though it stuck in his craw I can tell you. Yes, you are right, your father is a Godless bastard. But answer me this: if the Creator whom you and that wet-mouth Shmuelly worship holds it as a matter of urgency that the feelings of Aunty Hetty and Aunty Sandra are to be considered of no account because their husbands are defiled by the prepuces which were His fucking invention in the first place, what the Christ are you doing giving credence to a word He says?

Honouring God isn't compulsory, you know, even if He exists. You may choose not to.

That was our big contribution however many years ago. We discriminated. We chose. With plenty to choose from, we chose Him. And because we knew how touchy He was we went along with the pretence that He was choosing us. But it is open to us at any time to go back on our decision. 'Sorry about that but we've changed our minds. Your Own fault. You've gone off.'

Think of it this way: worse by far than a universe without a trace of a divine spark is a universe manifestly driven by One

All-Powerful God who happens not to be worth a pinch of shit either as a judge or as an exemplar.

Receive then as my wedding present to you, my darling, my annual report on your progress in Theology and Human Relations:

COULD DO BETTER.

FINALE

I came back to New York City without a wife ... Three years of sunshine and brown grass had left me unfit for the battle zones of Manhattan's West Side. Taxicabs would dive out of the curbs like so many sharks' noses: I saw teeth behind the grilles, and I froze, unable to step off the sidewalk. I couldn't go underground: the scream of subway cars frightened me ...

Isolated, morose, I turned to ping-pong –

'Ping-Pong in New York', Jerome Charyn

THEY SPEAK A different language in Manchester today. G-MEX was where I was told I would find the World Veterans' Ping-Pong Championships. Standing for Greater Manchester Exhibition Centre. Take the METROLINK to G-MEX. It used to be Central Station, but that's not how they name amenities in Manchester any more. Central Station would be CENTRAX. And the Free Trade Hall? Well there wouldn't *be* a Free Trade Hall. Free Trade was an idea, a principle, and who would dare associate a building with a principle these days?

There is a new concert hall in Manchester. The Bridgewater Hall, named after the canal over which it decorously presides. It could have been worse. It could have been BRIDEX or MANCON. But as a one-time resident and sometime re-visitor

I'd have preferred to see it called Edification House, or the Elitism Room, or even Le Grand Théâtre des Spectacles Artistiques if the English language is no longer capable of expressing a big idea. Something for Mancunians to be proud of. Something that's not G-MEX or Boogart 'Awl Cloof.

You can see G-MEX from the Bridgewater Hall. Position yourself on one of the upper floors and look across Lower Mosley Street (Lower Oswald Mosley Street?) and you get a good view of the grand rainbow sweep of the glass and iron fantasy that was Central Station. Catching a train meant something in those days. Departure and arrival, too, were ideas, principles, deserving of a Hall. And what a hall! Wonderful, the confidence Victorians enjoyed in their capacity to enclose any space, no matter how vast, and shelter it from nature.

I made do with the external view for a while, leafing through postcards in the concert hall shop, picking up and putting down items of useless stationery, shmying just like my old man, except that I shmy only in arts-related environments.

I bought a birthday card with a cello on it, although it was no one's birthday. I didn't yet have the courage to cross Lower Mosley Street. I hadn't seen ping-pong played in Manchester for close to forty years. I wasn't sure that my heart could take it.

Would it be like that unforgettable ping-pong virgin's view of the twenty tables in action at the Tower Ballroom? Would it live up to my first ever tournament when I pushed open the doors to the Sports Hall at Manchester University, and pow! – the Happy Valley, the Garden of the Hesperides, green, green as far as the eye could see, like the foothills to Heaven?

Reader, it was.

Reader, it did.

Only more so.

Did they know, the architects of Central Station, when they erected their magnificent vestibule for those arriving in the city of Manchester by train, that they were also designing a ping-pong palace to take the breath away?

Forget twenty tables going at once. Forget fifty. Forget even seventy-five. One hundred. *One hundred* – that's how many matches were in progress when I finally summoned up the courage to cross Lower Mosley Street, negotiate the METROLINK tracks, buy a ticket, pass the bouncer (for that's what Manchester has come to: it has bouncers even for ping-pong), and go in. Oof plock, oof plock, times one hundred.

Did I wish I was playing? Did the hand that once had held the racket itch?

Yes.

No.

Yes.

But itch is not the word. More a longing, if a hand can long.

Leave the hand out of it. *I* longed. I wandered between the tables, up this row, down that row, paused, watched, clapped, walked on again, the whole time trembling with longing. Not for the game itself, though, not first and foremost for ping-pong, entrancing as it was to see it played expertly again. First and foremost what I trembled with longing for was the fellowship, the company, the players. I yearned to be among them; I yearned to be of them. Of them *again*. For they were my age, you see. All of them. My age or older. Veterans. And where do you see large numbers of people your own age when you're my age? Where else on the planet could I have marched into a room the size of the Piazza del San Marco and found two hundred men and women at one hundred tables, and just as many waiting their turn, not a single one of whom was self-mutilated or self-conscious, zonked one way or another with the difficulties of being young? Leave aside what they were doing. Just concentrate on *them*. They were *of my time*. They shared my sense of the ridiculous and the tragic. And for that I loved them with a passion.

It's a wonderful provision of nature that we should go on loving people positioned at the same point between life and death as we ourselves are. It's good genetic economics. It means we look after one another. It means we don't hanker unseasonably after the young. And when we do, we know it's an aberration. The same would hold for hankering after the old, but of course no one does hanker after the old. Which is why we need one another.

Myself I'm picky about the age of the people I mix with these days to within a latitude of about eighteen months. It's very nearly all I look for. You're how old? Excellent. Me too. Let's be friends, lovers, whatever. Let's go on holiday together, let's buy a house, let's start a business, let's never part.

My emotional preferences aside, that it actually suited the *game* to be played by people the age I now was I would never have believed had I not seen it with my own eyes. It was as if I had come full circle. Here were my heroes again, the war-torn and the lugubrious, the pallid and the famished, the hollow-eyed indoor nihilists from Prague and Budapest whom I'd got to know from their clumsy black and white portraits in Barna's and Bergmann's instruction manuals, come alive half a century later in G-MEX. I am not speaking fancifully. I am not talking resemblances. Some of those very men were actually here. Don't allow the venue to take away from the eminence of the event. This was a *World* Championships. You could go away from here in a week's time and be World Over-Forties' Champion, World Over-Fifties' Champion, Over-Sixties', Over-Seventies', Over-Eighties' even. The honours justified the strain on the pension. So it stood to reason that many of the players I'd admired as a boy would be in Manchester, on the glory road again. But what was wonderful was that they had not adjusted to the times; they were not a modern version of themselves; except for the tracksuits which they wore instead of cardigans, and the surgical bandages in which they were ceremented, they were themselves as they had always been – just as morose, just as highly-strung, just as heart-broken.

356

The game looked like a pursuit of the jaded intellect once more, that's what I'm saying. Yes, the fat-nippled spam-thin bats had gone and would never return; yes, the technology had advanced to the point where even the glue with which you attached your rubbers to your blade had become decisive, a matter of subtle preferences and choices, so much so that you could be deemed to have gone too far, to have overdosed your bat, to have submitted it to substance abuse, the merest suspicion of which would have the tournament referee removing it from the hall and feeding it into a glue-sniffing machine positioned in the officials' area; and yes, one smash with a Yasaka Mark V rubber, which you buy packaged like a CD – 'Every shot aimed at glory' it promises on the sleeve – and that was that, point over. But despite all this, the deportment of the veterans themselves restored the game's Old World raffish European dignity. Every player looked like an academic philosopher again. And played like an academic philosopher too. There was Althusser hitting shots behind his back, and Derrida putting wiggle on the ball. There was Steiner needlessly belting shit out of the softest of opponents. And look – bouncing in a little pleated skirt and Reeboks, Susan Sontag, playing safe.

Seventh heaven for me. I couldn't remember when, on behalf of humanity so to speak, I had ever experienced a sweeter mix of melancholy and elation.

On behalf of myself I was more circumspect. High up on that secret shaming midnight list of all the things I could have been had life only treated me differently was ping-pong player to end ping-pong players. The best the world had ever seen. The Mighty Walzer. Now, in the presence of a thousand and one adroit and plucky competitors from every corner of the globe, I had to swallow a bitter pill. I would never have come close. My talent was not extraordinary. It was not even exceptional. I had only ever been so-so.

Do I mean it? Even if I'd practised harder? Even if my

temperament had been sounder? Even if I hadn't fallen in love with losing at a susceptible age?

I mean it. I would only ever have been so-so. It is important to me to open that wound and rub salt in it. So-So Walzer. So-so and no more.

There was one consolation, should I have been small-minded enough to take it: the game attracted just as little interest among the lay public as it always had. The only spectators, apart from me, were other players not currently engaged in a match or already knocked out. We played for one another. Whatever applause there was came from our own number. No one else gave a damn. So even if I had been in possession of an exceptional or extraordinary talent, it would have blushed unseen, its sweetness wasted on a sour world.

I was sad for myself all the same. So-So Walzer. Fancy having to face up to that so long after the event. Something else would now have to fill the space on that secret shaming midnight list.

Because you cannot live without the idea that you are exceptional at *something*, can you?

Or can you?

I retired to the back of the hall where the seating was tiered and empty, dropped my head between my knees and fell into a contemplative mood, lulled by the oof plock, oof plock times one hundred.

Why *had* it mattered so much that I be out of the ordinary?

Why did it always have to be win big or lose big?

Why had the game been everything and then nothing to me?

Why had I turned against it?

Why, in a word, wasn't I still playing as the vets all were — for the fun and companionship of it, all in it together, content, most of them, *not* to be out of the ordinary?

I mustn't idealize. There was plenty of the old spermed-up

tantrum throwing, even among the altie kackers. The bat-slapping, the complaining about injustice, the screams of 'No!', the irritation with yourself, the irritation with your equipment, the anger with the ball, the anger with opponents whose games were too leisurely or too rushed, the gracelessness. 'I know, I lost it,' I listened to a woman with overlapping thighs saying to her friends, in the hearing of the person who had just beaten her. 'She didn't win it, I lost it. I know. It's my own bloody fault. I'm too fat. I was knackered by the middle of the second game. I'm probably better off in the consolations anyway.'

Especially bad, the women. One match was becoming so ill tempered I could hear it from the top of the tiered seating, even though it was in progress at the opposite end of the hall. I hurried down to see what was the matter. A rather attractively out of focus furry Iranian woman now playing for a club in Middlesex was locked in a bitter point by point dispute with an ostrich of a New Yorker called Rhea. Rhea would put her hand up to say she wasn't ready every time Shanda crouched to serve. Shanda would then turn her back on the table and make an appeal with her big dark blasted eyes to a personage whom I took to be her husband on the grounds that he looked worn out and kept shouting at her to calm down. Then she would go on a short raging walk, swing around suddenly, and crouch to serve again.

'Are you ready *now*?'

Rhea nodded.

Shanda threw up the ball.

Rhea put up her hand.

'Stay calm,' Shanda's husband said.

Shanda towelled herself down, threw the towel at her husband and went on another walk.

'Keep calm,' he said again. 'You'll lose it if you don't stay calm.'

'How you expect me to stay calm? She keep saying she not ready.'

'Take no notice. Just do the business.'

'Every time I serve.'

'Shanda!'

'What else you expect of a damn Yankee?'

I watched Rhea think about hurling her bat. Had there been an official referee umpiring the match she may well have lodged a complaint. But this was only round one, when any old person does the scoring. She nodded, instead, to signal she was ready.

Shanda crouched to serve. Threw up the ball.

Rhea put up her hand.

Shanda won in the end. On a net cord at 20–19 in the third.

They did not shake hands.

Wherever I went for the next hour, there was Rhea biting her ostrich lip, her long neck white with rage, describing her match to whoever was prepared to listen. You could hear her too, from the opposite end of the hall, pawing the ground and rattling her quills. Eventually a loud series of bangs brought a cry of let! from all one hundred acting umpires. Had there been an explosion? No, it was just Rhea throwing everything she owned into a rubbish bin – her coffee cup, her tournament programme, her towel, her plimsolls, even her bat.

No, I mustn't idealize. But I mustn't sell the occasion short either. It was an old persons' love fest. They had seen a way of entwining ping-pong with their affections, these globe-trotting veterans, of making it a thing of beneficence to themselves and others. They had set sail on a circuit of the emotions, meeting up every other year in a new corner of the ping-pong playing world; shaking hands, embracing, kissing, laughing, sharing news, exchanging photographs. 'I'm a grandfather now,' I heard an ex-Romanian international telling a diminutive Taiwanese lady pusher who had butterflies on her skirt. 'Oh,' she said. 'Oh, oh, oh' – like little bells going off. Then she put up her hand, just as Rhea had, rummaged in her sports bag, and brought him out a gift, already wrapped and ribboned, just in case. For grandpa.

There would be a lot of new grandpas and grandmas you had to remember to bring presents for on the veterans' circuit.

Sometimes players exchanged gifts after a game – a wine glass from Bavaria, a set of ornamental chopsticks from Japan – even though they'd never met before today. Next time they'd be friends. They posed with their arms around one another for a picture. You finish? Now I take.

I felt like a ghost at a banquet. Some advantage – being invisible! Some advantage, when the tables creaked with good things and you weren't able to taste a morsel!

I was becoming tearful. The elation/melancholy mix was losing its elation. How much more upset could I take? Everything I saw was as though a lesson or a reproach to me.

Why, there were men here, playing in the over-eighties' competition, wearing knee-supports and elastic hose and bandages round every joint, so arthritic that they required the assistance of a third party to retrieve any ball for them that didn't finish up in the net. They had to hold on to the table between strokes, some of them, so that their own momentum wouldn't knock them over. Could *their* imaginations still be rioting in futurity, looking forward to the day when they'd be world beaters?

In Grand Central Station I sat down and wept.

It was afternoon teatime on the first day of the Ninth World Veterans' Championships, and there was still another week to go.

I could, of course, have called it quits and flown back to Venice. I had come to Manchester for a wedding, not to have my neshome ripped out. But I never once considered it. I would take my punishment like a man.

I stayed with my mother, in my old room, returning late in the evening and going out again early the next morning, so that she wouldn't have the chance to make another apology for having given me life.

Two nights in my old room were usually the most I could take. It's probably not a good idea for a grown man to return to the room he slept in as a boy. Especially when half his old things are still there – the jigsaws and the crossword books my aunties bought me; the dice for the snakes and ladders; a photograph of my grandmother holding my hand outside the butchers on Waterloo Road; my framed letter of acceptance from Golem College; three certificates from the ice-cream company citing me as salesman of the month; those Collins Classics that weren't suitable to take to Cambridge; my Manchester and District Table Tennis League Yearbooks; albums of press-cuttings; my cups and medals – all on the very shelves my father had put up for me, hyper-heavy-duty planks of eight by two hard-as-it-comes-hardwood – railway sleepers they had probably been – secured to the walls with ten-inch industrial screws and brackets strong enough to hold up the *Titanic*, just to be on the safe side. Even the old hoop-la board, with the rubber rings rusted to the hook marked 20, was still hanging where it had last been played with in 1950-something, on the same six-inch galvanized nail which my father had hammered into my bedroom door, just to be on the safe side.

Best never to see all that stuff again. It doesn't do to have material evidence of the little that goes into making a life.

Or to be reminded of the impossibility of ever putting any of it behind you. Of ever putting *you* behind you.

That was my usual position. Two nights and gone. But this time I was in no hurry. If that's what makes a life, that's what makes a life. Look at it, Walzer. Be grateful. Say Got tsedank.

I was in a softened state. The veterans had got to me. Instead of immediately turning off the light and falling into troubled sleep the way I usually did when I was back in my old room, I sat up late going through the contents of my shelves, blowing away the dust, easing apart pages that had stuck together, wiping the thumb prints off ancient photographs, and where they were torn, putting them back together.

'I'm glad you're sorting through your old things,' my mother said.

I didn't know about 'sorting'. All I was doing was looking. Re-acquainting myself. And doing a little repair work.

I didn't know about 'things' either. Things? Mother, these are the tsatskes of the heart.

Then it was back every morning to G-MEX for more upset.

Was it only the third day, was it only midway through the afternoon of the third day while I was climbing to the top of the tiered section of seats to get a commanding overview of one hundred games of ping-pong, that I heard someone trying out my name – 'Oliver? Oliver Walzer?'

I swung around. I'd expected to see people I knew from the past here, but so far the ones I recognized hadn't recognized me. No one important. No one I could realistically have expected to remember who I was; though their failure to do so underlined the bitter discovery I had already made. That as a ping-pong player, to take it no further than that, I had been unmemorable. So-So Walzer. But now it was my turn not to recognize. If the person who was following me up the steps reminded me of anyone it was Placido Domingo, and I wasn't expecting to see him at the Ninth World Veterans' Table Tennis Championships.

I looked harder. He was a person about my own height and possibly five or six years older. Like me he was in civvies, not here to play – unless he'd played already and crashed out of everything. There was something just the smallest bit old-fashioned about his appearance, for the reason that he was kitted out to look cool and that always dates you if you don't get it spot on. Black leather jacket, black trousers, open-necked striped shirt, circa 1966. He looked tired. Life-tired. Not bitter – that's too active. But ingrained with disappointment; not on the look-out any more for anything else. And somewhat uprooted. A bachelor, like me.

Maybe another bachelor whose children had been brought up by someone else. But I was damned if I knew who he was.

'It's Theo,' he said.

Theo? I looked at him. Theo? Did I know a Theo?

I was ready to throw open my arms and say, 'Theo, how the hell are you?' to save us both the embarrassment. Eventually he'd let slip something which would give me a clue to the particular Theo he was.

But then he changed his name to make it easier for me. 'Twink,' he said. And it was all I could do not to fall at his feet.

I was right about his being on his own. You can always tell. It's the air of time hanging heavy.

He'd been married. Perfectly nice girl. Three children. All boys. All doing well? Listen, these days you're doing well if you've got a job. So touch wood, yes, doing well. The only one who didn't have a job was him.

I don't know why but this made the black leather jacket somehow more affecting. How old was he now? Fifty-seven, fifty-eight? Pushing sixty and no job, but still in a leather jacket. Didn't that have to mean that he was not prepared to go quietly? That he was still showing a bit of the old rebel?

Or was it only because I would soon be a little old man myself that he heroically didn't look like a little old man to me? Did we both look like little old men to other people?

I didn't want to ask what the job was he no longer had, just in case he'd gone back to working his button machine after national service; I didn't want to embarrass him. But it came out in the saga. He'd lingered in the South-West once they'd demobbed him from the army – for sweetheart reasons, I gathered – managing a record shop in Bournemouth. He came back to Manchester for his father's funeral and met his wife. Then he went into business with her brothers. Wallpaper. A wallpaper warehouse on Great Clowes Street. Then her brothers had done the dirty on him. You wouldn't think it, would you, your own brothers-in-law? Yiddisher boys! But they had. They'd taken his money, removed him slowly from his savings, then nothing like so slowly removed him from the firm. How? Don't ask him how. His wife took their side. Blood's thicker than water. So that was the marriage kaput too. Listen, there was no point going over it. He'd seen with his own eyes what harbouring a grudge had done to his father. He wasn't going to go that way. They could rot in hell, he wasn't going to think about them. You wouldn't imagine your own brothers-in-law would do that to you, but that was then and now is now. You have to be philosophical. The ganovim!

'I always thought you were much taller than me,' I said.

'Well, I was then. You were a kid.'

'No, I mean I always thought of you as really tall – over six foot.'

He shook his head sadly, as though that was something else that hadn't worked out – his height.

'But your health's good?' I said. 'You look well.'

'Listen – I've got a lazy bowel and a hiatus hernia and I'm on Prozac for worry. But think of all the people we used to know who are dead already.'

I didn't ask him to name names. I didn't want to know.

We hadn't moved from where he'd found me. Match after match of high-quality geriatric ping-pong had been won and lost before our very noses while we talked, but ping-pong was the hardest subject for us to broach. It was as if we were old lovers meeting in a bedroom for the first time in nearly forty years, not daring to look at the sheets.

In the end we broke the truce at the same time, applauding a fusillade of exquisitely timed whipped forehand smashes from Marty Reisman, the great American exponent of pimples who would undoubtedly have become World Champion forty years ago had sponge not happened. He'd been robbed by history, everyone agreed about that. 'Beautiful to see,' we said together.

Beautiful to hear, too – the old plock plock, plock plock.

Reisman touched his familiar black beret in acknowledgement of our acknowledgement of his genius.

Setting aside the small matter of that genius, he was me with staying power. He was nearly seventy but he could still hear a hand clapping on another continent; his eyes were going but he could still find a fan in a haystack.

'Did you ever make the change?' Twink asked me.

'Yes, but I was never really comfortable. I think that's why I gave it away in the end. I was essentially an old-fashioned player.'

'You're telling me? I remember saying to you, "Oliver, you're going to have to adapt." Do you remember when you won the Manchester Closed for the first time? I said then that you'd made too much of a megilleh of beating that Finn. "You're going to have to learn to mix your game up, Oliver," I said. Do you remember that?'

I didn't, actually, no. But I said yes, of course I did. And I was touched that he'd remembered my first final, even if he hadn't remembered it as I'd remembered it.

'The thing about your game,' he went on, 'is that you were never really a natural ball-player like me. I played football, cricket, squash, snooker, golf. I was good at all of them. You were a one-game player. I sometimes thought that that made you concentrate too hard. You remember me saying that to you, don't you?'

I didn't, actually, no. But I said, yes, and what about you, Twink, did you change your surface?

It cannot be of interest to anyone else what we discussed for the next hour or more. We had both only ever been so-so players. Every time Reisman wound up his 1949 forehand we fell quiet and thought about our limitations. But the game had been everything to us for a while, and we went through the textures and the thicknesses of our bats, the strengths of our team, the weaknesses of our opponents, the drives to the venues, the scores, the scandals, the nobbels and the moodies, with the passion with which old pals remember the names of their first girlfriends and the tunes they kissed to.

It was a worry to me that I couldn't recognize him. I knew him all right, knew his slightly put-upon way of looking at things, knew his exasperated Laps' drawl, as though every word had an extra half-syllable appended to it (necessary because no one was ever listening), and I recalled what he recalled (except when he was recalling it about me), but I couldn't place him. If he walked past me tomorrow I would once again not know that it was him.

Could it be that too much time had gone by? That the stuff on the shelves in my old room was lying and that I was no longer living the life I'd started out on half a century before?

If I closed my eyes and opened them again would he still be there? Would he ever have *been*?

'So what about the opera?' I asked. 'How are the tenors going?'

'You remember that?'

'What do you mean, *remember that*? Jesus, Twink, we talked more tenors than we talked ping-pong.'

'I thought that was Aishky.'

Aishky.

There, we'd named him.

I went very cold. Had Twink been looking he'd have seen the chill creeping up my arms, like the mist rolling in over the Grand Canal. So far he had said nothing of Aishky, had been careful to say nothing, it seemed to me, and I'd not dared to ask, fearing what the silence meant.

But now the name was out, I had to know.

'Me and Aishky,' I said. 'The three of us. He was Lanza, I was

Björling. And when he wasn't around I was Lanza *and* Björling. Are you in contact with him?'

I had to wait for my answer. One of the great Chinese players of the past, now living in Germany, was about to begin his match. Lesser players on neighbouring tables stopped their games so that they could get a look at him again.

'I saw him at the Free Trade Hall years ago,' Twink said.

'Aishky?'

'No, Liang.'

'What about Aishky, Twink?'

'It's funny you should mention him. How often do I see Aishky? You know what he's like. He says he'll be in touch and then you don't hear a word for twenty years. Once in a blue moon he rings me to see if I feel like a game of kalooki. Then suddenly – listen to this – I see him twice in one day! First when I'm visiting my uncle in Marilyn Kaprowitz House –'

'What's Marilyn Kaprowitz House?'

'It's the old people's home on Crescent Road. It used to be Hillel House. Don't you remember? We played against them a few times.'

'No, I don't remember. But look, are you telling me Aishk is in an old people's home?'

'He works there as a porter two mornings a week. The rest of the time – are you listening? – he's a security man for an insurance company in Spring Gardens. That was where I ran into him later the same day. I nearly collapsed. I'm coming out of Lewis's and there he is, standing like a shmulke in the rain. Hat, silver buttons, big black boots, the lot. I say to him, "Aishky, you're getting wet." He says, "I'm paid to get wet." I say, "Can't you stand in the doorway at least?" He says, "I'm guarding the doorway." How do you like that?'

'Aishky is a security man?'

'Well, that's what I want to talk to you about. I'm worried. You know Aishky. I went past there again last week and someone else was standing outside the door. A shvartzer. Wearing the same uniform . . .'

It was all moving too fast for me. 'A shvartzer wearing Aishky's uniform?'

'I'm telling you . . . I asked him if he knew where Aishky was and he said he'd left. But I didn't like the way he said it. You know how you get that feeling that something's wrong?'

'What do you think might be wrong?'

'The usual. Nerves.'

'So have you rung to see if he's all right?'

A queer expression passed over his face. 'It's not easy for me to ring,' he said.

I decided not to look into that one. 'Have you tried Marilyn Kaprowitz House?'

'If I go there I have to see my uncle.'

'So is Aishky married or what? Is there someone to look after him? Has he got kids? Is he on his own?'

'He had a lady. But I think something happened. He doesn't talk about it. I get the impression he's on his own. Ask him yourself.'

'Do you think he'd welcome a call from me?'

'What are you talking about? 'Course he'd welcome a call from you. I'd like to be there with him when he picks the phone up. I'd like to see the look on his face. He won't be able to believe it. Like me – I nearly collapsed when I saw you.'

'Why don't the three of us go out one night? Like old times.'

The same queer expression passed over Twink's face. 'It's a bit awkward for me,' he said.

And then I realized what it meant. He couldn't *afford* a night out. He couldn't even afford to make a phone call. He was stony broke. I again took in the still creaking 1960s leather jacket and the carefully pressed striped shirt and I wanted to burst into tears. I touched him on the elbow in a manner I recognized as belonging to my father. When had I acquired that? Had I picked it up years ago and been saving it for a rainy day?

'I'm flush at the moment,' I said. 'We'll all go out and I'll look after it.' Pure Joel Walzer. The hand reaching out to take the bill. The big fist closing over it. *I'll look after this.*

Meanwhile the money to look after it with was in a brown paper bag in a phone box.

And did it work? Of course it worked. Hadn't they all loved my old man for his big heart?

'Thanks for your understanding,' Twink said.

It must have been a nice experience, being my old man.

We caught a taxi back to his place in the wrong part of Prestwich so he could show me his records and CDs. He wanted us to take the METROLINK for which he had any number of concession cards – even one relating to his lazy bowel – but I wasn't prepared to travel on anything called a METROLINK. 'I'll see to the taxi,' I'd said.

In answer to my earlier question, yes, the tenors were going as strong as they'd ever gone. Stronger. Opera on record was the beginning and the end of his life. If you wanted to estimate Twink's material value you would have had to weigh him in a scale against his operas. They were all he owned. The tiny flat was rented. The television was rented. The phone only worked if you rang in. The carpets, he told me, had come from his oldest boy's house. All the clothes he possessed he was wearing. At the end of nearly sixty years as a son, a soldier, a husband and a father, he was down to just his operas. And the wherewithal to play them.

'What else do I need?' he said. 'I come in, I turn on the stereo, I sit down, I listen, I go to bed.'

The stereo was clearly such as only the most single-minded listeners treat themselves to. 'Is this a Bang and Olufsen?' I asked. As if I knew from anything.

I won't bother repeating his reply. For a start, Bang and

Olufsen wouldn't like it. And to be honest I didn't take in very much of what he told me about the rarity and fragility of the valves or whatever on which his system depended. Some of the components were covered with tablecloths when they weren't in use, I observed that. And there were places Twink was anxious that I didn't stand. Otherwise I have nothing to report regarding the technical specifications of his equipment.

That it sounded good goes without saying. La Scala, in the wrong part of Prestwich, that's where we were. The Metropolitan, just off Sandy Lane.

But it was the collection itself that took my breath away. Not just the extent of it – though it is not often you see all four walls of a council flat given over to boxed sets of opera from *Ariadne auf Naxos* to *Zauberflöte*. And not just the irreproachable library system according to which it was arranged, so that Twink could lay his hands on any single tenor aria sung by any single tenor in a matter of seconds. No, it was the comprehensiveness of the passion it represented which impressed me. There wasn't an operatic argument that Twink didn't have the means to put or to refute; not a conceivable operatic comparison, and not a song cycle or cantata comparison either, he didn't have the source material to mount. It was all here: everything there was and everything Twink felt and thought about it.

As to the quality of his judgement, as we used to say at Golem; as to whether his mind was rich or poor, musically – I am in no position to comment. My own interest in opera had always been fitful. As a boy I had loved it because Twink and Aishk had loved it. At Golem I had revered Mozart because Yorath and Rubella had revered Mozart. Tenor arias of the romantic sort I had gone on loving independently of Yorath and Rubella because they spoke the language of my soul. *E lucevan le stelle*? – sure they were, not a star in the heavens that didn't shine upon the head of the Mighty Walzer. But then came 'Nessun Dorma' at the World Cup in Italy, and that pretty well put paid to all tenors and all arias at once. The association of opera and football was too hard to bear. The spectacle of the ignorant suddenly discovering and delighting in an aria the rest of us had been humming since the cradle, simply because it was now bellowed on a football pitch, disgusted me. *How could they not have heard it before?* And the subsequent transformation of the once sweet-voiced Pavarotti and the once subtly lyrical Domingo into screamers for the masses, competitive sperm-chuckers from the Black Lagoon, was the last nail in *my* operatic coffin at least. So I was not the one to sit in judgement on Twink's taste.

He would not have agreed with me, anyway, that civilization died the day Pavarotti puffed out his barrel chest and skvitshed what no one had ever sung more feelingly than Björling, out of context, out of season, out of place, for the cameras of a lost footy-fevered species. He was not a Yorath and Rubella man. He was not a cultural Domesday merchant. When I caught myself thinking the worse of him for that, I wondered if I hadn't myself died the day Golem College let me in.

We sat in the dark, just as we had when we were boys, comparing liebestods – Nilsson good, Nilsson powerful, but oh God, the wine-dark anguish of Flagstad! – and by the flickering lights of his thousand-valved amplifier I could see he was transfigured.

At last I recognized him.

When I got home my mother had retired but there was a message waiting for me on my pillow. Sheeny Waxman had rung – Jesus, how much more! – Sheeny Waxman, if I remembered who he was, had rung to say that Phil Radic, if I remembered who he was, had thought he'd seen me leaving G-MEX the day before and had mentioned it to Sheeny on the golf course that morning. If it *was* me and I *was* back, would I ring —.

Sleep on that, Walzer! All I needed now was for Selwyn Marks to enter my bedroom in a winding sheet and we'd have been complete, the Akiva team up and running, ready to take on anybody.

I woke early, in something of a quandary. Who ought I to ring first – Aishky or Sheeny? It mattered, the order in which I rang, because I believed I would feel differently about the one after speaking to the other. Aishky enjoyed precedence in the sense that his name had cropped up earlier in the day. But Sheeny had rung *me*. On the other hand, although I had no idea what Sheeny had been up to for the last thirty years or more, I doubted he was working as a doorman. Therefore, I reasoned, he needed my call less.

I was reasoning needs, now? I was weighing them up like a soup-kitchen ladler?

Of course I was. We were old men. There was nothing left of us but needs.

I rang Aishky, because he came earlier in the alphabet.

He didn't seem all that surprised to hear from me. 'Yeah, Oliver, Oliver Walzer, I remember, you had a good backhand.'

'You too,' I said. 'You had a wonderful backhand.'

'*And* I had a good forehand,' he said, 'before my accident. You probably don't know about my accident.'

'Aishky, I was there.'

'No one was there. That was the trouble.'

'I was as good as there. I've never forgotten it. But listen, how are you?'

'I've had three tragedies. My mother, alav ha-shalom, died. My father, God rest his dear soul, died. And the young lady I was seeing, alav ha-shalom, she died.'

'Aishky, I'm so sorry.'

'Yeah . . .' His voice went dreamy. 'I took my mother's death very badly. My father's even worse. Elizabeth's very, very badly. I never did so much crying in my life over three people. It affected me. I had a breakdown. You're not going to believe this – I've had a breakdown every single day since my father passed away.'

'Oh, Aishky –'

'I'm not even well now. I've got some meshuggener illness. I say things that don't make sense. I'm tsemisht. I get a lot of headaches. The doctor says I probably do too much reading. I read all the time.'

I asked him what he was reading. A Yorath and Rubella question. Was he reading what he *should* be reading. But when all's said and done, what else could I ask him?

'The Holocaust. I've been studying it for forty-three years. I've gone way beyond Martin Gilbert. The only difference is that I don't have initials after my name.'

'So get initials after your name. Do a degree, Aishky. It's the age of the mature student.'

'To be truthful with you, Oliver, and don't take this the wrong way, I'd like to be teaching myself. I know everything there is to know about the subject. The only thing is, I get klogedik sometimes, very very bitter. I have terrible thoughts.'

'What sort of thoughts?'

The phone went quiet for several moments. Then he said, 'I hate the enemy. I hate the people who murdered our people.'

'You're allowed.'

'When I say my prayers at night, I have terrible thoughts.'

I was out of my depth. Prayers floor me every time. Too private, prayers. 'So listen,' I said, 'when are we going to get together, the three of us?'

'Well it's hard for me because of the hours I work. I work late every night.'

'I was going to ask you about that. Twink said he saw you in Spring Gardens the other week and then suddenly you weren't there any more. Instead of you there was a shvartzer. He was worried.'

'Was he a tall shvartzer or a short shvartzer?'

'I don't know, Aishky. Twink never said. Just a shvartzer.'

'It was probably Clive. He's a very nice person, actually. But, yeah, no, I've moved. I'm in Dukinfield, now. You remember the Jam and Marmalade works where we used to play table tennis? – you'll split your sides at this –'

'That was my first ever league match, Aishk, I'm never likely to forget it.'

'Yeah, well I'm a security officer there now. What do you think of that?'

'I think it's a long way for you to travel, especially in the fog.'

'It takes me three buses, door to door.'

'Is that mamzer Cartwright still there?'

'The one with the shmatte bat?'

'The one who was always complaining about our shmatte balls.'

'I think he died a few years ago.'

'Listen, Akishky, do you work late every night?'

'Of course. I'm a security officer. Mondays, Tuesdays, Wednesdays until midnight. Thursdays and Fridays until 9.30.'

Today was Thursday. 'Then we'll pick you up there tonight at 9.30,' I said. 'I know the address.'

And before he could put any obstacles in my way or add to the list of dead loved ones – dead hated ones, too – I rang off.

Then I said a prayer of my own.

My call to Sheeny Waxman was less metaphysically vexing. I reached his secretary. 'Mr Waxman said that if you called I had to tell you to jump straight in a taxi at his expense and ask to be brought to Gallery W in Wilmslow. He will be here all day. Oh, and he also said to say "Oink, oink."'

I rang Twink on his receive-calls-only telephone to tell him what I'd arranged with Aishky, mentioned Sheeny Waxman about whom he was as incurious as he had always been, then did the extravagant thing I'd been told to do and jumped in a taxi. Gallery W? I was unable to make a single reasonable stab at what Gallery W made or sold. Mirrors? Greetings cards? Wedding stationery? Tsatskes, I was certain of that. The higher swag, as befitted the mock-Tudor, mock-Georgian, mock-Edwardian village of Wilmslow. Heavily varnished prints of English country scenes in gaudily gilded frames? Twelve-branched chandeliers? Reproduction antique furniture even? But really I was at a loss. I suppose I was also in shock. Too much of the past in too short a time. Too many memories I couldn't be absolutely sure were mine.

And too many I could, come to that.

I saw Sheeny before I saw Gallery W. He was standing on the pavement looking up and down the street. For me? How touching if that were so.

We fell into each other's arms. His doing. I felt slightly over-whelmed by him again, just as I had when I'd first encountered him and he'd put me down for being a kid. And now to go with the alarming tic and the KD demeanour was a killingly contemporary London haircut – parted not quite in the middle, fuller on the top than the sides, like a headless partridge flecked with copper highlights – and an abstemious black curatorial suit, worn over a crisp white cod muezzin shirt with no collar.

'Jesus, Sheeny,' I said, backing out of his embrace, 'you look as though you've just come from judging the Turner Prize.'

Had I thought about what I was saying I wouldn't have said it. What would Sheeny Waxman know about the Turner Prize?

But then I wouldn't have said it had Sheeny Waxman not looked like what he looked like.

'You're talking to a man who's gone one better than that,' he said, hoarser than ever. 'You're talking to a man who's just got two of his artists on to the shortlist for the Turner Prize. Eh? Come in and I'll show you.'

I looked at Sheeny's priestly get-up, belied by his festive roistering expression, then I looked over his shoulder into the window of Gallery W where was laid out an installation of sacks of rice and mutilated parts of women together with a bank of video screens showing me looking at those sacks of rice and mutilated parts of women, and in the words of my old friend Twink Starr, I nearly collapsed.

Sheeny Waxman was become an art dealer! What is more he was become an art dealer at the very cutting edge of the market. Heavily varnished prints in gaudily gilded frames? Ha! – I'd got that wrong in a big way. There wasn't a frame in sight. And nothing that could *be* framed. Floor art, that was Sheeny's passion. Ideational tsatskes. Shmondries you moved around. It looked like the Tate kindergarten in there. So, yes, the higher swag right enough. But never in a thousand years would I have imagined Sheeny *this* high.

'Well? Is this a good flash or is this a good flash?' he asked.

'It's a fantastic flash,' I said.

'Charles Saatchi, eat your heart out!' he laughed.

'So is that your ambition, Sheeny?' I asked. 'To become the next great shaper of the contemporary aesthetic?'

I heard my own words but could scarcely believe I was uttering them. It was too eerie. Conversations of this sort I did not have with Sheeny Waxman. The subjects of my conversation with Sheeny Waxman were the Kardomah, keife, and pigs. His job was to sit in the back of the van with his shmeckle out, looking not unlike a piece of pork itself, while I drove us to a ping-pong match, slowing down for any bit of skirt we happened to encounter on the way.

But if I was at a loss to know where or who I was, Sheeny didn't look troubled. He was the right way up and utterly himself.

'What's with this "become"?' he said. 'I'm already his only serious competitor. I might not have his funds but I've got better taste than he has. And I'm more loyal to my artists. You come to Sheeny Waxman, you stay with Sheeny Waxman. What do you think of these?'

He had linked arms with me, for all the world as though we were a pair of AC/DC Greenwich Village dilettantes in polka-dot bowties, and was walking me around, showing me work which was strictly speaking not for sale, his private collection. 'These' were a stand of dripping monoliths, made of something that resembled candle wax, vaguely reminiscent of termite mounds which had started to bubble over.

'They're interesting,' I said. 'I like the way they appear to be humming.'

(Good, Walzer – now go out there and sell, men!)

Sheeny's eyes were dancing. 'I love this sort of gear,' he said, reaching over and stroking them. 'They're much less grainy than you'd think. Go ahead, touch. Does that get you going, or what? You know, I picked these up for next to gornisht in Switzerland. The artist had gone mechullah. Guess how much I paid for them?'

I had no idea.

He pulled me to him and whispered a modest figure in my ear. 'For all three! Is that cheap or is that cheap?'

'That's cheap, Sheeny,' I said.

He was laughing now. 'It cost me fucking twice as much to ship them over.'

But there was no vulgar triumph in his laughter. He hadn't got the better of anybody. The earth had yielded up its bounty, and he, Sheeny Waxman, adventurer extraordinary, had gratefully accepted.

If the bargain hunting was important to him, it did not determine how he bought. It simply went with the territory; it was integral to his innocence. He loved the work and should there be a story of adventitiousness attached, well he loved to tell that too.

You'll have noticed I'm defending him. From whom?

From Yorath and Rubella, that's whom. From me, from the me who cleaved to Yorath and Rubella – that's if there had ever been a me of any other sort.

But sentiment apart, now, how good was Sheeny's taste? Was *he* intelligent? Was *his* mind good?

Lig in drerd, Walzer! Lie in the cold earth!

I spent half the day in his company, my feet never touching the ground. I saw no more than one-tenth of what he showed me – the voluptuously guggling obelisks I was invited to be turned on by, the heads in formaldehyde, the moulds of chairs commemorating places where people had once sat, the videos showing nothing happening (or were they?), the empty spaces filled with sounds of moaning women (labour or orgasm? – aha!), the lifesize mutilated fairies which would have served my purposes admirably in the old cut and paste lavatory days. (Thank God I wasn't a kid growing up now.) And I heard no more than a tenth of what he told me – the partnership with Benny the Pole (did I remember him?), the Jaguar concession, the marriage to the daughter of a Derbyshire natural form sculptor he'd picked up in the Kardomah, the grand tour of the great European galleries, the awakening, the passion. Too much, too much to take in all at once. I would need to go away and think about this. I would need a further fifty years to sort it out in my mind. I knew how Aishky felt. I was tsemisht. But it was a warm tsemisht, akin to a wet rubber sheet when you're eighteen months old.

He gave me another hug before I left and repeated his offer to look after the taxi. I saw that he was relieved when I refused, not because it saved him a few quid but because it signified I wasn't short. He wanted us all to be having a good time together.

'So what do you think?' he asked. 'Is it a nobbel, or what?'

I knew what he meant. He meant all this, the gantse geshecht – what had become of him, what he was, what he did, the *transformation*. For he too thought it was a tremendous joke.

'Sheeny, I think it's the greatest nobbel on earth,' I said.

He pulled off his most spectacular twitch ever, both eyes on a simultaneous sideways roll, the Muslim shirt gulping down the entirety of his neck, one shoulder jerking up as far as

379

the headless partridge which Vidal Sassoon had deposited on his head.

'You know something – I really loved your old man,' he called out, as my taxi pulled away.

Aishky was in hiding when we arrived to collect him at the gates of the Allied Jam and Marmalade works.

The place was silent and ill floodlit, surrounded by high wire fencing, the car-park yard cringeing and cold, even in June, criss-crossed by angular shadows. Belsen, I thought. What was Aishky doing working somewhere that resembled Belsen?

I'd forgotten that you don't have that many choices in Greater Manchester, where every workspace has been desolate for decades, waiting to be cleared to make room for that Olympic Village which, thanks to what my father did in 1933, will never be built.

'He's over there,' I said to Twink. 'I can just see him.'

I recognized the shape of his head peering out from behind a wall, the beaky profile silhouetted like a Pulcinella mask on the factory yard. Remarkable that I should know it after all this time. Remarkable it should have changed so little.

'Aishky, what's the matter with you?' Twink called. 'Oliver's here to see you.'

Something else that hadn't changed – Twink enjoying having a nervous system more fragile than his own to show consideration to.

'Shemedik,' Aishky called back from the shadows, half amused, but only *half* amused, by his own bashfulness.

'Shemedik! Since when were you shemedik?'

'Me? I've always been shy.' He had appeared now, come out from his hiding place to see us, beaming, carrying a torch and wearing his security officer's uniform. A cap, even.

He was the same. Twink I'd had to piece together again, painfully slowly, never sure that I'd ever really be able to get him to re-form. Now here was Aishky, older to look at than Twink, settling for being an old man, as Twink decidedly was not, yet unmistakably the person I'd known a thousand years before.

Whether that was a good thing or a bad thing I had no idea.

As for the kind of security officer he made – well, you'd have thought twice before breaking into any building of which he had charge. You'd have thought twice and then done it.

But maybe nobody was into stealing jam these days.

We crossed the road to a dismal pub Aishky claimed to know, though when I asked him what he wanted to drink he was at a loss to remember the name of a single tipple.

'Lager and lime?' Twink helped out. 'Shandy? Club soda? Bitter lemon?'

'What are *you* having?' he asked Twink.

Twink turned to me.

Nice as it was to be back in the fifties I had a yen for a contemporary drink. 'I'm going to have red wine,' I said.

'Yeah, I'll have that too,' Aishky said.

Twink looked worried for him. 'It won't be sweet, you know, Aishk.'

'Won't it?'

'Why don't we all have whisky?' I suggested.

So that was what we did. Whisky we all knew, from weddings and funerals. And of course from circumcisions. That's your first touch of the hard stuff, a suck of Scotch from your father's finger to take the pain away from your guillotined little in-between on the eighth day of your first and only life on earth. No wonder we're not drinkers.

There was no one in the pub but us, yet the noise was deafening. In the absence of anyone to prompt it, the jukebox played its own favourites. The fruit machines made horrible jeering electronic sounds. The bar staff rattled glasses. Anything not to have to hear silence.

We sat by the door where it was quietest and raised our whisky glasses to one another. The three musketeers.

Now what?

I looked into my glass. Aishky looked up at the ceiling.

Could it be that we no longer had anything to musketeer about?

Glory be to Twink. 'Guess who I saw the other day at G–MEX,' he said, 'just before I ran into Oliver? Charlie Williamson. Remember him, Aishk? From Mather and Platt? Used to play in wellingtons?'

'Very hard to beat,' Aishky said.

'I'm not kidding you, Oliver, this feller would turn up on a motorbike and come to the table in leather trousers and wellingtons . . .'

'A mad defender,' Aishky said.

'That's right. Still is. He'd come to the table in wellingtons, isn't that right, Aishky? – it was very hard to keep your face straight.'

'The other one that got me,' Aishky said, 'was John Smedley who used to play in his socks.'

'*Jack* Smedley.'

'Jack Smedley, that's right. Played for the Tax Office . . .'

'Social Security.'

'Social Security, that's right. He had this meshuggener backhand which he'd hit while he was sliding about in his socks.'

'Also hard to beat.'

'That's what I'm saying. You couldn't tell what his feet were doing. You couldn't hear him.'

'Didn't you lose to him once, Aishk, in a cup match?'

'*Nearly* lost to him. Until I changed my game at seven–nothing down in the decider.'

'That's right. I remember. We were all having heart attacks.'

'What did you do to change your game, Aishky?' I asked.

'I took my pumps off and played in *my* socks. So now he couldn't hear *me*. It was one of the quietest games of table tennis ever played.'

'That reminds me of Pawel Trepper from the Polish Circle, do you remember him? A mute. Very good-looking guy. He could have been a model. But deaf as a post. If you were umpiring you had to write the score in the air with your finger.'

'Also hard to beat,' Aishky said.

'*Very* hard to beat. Though he always liked to win with a smash. Sometimes he'd put five or six off the table trying to clinch it.'

'That's how I beat him,' Aishky remembered.

'Mind you,' Twink continued, 'even you at one time, right, would think nothing of hitting five or six off the table. Am I right?'

Aishky waved the recollection away with his hand. For the first time I noticed the missing fingers. Not so bad as I'd remembered. Only the tips were gone. And what was left had healed over nicely.

'Those were the days,' Twink said.

Aishky had fallen quiet.

But not Aishky's uncle Twink. 'So do you look back on it all fondly, Aishk, the way we do?'

'Sometimes I do, sometimes I don't,' Aishky admitted. 'I'm full of emotions you know.'

'I know,' Twink said.

'I took the death of my parents very badly.'

'I know you did,' Twink said.

'When my father was put in the nursing home I went off my rocker.'

'How old was he?'

'Eighty-seven.'

That's a good age, Aishky.'

'No – it's what happened to him that made me ill. He finished up with blood dripping in his head. I loved my father. I can't bear it even now. You'll think this is mad, but some nights I bang my head against the wall. I say meshuggener things to myself.'

He was well on the way to saying meshuggener things to himself this night. He had stopped noticing us. We needn't have been there. I didn't begrudge him a soliloquy but I already knew the gist of the mantra from our phone call. Next it would be the Holocaust. He was all right so long as we could keep him away from death and the Holocaust – aren't we all all right so long as you can keep us away from death and the Holocaust? – so I interrupted Twink who was trying to reason him out of it ('You can get too far in, Aishky, you know that yourself, you can think too much about your parents however much you loved them') by asking Aishky if he still listened to Mario Lanza.

It worked. The old shy Esau smile returned to his face. He took his security officer's cap off for the first time. Not bald, I was pleased to see, stubbly but not bald. 'Do you remember this one?' he said. '*M'appari, tut amor . . .*'

'I've got the best recording of that,' Twink said. 'Carreras. Before he took ill . . .'

'O, my babby, my curly-headed babby,' Aishky half-said, half-sang. 'I always loved that.'

'Paul Robeson,' Twink said.

'I'll tell you who was one of my favourites,' Aishky said. 'Peter Dawson. Do you remember "On the Road to Mandalay"?'

'Sing it for us, Aishk,' I said.

'Isn't there too much baritone in that for you, Aishky?' Twink fretted.

Aishky didn't think so. Me neither. We were in need of some deep notes. He looked around to see who was listening, saw that no one was, cleared his throat, and sang it for us – Peter Dawson, Peter Dawson as I live and breathe.

By the old Moulmein Pagoda, lookin' lazy at the sea,
There's a Burma girl a-sittin', and I know she thinks of me . . .

I drifted off on the extravagant wings of song. Aishky in Mandalay. Aishky gone from Mandalay and the Burma girl a-sittin', not knowing that her British soldier was in Cheetham

Hill, carrying a night watchman's torch and saying meshuggener things to himself.

The dawn would have come up like thunder for a second time had the barman not broken all our reveries ringing his accursed bell.

Aishky jumped. 'What was that?'

'Last orders, Aishky.'

He looked bemused. *Last orders?*

Is that not wonderful – that you can get to sixty and not know that there is such a thing as last orders? Sixty and never once have been in a public house late enough to hear the bell? I leaned across and kissed the top of his pate, tasting the old ginger stubble which was softer than maybe it should have been and miraculously smelt of newness, like a baby's.

'Does that mean we have to leave now?' he asked.

'It means we have to drink up. We've just got time to get a couple more songs in,' I reckoned. 'One or two from the old Brindisi collection.'

So that was what we did, even managing to persuade Twink to join us in the odd chorus, though he had always been more the collector than the performer – yes, before they could turn us out on to the blank songless streets of Manchester, a million miles from Mandalay, we bel canto'd one last time with feeling whatever we could remember of our favourite drinking-up songs, the 'Libiamo' from *La Traviata*, the knock-it-back-quick from *Cavalleria Rusticana*, Lucrezia Borgia's 'The Secret of Bliss is Perfection', and Mario Lanza seizing the day as the carefree student in Heidelberg, destined one day to be a king and never to carouse again.

Ein, zwei, drei, vier . . . *Libiamo ne'lieti calici*, for life is but a tsatske and tomorrow we may die.

And that ought to have been that. Enough. Enough, even for a glutton for punishment like me. The next morning should have seen me back on Alitalia, scampering for the clear uncluttered blue of my little pigeon loft on the Via Dolorosa, coffined gondolas or no coffined gondolas, as quick as my Walzer shanks would carry me. Enough already.

But you don't always have the final say in matters of the heart. You can't float into your old home town, sleep in your old room among your old shmondries, shove your nose into your daughter's wedding, pootle along to the Ninth World Veterans' Table Tennis Championships and not expect some of the shit to stick.

You can't monkey around with your feelings *and* with ping-pong.

I actually had my ticket in my pocket when I turned up at G-MEX for the finals. My flight was at 5.30 so there was a fair chance I wouldn't get to see all of the later matches. But I'd take whatever was on offer. It was going to have to last me a long time.

During the mid-morning break between the two men's doubles semi-finals and the two women's, I ran into Phil Radic. I recognized him immediately. Another one who hadn't changed. We hadn't met since I'd served off the table to Royboy Roylance in a pet, and we hadn't spoken since I'd said 'I don't think there's anything to discuss, Phil,' also in a pet, but I knew he wouldn't be harbouring a grudge. I'd written glowingly of him in my manual, recommending his game as a model to anyone wanting to play ping-pong the way it was originally meant to be played, with mercurial wit, and although no one ever bought or read that publication, apart from my father who made it to the bottom of the acknowledgements page, I was aware that books had a marvellous way of always landing on the desk of whoever they happened to mention.

We shook hands. He had his old Irgun tan and looked mighty handsome, shone up like a conker, in a black and grey loose weave jacket and a tie I recognized as Ferragamo from a shop on the Via Veneto. There was a lady on his arm. Not quite his style, I thought. Anderer, for a start. (Phil had refused to play for England on a Shabbes, remember.) And although my age, I guessed, and therefore younger than him, somehow too old for him at the same time. Grey haired, full figured, an eensy bit florid. Someone who had crossed over, in the Italian style herself, from being decorative to being functional. Done lovely, now doing motherly. An admirable portioning out of seasons, it always seemed to me; something Italians did well. A problem for the men, but then what isn't? She was not someone I could imagine Phil Radic showing off around the pool in the King Solomon's Palace Hotel, Eilat, that's all I'm saying. Not any more, anyway.

'Oliver, I don't know if you ever met my wife,' he said. 'Oliver, Lorna.'

We bowed.

It did for one mad moment pass through my mind to say, 'Your wife's maiden name wouldn't happen to be Peachley would it?' But the question was redundant. I had not the slightest doubt it was her.

Changed beyond recognition, but her. Her. Oh yes, her.

I surely don't need to explain how I knew. Magnetism, that's how. The same way a bird born on the Manchester Ship Canal knows, come September, the quickest route to the Zambezi.

For a millionth of a second I ceased to be a living person. For a millionth of a second I was medically dead. No human frame could have turned that cold and gone on harbouring life. But let no one tell you differently – worse by far than the moment of death is the moment of resurrection. A terrible nausea seized me, as though nothing I had ever done or felt had the slightest meaning. I am still not sure how I managed to stay upright.

And her? From her not a flicker. Had a fly been resting upon her eyelid it would not have registered the slightest encouragement to be gone.

And had the fly been resting on her heart?

Ditto.

'Well, good to see you, Phil,' I said.

'You too, Oliver.' Then he laughed. 'Maybe in another forty years.'

And I laughed. 'Maybe.'

Then I bowed to Lorna.

And Lorna bowed to me.

Later in the day I was sitting thinking about my plane, looking at my watch and waiting for the men's singles final to start, doubting whether I'd get to see it all, wondering if I cared, when I became conscious that Mr and Mrs Radic were taking up seats in the row behind me. I didn't turn about to look. But I sensed them through my back, climbing over knees, fussing. Then I felt a hand – a woman's hand, full of rings – quickly tousling my hair. No lingering. No pressure. Just the gentlest of ruffles. Such as you might give, without thinking, to a favourite child.

Denoting, in my view, what?

That she loved me after all?

Of course not.

That she forgave me?

Not that either.

Just that she remembered who I was.

Which is all any of us Walzers has ever asked.